THE
PHOENIX
EFFECT

PART III: PURSUING ECHOES

THE PHOENIX EFFECT

PART III: PURSUING ECHOES

MARGARET M. MACDONALD

DRAGONBRAE

DRAGONBRAE

An imprint of Roan & Weatherford Publishing Associates, LLC
Bentonville, Arkansas
www.roanweatherford.com

Library of Congress Cataloging-in-Publication Data
Names: MacDonald, Margaret M., author.
Title: The Phoenix Effect: Pursuing Echoes | The Phoenix Effect #3
Description: First Edition | Bentonville: Dragonbrae, 2025.
Identifiers: LCCN: 2025936609 | ISBN: 979-8-89299-019-6 (hardcover) |
ISBN: 979-8-89299-020-2 (trade paperback) |
ISBN: 979-8-89299-021-9 (eBook)
Subjects: BISAC: FICTION/Dystopian |
FICTION/Science Fiction/Genetic Engineering | FICTION/Science Fiction/Military
LC record available at: https://lccn.loc.gov/2025936609

Dragonbrae trade paperback edition January, 2026

Cover Design by Casey W. Cowan
Interior Design by John Bredesen
Editing by George "Clay" Mitchell & Lisa Lindsey

To Hillary and Heather,
for looking after me when I didn't have enough teeth

ONE

THE FOREST WAS peaceful until the tank arrived. Birdsong ceased as low rumbling emanated from over the hill. Wet squishing soon followed as the treads flattened their way across the muddy plateau. Would they notice how unusually flat the land had suddenly become? Would they think the leaf litter was a bit too fresh and even?

A pair of voices rose up above the rumbling and squelching. Two of the three guards in front of the tank were engrossed in conversation as they casually strode ahead. Lia attuned her ears to their voices.

"They're just violent, you know. Come at you for no reason," one guard grumbled.

"They've got to have a reason," the other responded in high-pitched protest.

"They don't. They're just whacked." It was then Lia realized they couldn't have been talking about the Resistors. There was no doubting their reasons to attack.

"So, do they run around naked then?" the guard with the high-pitched voice asked.

"What's that got to do with it?"

"It's been fifteen years. More in some territories. Clothes don't last that long. If they are whacked, then they wouldn't bother wearing anything. They'd be attacking in the buff."

Those tin cans' minds could not be further from their job, Lia thought as she lined up her shot.

The front man spun around to chastise them. "We're on disputed territory here, transporting enough weapons to flatten an entire town of Scavs, and I'm not about to let it get into the wrong hands. Now, keep your eyes open and your mouths shut."

The voice of reason had spoken.

Unfortunately for the Unis, it had not happened soon enough. As he turned back around, Lia pulled the trigger. He crumpled to the ground before the crack of her rifle cleared the air.

"Weapons up! Now!" the high-pitched voice shouted. Their gun barrels pointed in all directions, but there was not a single target to be seen. A moment of confusion was followed by a ripple of uniform movement as they looked up at the onslaught coming down from above.

Thud! Thud! Thud! The balls of mud hit each window on the tank, dead center. The tank slipped to a squishing halt. The ring of guards did another frantic search for their enemies in the trees. Lia didn't worry about anyone being spotted. She had trained them all to become invisible. Now, all they had to do was wait.

As the tank hatch swung open, she whispered the order "Driver."

Zip! A bullet from the other side of the clearing dropped the driver halfway out the hatch. Her limp body fell out and flopped into the mud. That giveaway of her sniper's position could have ended his life, if it hadn't been for the perfectly timed onslaught that followed. The flying mud balls were big enough to take down two Unis at a time. No doubt a few rocks had been added to the mix. They all would have been able to get back on their feet, if not for the wads of sticky slop that flew down next.

Harris must be pretty proud of himself, Lia thought as she saw how perfectly his plans had panned out. Yes, it had been worth building the catapults. The poker faces were still writhing around, clawing mud from their eyes and slapping at the ground to retrieve their fallen weapons, when the surrounding forest burst into motion.

There was no need for guns. The third wave came in with steel. After a few gargled cries and wet thuds, there was only one tin can left alive.

Roland had his sword at the soldier's throat before he had found his fallen gun. "On your feet," he said with the undeniable confidence of a man with the upper hand. "Where are you taking the weapons?" he asked as the soldier rose.

He glanced around, taking in the sight of his fallen comrades and the surrounding ring of Resistance soldiers with swords, but said nothing.

"I have no qualms about leaving you in the mud with the rest," Roland said with a quick flick of his blade to the nearest uniformed body.

The soldier's second glance around gave Lia pause. Since when did a lackey poker face make any assessments before acting? She shouldered her rifle and began to climb down from her position, but kept a firm eye on the situation as she lowered from branch to branch.

"I don't know," the soldier finally said.

"Am I supposed to believe you were escorting your cargo around completely blind?"

"Our Sub-Command gave the orders day-to-day. Map is in the tank."

Roland poked his sword up under the lackey's chin. "Then, why don't you go ahead and get it for me?"

The soldier turned and began to climb up on the tank. His sudden change from inaction to action, without a second thought, concerned Lia even more. She stopped her descent from the tree, steadied her back against the trunk, and took aim at the poker face, just in case.

Roland followed him up, remaining within severing distance, sword at the ready. "This gives me a bit of reason to debate your usefulness," he said as he rounded to the opposite side of the tank hatch. "Think about what you might have to offer me that the map does not." He gestured with his sword for the soldier to climb inside.

That's when the soldier reached into his pocket. Before Lia could secure her aim, before Roland could pull the sword back for a killing blow, the Uni had triggered and released a grenade. A tiny tink sounded out as it struck the side of the hatch before dropping inside.

Lia pulled the trigger, but it was already too late.

The massive shock wave that followed the bone shaking boom was like a tornado wind. Lia found herself flat on her back in the mud, completely deaf and without her rifle. What had happened to Roland? She scrambled up and raced toward the tank, tearing through the rainfall of freshly loosened leaves.

In the clearing ahead, Roland lay on one side of the smoking tank, the poker face on the other. Roland's sword lay between them.

As the already healing poker face began to sit up, Lia's anger took hold of her body. She ripped Roland's sword from the mud and stabbed it straight into that tin can's chest.

Crunching past his bones had been easier than she thought possible. He slapped back into the mud with Roland's sword poking out of his chest like a flagpole. The brief hint of struggle for life in his eyes was enough to tell Lia he would not heal this time. She raced to the other side of the clearing and dove to her knees at Roland's side.

Worse than the burns on his flesh, than the shaking of his muscle as he struggled for each breath, than the trickle of blood from the corner of his mouth, was that same struggle for life in his eyes.

BEFORE THE PAIN took over, there was thought—the thought that he should have known that soldier's plan long before it had come into action. Perhaps he had forgotten to look straight into his enemy's eyes so long ago, that it was inevitable he would receive a harsh reminder. There was the thought that Lianna had never looked so enraged as she did the moment she took up his sword and that, as she arrived at his side, she had never looked so frightened. There was the thought that the pain ought to have arrived long before the dull whine from his busted eardrums drowned out the panicked orders shouted out over his body. And just before the agony flooded in and shoved out all other thought with its screams, there was the thought that this forest looked so much like the one he had been wandering through the day he met her.

ROLAND

HE DIDN'T REALIZE how thirsty he was until a huff of exhaustion forced the smell of his own rancid breath up his nose. The hours without water had turned his spit into a stinky paste. The road had veered away from the river so long ago it was too far to go back now. The surrounding trees were still lush, but there was not so much as a creek to be seen.

Then, as if the forest could feel his need, his foot sunk into a patch of mud. Roland crouched and began to claw at the mud. The thick mud gave way to a sloppy wet mess. He kept digging, squeezing each fistful of mud as he shoveled it to the side. Eventually the hole he excavated was full of dark brown water. He cupped the liquid into his shaking palms and sipped up the murky water.

A sound filtered through the trees. Roland froze and tilted his ear up to the sky. It was voices. He ducked off the road and scrambled to hide among the saplings. He stilled his shakes and watched from between the tiny trunks as a group of Unity soldiers walked down the road. They were not marching, but at ease, chatting to each other as if they were out for a pleasant stroll. Roland wondered if they were telling stories and making jokes about all their recent conquests. Of course, they wouldn't be able to laugh even if they were.

He waited in stillness as their voices drifted away, then through another moment of silence for good measure.

Roland began to stand and, as his view cleared the top of the saplings, a pair of hands grabbed his arm and yanked him back to the ground. An arm clad in black leather snapped around his chest, binding his arms. A hand slapped across his mouth, and a soft voice whispered into his ear, "Shh. There's more."

He managed to still the panicked bursts of breath escaping his nostrils as another group of Unity soldiers came into view. This group walked in silence, without marching, but with an air of caution, as if they knew there were eyes on them.

Roland waited as the arm kept him still and the hand kept him silent. The Unity soldiers disappeared from view. The dulcet sounds of the forest took over. As the arm began to release him, he broke free and sprinted into the forest.

The stranger chased him, speeding around the trees like a black wolf bounding after a rabbit. Hands snatched his belt and tackled him to the ground. One of his arms crunched up under his body as the stranger pinned him down, but the other was still free. He pulled his knife from its sheath. The stranger flipped him over. Roland slashed at the air in front of her face. She snatched his wildly slashing arm and slammed it to the ground. His knife tumbled away.

"What kind of shatz are you trying to pull, kid?" the stranger shouted. Roland finally focused on her face. She was a young woman, with hair as black as the leather body armor she was clad in. Piercing eyes stared down at him in accusation. "Someone saves your ass from getting picked up and taken to one of those government kiddie camps or being used for target practice, and you repay 'em by slashing at 'em with a hunting knife?" She scooped up his knife and held it defiantly in front of his face.

Roland found himself unable to move, let alone speak. He wasn't even sure he was still breathing.

The stranger stood up and stretched out her back muscles. Roland took in her full appearance. She had a rifle strapped across one shoulder, and a travel pack slung over the other. "What are you doing out here anyway, kid?"

Roland had to swallow in some air before he could answer. "I ran."

"From?"

"From my farm. From the soldiers."

"And your farm is?"

"Willowdowns."

A look of both recognition and shock registered on her face. She knelt down beside him.

Roland found the strength to sit up.

"How long have you been out here?" she asked.

He had to search his memory for the count of sunrises he'd seen. "Twelve days."

"Where are your parents?"

He tried to breathe calm into his body but could not keep his jaw from quivering as he answered. "They killed my father. He tried to fight but—"

"It's okay, kid."

Cutting him off had saved Roland from shedding any tears. He blinked the sting of salty water out his eyes.

The stranger looked him up and down, as if assessing him. He considered how he might have appeared, small, scared, dirty, and—if his breath was any indication—smelly. He must have looked like a half-dead baby rodent to the wolf-woman staring at him now.

"You been sticking to the road?" she asked after a long assessment. Roland responded with a nod.

"Where are you going?"

"Wherever it goes."

She twisted her travel pack around to the front, reached in, and pulled out a canteen. Roland must have looked at her as if he were sure it was poison. She shook it in front of his face, making its contents slosh about. "It's only water, without the mud."

Roland's hesitance quickly turned into an abundance of relief as the clean water washed down his throat, taking with it the paste of thirst. He only realized how much he had drunk as he felt his head tipping back for another mouthful. He stopped just short of finishing the entire canteen. Words didn't suffice to express how he felt after that, but he still uttered, "Thanks."

She wore a slight smile as she took back the nearly-empty canteen. "Don't mention it." She stowed the canteen in her pack, along with Roland's knife. He watched until its carved handle disappeared beneath the ties. "The name's Saphron. Saph for short." She held out her hand.

Roland was a bit embarrassed to present the scabby crusted mess that his hands had become, but did, nonetheless. "I'm Roland."

"Well, Roland," she said very matter-of-fact, "I think you should come with me."

Lifting his legs over the uneven ground of the forest floor was a huge effort after days on the flattened road, but the trees felt as if they cloistered him from harm. He watched Saph trudge on ahead and wondered how well she knew how to use the rifle on her back. It certainly seemed like another appendage of her body, something she could wield at a moment's notice if necessary. The sun was low, and the trees were casting long, lean shadows between strips of golden light when they finally reached a clearing.

Saph held up a hand, halting Roland at the tree line. Roland peered between the trunks, half expecting to see a Unity encampment, but the clearing only contained a budding campfire being tended by a lone man. He was huge and hulking, with ginger hair and beard to match, dressed in body armor like Saph.

Roland took one step forward and snapped a tiny twig underfoot.

The man whipped a gun from his belt and pointed it straight in Roland's direction.

Saph was quick to tug something from her breast pocket, a small mirror. She found a ray of sunlight and flashed the beam across the man's face in a sequence of three and three.

He lowered his gun.

Saph emerged from the trees, beckoning Roland to follow. He kept a safe distance behind her as the man approached, looking him over with a scrutinizing glare.

"When I told you to hunt, I meant for animals. I don't think we're that desperate yet." His voice was alarmingly gruff. It brought Roland to a standstill.

"I found him by the road, alone." Saph's voice sounded even softer after the harsh tones that proceeded it. "Has been for days. They killed his father."

"Along with a lot of other people."

"He's been surviving out here by himself. Running from the Unity. You know that ain't easy."

"Even harder when you've got more people to hide, not to mention feed. I know where you're going with this, so I'll just say it before we get there. No." He turned back toward the fire.

Saph followed.

Roland kept his distance but was close enough to hear their only semi-whispered conversation.

"He's got nowhere to go, Red. No one to help him." Her voice was soft and warm.

"The Unity orphaned him, and they can take care of him, along with all the other kids they did the same thing to. They are not our problem." His voice was rock hard and icy.

"He was in Willowdowns."

That one statement elicited the same shock in him that it had in Saph. The man named Red gave Roland his own assessment before turning back to Saph. "Are you sure?"

"He didn't say much about the night they came. Only that they killed his father and that he got away using this." She twisted her pack around and pulled out Roland's knife.

Red turned it over in his hands as if he were making sure it was real.

"He fought back?" Red asked without taking his eyes off the blade.

"You think he'd be standing here if he didn't? He's strong, fast. Almost outran me. He's got a lot of will to have made it this far."

Red gave her words a moment's consideration, then shook his head. "I've got more important things to do than babysit." He attempted to turn his back.

"I can watch him," she said blankly.

Red whirled back around with an incredulous look on his face. "Come on, darlin'. Hollis has got more nurturing bones in his body than you do."

"Wanna bet?"

"This isn't a game."

"An agreement then." Saph stepped in close to Red, making another attempt at whispered conversation, but Roland could still just hear her over the crackling of the fire. "We take him with us. I'll watch him. If he slows us down, we'll leave him in the next city. You have my word."

Red shook his head as if disagreeing with himself. "You know, one of these days you're not going to get what you want out of me."

Saph smiled. "I'll believe that when it happens."

Red waved Roland over with the knife and pointed to a spot by the fire, a clear instruction to sit. Roland was happy to finally rest his legs but incredibly wary of what might happen next.

Red towered over him. "Listen up, kid. If you're going to come with us, there's a few simple rules. Number one, I'm in charge. You do what I say without question. You don't like something I tell you to do, then by all means, head off on your own. It makes no difference to me. Number two, keep up. I am not going to wait around for anyone. And number three, if you want something, you're going to have to earn it. You want to eat, get your own food. You want to sleep, make your own camp. You want a fire, build one. You want anything from one of us, earn it. Understand?" Red had been gesturing with Roland's knife as he spoke. It was very distracting, but not enough to keep Roland from listening. He knew his survival depended on it.

"Yes," Roland answered in the most confident voice he could muster.

Red straightened up and looked down his nose at Roland. Was he searching for fear?

Roland stared back, unblinking, determined to show none.

When Red finally seemed satisfied, he gave him a nod and took a seat on the other side of the fire.

Saph glanced back and forth as she settled to the ground in between them.

Roland felt a need surfacing, a desire to ask something even though he knew it would earn him no good will. The words finally broke free. "Can I 'ave my knife back?"

The look Red gave Roland over the flames was inscrutable, but his words were perfectly clear. "Earn it."

More and more armed and armor-clad people emerged from the forest as the sun lowered. They were a motley mix of faces and ages, but all with a hard edge that seemed either inherent or honed. One by one, their confusion upon seeing Roland was met with a short, grumbled response from Red. From that point on, they seemed to ignore him as a rule. Roland was fine with that. He wasn't too keen to tell anyone his story, just happy to be sitting by a warm fire.

The last man to appear cut a long, lanky silhouette against the final rays of sunshine. Red approached him with his hands up in anticipation. The lanky man reached into his pack and pulled out one tiny, dead chipmunk.

"Dammit, Hollis! You think this is funny?" Red growled out in frustration.

"Hardly. I wouldn't have even picked up this scrap if it hadn't been the only thing I shot all day." He gestured with the chipmunk, making its limp body flap around.

Red tugged at his beard and turned back to address the odd group now gathered around the fire. "What is wrong with you all? You're supposed to be survivors. The toughest of the tough. You're telling me you can't even bring down a bunny rabbit?"

"It's not as easy as it seems, Red," said the man named Jarrel. He was small in stature, but had a hard, scarred-up face that made him look as if he had been carved out of wood.

"Yeah, these things are fast," the lanky man named Hollis added with another flap of the chipmunk.

"You get 'em in your sight and next thing you know, you're shooting at nothing but leaves. Right, Saph?" Jarrel gave her a light whack to encourage agreement.

Before Saph could confirm, the buxom woman named Madge chimed in. "Don't ask her. She was too busy filling out adoption papers to go hunting."

"I didn't see you bring back anything," Saph was quick to respond.

"Hey, where did he come from?" Hollis asked, having finally noticed Roland sitting by the fire.

"I'll explain later," Saph said in a pacifying voice.

"Enough!" Red's shout made everyone flinch. Roland sat bolt upright as if he had just been yelled at by a school teacher. "I don't want to hear it. If you can shoot those bulletproof shields the Unis call men, you can sure as hell bring down a nice flesh and blood deer."

"Ain't no deer." Roland didn't realize he had spoken until he saw all eyes around the fire staring at him.

"What was that?" Red asked as if he was grilling him for information.

"Ain't no deer. They's grass eaters, take to the plains. Don't like the growth 'round these parts."

Red looked as if he was going to crack his own teeth under the force of his clamped jaw.

Saph stepped in and knelt in front of Roland. "But there's got to be animals, right? Something we can hunt?"

"Hunt? No. All them critters 're too fast. Got too much cover." Roland was just telling the truth, but every face around him looked as if what he said was an insult.

"I don't think you know who you're talking to, kid. They may be too fast for you plow mules, but we're a little more experienced," Jarrel said, explaining the looks he had just gotten.

"A second ago, you seemed to agree with him," Hollis said.

"Are you going to let grade school over here tell you what you can and can't shoot?"

"He's just trying to help. Isn't it obvious he's as hungry as we are?" Saph said on Roland's behalf.

"Oh, I'm sorry. I didn't realize you snatched up this bush baby so he could give us hunting lessons." Jarrel was getting annoyed. Roland found himself suddenly afraid of what that might lead to.

"Can it, Jarrel." Hollis was clearly not afraid.

"Or what, Hollis?"

It seemed as if the tensions were about to break out in a fist fight, but Roland remembered, "You can trap 'em!" All eyes turned back on him again. He didn't wait to be grilled for information this time. "All you need is simple traps, deadfalls 'n such, circled 'round the camp. Come day, you'll 'ave the critters came durin' the night."

The look that passed around the circle this time was one of embarrassment.

"All right, kid. We'll give it a shot," Red said as if it were only a suggestion and not the sure-fire solution no one else had thought of. "Is that what's been keeping you alive?"

"Well, no. See, I was movin', runnin'. Can't set traps if you can't come back to 'em."

"So, what have you been eating?" Red asked with interest.

The sun had set by then, so Roland decided it would be easier to demonstrate than to explain. "I'll show you." He took off into the trees. The entire group followed, keeping their distance as Roland whacked a stick around the underbrush. He probably looked like a kid playing an imaginary game to them, but he was determined to prove otherwise. A bright flash of yellow under the leaves revealed what he had been searching for. He reached down, snatched the slimy, wriggling slug from the mud and held it up.

A collective gasp of disgust went around the group.

"That's what you've been eating, Roland?" Saph sounded horrified.

"T'ain't nothing wrong with 'em. They's protein. Easy to catch."

"Yeah. I bet it just slides right down," Hollis said with a chuckle.

"That's shatz, kid. You're just messing with us. They're probably poison." Jarrel seemed certain he was being played.

"What reason would he have to poison us?" Saph rightly asked.

"Oh, didn't you know? The poker faces started planting double agents across the country in the form of orphan kids who trick you into eating poisonous slugs." Madge rolled her eyes at the whole situation.

"You try it then," Jarrel said, challenging her.

"I'll save my appetite for the next course," Hollis added, laughing even harder.

"Nobody eats a thing until the kid eats it first," Red said, looking back and forth between Roland's eyes and the fat yellow slug wringing in his fist.

"He's not a lab rat, Red," Saph protested.

"How else are we gonna to know?"

She didn't seem to have an argument against that.

All eyes turned on Roland and his fistful of protein. He had intended all along to show them what to do, so he simply shrugged and shoved the entire slug into his mouth. Another gasp of disgust went around the group. He could feel its tail wriggling out of the corner of his mouth as he took the final chomp down on its head with his back teeth. The resulting gush of innards made a foamy slime dribble down his chin. He leaned his head back, swallowed it down, then wiped the slime off his chin.

They all looked at him like he had just peeled the skin off his face.

Hollis burst out in manic laughter. "Oh, we're axed now."

"All right, everyone," Red said very calmly.

"Here it comes," Hollis added between guffaws.

"Let's find some slugs," Red concluded.

After a few cold shudders and quiet exclamations of disgust, the group began to search through the underbrush. Hollis had to let his manic laughter die down before he could join them.

Roland was just bending down to join the search, when Red clapped a hand onto his shoulder.

"You can relax. I'm sure there will be plenty leftover." Red slid Roland's knife out from under his belt and presented it to him in an open palm.

He looked back and forth between the knife and Red's face, certain it might be snatched away from him any second, but Red's palm remained open. Roland dared to reach out and wrap his still slimy hand around the elaborately carved handle. As he looked back up into Red's face, he could see one upturned corner of his mouth peeking through his beard.

THEY NEVER DOUBTED Roland's advice again, at least not when it came to what and what not to eat. It helped that the few traps they set that night delivered a hearty breakfast, one that didn't include slugs. His willingness to set all those traps, get the fire started, and cook the next morning certainly helped to win them over. He didn't mind becoming their cook. He was just happy to no longer be alone.

No one wanted to talk about their occupation of choice in front of Roland. Secretive conversations about where they were headed and the plans they would enact when they got there took place well out of Roland's earshot, but he knew who they were and what they did. Any Resistance fighter, even one that came from as questionable a background as Jarrel, was a hero in his eyes. As he faced night after night of seeing his father's murder over and over again in his nightmares, he began longing to fight by their side. It would take some convincing, but Roland was willing to bide his time.

It was on one of those perfect days that followed, when the sun was warm and the air was sweet and cool, that Red presented Roland with his first challenge on the road to becoming a Resistor. Roland had taken on the job of foraging as they traveled. Once the trees had given way to bushland, there was much more to be found, and he was as keen as they were to eat more than slugs and rabbits. He didn't think anyone else had been keeping an eye out for food until Red called out to him.

"Hey, kid." Roland followed the gruff shout and found him stooped down by a well laden berry bramble. "These are the edible ones, right?"

"Right, ya," Roland responded and began to pick the bounty to add to his stash.

"That means yes, does it?" Red asked, one eyebrow raised.

Roland was thrown by the question but answered, nonetheless. "Right. Yes."

Red gave him a little nod, then joined him in the task of stripping berries out of the bramble. "Why do you talk like that, kid?"

"Like what?"

"You add all those yas, ays, and ois to simple statements. And when you're not doing that, you smash all your words together like a train wreck."

"'S how everybody I know talks. T'ain't nothin' strange about it."

"You mean there isn't anything strange about it. That's how you should have said it."

What difference does it make? Roland thought, annoyed. "You still savvy what I said."

"How you talk to people is not just about being understood, kid. It's a big part of how you present yourself, what people believe about you... beyond your words."

"What'u mean?" Only then did Roland realize he had said that as one long word. He had always asked his questions like that, and no one had ever wondered why before.

"If you want people to believe you're smart, then act like you already know everything the world could possibly teach you. If you want people to believe you're strong, never show them your weak side. And if you want people to listen, then every sentence has got to sound like poetry. People should be hanging on your every word, not trying to discern one from another. You savvy that?"

Roland nodded. He understood, but he still didn't know why it mattered.

Then, Red dared to ask, "Do you know how to read?"

"Yes!"

"Whoa. Okay, kid." Red looked oddly pleased that Roland had shouted at him. "Try talking the way people do in some of the books you've read as an experiment. See what kind of reaction you get. Chances are, people will treat you differently. They won't just think you're some uneducated, backcountry plow pusher."

A surge of anger rose up inside Roland. "I am a plow pusher! And plow pushers ain't uneducated. You 'ave to know lots to farm. Seasons, land conditions, crop types. You 'ave to learn how to treat an' protect the land, what to do when the seasons turn early an' the crops t'ain't ready, an' heaps more an' you'll ever know!" His pulse was pounding into his ears. He could feel his nostrils flaring with each breath he forced out and the heat of anger clamming up his palms.

Red looked at him and smiled. "You were a farmer. You're not anymore. Now you can be whatever you want to be. And if you treat everything you do with as much pride as you showed just now, you could even rule the world someday." He cinched up his satchel of berries and walked off to join the others.

Roland stayed behind, listening as his pulse calmed back into a steady rhythm. Was Red just amusing himself? No. He wasn't like the others. He wouldn't have said anything he didn't mean. It was at that moment Roland determined to prove him right.

HE HAD MADE it through the jerky journey across the forest and down into the sheltered recess of the valley. Even though he had to force every breath in and out of his body, even though he had to clench his jaw against the pain that must have been overpowering, Roland's eyes were still open. It wasn't until they laid him down in the medical tent that his lids began to flutter shut.

"Hey! Roland!" Harris shouted "Come on. Stay awake." He willed them back open, but the glimmer of active thought had left. They were starting to lose him.

Harris made quick work of peeling off his body armor and cutting away the last layer of fabric. All movement in the tent came to standstill. Harris didn't know how many soldiers were still at his back, but the gasp of shock came from every angle over his shoulders.

The entire side of Roland's body was torn apart. Blood oozed from every patch of flesh that wasn't blackened by burns.

Lia's face, hovering in the corner of his eye, turned pale as milk.

"Everyone out." Harris didn't hear any movement. He whipped around "Out! Now!"

The soldiers scampered out like rodents.

Lia was still sitting on the ground, too bloodless from shock to move.

As soon as the tent flaps shut behind the last fleeing soldier, Harris began his hunt through the equipment.

"What are you going to do?" Lia asked in a whisper.

"The only thing I can," Harris said as he found the metal box he had been searching for.

Roland's eyes fluttered shut again.

Lia crawled to his side. "Roland!" She looked as if she wanted to reach out, to shake him awake, but was afraid to touch him.

Harris snapped open the latches on the box with a desperate speed and pulled out one of the injection needles.

Lia's eyes widened at the sight of the formula in Harris's hand. "What is that going to do to him?"

"Same thing it did for me." Harris put one hand down over Roland's heart, clasped his other hand around the needle, steadied his breath, and jabbed the needle straight down into his chest.

Roland's eyes shot open before Harris had even finished injecting the silvery substance into his heart. As he yanked out the needle, Roland took in a heaving breath. He let it out as an anguished cry through clenched teeth.

Harris could only imagine the amount of pain that had just rushed back into Roland's body, but this was the only surefire way he could think of to save his life.

Roland's body begin to seize. All Harris could do was hold him down. "Help me!"

Lia clasped Roland's arm against her body. "Roland, look at me. Look into my eyes." By some miracle, he did. "You will get through this. You will survive. For us. For Malcolm."

His sharp panting slowed. His trembling muscles stilled. She couldn't know how much pain he was feeling, but she had found a piece of his mind that sat beyond the physical. She had tapped into his sheer will to live. He kept his eyes focused on her until his body's only defense against the pain switched on, and he passed out.

TWO

HIS EYES OPENED so quickly that Lia thought he might snap upright, but all Roland did was look around, orienting himself back into the world. She gently rested her hand on his chest to let him know she was by his side.

"Try not to move," she whispered.

Roland turned his head slowly and stiffly in her direction. There were blood stains pooled into both of his eyes, but the life had returned to them.

She propped herself up onto one elbow, so he could see her without twisting too far.

"How long?" his voice croaked out.

"About four hours now."

He tried to ask another question, but his throat closed up around the words.

Lia sat up and hunted for her canteen. She dribbled a tiny trickle of water into his mouth. Even that pittance seemed to be a huge effort for him to swallow. Rather than watch him struggle, she filled the silence. "Harris has done his best to quiet the murmurs of your inevitable death. The camp has been calm for a while now. Whatever he conjured up must have worked."

Roland stared up at the canvas, thoughts processing behind his damaged eyes. What were they? Regrets? Doubts? Fears? If he ever experienced such thoughts, they would be with him now. He finally said, "Now I know what it feels like."

"What?"

"To be at death's door the moment the formula enters your body. That kind of rebirth is something I never want to experience again. Or impose upon another... again."

He could have been thinking of anything. Lia never guessed it would be of her. She didn't know what to say. "Try to rest." Those were the only words that surfaced.

His blood-spotted eyes followed as she lay back down by his side and rested her head on her arm. He forced a deep, wheezing breath in and out before speaking again. "You took up my sword."

She didn't think he had seen that. "It seemed like the thing to do." "You hate blades."

"Proved to come in handy. Don't worry, I remembered to bring it back." She had, in fact, clutched to the hilt through that entire uncertain journey to get him back to camp, as if holding his sword would keep him alive.

Somehow, Roland found the strength to smile. With slow and careful movement, he reached his arm up and placed his open palm on the ground between their shoulders.

Lia slipped her hand into his. He gave her fingers a gentle squeeze and allowed his eyes to shut again.

BY THE TIME they reached the edge of the bushlands, Roland had made himself an essential member of Red's team. He didn't mind getting up before dawn to check the traps and light the fire. He didn't mind foraging throughout the day. He didn't mind serving them all with care and humility. What he did mind was being left alone as they went about whatever secret mission had been their objective on this land... and the next... and the next.

They wouldn't let him near the Unity encampments he knew they were wiping out, let alone the villages they were aiming to free. It was true it could go wrong at any moment, that one misstep would see Red's entire team killed, and Roland would be alone again. He still longed to see, first hand, how successful they really were. He had gotten pretty good at feigning deafness to the conversations that slipped out in his presence. He had never betrayed his desire to join them out loud, but his frustration was building. Perhaps that's why his emotions emerged in the unexpected way they did that day.

Roland could feel everyone watching the spit as he turned it. Yes, the sight of lizards roasting whole, tails and tongues flopping with every turn, was less than appetizing, but he knew that once charred up, they would be pretty palatable.

Madge finally said what everyone had been thinking. "I can't believe this is really our dinner."

"The fires scorched what little vegetation was out here. I don't even think those scrawny jackrabbits could survive." Saph always came to Roland's defense, even when the others' comments were obtuse insults at the most. Part of him wanted to get annoyed at her for never letting him fight his own battles, but her protectiveness was actually quite endearing.

"Doesn't bode well for the village over the ridge," Jarrel said as he tossed another pebble over the fire, which whizzed a bit too close to Roland's head.

"They'll have food, processors, plenty of supplies." Red sounded exhausted.

"Maybe even a little liquid golden love," Hollis added with the usual energy that only he always seemed to possess.

"How can you think about drinking with those slimy little things roasting in front of us?" Madge asked.

I'll gladly eat your share, Roland thought.

"Easy. I just keep thinking, at least they're not slugs." Hollis's statement sent a murmur of agreement around the fire.

Saph knelt down by Roland's side. "Why don't you let me do that for a while?"

"I really don't mind."

"Quit being such a gentleman and go sit down before you singe off your eyebrows." She gave him a warm smile that couldn't be argued with.

As Roland stepped away from the fire, he realized how wonderfully cool the evening had become. He stripped off his jacket to feel the relief provided by the air. As he tossed it to the ground, his satchel of seeds, the only remnant of his former life and his family farm, tumbled out of his pocket and landed right at Jarrel's feet.

"What's this?" Jarrel snatched up the satchel and peered inside. Roland lunged at him, one arm outstretched to snatch it back, but Jarrel stood with lightning speed. "Have you had this all along, kid?"

"Give it back! It's mine!" Roland took another leap at him, but Jarrel's arms were just long enough to hold it out of his reach.

"Oh, I don't think so."

"What is it?" Red asked.

Jarrel showed Red what was inside.

"It's seed, grain, a crop field's worth." The satchel was within reach now, but Roland didn't dare snatch it out of Red's sight. "You've been holding out on us, kid. Making us eat creepy crawlies for your own amusement while you got a bounty all to yourself."

"He wouldn't do that, Jarrel." Saph came to his defense as always.

"Oh no? You think he picked all this up on the trail? He's a thieving little rat."

"I said give it back. Now!" Roland could feel his jaw tightening, his fists trembling. The forethought and control he'd maintained over those last few months was suddenly absent from his mind and body.

"Don't you dare give me orders, you dirty little plow pusher."

Whatever force had shoved thought and control out of him took over his actions. Roland whipped his knife out of its sheath and held it against Jarrel's throat.

"Roland, don't!" There was genuine fright in Saph's voice.

"I said give it back," Roland said with a calm command completely opposite to how he was feeling.

"Are you joking, kid?" Jarrel was looking at him with the eyes of a man who couldn't be threatened by anything, but that did not deter Roland.

"Now." He pressed the blade harder against Jarrel's throat.

"Come on, Red. You're not going to let him get away with this." Perhaps he was starting to feel a bit threatened after all.

"I don't know, Jarrel. He seems pretty serious to me. I think you'd better give it back to him." Red sounded rather serious himself.

"What?"

"Just give it back." Saph sounded like she was ready to draw her rifle if need be.

Jarrel slowly lowered the satchel of seeds until it was dangling in front of Roland's face.

He snatched it back, shoved it deep into his pocket, slid his knife back into its sheath, and returned to the fire to continue turning the spit. He didn't say anything about the satchel of seeds, and no one bothered to ask.

After they ate, Roland found himself actually wanting to be alone for the first time since fleeing from his family farm. He found solace on the nearby hillside but stayed within view of the camp. His fear of being abandoned still far outweighed his desire for solitude.

It wasn't long before he saw Jarrel's compact silhouette climbing up the hillside toward him. Roland pretended he was invisible.

"Mind if I join you?" Jarrel asked, as if he would oblige if Roland said no. He took Roland's silence as an invitation and sat down beside him. "Listen kid, if you're going to pull a knife on someone, you gotta make them believe that you intend to use it, otherwise they'll know you're just putting on a show."

"I did intend to use it." Roland wasn't sure if that were true, but he wanted Jarrel to believe it was.

"That's tough talk, but it's shatz. You wouldn't have done a bit of damage with that knife, not the way you were holding it."

"How would you know?" Roland shot an angry look at Jarrel and was instantly reminded of the distinct scars on his face. He would probably know better than anybody.

"Let me see the knife." He held out his hand.

Roland leaned away. "No."

"What am I going to do, kid, run off and bury it under a bush? Let me see it." He gave an insistent flick of his awaiting fingers.

Roland glanced down at the rest of the group. They were chatting by the fire, not paying attention, probably too far away to see much of anything in the dark. Not even Saph was looking in their direction. Roland slid the knife out of its sheath and passed it to Jarrel.

He tossed it back and forth from hand to hand and gave it a quick flip, catching it delicately by the blade. Yes, he definitely had some experience with a blade. Just when Roland was certain that all Jarrel wanted to do was impress him with a few showy tricks, he lunged forward and held the knife to Roland's throat.

"Now, you were holding the knife about here. Right against my windpipe. You feel that?"

Roland summoned the courage to give him a little nod. It felt as if anything more would have sliced him right open.

"That's the hardest part of the throat to cut, especially at close range. It's tough, stringy. If you want to do instant damage, you hold it here." Jarrel slid the blade around to the side of Roland's throat. He instantly felt the difference as the steel pushed against his soft, vulnerable skin. "That's the jugular, a main vein. One good slice, and you're drained pretty quick. You threaten any man with that, and he's bound to take you seriously. And you can push pretty hard before you even break the skin. Just like that." Jarrel pressed the blade into Roland's skin. He was certain he was going to be bleeding to death any second. Jarrel looked at him with those same fearless eyes. "Got it?"

Roland found enough space between him and the blade to nod again.

Jarrel retracted the knife as quickly as he had wielded it.

Roland couldn't help but feel his throat. There was a horizontal indent in his skin but not the slightest hint of blood.

Jarrel presented the knife to Roland, handle first, as if safety were his primary concern. "It's too big for you, anyway," Jarrel said casually as Roland stowed the knife. "Was your dad a big guy, tall?"

Roland looked away as he nodded. He hadn't quite recovered from the fear yet, and he really didn't feel like talking about his father.

Jarrel went on talking anyway. "You'll grow into it then. Right now, it kind of looks like a little sword in your hands. Bet you could use it like one, you're fast enough anyway." Had Jarrel actually just complimented him? "Know anything about swords?"

Roland had to swallow before he could answer. "You mean those ancient weapons?"

"A weapon's a weapon, kid. Just because a new one was invented doesn't mean the old ones don't still work." He stood up and headed toward the nearby bushes. He broke one of the low branches off with a stomp of his foot and snapped it in half over his knee. "Come here. Take one of these."

He stripped the branches and presented one to Roland.

He really didn't know what to expect but suddenly felt very compliant, especially to Jarrel. He stood up, took the branch, and mirrored the upright position Jarrel was holding his in.

"Now, it all begins with first position."

IT TURNED OUT Jarrel knew quite a lot about swords. Roland never asked where he had learned his skills, and Jarrel never volunteered that particular bit of information, but he willingly taught him all that he knew. Roland was happy to have the distraction. The task of cobbling together their wooden practice swords kept his mind busy, and their regular matches helped to vent some of his frustration. Saph was watching that afternoon, so he was determined to win.

"Come on, Roland! You're faster than him," she shouted from the sidelines.

"You're asking for it, sweet cheeks," Jarrel said with a quick point of his sword in her direction. That distraction gave Roland plenty of time to sidestep Jarrel's next jab at him.

"He's proving me right," she said with a smile.

Roland's body buzzed with adrenaline and pride. Jarrel came rushing at him with immense speed. Roland ducked down and tripped him over with a whack to the shin. Before Jarrel could stand, the point of Roland's wooden sword was at his throat. It was his first win. Saph had proved to be a very motivating audience.

"That's what you get for calling me sweet cheeks." Saph nudged Jarrel's back with her boot.

"He caught my blindside," Jarrel said dismissively as he stood up and dusted himself off.

A nearby splash grabbed their attention. Hollis was trudging across the river with a full-grown deer slung over his back. Jarrel and Saph rushed over to help him offload his kill.

"Oh, she's a thing of beauty." Jarrel was practically drooling as he ran his hands over the deer's flank.

"We can smoke rations for weeks," Saph said.

Roland would have joined in their exclamations of excitement but found himself transfixed on the bullet hole in the deer's head. A single, clean, kill shot had won Hollis his prize. Suddenly, there was another skill Roland longed to learn.

"I found their grazing land," Hollis said. "If we have to hold up here for a while, I can bag us another one."

"Can I come with you? Learn how to shoot?" Roland asked.

Hollis opened his mouth to answer but didn't get so much as a sound out.

"No," Saph said instantly.

"Definitely not," Jarrel added with a chuckle of disbelief.

"Now, wait a second," Hollis countered. "It's a good skill for the kid to know. Serves us with more than just hunting."

"It's too dangerous." Saph's face had grown very serious.

"I'll be careful," Roland attempted to reassure her.

"Famous last words," Jarrel facetiously sung out.

"You're the one teaching him swordplay," Hollis said.

"Swords don't go off and shoot you in the back." They were about to launch into an argument, if not for Roland's sake than for their own amusement, but Saph was suddenly lost somewhere in a cloud of dark thoughts. She really didn't want to see a gun in Roland's hand.

"It's okay," Roland said loudly enough to cut their argument short. He looked up into Saph's eyes as he said, "I'll wait."

A smile returned to her face. "That's all I ask." She lightly stroked Roland's cheek, encouraging a smile out of him, too.

The waiting turned out to be very short. Either Roland's frustration was too obvious to ignore, or Hollis simply felt sorry for him. It was on their very next fishing trip that Hollis decided to teach him about the mechanics of a gun. He demonstrated with his six-shooter, the "just in case" weapon he kept tucked in his boot. It looked tiny in Hollis's hand as he opened and shut the various chambers and instructed Roland in the proper order of operations when handling any gun. Roland expected that to be the end of the lesson, a simple introduction only, but he must have looked at Hollis the way a starving man would look at a steak.

Hollis let out a long sigh as he said, "All right, fine." He led him to the river's edge, placed the six-shooter into Roland's palm, and wrapped his fingers securely around the handle.

It looked much bigger in his hands and turned out to be much heavier than he thought.

Hollis forced Roland into position like a scarecrow, locking his elbows and bending his knees, then stood behind him. "You only shoot into the water, you hear me? Not the trees, not the air, and definitely nowhere in my direction. You got that?"

"Got it," Roland said without shifting so much as his eyeballs.

"Okay… go ahead," Hollis instructed.

Roland looped his finger into the trigger and took his first shot. The recoil rocketed straight down his locked arms, making his shoulders lurch. He stepped back to keep from losing his balance and felt Hollis's huge hand grab onto his shoulder.

"It's okay. I got it!" Roland was quick to say, lest Hollis snatch the gun away.

Hollis had enough faith to remove his stabilizing hand, but muttered under his breath, "Famous last words."

Roland took a wider stance and pulled back the trigger again. He remained perfectly still and statuesque through the next shot. Part of him wanted to turn and receive some acknowledgment, but his desire to keep shooting outweighed any need for praise. He took a few steps forward, wading into the cool of the river. Something drove him to take the next three shots in a row. Three tiny spurts of water shot up in a neat line.

"Easy, kid," Hollis said.

Roland nodded but didn't turn around. He waded deeper into the river. A light slap at the surface caught his ear. In a shallow bend a few paces ahead, the fish were jumping up to snap at the cloud of bugs hovering over the glassy surface.

Roland began a slow stock toward them.

"Get real, kid," Hollis called from the bank, but Roland waded farther in, undeterred.

He got close enough to pick out the shape of each individual fish twisting and turning under the surface. Roland pointed the barrel of the gun toward them, lined his view up behind the sight, and waited.

One fish broke away from the others to swim toward deeper waters. He followed with his sight, held his breath, and pulled the trigger.

The water exploded. The fish scattered. Before the ring of ripples even reached the riverbank, one dead fish bubbled up to the surface. It had a perfectly round bullet hole in its side.

Roland was already smiling before he heard Hollis's applause coming from the bank behind him. He splashed over to collect his prize, and then turned back to receive his praise.

He really did think that bringing a bounty of fish for dinner that night would keep anyone from being angry with him, but the darkness returned to Saph's face as soon as Hollis told them how Roland had managed it. He sat down by the fire and let the argument ensue over his head. This part of his fate was not in his hands. Not yet.

"You can't pretend he doesn't need it, Red. For protection," Hollis attempted to say as discreetly as his loud voice allowed.

"I keep him well away from those tin cans, and you know it!" Saph snapped back at him.

"You can't protect him forever, Saph," Red said.

"See. He agrees with me."

"But he is just a kid, Hollis."

"He's got mad skills for a kid," Madge added, not seeming to take either side of the argument.

"Am I hearing crazy here?" Roland thought the demonstration of his skill would have won Jarrel over, but he was still firmly on the side of no.

"When was the last time you hit a target like that?" Hollis asked as if he knew what Roland was thinking.

"Enough." Red's voice had brought about silence, as always. He took a knee in front of Roland and waited until he was looking him in the eye. His look was, once again, inscrutable, but his words were clear. "The day you need a gun, kid, I'll hand you one myself."

IT SHOULDN'T HAVE surprised Harris to see the flesh on Roland's side had already sealed. He knew from first-hand experience how quickly the injection worked the second time. Of course, he also knew how long it took for the pain to subside. Deep red scars and blackened bruises were the only vestige of what had once been near fatal wounds, but Harris kept that secret hidden under the bandages. Roland didn't need any encouragement. He was already trying to stand, against Harris's advice, when Lia entered the tent.

"Don't!" That was all she needed to say to freeze him in place.

"I'm not accustomed to being idle." Roland's voice had also recovered quickly.

"You're not strong enough for that yet," Lia argued.

"Which is exactly what I told him," Harris added.

"And what would either of you do if I told you the same thing?" It was a fair point, one that encouraged both of them to help him stand up. He cringed as he stretched up his spine.

Harris stepped away, but Lia kept one stabilizing arm around him. "We should be getting ready to move."

Harris had prepared for this argument. "We can't. As far as everyone knows, our Commander is only in stable condition and won't move for days."

"I'm moving now," Roland grumbled through another cringe against the pain.

"Even the most miraculous of known cures doesn't work that quickly."

"We're vulnerable this close to that explosion. They could find us in a matter of hours."

"We have eyes surrounding the camp. We'll be ready if someone approaches."

"That won't give us enough warning." Roland tried to take a step away from Lia's supporting arm. The pain made Harris's point for him. Roland doubled over. He allowed himself to be led back to the bed to sit down, though neither of them even attempted to convince him to lie down.

"If you want to keep what you have left of a rib cage, we have to hold," Harris declared.

Roland was about to throw another argument back at him, despite his pain, when Lia spoke up. "The best thing we can do now is relay an order that comes straight from the Commander."

Her suggestion was inspired. It set Roland with a task. Now his mind was occupied with something other than forcing his body into compliance.

"Take your lead team back to the site and look for scouts. Find out how many and what they know. Stick to the trees and cover your tracks." His voice had found its calm authority again.

"Yes, sir." She turned to leave, but Harris had an idea to add.

"And Lia, a few traces of a false trail in the wrong direction could also buy us some time."

She looked to Roland. He gave Harris's suggestion a nod of acceptance.

"Yes, sir," she said again, without making it obvious which one of them she was speaking to. It was a skill she had instantly mastered the day they set off to war. Lia disappeared through the tent flaps.

Harris considered what more he could say to Roland. He wasn't going to rest, no matter how much Harris encouraged him to. He was going to stand up again. He was going to push his body to whatever limits his pain would allow. He was probably going to look under his bandages and discover how fast he had actually healed. The only thing Harris could do was tell him the truth.

"You felt everything." That statement alone captured Roland's rapt attention. "The moment that stuff hit your heart, you were suddenly aware of every single sensation in your entire body. And if the pain hadn't been intense enough to knock you out, you would have felt every stitch I put in your side, every broken bone shifting in and out of place, every severed nerve firing, and every bit of skin that was burnt to a crisp. Just like I would have felt those bullets being pulled out of my chest if the Doc hadn't put me under. And now, that stuff is running through your veins telling you to get up and move, to ignore the pain, because you know how great it will feel once you're on the other side of it. It makes you want to run when you should walk. It makes you want to fight anything and everything. It makes you want to… do all kinds of stupid things." Harris had to fight the urge to turn his eyes down. Roland was hanging on his every word. "Patience is one of your greatest strengths, Roland. Don't forget that."

Roland took a moment, then gave Harris a small nod of understanding. "How long does it last?" he asked with that same calm authority.

Harris considered how he could explain, how he could possibly elaborate on everything he had experienced since that second injection but had never said a word about to anyone. There was only one explanation to give. "I don't know yet."

Roland gave him another nod. It was enough to encourage Harris to leave him alone in the tent, even though he knew his words of caution would only last so long. Whether due to the force of the formula surging through his veins or to Roland's own willfulness, they would be moving again soon.

THREE

PEACE HAD RETURNED to the forest. Other than the few squabbling crows that had discovered the bodies lying in the clearing, there wasn't a single soul to be spotted. Lia scanned the ground again, making sure there were no fresh prints in the mud, but not even the leaves that rained down in the explosion had found a breeze to move them.

"Perimeter check," she said into her radio.

A series of voices each responded with, *"Clear."*

"One more hour. Then, we return to camp."

Lia had just allowed herself enough movement to crack the kinks out of her neck, when an alert voice whispered in her ear. *"I've got movement in the North. They're headed your way, Sub-Commander."*

Lia mounted her scope onto her rifle, pushed back into the security of the shadows, and steadied her aim into the clearing.

Crunching footfalls became rustling leaves and then snapping branches as the Unity soldiers emerged into the clearing. The crows scattered as the tin cans spread out to examine the bodies of their fellow soldiers.

One of the sticky-beaked birds landed beside Lia and gave her a suspicious side eye. She put a silencing finger to her lips. He may have only been a crow, but she was certain he understood.

Lia focused in on the soldier that was examining the explosive-throwing ass she'd seen fit to kill with a sword. The gaping hole through his chest was undeniable as his cause of death.

The soldier hovering over him called back to someone who was still in the trees. "You were right, Commander." Lia followed her eye-line toward the trees and focused on the face of their Commander as he emerged into the clearing.

It was Martrim.

"I knew this one would be too tempting to ignore," his voice slithered.

An instant chill down Lia's spine was accompanied by the phantom sensations she could still feel in her nightmares, the explosive pain he'd inflicted upon her eye sockets, the repulsive crawling of her skin as his hands traced her scars.

The crow took off with a cry of alarm, calling the others up into the air with him. Even the birds seemed to know this was not a man to linger around.

Martrim crouched beside the soldier's body, analyzing the open wound. Once he was satisfied by what he saw, he stood and whistled into the trees.

Unity soldiers began to emerge, their numbers increasing by the second, like an infestation of black locusts.

"Fan out! Find their trail!" Martrim ordered with a cold shout.

"North, how many do you count?" Lia whispered.

"More than we can take before they scatter. And more coming still."

"They're starting in from the West, too," another voice added.

Lia fixed her focus on Martrim's head as he commanded one group after another with a cryptic whip of his hand, this way and that. "And if I took out their Commander?"

"There are still more coming. We can't cover that."

"There aren't enough of us."

Lia caressed her trigger. Would it be worth watching Martrim's skull blow open, even if it was the last thing she ever saw? No, that would be going too easy on him. She pulled her hand away from temptation. "All right. Retreat formation. Stay in the trees and stay invisible."

Many relieved affirmations sounded out in her ear. She climbed away into the dense cover of the treetops, leaving Martrim behind.

Their false trail was good enough to buy them some time, not that they would need it. As soon as Roland found out who was on their tail, he would be instantly ready for battle, and there would be no convincing him otherwise.

BY THE TIME they reached the badlands, Red's group was always well fed and mission ready. They had finally stopped being delicate around Roland and began talking openly about their plans, but he was still left behind whenever they would head off to enact them. He considered trailing them, even if it was only to see a glimpse of the action, to watch at least one of those tin cans fall, but uncertainty about how Red would react if he was discovered kept Roland from wandering too far from their campsite.

They had taken a particularly long time to get back that morning, and the fine sand proved to be very unforgiving ground for building a campfire. His third attempt at structuring a peak out of the few twisted branches he could find, collapsed under its own weight. Roland kicked the pile. He gained some relief from frustration as he watched the branches fly up into the air, but when the soft slope of the hillside sent every single one rolling gently back to his feet, Roland launched into a rage. He picked up the largest branch and smashed it down on the others like a club. The loud cracks and bits of bark flying up into the air offered him more relief than he'd felt in quite some time.

"Relax. It's just firewood." The sound of Saph's soft voice instantly washed away his frustration. She looked flushed and excited, fresh from the fight.

He scrambled up the sandy slope to meet her. "Did you find them? Did you fight? Is everyone okay?"

"Slow down, Roland. We're fine. We're better than fine. None of those Unis are ever coming back!" Her shout encouraged whoops and hollers of triumph from the others as they followed her into the sandy valley.

"How did you do it? Did you catch them by surprise? How many were there?"

"Roland," Saph said with a cautioning tone.

"You can tell me. I can handle it."

She took the time to drop her weapons and stretch her back as she considered. The others were already buzzing with conversation as they approached. Whether it would be due to the adrenaline pumping through their veins then, or the inebriation that would take over later, it wouldn't be long before Roland got the entire story out of them anyway. "Look, we'll tell you all about it, but why don't you make a run to the creek for us first." She was still trying to shelter him, but he was also still dedicated to being their dutiful caretaker, so he appeased her with a smile and a nod.

"Let someone else get the water, kid. I've got an assignment for you." Red had popped up at Roland's shoulder. Before he could even register the surprise of Red's appearance, let alone the fact he actually wanted something from him, Saph stepped in between them.

"What assignment?"

"An important one. And no concern of yours." He looked around her to address Roland. "Grab your gear, kid. We're going on a little hike."

Roland scrambled to gather up his things. Whatever it was, he was not about to question Red, but Saph certainly wasn't done yet.

"What are you going to make him do?" she asked with deep suspicion in her voice.

"Nothing the kid can't handle," Red said with that same inscrutable look in his eyes. He directed Roland to follow with a jerk of his chin. He could feel Saph's eyes watching as they wound up the sandy slope and out of sight.

Red didn't say anything throughout their entire hike. Roland didn't have the courage to start a conversation, even a seemingly harmless one. If this was a test, he would not fail. So, if Red wanted silence, that is what Roland would give him.

The sandy peaks gave way to rocky ones. The undulating land began to open up into crevices. Red took a scramble up a rocky slope and waited at the top. *This is it*, Roland thought. He followed in his footsteps and prepared for his destination to appear.

The tiny box canyon on the other side of the slope was littered with bodies. Deep purple stains spattered the rocky walls. Blood formed shiny pools in the dust. Blank faces of dead Unity soldiers stared up into the sky, mouths and eyes fixed open. Others were crumpled face down, nothing but a heap of black fabric. Flies buzzed through the otherwise silent air.

"They're all dead," Roland heard himself say.

"That's what victory means." Roland had no idea how long he had been staring at the bodies before Red spoke up again. "Not a one is coming back, so you don't have to worry about that. Some nice precise kill shots took care of the ones that were still moving. Go ahead, hike on down."

Red gave him a little shove on the shoulder. It forced something to surge up inside of Roland. He whipped around and shouted, "Why'd you bring me 'ere?"

Red didn't seem to care that Roland had shouted at him or that he had slipped out his carefully practiced speech patterns. He launched straight into his plan. "You see those bikes over there?"

Roland followed Red's point, glancing past the bodies and into the darkened end of the canyon. Several motorcycles were lined up in a tidy row, waiting to be driven.

"Now, I count twenty-one bikes and twenty-one bodies. Which means there are twenty-one keys, one on each body. I want those bikes. Your assignment is to get me those keys."

"Didn't you already search the bodies?" Roland asked without taking his eyes off the motorcycles. It was the one crevice of the canyon free of blood.

"We took their weapons and ammo, but I told the crew to leave the keys. That's your job."

Roland still couldn't move his eyes.

"Take as much time as you like. Take all night if you want, I don't care. But don't come back to camp without those keys." Red signaled his departure with a pat on the shoulder, then turned to leave without another word.

By the time Roland was able to move his eyes again, Red's figure was already getting smaller in the distance. He glanced back and forth between Red's shrinking shape and the gruesome sight below him. It felt as if there was an invisible barrier between him and the canyon floor. It wasn't until Red disappeared over the horizon that Roland felt the barrier drop away. He took in a deep breath, unstuck his feet, and hiked down into the canyon.

Roland had steeled himself to enter the canyon, but the body tucked under the base of the rocky slope took him by surprise. He side-stumbled his way down the last few steps in an attempt to keep from landing right on top of him. The man was face down with a halo of blood around his head. Roland crouched and watched the flies buzzing around the man's dusty hair and the sticky red pool. His stomach was beginning to turn, so he dared to turn his back on the body, even though part of him was still afraid it might get up at any moment.

Roland spotted a scrubby bush growing out from under the rock face and gleaned an idea. He snapped one of the branches off with his foot, just as Jarrel had done to create a makeshift sword, and turned back to the body, armed with his branch. Holding it at arm's length, he poked into the man's pants pockets. There was no sign of a key tumbling out, not even a light jangle from inside. Perhaps it was in his jacket, but all those pockets were on the front. Roland tried to lever the body over with his branch. It instantly snapped in half. He dared to slide his foot under the man's hip and lift with his toe. The sensation of his full weight against Roland's foot made him instantly retract. The body rocked but did not turn over. Roland breathed his fear away in short bursts, tucked his foot back under the man's hip, and lifted with all his strength.

The body flopped over. Roland fell to the ground in horror.

Where there had once been an eye, there was now nothing but a gaping hole with a grayish mush trickling out of it. The eye itself was dangling near the man's ear from a thin red strand. Blackish blood formed crusty trails out of the man's nose and mouth.

Roland crawled back to the bush and vomited all over its branches. He stayed on all fours, trying to breathe away the dizziness that threatened to leave him lying on the ground with the rest of them. When he finally felt the blood return to his limbs, he stood up on wobbling legs and turned back toward the body.

He looked at it out of the corner of his eye, slowly reintroducing the sight, as if every detail of what he had just seen wasn't already burned into his memory. A glimmer of sunlight off a scrap of metal caught his eye. There was a key attached to the man's belt.

Forgetting his fear in triumph, Roland rushed over to the body, dropped to his knees, and yanked the key off his belt. Roland stared at the scrap of metal as if it were a priceless jewel, lost in the warmth of victory, until a cold, creeping sensation sneaked up from below. He was kneeling in the pool of blood.

Roland jumped up and backed away, but contact with the lifeless liquid had already been made. Two perfect circles of red stained the knees of his pants. He touched his fingertips to the spot. It was wet, cold, and sticky. He had expected it to feel different. He had convinced himself that Uni blood was like a strange toxin, instantly harmful to all other lifeforms, but this blood felt no different than his own.

He turned and looked over the rest of the canyon. Some of the bodies had gaping wounds, exposing innards to the open air. Others had nothing but neat bullet holes in their temples, but every body had bled until it no longer could. Roland told himself he had already seen the worst of it. He took comfort in the fact that his enemy's blood had caused him no harm. There was nothing left to fear, only an assignment that needed to be completed. He pocketed the first key and began to search for the rest of them.

As the day wore on, Roland found a way to keep his mind occupied against any thoughts of how long it took each of those soldiers to die. He would, instead, try to assess where each of them might choose to keep their keys. Was this the sort of man who liked convenience and would keep everything within easy access? Was this the sort of woman who didn't trust any of her fellow soldiers and would stash her belongings in an inside pocket? He also found himself trying to figure out who had been responsible for each kill. He was certain those neatly disposed of with a single shot to the brain must have been killed by Saph. She had the skill and the grace for it. The messier kills were more likely to be Jarrel's. How Red might choose to go about killing was still a mystery to him.

The sun was beginning to set when he approached the last body. The gaping wound in the man's chest had caused Roland to circumnavigate him throughout the day, but his assignment would not be complete if he didn't collect that last key. The crows had made their claim on this body, while he had been busy with the others, and were pulling rubbery bits of flesh out of the wound with their beaks.

Roland had to turn his eyes down and swallow back a sudden rise of bile. He began to examine his own body. His pants were now soaked from the knees down in blood. There were dirty smears on his thighs where he had wiped his hands. His knuckles and nails were crusted over with a blackish paste, the combination of dried blood, sweat, and dirt. He was not so different from the crows after all.

Roland tossed tiny rocks at the protesting birds until they were annoyed enough to fly up and out of the canyon. He stooped in front of the body and, without looking into the man's face, searched through his pants pockets, followed by his jacket. After turning up nothing but lint, he tucked his fingers into the single breast pocket that remained untainted, sending a trail of ants scurrying away in panic. He felt the hard edge of an I.D. badge and began to slide it up out of interest. When the top of the man's image emerged, he thought better of it and tucked it back in. There was only one pocket left to check.

Roland methodically unbuttoned each silvery button on his uniform until his jacket fell gracefully open. Whatever color shirt he had been wearing underneath was now beet red. Roland pushed his hand toward the inside pocket without looking. Some part of what had once been the man's chest was dangling like a medal of honor. He slid his fingers past the slimy, unidentifiable lump and into the pocket. A single key emerged, covered in a substance that looked like red porridge. Fighting the rise of bile once again, Roland wiped the key off on his already ruined pants. As he looked at his victory key, a never-before experienced desire, a pressing need, rose up inside of him.

He would stake his claim.

Roland walked over to the neat row of motorcycles with the last key in hand. He tried it in each one along the row, one by one, until it finally slotted in with a satisfying click. The engine roared on and headlights flooded the canyon, sending the crows and creatures that had emerged with the dark scampering for cover. The low hum of the engine was exhilarating. Roland walked around the motorcycle, leaving dirty streaks on its shiny body as he felt its cool, smooth surface. He placed both his hands on the handlebars, testing his grip. It felt just right. He threw his leg over the seat. His toes barely touched the ground. He closed his eyes and felt the vibration of the engine travel up his spine. Yes, this one was his.

Roland pushed forward with his toes. The motorcycle wobbled but did not free from its stand. He put one foot flat to the ground and pushed with all his might. It refused to budge, but so did Roland. He pushed and pushed without taking a breath. Just when he was about to run out of oxygen, the motorcycle dropped free, and the stand clicked up. Roland jumped into the seat and struggled to balance its weight between his thighs. Once balanced and breathing, Roland revved the engine and began a slow and wobbly ride back to camp to report that he had completed his assignment.

He didn't feel anything throughout that ride. He didn't feel the wheels bumping over the rocks and slipping in the sand. He didn't feel his face smacking the ground when he fell, or even the burn from the engine on his leg. He didn't feel the muscles in his back straining as he lifted the heavy machine upright. The desire to ride back a complete success caused him to push all pain from his mind. He could let himself feel it later.

All eyes were turned his way as he stomped down the sandy slope. A few of them were brandishing their weapons. They must have heard the engine approaching. No one would have guessed it was Roland.

The only person who seemed at ease was Red. He sat on the opposite side of the fire, eyes following as Roland marched into the circle of light.

Roland tossed the sack of keys at Red's feet. "Twenty keys." He held up the one that had won him his prize. "This one is mine," he said and slipped it into his pocket.

Everyone began talking all at once.

"What happened to you, Roland?" Saph asked, a bit breathless.

"You can't be serious, kid." Jarrel was vocal with his negativity, as always.

"Do your feet even reach the ground?" Hollis asked him.

"They obviously don't," Jarrel responded for him. "You can tell just by looking at him how many times his face hit dirt."

Only then did Roland begin to feel the sting from the scrapes on his cheek, but he didn't show it. His eyes were fixed on Red's, and Red's on his.

"I can't believe you thought this was a good idea," Saph said through her teeth. She sounded angry enough to slap Red right across the face. "Look at him!"

"It's yours," Red declared loudly enough to bring about silence. "But you need to do a couple of practice rides before you take it on a long haul. All right?"

"All right," Roland said with a nod. They looked at each other a moment longer as everyone else looked on in silence.

"Why don't you help him get cleaned up, Saph. Then, you can come back and have something to eat."

Roland finally broke his gaze and allowed Saph to lead him away from the camp.

The fresh creek water felt like acid as Saph wiped the dirt from his collection of scrapes and burns. He clenched his jaw, refusing to flinch. It would have only made her feel guilty. He didn't even feel how cold the night had become until she pulled the blanket up over his bare shoulders. He snatched the fabric and held it close to his chest, allowing warmth to return to his body.

"You didn't have to do that," Saph said as she coiled a bandage around his leg. "You could have said no. You could have come back."

"I had to pass the test."

"It wasn't a test. Red expected you to turn around. He didn't actually want you to do it. He was just trying to show you how brutal these battles really are, trying to let you know, once and for all, that you're not ready." She cinched the bandage up a little too tight, but he still refused to show any discomfort.

"Doesn't matter. I wasn't ready when they came for our land. Wasn't ready when they killed my father. Didn't stop it from happening. It won't stop happening. Not unless we make it stop. Doesn't matter if I'm ready or not."

Saph looked into his eyes with that same darkness in hers, but he felt no instant desire to vanquish it this time. "You're still just a kid," she said softly.

"That doesn't mean I don't understand."

"What is it that you understand?"

"We're all the same. They aren't stronger. They aren't invincible. In death, we're all the same, nothing but blood and guts, dead animals destined to be meals for the living ones. The only difference is... they deserve to die."

It looked as if a cold chill went down Saph's spine. A desire to offer her some sort of comfort returned to him.

Roland reached one hand out from under the blanket and offered it up to her.

She slipped her hand into his and gave it a squeeze. That removed a bit of the darkness, but Saph never looked at Roland the same way again.

None of them did.

SMASH! BITS OF the supply crate flew up into the air. Harris and Lia both stepped back, practically against the canvas, as Roland took over the tent with his pacing. Harris didn't find it surprising that Roland had picked up his sword, but the fact that he'd found the strength to swing it was entirely unexpected. The pain had to be excruciating, but he didn't so much as flinch.

"Were there even weapons in that tank, or was it just a trap?" he asked Lia without slowing his stride.

"We couldn't get close enough to find out." Her eyes followed as he paced past. It was obvious she was worried, but she knew, just as well as Harris, that they couldn't convince him to slow down, not after hearing the name Martrim. "They took the bait. Our eyes saw them heading East. We have a while before they puzzle out that it's a false lead." She was attempting to give him a reason to relax, but all he did was whip around and point at Harris with his sword.

"How long will it take us to divert through the mountain territories?"

"Four days."

"Then that's our next move."

Harris had already assumed that was going to be Roland's solution. He hadn't thought of a better one to offer. He didn't exactly want to sit around and wait for Martrim to attack either, but he made the one argument he had against it, nonetheless. "How are we supposed to get you up there?"

"I will ride, just as I have been."

"So, the Commander who was nearly dead yesterday is now going to lead a full speed charge up a mountain?"

Roland took another lap as he considered. Harris knew Roland never wanted to be more than a leader. Making a miraculous return from death's doorstep had never been part of his plan, even after it had become a very real possibility. He lifted his sword and held it perpendicular to his body at the full stretch of his compromised arm. The tiny muscles in his jaw were quivering. Sweat beaded up on his brow. He must have been in agony but was refusing to let it surface. He finally allowed his arm to drop with perfect control and took a cleansing breath. His experiment with pain had brought him to one determined conclusion. "I do not intend to stop simply because that's what's expected of me. We move at dawn."

Harris wouldn't have slept that night, regardless of how much time it took to ensure the camp was packed and every unit was ready to move. Roland agreed to leave the medical tent up to maintain the illusion that he was still in recovery, and by the force of her incomparable stubbornness, Lia had managed to keep him inside, but their attempts to maintain secrecy had only created an air of mystery. Now, the only thing anyone seemed to be waiting for was the moment Roland would appear. Harris wondered if they wouldn't have been better off letting him go ahead and lead a full-scale attack on Martrim that very night. Of course, Martrim would have won. Roland's ability to push pain aside did not equate to an ability to fight. Harris could only hope he was fully healed by the time Martrim did finally catch up with them.

Harris could feel the eyes on his back as he packed up Roland's motorcycle. He secured the last pack in place just as Lia finished with hers. They gave each other a knowing look.

"You ready?" she asked without turning toward the camp.

"As I'll ever be." Harris wasn't about to turn around and look at that sea of faces either.

Lia entered the medical tent.

A sense of silent anticipation thickened the air like an invisible fog.

Roland emerged, in full gear and armor, with his sword strapped to his back.

A collective intake of breath traveled around the camp. Harris, on the other hand, let out a huff of frustration. Roland hadn't listened to one word of his advice. As accustomed as he was to being the center of attention, the look on Roland's face indicated that he hadn't expected to see quite so many eyeballs waiting for his return to the fold. He straightened up to his full height, which couldn't have been easy with that much extra weight on his barely-healed bones.

It only took a moment of thought for Roland to find the words those faces were waiting to hear. "Let this serve as a reminder. No weakness, no fear, not even the threat of death, will stray me from my chosen path."

Perhaps, Harris thought, *Roland does want to be more than just a leader after all.*

The faces that looked on were gripped in silence as Roland mounted his motorcycle and let the engine roar to life. Harris and Lia did the same. They rode off together to face whatever challenges lay ahead. Of course, Roland had already decided for them that nothing would stray them from *his* chosen path.

THE ROAR OF all those engines at once was nearly deafening, but the sensation that vibrated into Roland's ears only made him laugh. So did the joy of finally being on even ground with the rest of Red's group. Not everyone was convinced that the single morning of practice rides Roland had gotten in while they went to claim their own bikes was enough, but they had to either let him ride now or leave him behind. He had become too valuable for anyone to consider the latter.

"Move 'em out!" Red ordered over the din of motors and they each took off, one by one, kicking up dust as they went. Red grabbed Roland's handlebar before he could rev up and take off after them. "I want you to bring up the rear with me, Roland."

They both hung back in the cloud of dust that was left by the others. Red waited until the worst of it had settled before he released Roland's handlebar. He reached under his jacket and unfastened something from beneath. His hand emerged with a pistol tucked into a leather holster.

Roland glanced between Red's eyes and the pistol in his open palm.

"Go ahead," Red assured him.

Roland picked it up with reverence, using both hands. He slid the pistol out. It was made of dark iron with a long barrel and had a carved wooden handle, just like his knife. It was weighty but well balanced, and the perfect size for his hand. This, too, was his.

"It's too heavy for a pocket, so keep it clipped to your belt, just behind the hip." Red pointed to the spot next to Roland's knife.

Roland clipped the holster into place and slid the pistol back into its securing hold.

"You ready?" Red asked.

"I am," Roland responded.

Red offered him the lead with an open arm. Roland took off, slow but steady, becoming one with the hum of the engine. Red soon glided up by his side. They headed off together to face whatever challenges lay ahead.

FOUR

THE GRAVEL PROVIDED enough grip for their ascent, but the spine-tingling vibrations were getting tiresome. Lia was glad she had convinced Roland to shed the extra weight of armor. Whatever discomfort he might still be experiencing, he wasn't about to show it.

In fact, the only one to complain out loud was Harris. "This picturesque town better be worth what the trip is doing to my shocks," he shouted over the hum of their engines and the grinding of their wheels.

"I can't promise a bed, but the people are welcoming, and the ale never stops flowing," Lia said with a smile.

"Now you're talking." Harris sounded convinced enough to stop complaining.

"I hope they're not too pickled to prepare for the Uni troop headed their way." Roland would not have admitted he was in pain, but Lia could hear it in his voice. There was only one thing she could do to help—give him a little extra motivation to get the ride over with as quickly as possible.

"There's only one way to find out," she shouted over the engine as she shifted into high gear. "I'll meet you snails at the tavern!" She took off at twice the speed. *That ought to do it.*

The fresh mountain air blasted into her face as she sped upward. It smelled lush with life, just as she had remembered. The engine whined as she banked around the final curve. No matter, Cleanair was just ahead.

As the road straightened out, the tiny town nestled into the massive trees began to come into view, but there was something different about it. This wasn't the kind of difference created by time. The tidy buildings and clean streets were exactly the same. It wasn't until Lia entered the center of town that she realized what had changed.

The town of Cleanair was completely empty.

She skidded the motorcycle to a twisted stop in the middle of the road. Roland and Harris were not far behind, but she was already walking away as they pulled up behind her.

"Arm yourself," Roland warned.

Lia pulled out her gun, but it just became a dead weight in her hand as she spun around, looking into the buildings.

Each door had been left open, exposing the empty inside of each and every home and business. The windows were black squares, no lights or life to be seen through any of them.

"Are we too late?" she asked the air.

"There's no evidence of gunfire. Not the slightest hint of a struggle," Harris answered. "It looks like they abandoned the town."

"These buildings haven't been empty long. This smells more like a trap." Roland's words should have put Lia on edge, but suddenly all she wanted to do was find some hint of life, some familiar face that could unravel this mystery. She raced off to the one place she knew better than any other.

The tavern door was standing open, just like the others. His favorite chair was still sitting on the porch, empty. She could hear Roland and Harris climbing up the porch steps behind her, but she did not stop to explain. Inside, the same old chairs were turned up onto the same old tables. The stack of glasses was neatly arranged on the bar, clean and ready for the day's patrons, just as he had always left it, but there was not a patron, not a bartender, not a single soul in sight.

Lia spun around to face them. "Where is everybody?"

LIA

IT WAS THE most beautiful town she had ever seen. The trees were like towering skyscrapers, bigger and grander than even the oldest in Waterford. Halos of green branches embraced the tidy buildings, all of them matched in style, just like a village in a fairy tale. It was obvious from the way she was dressed that she was not at all local, but she was still greeted with smiles and nods as she wandered her way toward the town center. People occupied themselves with chatting and trading. Children darted in and out of the trees, playing games. The town was full of life. Real, untainted life.

This was the perfect place to escape to.

There was a wide and commanding building in the center of town. That had to be the tavern. It always was the heart and soul of a small town like this one. The sign dangling above the porch read *MANNY'S*. A tiny one dangling beneath it read *Barhand Wanted*. In the shade of the porch sat a hulking man with a long curly mustache. He was leaning back in his chair, no doubt putting a fair strain on its back legs, and simultaneously fanning himself while swatting at flies.

Lia marched up the porch steps and straight toward him with a determined stride. "Are you Manny?"

"'S'right," he said without missing a swat.

"I'm Lia, your new barhand." She extended a hand.

He gawked at her. "How old are you?"

She had to stop and remember the birthday that had slid by while she was busy with distractions she'd rather not think about. "Nineteen."

He laughed, hearty and full bodied. It was contagious. Lia would have laughed herself, if she hadn't been the thing he was laughing at. "Listen, sweetheart, this ain't the job for you."

"Who says?"

"I says." He pointed at himself with a thick thumb. "I need someone who can haul at least three barrels a night from cold storage up to the bar. I can tell just by looking at you that you don't fit the bill, unless them little stems are made out of steel." He loosely gestured down the street. "Why don't you try the tailor? They always need an extra hand."

"Don't know how to sew."

He looked at her as if she had seven heads.

"Pardon me. I didn't realize it was such an essential skill."

"Well, whatever it is you know how to do, you're going to have to find some other place to do it."

"What I know is how to serve drinks. I know my liquors, and I know my ales, and I've been serving them up since I was twelve."

He looked at her as if she had just grown three additional heads.

Lia refused to break, holding a hard stare down the bridge of her nose.

"Listen, when I'm not hauling barrels up the stairs, I'm hauling steins and bottles across the bar. Or hauling furniture, so I can mop all kinds of liquids off my floor. Or heaving the drunks off my porch. So, unless you can toss a weight about three times your size, you aren't any good to me." He went back to fanning and swatting, expecting her to disappear.

A moment of inspiration struck. She knew how to win him over. Lia dropped her bag and shoved open the tavern door.

"Now wait a minute!" Manny called out.

She knew it was going to take him a minute to get his girth out of that chair, just enough time. She spotted the door down to cold storage and burst through it. Lia already had the barrel on her back by the time she heard him pound inside. Now to conquer the stairs. Her stems certainly weren't made of steel, but she had always been stronger than she looked. It was a shaky ascent. Her thigh muscles began to quiver, but there were just three stairs to go.

The first thing she saw as she came through the door was Manny's slack jawed face. It infused her with just enough strength to finish the job. She got the barrel as far as the taps, then dropped it with a clunk.

She caught her breath before turning around to face him. "Got any drunks you need me to toss?"

The gaping maw underneath his mustache turned into a smile, then he laughed that same full, infectious laugh again.

This time, Lia joined in.

Manny's patrons turned out to be much more polite than the picture he had painted. They were an easy-going people who had worked hard throughout the day and just wanted a place to relax at night. Serving those smiling faces turned out to be much more pleasant than serving her father's sycophantic advisors had ever been.

That was, until she felt the beady eyes of the skinny man at the corner of the bar watching her every move. Like any woman who found herself the subject of an uninvited gaze, she pretended not to notice, but that only ever lasted so long. The skinny man sidled up in front of her, and greeted her with a ragged smile. Like any woman who was about to receive an unwanted advance, she responded to his smile with a matter-of-fact stare.

"You're new." In all the time he had spent staring at her, that was the only opening line he seemed to have come up with.

"Very observant. What can I get for you?" she responded in a tone that matched her stare.

"Straight to business, huh? Make it a double golden straight up. Nice and strong, just like me."

Lia managed to turn away before her inevitable eye-roll could be seen. She spun back, slid the glass across the bar, and poured from an impressive height, just like Papa taught her.

He looked down at the glass. "Aw, come on, I can handle more than that."

Lia was about to do another acrobatic pour when she noticed the bottle was nearly empty. She plunked it down beside his glass. "There you go."

"What? Don't you believe in service with a smile?" He demonstrated with his own.

Lia forced out the well-practiced smile that anyone with half a brain would know was fake.

"You're pretty as a picture when you smile. Just like I thought." He leaned onto his elbows, forcing a closeness she couldn't escape from behind the bar. "Guess that means I was right about everything else I was thinking. You want to know what that was?"

Lia was weighing up the instantaneous loss of her job against the instant gratification of breaking the bottle over his head, when the shaggy haired man at the other end of the bar spoke up.

"I don't think anyone wants to know what you were just thinking, Scrimjaw, especially not the lady."

"I don't recall inviting you into this conversation, Junior," the man appropriately named Scrimjaw said back to him.

That's when Lia noticed how young the face hidden under the shaggy hair and slightly less shaggy beard was. He was indeed a junior.

"I don't recall the lady inviting you into conversation either," he responded with a confidence that also concealed his age.

"That's up to her, ain't it?" Scrimjaw looked back at her with that same uneven smile on his face.

Lia thought of something better than breaking a bottle over his head. "I'm always happy to be part of a stimulating conversation." She allowed enough time for Scrimjaw to give the young man a cocky nod before she finished with, "You, however, are far from stimulating."

The young man snorted with laughter. It was adorable.

Scrimjaw made a show of picking up his glass and his bottle. "Good luck getting tips with that attitude." Lia watched him saunter across the tavern, attempting to walk away from his wounded pride.

The young man took his opportunity to slide into Scrimjaw's place. That was an advance she didn't mind. "I wish I could tell you that's the last you'll see of him, but he makes at least eight attempts at every female he gets in his sight."

"I can handle it."

"So it seems." A smile emerged from under the beard. That, too, was adorable. "I'm Sebastian."

"Lia." She could feel herself blushing.

"So, what brings you to Manny's, Lia?"

"Needed a job."

"Well, you found a good boss, even if some of his customers leave a bit to be desired."

"You're a customer, too."

"Fair point." Now he was blushing. "Where you from anyway?"

Lia turned her eyes down and began to wipe the already clean bar. "Um, Havitstown."

"Really? My father trades there all the time. What street did you live on?"

"I didn't live there for very long."

"Well, where were you before that?"

"Orderville," she grumbled out, assuming he might not hear.

"Been there to trade, too. Do you know James Franklin?"

"No." Now she was giving Sebastian her best matter-of-fact stare, but he was too busy digging up names to notice.

"I thought everybody there knew James. At least, that's what he'd like us to believe. What about Miss Arina? My father does a lot of trading with her circle."

"Well, is there anyone or anyplace he doesn't?" Lia snapped. Maybe this was how she was going to lose her job on the first day.

"Sorry. I didn't mean to pry. I'll let you get back to work." Sebastian turned away from the bar, his shoulders hunched.

Lia felt like she had just scolded a puppy. "Waterford. I'm from Waterford."

He turned back, a slightly more cautious smile on his face. "Now see, I've never been there."

"Feels like a long time for me, too."

He straightened away his hunch. "That's near one of them Unity cities, isn't it?"

"Io City."

"Ever been there?"

This time, Lia occupied herself by drying glasses. She really didn't want to send him cowering away again. "Once or twice."

"What's it like? I heard they're quite a sight."

"Shiny, clean, boring…. They build these great big glass towers, and then everybody lives inside of them, hiding from the sunlight. There's no children playing in the park, no people laughing on the street…. It's like a nightmare." She didn't realize how far her mind had wandered until she saw how well and truly dry the glass in her hand was. She flicked her eyes back up to Sebastian, assuming he was on the verge of backing away, but he was focused entirely on her. "I like it much better here. There's a lot of life in this town. Good life."

"Does that mean you aim to stay a while?"

"As long as I can," she said with a smile.

"The people of Cleanair are lucky to have you." He raised his glass to her and gave her that same adorable smile.

Yes, this was the perfect place to escape.

LIA RAN HER hand over the top of the bar. Years of wear had put even more pits and dips into the wood, but it was nothing those fat bottom steins couldn't stand up on. The bottles were stashed on the same shelves at the back, the dish towels hung on the same hooks. Where was the man who put them there? She walked out onto the porch. All these years, and his favorite chair had never broken. That was the kind of craftsmanship you only found in a town like this. But where had all the craftsmen gone?

The streets were filling up with their soldiers, looking for trails, for clues, for anything at all. The rest of them were backed up down the road, waiting for either an all clear or a call to arms. It was hard to know which was more likely.

Lia spotted Harris charging up the center of the road. If anyone found something, it would be him. She joined him in his authoritative march across the town. "Anything?" she asked.

"There are trails leading into the woods."

"That's just how they get to the neighbors out here."

"I mean fresh ones. Lots of them." He was keeping his voice down. "It's like they scattered into the trees."

"But why?"

"You're the only one that's ever been here. You tell me."

Lia didn't want to admit she had no idea.

Roland's voice vibrated into their radios. *"South end of the town. Come alone."*

They found him standing where the main road forked off and led down to their gathering hall, which was settled into a niche in the forest floor. Its pitched roof poked up through the greenery.

Roland looked very serious. He began leading them toward it without any explanation "Do you know what this building is?" he asked without turning around.

"It's their town hall," Lia answered.

"I guess they thought it was the best place to leave a message." He pointed toward the entry. There, etched and then burned across both wooden doors, was a very clear message.

WE WANT NO PART OF WAR
PASS IN PEACE
DO NOT RETURN

"How did they know the Unity was tailing us?" Harris asked.

Lia finally understood why everyone had left. "This message is for us."

THE NIGHT WAS quiet, just a few murmured conversations among sparse groups dotted around the tavern. Lia made sure everyone had a drink in their hand, and then got into her own close conversation with Sebastian. She liked hearing about his life. He worked for his father's lumber trade, chopping trees, planting new ones, letting the earth tell him where it was ready to be resewn, and where the old growths needed to be left alone. He spent long days out in the woods and pleasant nights in the comfort of Cleanair. It all seemed so simple. He was not one to talk about himself, but Lia had gotten fairly good at circling the conversation back to him whenever he started asking about her. She would tell him everything… someday.

Manny pushed into their conversation by shoving a tray full of glasses between them. "Best get to washing those."

"We have plenty of clean ones."

"And no customers waiting for them to be filled. So, I say we get a jump on cleanup now, so I can close those doors and my eyes at a decent hour this evening," he said with a commanding point at said doors and eyes.

"Aye, aye cap." She gave him a playful salute.

Manny shook his head and went back to his cleanup.

Lia scooped up the tray and signaled her desire for Sebastian to stay right where he was with a smile. She plunked the glasses in and filled the sink. As soon as she shut off the whistling tap, the tense conversation from the other side of the bar began to float into her ears.

"I'm telling you, that was the last healthy animal I had left. I'll be lucky if I can get the ones I still got to breed." It was a man Lia had never seen before, but he was rather robust, probably a farmer.

"I know how you feel. Every winter, them Unity soldiers barely leave me with enough leather for one decent coat, let alone enough for the whole town. Any worse, and it'll get so I have to ration clothes for them that need it most," said the tailor from down the road.

Lia kept her hands occupied under the water, but her ear tilted toward their conversation.

"At least you two still got a business to speak of. Last year, them soldiers burned down half my trees. Claimed the land for a new crop. Says mine isn't valuable enough. If you can't make more than one thing with your land, then you don't get to keep it."

"They can't do that! This ain't unified land." The farmer was suddenly flush with anger.

The tailor responded with a practiced calm. "It's all unified land to them. It's just a matter of whether they use their soldiers to protect it or pillage it."

"Why don't you stand up to them?" Lia didn't realize until they had all turned her direction that she still had her hands in the sink. She shook off the water and forced her way into their conversation. "Why don't you fight back? It's well within your rights to protect your property."

"We can't fight them." The tailor was still calm, even though her friends were both looking at Lia like she had just spoken in tongues. "That's why they take from us because we can't do anything about it."

"But you can. They can be hurt. They can even be killed. You threaten that, and they'll back down."

"Or just take twice as much," said the farmer, who was even redder now than he was before. "They do that to me now, and I might as well give up on everything!"

"Aye. After what happened last year, I ain't inviting any more violence into my life," added the other, slightly less ruddy, farmer.

They turned toward a table to escape Lia's uninvited opinions, but the tailor saw fit to give her a concluding remark. "Best keep your big city notions of rebellion to yourself, miss."

Dejected, she turned her dripping hands back toward the sink.

Sebastian had taken the nearest seat while she had been distracted. "It's not unusual, you know. They show up at my father's place every once in a while, take at least a third of his lumber."

"And he just lets them do it?"

"He figures he's lucky to still have land to take from."

Lia's instinct to shake Sebastian's innocent face until he understood what those soldiers were really capable of, became instantly squashed by another—self-preservation. She dried off her hands, flung the towel aside, and escaped the confines of the bar to talk to Manny. She was pretty confident Sebastian wouldn't go anywhere in the meantime.

She found him in the midst of wiping down the empty tables. "Manny, those Unity soldiers, the ones that come into town and take from everybody, do they ever come in here?"

He responded without looking up or missing a crumb. "Not often. My services don't render the same kind of forgetfulness in them that it does in my other patrons."

"Well, if they ever do come in, I won't serve them. I don't even want to be in the tavern when they are."

He finally looked up from his cleaning. "Feel that strongly about it?"

"I do."

"Well, I've never been one to let my political convictions mix with business. But seeing as how you're the best barhand I've ever had, I guess I can make an exception. As long as you keep up the good work, aye?"

His slyly placed compliment helped her to relax. "You have my word," she responded with a smile.

"Aye." He passed over another tray full of glasses as an immediate test of her promise, then flicked his nose toward the bar. "Is that Sebastian Collins Junior still sitting over at that bar? You know, he never used to come in here more than once a week. Taken to a lot more visits lately. I wonder why." One corner of his mustache curled up in a smile.

"I'll get to washing those glasses now."

"Aye."

THEY KEPT A brisk pace and close quarters as they headed back to the center of town.

"You said yourself these people had more reason than anybody to hate the Unity." Harris said it as if he suspected Lia of concealing something from them.

"They survived by backing down whenever the Unis showed up. We have no reason to believe that's changed. Nothing else about this town has."

"That was before they had an army to protect them. We can fight for them, fight for their land. Why would anyone refuse that?" It sounded as if Roland was taking their passive resistance personally.

"Maybe this is their way of protecting it themselves." It was the only reason Lia could think of.

"Regardless, no one is here to explain it to us. We keep this to ourselves. Concentrate everyone on this side of town. No one needs to know we're not welcome here." Roland was definitely taking this personally.

They maintained silence as they entered the center of town. Roland took advantage of the dominating structure of the tavern to step onto the porch and address the crowd of soldiers. "The mystery we face here remains unsolved for the moment. But this town offers the shelter we need. We stay here for the night. Everyone is to remain in the center of town. We keep togeth—"

"You will not remain here," a voice shouted out of the trees.

"You were told to pass through," another joined in from the other side of the road.

"Your kind are not welcome in our town," yet another voice called from another direction.

The voices were loud and clear, but their sources were totally invisible. It would seem the craftsmen had been busy making tree hides for some select sentinels. They had been watched from the moment they arrived.

Several of the soldiers had armed themselves on instinct and were pointing their guns up into the trees.

"Guns down!" Roland shouted. "We do not fire on our allies."

"We are no allies of yours," the first voice was quick to say.

"Take your weapons and your war elsewhere," said the voice down the road.

"Do we not deserve a chance to be heard?" Roland called up into the air.

"There is nothing we would hear from you." The first voice was even angrier than before.

"A chance to rest then, same as you would offer any weary traveler."

There was a pause, as if the voices were discussing it in silence.

Then, a new voice called out from the trees above the tavern. "We have no beds for you here."

Lia knew that voice. "Manny!" Her shout cut short Roland's conversation with the trees. She walked into the center of the road and shouted up at the broad branches hovering over the tavern roof. "Manny, it's Lia. I'm here. I've come back."

There was another pause, another silent discussion.

"Manny, please. Please, come out here and let me see you."

Another pause was followed by a light rustling of branches. No one dared to move or speak.

Then, a hulking man with deep smile lines around a gray curly mustache appeared from behind the tavern. "Is that really you?" Manny said as he stepped out into the sunshine, his eyes sparkling with surprise.

Lia darted down the road and launched straight into his giant arms. "Yes. Yes, it's me."

He hugged her tight, lifting her right off her feet. His shock soon melted into a full-bodied laughter. It was just as infectious as it had always been.

THE VOICES TURNED out to be those of the town council, who had been trusted to guard the town while its occupants holed up in the nearest valley. With a bit of encouragement from Manny, they allowed the Resistance soldiers to set up camp in the woods, but at a distance barely within sight, let alone earshot of the town center. It took a great deal more encouragement before the people of Cleanair began to return to their homes.

The looks Lia received as they skirted around her were a far cry from the smiles and nods she'd received all those years ago. She was the only one of "their kind" that had been allowed to stay within the town. She bore their mistrustful stares as she patiently awaited the time Manny had promised to her.

There were a few people in the tavern when she entered, but they went silent as she neared, as if the air around her were swallowing up conversation. After they settled into Manny's favorite corner, the voices behind her gradually returned to a normal volume.

She bided her time. Manny wouldn't hide the truth from her, but she certainly wasn't about to force it out of him. She let him guide the conversation, this way and that, probably being more amiable than she ever was all those years ago. Maybe he would chalk it up to her maturity. She had, after all, grown up quite a lot since then.

It wasn't until she began to tell him about Cambria that she saw the opportunity to gently take the helm. "Street after street of magnificent houses. Farms as far as they eye can see. It's the most beautiful city I've ever seen, Manny."

"Aye. I've heard some tell of it."

"And there could be so many more just like it. Free and proper cities. Places for all of us to call home, without our land being threatened. That's what we're fighting for. Why wouldn't you—"

The interruption of his barhand arriving with drinks actually came at the perfect time. Manny had just started to show some discomfort.

It doesn't matter, Lia thought. *I can bring him around.*

The barhand was a slight young man, but he still had the strength to carry two steins in one hand. "I see your expectations for your staff are still high as ever." Lia gave Manny a smile, inviting him to relax back into conversation. "Thanks much," she said to the barhand with a raise of her glass.

He responded with a curt and short smile, then walked off without a word.

"Though I'd like to think I was a bit friendlier."

"You'll have to forgive them, sweetheart. None of them have ever seen an honest to goodness Resistance soldier before." He loosely gestured at her.

She looked down at herself. Perhaps removing her weapons would have reduced the number of stares she had received. "Sorry. Force of habit." She slid her gun holster around to her back.

"Did I hear right? Are you really a Sub-Commander?"

"That's right. I'm the head of the sniper force."

"What fool put you in charge of that?" He was wearing a cheeky smile, just like he always had when he teased her.

"Hey, I could out-shoot you any day, old man."

"So says the student to the teacher." He was finally acting like his old self again.

"You gotta learn from the best to be the best. Right?" So was she.

"Is that what you think you are now?"

"My rifles are a bit more accurate than big blue. Do you still take her out when the life of a bartender gets you down?"

His smile dropped in an instant. "Not in a long while. Ammo's run low over the years."

"I can fix that."

"Not necessary."

"You can take a crack with one of mine then. See if you've still got what it takes to beat me. Though I doubt it."

His smile didn't return, nor did his teasing jibes.

Lia leaned over the table, determined to hold him captive to the conversation. "You've got a lot of fight left in you yet. I see it in your eyes. Why not use it?"

He responded with a dismissive wave of his hand. "I'm an old man now. Best I can do is stay out of the way."

This didn't sound like the man she once knew, who was more likely to insist on going about business as usual, even if he had two broken legs. This wasn't the kind of change brought about by age, but by something much more sudden than the passing of time. She didn't realize they had both drifted out of the conversation, until Manny brought himself back into it.

"So, tell me what other kinds of trouble you've created over these last few years."

A slight smile had returned to his face, inviting her to relax again. "Well, you probably won't believe it, but I'm a mother."

"You are?" His smile dropped away again.

"I have a son. He's three now."

"With that man? Your commander?" He pointed in the direction of the unwanted encampment outside of town.

She felt as if she was being accused. But of what? "He's my husband."

Manny turned his gaze toward the tavern, eyes wandering in search of an out.

Lia wondered what could be so wrong with her act of becoming a mother. She thought of all she was about to tell him about Malcolm, all the things she was proud and excited to share with a man whose opinion she so valued even after all these years. It seemed unfair to have whatever tainted his thoughts of "their kind" to reflect on her son. She suddenly found herself wondering what Malcolm looked like now in his tender third year of life.

Manny cleared his throat loudly enough to make Lia's thoughts jump back into the present. "Time has raced past me tonight. I'd best get to cleaning."

"You used to stay open until sunrise."

"My old bones can't hold themselves up that long anymore." He pushed himself to standing. It certainly didn't look as if it took him any longer or required any more effort than it used to.

Lia looked to her half-finished drink for answers. She found none. "I guess your customers would appreciate it if I went back to camp," she said as she stood.

He put an apologetic hand on her shoulder. "Take care. Aye?"

She responded with a smile, then walked past all the suspicious eyes following her, out of Manny's tavern, out of the picturesque town of Cleanair, and into the dark of the forest.

She entered from the cold blue of night into the orange glow of their tent. Roland was in the midst of attempting to claw off the bandages that Harris had intentionally tied out of his reach.

"Stop," Lia commanded.

He put both hands up in the air.

"Your body has been under too much strain. Those bandages are there to remind you to rest."

"I can barely breathe in this cocoon," he growled. "One night's sleep without them is all I ask."

Lia didn't bother to argue. Her stubborn insistence had worn thin. She untied the knot at his back and unwound the coils of fabric from his torso.

Roland sucked in a breath like he was surfacing from the deep. His skin resembled the strata of an ancient mountain, all shades from sulfurous orange to deep purple, with raised ridges of bright red crisscrossing throughout. It was hard to believe he could move at all, let alone ride up a mountain. Roland clasped her hand, pulling her attention away from the landscape of his injuries and up to his eyes. "What did he tell you?"

"Nothing."

"There had to be some indication as to why they have such disdain for us."

"None. He said so little that I can't help but think that something happened to them. Something sudden… and secret." She stripped off the guns and armor that had made her the target of many mistrustful stares. Though free of the extra weight, her body itself felt too heavy to hold up. She allowed herself to sink down onto the blankets.

Roland hovered over her. "It was by his influence that we were allowed to stay. He must know the reason."

She let out a little chuckle. "Since when does a bartender not know everyone's troubles?"

"Do you think he'd be able to gather them for us? To allow us an opportunity to make our case?"

"I don't know. Just having me there compromised his popularity."

"It may be our only chance. Otherwise, we take our soldiers, our weapons, and we leave them on their own. There's no telling what will happen when the Unity comes through. They could lose everything."

Lia finally looked up at him. It was more than personal. Roland really was afraid for them.

"I'll try." In the wake of the mystery they were facing, it was the most she could promise. Lia lay back and stared up at the canvas.

Roland slowly lowered himself to her side. It sounded as if it took a considerable effort. She should have helped him, but he probably would have refused if she had tried. He was still sitting up, his eyes burning through her. "Lianna."

She turned to look at him. Somewhere under the pain he was tamping down was the worry, for them, and for her.

"I won't let it happen again. Not as long as we have the power to stop it."

"I know." She turned her eyes back up and tried not to think about what they didn't want to happen again. It was hard not to. It had happened in that very forest.

FIVE

ORANGE RAYS OF late afternoon sunshine beamed through the windows. The gentle turning of seasons had brought the sun low enough to break between the trees.

Lia leaned against the bar, staring at the particulates floating through the beams and wondering what the coming winter would be like. *These mountains must get buried in snow*, she thought. She'd have to play down her "big city notions of rebellion" in order to get a heavy coat from the tailor. She drifted into visions of long nights by the fire with Sebastian, hoping winter would bring them closer together.

Manny cleared his throat to grab Lia's attention. She snapped back to the present and glanced around at their handful of early customers.

It turned out Manny was the only one who needed something. "Suppose you could bring me a glass of motivation?"

She obligingly filled up a stein and brought it over to his favorite corner seat, where he was immersed in the task of balancing his books, or so it seemed.

"That Collins Junior going to come in tonight?" he asked without looking up.

"How should I know?"

"Thought he might have mentioned it."

"He didn't."

Manny dove into his first sip.

Lia took that as the end of the conversation and turned back toward the bar.

"Miss Johnston said she saw you two today."

She turned back.

Manny was eyeing her over the rim of his stein. "Walking down by the river," he added before going in for another sip.

"Did she?"

"Were you?"

"Maybe."

"I see." Manny sucked the suds out of his mustache.

Lia made another attempt at escape.

"He's a good kid, that Collins boy. His folks are right proud of him, as well they should be."

She turned back, acquiescing to the fact that Manny would make whatever point he was aiming at, whether or not she participated in the conversation.

"He's attracted a fair share of fillies, too, which many other men would take sinful advantage of, but Junior isn't like that. He's more…."

"More what?" She was suddenly very suspicious of his motivations.

"Old fashioned. A romantic at heart. Believes in taking things slow. It takes a special lady to turn his head," Manny said, mostly to his beer, as if he couldn't look her in the eye.

"Uh huh." Lia was certain she was about to be told she wasn't good enough for Sebastian. She had seen it in the stares and heard it in the whispers that circled around them whenever they walked through town together. The words "city girl" and "sinful liquor slinger" had floated around, even though there wasn't a person in town who didn't have occasion to visit Manny's. Their opinions didn't matter to her, but if Manny was about to agree with them, he was also about to end up with that stein emptied over his head.

Manny took another sip.

Lia attempted to walk off again. It was better not to let him finish his point, than to lose her job.

He managed to swallow back his sip rather fast. "All I'm saying is—"

Lia whirled back around. "What? What exactly are you trying to say? Because if it's about my big city notions, or me being nothing but a liquor slinger, then I don't want to hear it."

Manny responded with a wide-eyed stare the likes of which she had never seen. The other patrons went quiet. She probably would have been better off emptying the stein over his head.

"Perhaps it's best you take a seat, young lady."

Lia flopped into the seat opposite his.

Manny loudly cleared his throat, directing the noise out into the tavern. The other patrons gently resumed their conversations. He leaned onto one elbow, hovering over his books.

Lia kept her eyes fixed on the tabletop.

"All I was saying is he's a right smart match for you. Not only for all the reasons I just mentioned, but also because he's the only bloke in town likely to treat you proper. The way you deserve."

"Oh." She couldn't bring herself to look up.

"So, I hope he does plan on coming in tonight. Even if he does spend a little less pocket money than the rest of these booze hounds."

"Oh."

"Think you can get back to work now without snapping any of my customers' heads off?"

She finally looked up. "Sorry."

A slight smile sneaked out under his mustache. "You can make up for it by naming your first born after me. After all, you did meet under my roof." He gave her a wink, helping to ease away the last of her tension.

The feeling of genuine warmth Lia carried with her for the next few steps was instantly drained away when a shadow flicked across the golden rays. A deep-seated instinct told her it was more than just an early imbiber. The brief flash through the window of a black silhouette in a neatly tailored jacket confirmed her instinct. There was only enough time to race behind the bar and duck into cold storage before the soldier's silhouette filled the doorway.

Lia dared to peer through the crack by the big iron hinges. It didn't take long to spot the distinctive insignia on the soldier's uniform. He was a bounty hunter, and an officer at that.

Manny was already standing. He approached the bounty hunter with a standoffish air. "What can I get for you?"

The bounty hunter looked Manny up and down, assessing his size. "I'm here on business."

"Then what can I do for you?"

He took a glance around the tavern. Lia couldn't see any of the other patrons, but they certainly weren't making a sound. "You tend this whole place yourself?"

"Have been for near fifteen years."

"It's a big place. Must fill up at night." He was still glancing around, as if he hadn't quite seen enough yet.

Lia took a step back, just in case.

"People in this town got enough patience to wait for drinks if they have to. But none of us have patience for meaningless chatter."

Manny's straight forward attitude seemed to have won him a bit of respect from the bounty hunter. He turned back to address him directly. "I'm looking for a young woman, passed through here some months ago."

"You're trailing a tad far behind."

Another shadow flicked through the beams. Had he brought reinforcements? Lia dared to put her face up against the iron and peer toward the front door.

The next person to enter was Sebastian. He came to a dead stop as soon as he saw a Unity uniform in front of him.

The bounty hunter gave Sebastian's non-threatening shape a quick glance, then turned his attention back to Manny. "It's also possible that she stayed a while. Might even still be here."

"You got a name?"

"Lianna McMillan."

Instant fright jumped into Lia's throat. Sebastian's innocence was only outweighed by his chivalry. She didn't know him well enough yet to know if either of them could take a back seat, but he said nothing. Neither did Manny.

The bounty hunter turned his attention toward the other patrons. Lia stepped back again but could still see each and every shiny button on his uniform dancing through the crack. "She's nineteen. Lean, stronger than she looks. Pretty. The type of young woman a group of men like yourselves would have noticed."

There was only a brief pause before a voice out of view answered.

"Yeah, I've seen her." It was that slime-ball, Scrimjaw. He had made at least six more attempts at her. She'd thrown every single one back in his face with resounding success. Was he about to get petty revenge by sending her to her death?

Sebastian's chivalry overtook his reason. He managed only one step forward before Manny blocked him with one of his trunk-like arms. Luckily, the bounty hunter was too busy assessing Scrimjaw to have seen it.

Scrimjaw's voice added, "It was a couple of months back. She went west, I think."

The relief that washed through Lia's body made her knees weak.

Even Sebastian's posture relaxed.

"Are you certain of that?" the bounty hunter asked.

"Hey, like you said, she was the kind of girl I'd notice. Believe me, I wish she'd stayed." He was so convincing, it made Lia wonder how many other lies he had pulled out of his ass over those last few months, but the bounty hunter was not yet sold.

"And what about the rest of you?" he asked the hidden portion of the tavern.

No one spoke another word.

"All right, then. Thank you for the information." He gave a slight nod to Manny. It was less of a send-off and more of a promise to return. Then, he walked out of the tavern.

Lia wasn't about to emerge from the safety of cold storage, so she backed silently down the stairs and awaited whatever came next.

It wasn't long before Manny's footsteps pounded down toward her. "Where is it?" were the first words that growled out of his mouth. Of course he knew. There wasn't a thing that happened in Manny's tavern he didn't know.

Lia pointed under the stairs.

Manny's hand fished around in the darkness and emerged with his shotgun. He checked the chamber. Yes, it was loaded. He gripped the barrel in an angry fist, and he shook it at her. "I taught you good aiming practice for sport. Not so you could start trouble in my place."

"I would never. I swear it. It was only if I had no other choice."

"And why would that be? Why is he after you?"

Lia was summoning the courage to answer when another set of footsteps flew down the stairs. It was Sebastian.

"What's going on?" he asked with fright in his eyes.

"You best get yourself back up those stairs," Manny ordered.

Sebastian's eyes didn't even shift in Manny's direction. "Why are they looking for you?"

"I mean it, Junior, get your arse out of my storeroom right now." Manny shook the shotgun at him, but Sebastian still didn't move.

"What did you do?" He was still looking at Lia with those deeply innocent eyes.

She suddenly couldn't even move, let alone speak.

"I'm not playing around here!" Manny's voice vibrated the barrel Lia had been clasping for comfort. It awoke her instinct to fight.

"I didn't do anything!" She shouted them both into silence. "I was never a part of it. I didn't know what was going to happen. I didn't do it… I didn't." She lost her words to the onset of panicked tears.

Manny let her sit in the storeroom until the tavern filled up enough for her presence not to draw all the attention, though it still soaked up quite a lot. No one asked her anything. Manny must have made it clear they wouldn't be allowed to stay if they did.

Sebastian kept a sentinel's post at the corner of the bar, watching her every move through a few silent hours. It wasn't until Manny had finally closed the doors for the night that she had a chance to tell them the story.

Manny was somber, Sebastian concerned. It was the first time she had ever seen that look on his face.

"How many died?" Manny asked after a long silence.

"One hundred and eighty-three. All recruits, most barely eighteen."

"Oh, lord."

"If I had known, if I could have stopped them, I would have." She was still trying to sell them on her innocence even though they were both already convinced.

"Don't they have to give you a trial?" Sebastian asked.

"It'll be a military trial, with a jury of Unity soldiers. It won't matter that I didn't know what they were planning. I gave them the keys. I made it possible. No Uni jury will see me as innocent, even if I get to trial."

"What do you mean if?" Sebastian really didn't know.

Lia didn't have the heart to tell him.

Manny stepped in to explain as gently as he knew how. "Those soldiers they send out for arrests, they can use whatever force necessary, even deadly."

"They found all the others already. Only half of them made it to trial. All of them were found guilty and...." She didn't finish her sentence. Sebastian had already gone pale. "I should leave."

"No. You can't." Sebastian gripped her hand as if she were already on her way out.

"He'll be back, as many times as it takes. Someone will tell him where I am."

"That's where you're wrong. Ain't none of these people going to turn you in. Not a one." There was a sudden return of confidence to Manny's presence.

"Aye, even that no account Scrimjaw lied for you. Without question." That same confidence was in Sebastian's voice now, too.

"You're one of us now. A part of our town, a part of our family, and we always take care of our own."

The warmth she'd been robbed of that afternoon came rushing in like a tidal wave. Tears of overwhelming emotion, of disbelief, joy, fear, dread, and hope ran down her cheeks. "I can't let you risk your lives for me," she whispered.

Manny took her other hand and gave it a squeeze. "We ain't giving you a choice."

Sebastian walked her home, just as he had on many other nights before, but on that night she didn't feel worthy of the polite kiss he had taken to giving her. She turned her eyes down as they arrived at her door. "I'm sorry for hiding the truth from you."

"I hold no grudge about that."

"I'm sorry for bringing this into your life. I shouldn't have stayed here for so long, but after a while I couldn't bring myself to leave."

Sebastian put a hand on her cheek, drawing her eyes up from the ground. "You should never be sorry for that. You have every right to take your life wherever you want, lead it however you choose. And I'm just as happy that you're here today as I was the first night I saw you." Those same tears flowed down her cheeks again. He gently brushed one away with his thumb. "You're making it awfully hard for me to leave you tonight. I've been struggling for hours to get over this feeling that something bad is going to happen the moment my back is turned."

"Then don't leave." She was struggling with the same feeling.

"I can't stay here all night." He was indeed an old fashioned romantic.

Lia had, on many occasions past, wanted to rant about how unheard of his behavior was in the world outside his own. Then, she would quickly remember how little typical male behavior had ever benefited her. It usually had quite the opposite effect. Sebastian was a rare gem and had never seemed more precious than he did on that night. It only made her that much more desperate to hold on to him.

"Just stay. That's all I ask."

So, he did. They lay above the covers on her tiny bed, letting the fire keep them warm. He allowed her to nestle against his chest. He smelled just like the trees.

This was the perfect place to escape to, even though it wouldn't last.

FOR SO MANY, dawn arrives with the promise of new beginnings. For Lia, that dawn dragged with it the burdens of the past. Something told her to get up, to gently leave the warmth of Sebastian's arms. Something told her to look out the window. She stared endlessly through the tiny break in the curtains, watching the light of day creep through the trees, until he stepped into view.

The bounty hunter stood in the middle of the road, his every breath making a tiny cloud in the frigid air. He wasn't about to leave. He would stay as long as it took. He would ask as many people as it took. He would coerce their cooperation if necessary. He would not stop until he had found her.

Lia watched him walk up the road from the safety of her tiny home, until he disappeared from sight. Sebastian was still asleep, peaceful as ever. She wanted more than anything for him to be able to stay that way, for his life to remain as simple and serene as it had been before she arrived, so she slowly opened the door and slipped out into the dawn.

The bounty hunter was standing in the center of town, scanning his surroundings, planning his next move. *I wonder what he would have done today*, Lia thought as she stood in the middle of the road, waiting to be seen. As he turned her direction, she raised her arms in surrender.

The look on his face could almost be interpreted as smug. He was in no rush as he approached, as if he wanted to give her time to reconsider. The hands that took hold of her wrists were ice cold. The handcuffs that linked them at her back were practically frozen.

"Did you think surrender was going to earn you some sympathy?" he asked as he double-checked her restraints.

"Hah. Sympathy, that's a good one." She felt a bit better after having found the strength for sarcasm.

He stepped around to face her. "What are you playing at, girlie? You've been on a pretty steady run till now. Why give up the fight?"

"Just didn't seem worth it anymore."

"On the contrary, you're worth quite a lot." He took a hold of her elbow and led her off the road, away from the picturesque town of Cleanair, and into the dark of the forest.

They crunched their way through the frost and into the depths of the forest in total silence. Lia saw no trace of a trail, no sign that transport of any kind had been through those trees. Was he going to take her away, or just dump her in the woods? The thought of Sebastian finding her battered body on the ground chilled her to the bone. Only then did the fright begin to settle in.

Lia stifled her shakes as best she could. "Where are you taking me?"

"I thought you didn't care anymore," he said without slowing his stride.

"Look, we both know you're not taking me to a nice little cell to face a fair trial. All I ask is that you get me out of here first. Then, you can do whatever you want."

"You've been here this long. Why so eager to leave now?"

A distant voice broke through the silence. The bounty hunter jerked her to a stop to listen. Sebastian was calling out her name.

"Ah, I see. You don't want your sweetheart to find you after I put a hole in your head." Sebastian was still shouting for her, but the bounty hunter kept forcing her ahead. "I should have known that's why you stopped running. No other reason to set up shop in a back end town. Did you really think you could live a happy little mud dweller life out here? Actually, the better question is, did you really want to?"

Between the fear that Sebastian was going to catch up with them, and the anger at being personally insulted by a heartless tin can who wasn't even capable of knowing what a happy life was, Lia was summoning the strength to fight. "Everyone gets a last request, right? So, are you going to give me mine or not?"

"Oh, I'll get you out of here, girlie. But the rest is up to your jury. See, I do intend to take you in alive."

"Why? You get paid either way."

"I'm a man of the law, and I follow it to the letter. Only a struggle warrants the use of force, and you are not struggling."

"Fine." Lia jerked her arm up as hard as she could. She slipped out of his cold grip. Her elbow made contact with what felt like his throat. She darted into the trees.

A gunshot blasted out. A bullet cracked into the tree beside her.

Lia kept running. She would either get away, or she would die trying. At least it would be over. What she didn't think about was how easy it would be to find them once the sound of gunfire led the way.

Bang! Lia's winding path evaded another shot, but a protruding root conspired against her. Her toe stopped cold. The leg she tried to catch herself with crumpled. Her face hit the ground.

Within seconds, the bounty hunter's icy hands had snatched her arms. He hauled her up and pinned her against a tree trunk. He yanked up the handcuffs, wrenching her wrists into a painful twist as he pushed her face against the bark. "Proving you want me to kill you will only keep me from doing it," he snarled into her ear. "Just makes me want to keep you around for entertainment."

The sound of running feet tore toward them. The bounty hunter's hands suddenly ripped away.

Lia whirled around. Sebastian had the bounty hunter on the ground. They were grappling for control of his gun. Within seconds, the bounty hunter yanked his gun free, took aim straight into Sebastian's chest, and fired.

Lia's scream drowned out the sound of the shot.

The bounty hunter rolled Sebastian's slack body aside. He lay on his back, struggling to breathe for a few precious seconds before life left him forever.

"No. No," Lia heard herself say, as if her denial would reverse time. She didn't know how she ended up on her knees, but she had put herself in the ideal position for execution. The hot barrel of the bounty hunter's gun pushed into her temple.

"Well, that was more entertaining than a trial," he said to her cowering form.

Lia closed her eyes and prepared to die.

A giant boom vibrated the air. Lia was left untouched.

She opened her eyes to find Manny standing before her, smoking shotgun in hand.

The bounty hunter was on the ground, pushing himself up. Manny took three giant steps toward him and boom! He fell back and gurgled out a mouthful of his own blood. Three more steps, and Manny was right on top of him. He shoved the barrel into the bounty hunter's forehead.

Lia looked away just before the final boom blasted out, and with that, his hunt was over.

LIA WASN'T INVITED to the funeral. As the processional passed down the main road, she could only watch from the security of her doorway. They wore white, as was the tradition when someone dies long before their time. She didn't wipe away any of the tears as they came. She didn't attempt to silence any of the voices of regret, of anger, as they sounded out in her mind.

Why did he have to follow me? Why did I try running at all? Why did I ever come to this town? Why did he have to suffer the fate that I deserved?

The couple walking behind the coffin must have been the parents that were robbed of their pride and joy. His father, with the same wayward hair and beard, showed her what Sebastian would have looked like one day, even though that day would never come.

Then, as if she felt Lia's gaze, the small woman by his side looked in her direction. They locked eyes. Lia thought it was a moment of understanding, of empathy. Perhaps his mother knew, the way a mother often does, how Lia felt about her son. Then, the small woman's face twisted with hate. She disdainfully spit on the ground.

Lia recoiled. Manny broke from the processional and took up guardianship at her side. They watched the others until they disappeared from sight.

There was only one thing left to do. Manny stood in the doorway as Lia gathered up the few belongings that had come into town with her. She chose to leave behind everything that had come into her life since.

"It's easy to get lost in those trees." It was the second time Manny had tried that argument. "Even people who've lived here for years still get turned around."

"It's the only way to cover my tracks. If I stick to the road, I have no chance at hiding."

"And there's no talking you out of this?"

She turned to face him so he would know there was no doubt in her mind. "I'm not letting it happen again. Not when it should have been me."

Manny stifled his urge to argue. He reached into his pockets and presented her with a small handgun and a fistful of bullets. "I know it's small, but that means it'll be easier to carry, easier to conceal."

"I thought you weren't a fan of my big city notions of rebellion either."

"As far as I'm concerned, the more poker faces you take out of this world the better. If you see one so much as threaten to kill another innocent life, you make sure you take his first."

Lia took the gun and bullets, stashed them deep into her bag, and hoisted it up onto her shoulder. "When the next one comes, tell him

I killed the bounty hunter. They want me dead anyway. What's one more reason?"

"You just promise you won't give them a chance to make that happen."

"I'll try." It was the most she could promise.

They said their goodbyes, and Lia walked away from her tiny home, out of the picturesque town of Cleanair, and into the dark of the forest to find a new place to escape.

THE STREETS WERE empty. Their walk from the far-flung campsite into the center of town met with no protest, not even a passive one. Perhaps Manny had managed to gather them all together. Maybe they would be willing to hear Roland out. Maybe their soldiers would be allowed to fight for Cleanair after all. Lia let her hope gently rise as they approached the tavern, but it dropped like a stone as soon as she saw the many empty tables inside.

Roland came nose to nose with Manny in the doorway. A toll had to be paid. "Thank you for allowing us this time."

Manny gave him a nod and readied to step aside, but Roland had more to say.

"And thank you for saving her life."

It was hard to tell from the look on Manny's face how he felt about that bit of gratitude. He stepped aside and gestured them inside. The conspicuous gaps in the crowd were too big not to acknowledge.

"Is this all of them?" Roland quietly asked.

"About a third of the town. Count your blessings it was that many," Manny answered at full volume. He promptly headed for his favorite corner seat.

Roland subtly gestured for Harris and Lia to space out. He didn't want to present them with an armed front, especially when there were so few of them. Harris stayed by the door. Lia shrunk to the back of the room. She didn't recognize any of the faces in the crowd, but that didn't mean they hadn't recognized her.

Roland took up position in front of the bar and allowed a moment's silent anticipation to build. "You are probably all well aware, just as you were of our coming, that a Unity troop is but a short ride behind us." His voice had commanded their attention, but his news did not come as a shock to anyone. "They blaze a trail as we speak, straight into the heart of our world, taking any land they can by force unless we secure it before they arrive. They bring enough weapons to war for years, and take enough from each territory to leave its people starved."

All eyes remained fixed on him, but each face also remained static.

"We came here, not to drag you into a battle you could have avoided, but to protect you from the one that will inevitably land on your doorstep." Roland began to walk among the tables, speaking to each individual set of eyes that followed him past. "They come, not simply to pass through and take what they will on their way. They come to take your farms, your sawmills, your mines, your businesses, your homes, the river, the trees, every grain of land you tread upon. If you allow us to stay and protect you from the Unity. To teach you how to fight and protect—"

Grumbles of protest began to ripple through the crowd.

"You mean the chance to be soldiers, forced to march off with the rest. What happens to our land then?" one of the townspeople called out.

"No one will be forced to—"

"And what of the next troop that comes?" a man behind Roland asked. "And the one after that? Will yee be with us then? They hear we're fighters, and they'll come after us like we are."

"You will be. We will train you. Give you weapons. No one will be left without protection."

"We won't take anything you have to offer. It comes at too high a price," a woman in the middle of the crowd said in a confident voice.

Roland's brow wrinkled. Was it in concern or confusion? "We ask nothing in return."

"So you say now. But once we've let you protect our land, then who's to say you won't try to control it?"

Noisy affirmations rose up from the crowd.

"That's right. Then, they'll be your farms, and your mines, and your trees."

"We'll be just like your soldiers and your citizens. Our sons and daughters forced off to war. Our very lives dictated by your laws."

"Our laws were created to protect!" Roland's shout instantly silenced the crowd. He took a moment to regain his composure. "That is all we want to do. To protect, so that not one of your lives will be lost at the point of a Unity gun."

Lia turned her eyes down. Her fingernails had clawed into the tabletop. She flattened her hands and tried to relax her posture.

Roland returned to standing in front of the bar. "Running and hiding in the woods will not protect you, but our army will." He took advantage of the silence he had forced into the room to let the air of anticipation build up again. "So, what say you, the people of Cleanair? What would you have us do?"

Silent stirrings filled the room as the townspeople looked to each other, but no one said a word.

A deep throat cleared at the back of the tavern. All eyes turned toward Manny as he stood. "I say this is our land and we should be the ones to protect it."

A short silence was followed by an "aye" from the middle of the crowd, then another and another as a wave of agreement crossed the tavern. Eventually, every voice had a say, and every voice said the same.

"Then, I can only hope you are able to."

Roland's eyes dropped to the floor. He walked out with a purposeful speed. Harris followed on his heels. Lia stayed seated at the back, trying to remain invisible. The rest of the crowd stood. Mumbles of discontent were shared among them as they headed for the door.

Manny played his role as the host, acknowledging each and every face as it left his tavern. He didn't realize anyone had stayed behind until he closed the door and turned around.

He started as he saw Lia standing up. "Don't give an old man such a fright."

She slowly approached, winding her way between the tables. "What happened to the man who told me never to let them take another innocent life?"

"This is different."

"What happened to the man who told me to fight?"

"That was before I understood the price you would pay."

"What price is that?"

"Your very soul!" His jaw quivered.

Lia was taken aback. "What do you mean?"

He pointed an angry finger at the door. "Those men you call your commanders, that man you see as your husband, is no man at all. They are lab creations, masterminded by one of the most evil inventors in this world." Manny's nostrils flared as he forced out an angry breath and then sucked in another. "And I hate to be the one to tell you, but you're the same, cast from the same mold, all at the will of your so-called great leader."

Lia felt like she was melting. "How did you know?"

Manny's face softened in shock. "You knew?"

"Who told you?" she whispered out with what felt like all of her breath.

"And here I thought you were just as innocent as the rest. I should have known you couldn't share a bed with a man and not also keep his devilish secrets." He turned his back on her and tried to walk away.

"I didn't know! Not for a long time. Manny, please listen!" She tugged him back with desperate hands. The sudden influx of oxygen it took to shout made her dizzy, so she held tight to him. "I was told against Roland's will. I never would have known otherwise. I didn't—I couldn't have told anyone else. No one would have believed me. And they never will tell any of them. They think it's too dangerous. That's why I must know, I *have* to know who told you."

The desperation was written all over her. Manny's hard stare dissipated into worry as he looked into her eyes. He took her by the shoulders and led her to the corner table. The weight of his hands pressing her down into the seat helped to restore her breath.

He sat and took a moment to restore his own before beginning his story. "He came through some months ago. Appearance of a traveler like any other. None believed his stories at first, not until he set about proving it. Proving that he had the ability in his blood, the one the doctor had given him."

"How?"

"Cuts sealed before your eyes. Broken bones mended within hours. It pained him every time, but he was determined to prove that he really had taken a bullet to the brain and survived." Those words sent such a chill down Lia's spine that she felt frozen to her seat. "Sooner or later, enough people believed. So, they started to listen to what he had to say about the legendary Resistance army… and your commander."

Lia stared down at the table as she tried to dig up some tangible reason, some logical explanation for what she just heard. "How do you know he wasn't lying? That he wasn't just some tin can putting on an act?"

"Aye, those thoughts were with me, too. But there were many nights shared right here with our people. Many stories told of joy and sadness, love and longing, pains old as time. No man can fake such emotion."

There was only one question left to ask. "Who was he?"

"Went by the name of Arin."

Every muscle in Lia's body went slack. Her eyes blurred under a veil of moisture. "Where is he now?"

"I'm not like to say."

Her desperate hands clawed at his arm. Her tears broke free. "I need to know! This isn't for revenge. This isn't so we can hunt him down. This is for me, Manny. Just me. Where is he?"

Manny leaned back in his seat. He lightly shook his head, as if he didn't quite believe his own thoughts. "'Tis true then. The stories and the feelings came along with them. He didn't fake any of that, did he?"

"Please, tell me where he is." The words came out with what felt like her last breath again.

He leaned forward and put a comforting hand over the one that was still gripped onto his arm. "Left some weeks ago. Can't honestly say where to. He left us with his words and let us do with them what we would. You see, sweetheart, we decided long before you arrived that we wanted no part of your commander's plans."

Lia slid back in her seat, allowing her arms to retreat with her. She looked down at the table as she waited for the strength to move and her tears to cease.

Manny waited patiently in silence.

When she could finally look him in the eye again, all she felt the need to say was, "I understand."

The fog rolled back into Lia's mind. The act of leaving the tavern, leaving the town, walking through the forest, was lost behind its obscurity. It might have taken minutes or hours to get back to camp, she couldn't tell. Three years had passed since she watched Arin die. Three years she had spent haunted by the ghost of a man who was still out there in the world. How was it possible? Why had he never come to her?

She entered the tent to find Roland and Harris in the midst of planning, and a sweeping wind of clarity brought at least one realization into focus. Someone had lied. They both looked to her, expecting some report about what she had discovered in their absence. She glanced back and forth between them, trying to surmise who was more capable of such calculated deception.

When she didn't speak up, Roland decided to share their plans. "We're going to stay into the night. If we give them a few hours—"

"We should leave now," Lia said without the need for any forethought.

"There are doubtlessly some who were simply afraid to speak up in front of the others. If we give them the chance to come to us."

"They won't. Trust me."

Roland turned to Harris for a confirmation. As the silent conversation took place between them, Lia could tell that neither of them knew what they were up against. However calculated this lie was, it had yielded an unexpected and entirely unknown result. They eventually came around to a conclusion.

Roland turned back to her. "If you're sure."

"I am."

"Very well. Spread the word."

Lia watched as they both prepared for the forthcoming duties of leadership.

She was standing in Harris's path as he headed out. He stopped beside her. "Are you all right?"

His concern was genuine, but she could no longer trust its source. "I'll be fine."

A tiny spark of suspicion flashed in his eyes.

Lia walked away to begin going about her own duties. She was content to leave him wondering.

The fog drifted in and out of her mind throughout the day. Hours lost in travel bled into hours setting up the next camp, which trickled into a long, exhaustive night. Lia sat up with her arms folded tight around her legs, letting her thoughts ebb and flow. The low spill of dwindling lamplight drew her focus to the blotchy field of color on Roland's side. Her eyes traced from angry red to deep purple, to patches of blue broken up by a sickly yellow. Just beyond, where his shoulder gently rose and fell with each breath, was the untouched hue of perfectly healthy skin.

Harris had given him another injection in a moment of desperation. Why would he believe that Roland was about to die when Arin had not? Even with that renewed strength in his system, Roland certainly hadn't healed before her eyes. Had Manny really seen Arin do what he claimed?

Lia's eyes traveled over to the pile of Roland's clothing at his feet. The tip of his gun-belt poked out above the jumble of fabric. She unfolded herself and gently fished into the pile, tracing the hard leather edge until she found what she had sought. Her hand emerged with his knife.

A flash of lamplight flickered off the blade. Lia looked back at Roland's sleeping form. His slow and steady breathing continued without interruption. She slid away from him, sat up on her knees, and gripped the knife tight in her fist. She summoned up her fearlessness with a few short breaths, then ran the blade across her forearm.

The sharp sting of pain was undeniable. She bore her teeth against the cry that wanted to emerge. She held her arm up before her eyes. Blood oozed from the open slash. She watched it bleed, letting it flow down her arm and drip off the point of her elbow. It did not stop.

Lia dropped the knife and rubbed blood away from the cut. There was no change. Blood rushed in to fill the open wound again. Pain began to radiate up and down her arm. Her injury was only getting worse.

A hand suddenly snatched her wrist. Roland's eyes flicked between her face and her cut, his fear apparent. "What are you doing?"

"I... I wanted to see how fast it would heal." How else could she explain it?

He snatched up the bandages he had discarded for his own comfort and began to wrap them tight around her arm. "You've been injured more times than I can count. You know exactly how much it hurts, and exactly how long you take to heal. Why would that be any different now?"

"I don't know." That was something she couldn't explain. He cleaned the blood from her hands as she stared down at the red stain at her knees.

Roland's hand tucked under her chin. He turned her face up and examined her eyes. "What did he say to you?"

Lia considered his questions. If Roland really had no notion of why she might suddenly wonder about the limits of her own body, of how a conversation with one bartender in one little town could elicit such emotion, then perhaps he wasn't the liar. She felt obligated to quell his concern. "It was just more of the same."

"Don't let this discourage you. I will do whatever I can to make sure all these people are under our protection."

"I know you will."

He wrapped his arms around her. She tucked into his shoulder and let herself relax against him. What little comfort she found in believing Roland was just as ignorant of Arin's survival as she had been, was enough... for now. Her eyes traveled down to the knife. She stared at the thin red line of her own blood on the edge of the blade and let one determination slowly seep into her.

She would find out what had happened to Arin.

SIX

HER DISTANT FIGURE was just a silhouette against the slate gray sky, but he still recognized every detail of it. One glance through the scope was all it took to pick out the distinct shape of a gun on each hip. She was using her scope to look up toward the mountain. What could she possibly see through the tree line? Very little, it seemed, as she lowered her scope with a frustrated heave of her shoulders. She shielded her eyes against the glare and looked up again, as if her own eyes would tell her more. After seeing nothing but trees again, she walked down the soft rise and disappeared back into the green of the valley.

He kept his scope focused on the bald peak of the rise, just in case someone else was about to appear. No one else did. It didn't matter, he had seen enough to know.

They had arrived.

Arin had anticipated their arrival but had not expected the first sign of it to be Lia's lone silhouette in the distance. He had prepared to shrink into the shadows again. He had steeled himself to confront them, armed and ready to fight whoever got in his path, if that's what had to happen. He had not prepared himself to feel a sudden desire to sprint over the foothills into Lia's arms and confess everything to her.

Arin turned his eyes to ferns on the forest floor far below the hide and turned his focus toward the facts he could surmise. Rather than march into town as an armed front, they had hidden themselves in the trees. That meant they had been pushed out of Cleanair and must have assumed Clearwater would do the same. Yet they had not circumnavigated the town and were keeping watch on their surroundings. At least Lia was. That meant they would attempt to win Clearwater over, to ally with its people, to put an army at their borders.

They would not succeed.

Arin could choose to watch this all unfold from the sidelines, or he could lead them in their charge against the Resistance army and make his survival, his abilities, and his years of subterfuge against Roland known to his entire army... and to Lia. A million different outcomes from either choice seemed to rush into his head at once. He couldn't decide yet. He had to erase that image of Lia's silhouette from his mind before he could be objective—if he ever could.

Arin climbed down from the hide, followed the winding footpath out between the ferns, and headed back into town. Just beyond the quiet of the trees, the town bustled with its daily life. He kept his eyes down, lest someone ask him if he had seen anything. He would tell them as soon as he knew what to do.

Desmond would want to fight. He would want to drive them out of town with pitchforks and torches like the monsters he believed them to be. Arin would have to talk him down before the entire town ended up in a war they would lose. Even with Arin on their side, his ability to fend off bullets could not protect them against an entire army whose leader wanted him dead.

The gushing of the waterfall told him he was close enough to look up now. With his focus on the little house tucked against the hillside under the mill, anyone who spotted him would just assume he was heading over for a neighborly visit. He jogged the last couple of steps down the stone path and cracked open the door without knocking.

A pair of little feet raced toward him from the hallway. Ewan always greeted him as if he were bringing a burst of magic into the house with him. Arin supposed that, to the little boy who had watched him instantly recover from the beating he had taken the day the riverbank gave way and the rapids had thrown him into every rock, he must be a bit magic indeed. Ewan threw his little arms around Arin's leg, forcing him to a stumbling stop.

Jania was not far behind him. At nine months pregnant, it took her a bit longer to navigate the narrow halls now. Her face dropped as soon as she saw Arin's. She knew what news he had come to share.

"They here?" she asked.

"They are," he confirmed.

Jania took a deep breath. "Ewan, sweetie, why don't you go have something to eat."

"Okay, Mama." Ewan obligingly trotted off to the kitchen.

"Don't worry," Arin assured her. "I won't let him do anything stupid."

"You mean you'll try," she corrected with a worried smile. "He's in the mill."

Jania stepped aside so Arin could squeeze past her and up the stairs. The slapping of the wheel against the water just outside the window and din of grinding from above grew with each step he took, echoing around the narrow corridor. Arin slipped through the crooked door at the top and into the heat and noise of the mill house.

Desmond dropped the sack from his shoulder as soon as he saw Arin. He, too, knew what he had come to say. He scowled, twisting the tip of the distinctive scar that ran down the length of his face and through every feature it touched.

"I need some time, but I will come up with a plan." That was all Arin could say for now.

Desmond wrestled with a response. He probably wanted to jump into action, to rally everyone and their pitchforks together, but Arin had earned his trust, so he stifled his words with a nod.

Arin crossed the room, skirting around the mill wheel, and headed for the broad window at the back. He put his foot up on the sill, stared down into the churning river below, and let his thoughts flow. Like the river, they came swiftly and glided around each and every obstacle. Only one thought remained constant as he formulated plans and envisioned each and every outcome.

I'll be ready this time.

ARIN

"ASK YOURSELF IF you are truly prepared to take the next step." Commander Hudson was in particularly good voice that day. He probably liked this point in basic training better than any other. It would naturally weed out the weak.

Arin kept his eyes fixed on the Commander's face, determined to show he would not be among them.

"Your education, your training, everything you've experienced up to this point in your lives can only take you this far, and not one step farther." Commander Hudson stood up tall, putting his face in line with the Unity symbol on the banners that flanked him.

Arin felt his own spine straighten up in tandem.

"Without injection, you cannot join our ranks. Without injection, you cannot take the Oath of Unification. Without injection, you will never be one of us." Commander Hudson's eyes swept the crowd before he continued.

Arin told himself not to even blink, lest it be misconstrued.

"This weekend is not for you to waste on meaningless activities, like sleeping well past dawn, eating whatever toxic junk you please, booze. Sex."

Someone let out an uncomfortable titter behind Arin.

"This weekend is your final chance to decide if you're going to back down and give up your chance at glory, or if you are truly ready to be one of us. Forever."

Arin could hear the shifting of his fellow recruits. Some of them turned to look at each other, but Arin kept his eyes fixed firmly on the Commander.

He was ready.

They hustled out quickly, most heading back to their bunks to pack for whatever debauchery they had planned for that weekend. Arin maintained the calm and steady pace they had been trained to keep throughout each day. The halls may have looked devoid of authority, but he was certain someone was always watching.

He thought the break room would be empty, but Vasquez, Frost, and Drake had secured a corner of it to engage in their usual less-than-highbrow discourse. Arin considered leaving but knew that would only draw the attention he was attempting to escape from. He did his best to go unnoticed as he headed for the nutrient machine. He focused on the machine's movement as it dropped the tiny cup and slowly filled it with the green-brown slurry, while today's choice of illuminating topic drifted into his ears.

"But if you can't get excited, then how are you supposed to, you know, get it goin'?" Frost asked in his uniquely simplistic way.

"Come on, dude. A breeze would get you going." Vasquez had made an art of being one of the boys by consistently undermining their anatomy. None of them were brave enough to throw a response of equal measure back at her.

"Why don't we ask head of the class here?" Drake said loudly, though he knew they would have been overheard regardless.

"Ask me what?" Arin responded without turning around. Even if he wasn't the only other one in the room, he would have known they were talking about him.

"Like he would know," Frost said under his breath.

"Humor me," Drake responded with no attempt to keep his voice down.

The machine spluttered out the last of the slurry. Arin scooped up the cup and turned to face them.

Drake sat up on the edge of the table, something he definitely wouldn't do if any of their professors were in sight. "We were just wondering, after the injection, if ah… doin' it would still feel the same."

"Doing what?" Arin hated innuendo. He wanted to make at least one of them say it out loud, but all he received in response was a collective snicker. He filled the break in conversation by slamming back half his slurry. That was the most he could handle in one gulp.

"I mean," Drake continued after he contained his laughter, "being intimate with a lady."

Vasquez and Frost snorted.

Arin waited for a pause in the snorts before answering. "Nothing about our basic biology will change. Functions essential to human survival all remain the same."

"See what I mean?" Frost said to Drake.

"He's a walking textbook." Vasquez waved a dismissive hand at him.

"I mean, sure it will function," Drake continued. Perhaps he really was looking for an answer. "Man, I hope it functions even better, if you know what I'm sayin'." Or perhaps not. "But will it feel the same?"

"Why wouldn't it?"

"What about all those scientists who say that, like, pleasure and pain, even though they're opposites, our bodies see them as the same thing. Those little guys are supposed to know we're in pain and stop it, right? So...." Vasquez was actually on to something there.

Arin could have told her what he had learned about the nanites' nerve response adaptability, that essentially the more sex they had the better the nanites would get at knowing the difference. Who wouldn't want to hear that?

Frost was quick to jump in and bring the conversation crashing back down to his level. "Oh, that's depressing." He began faking an orgasm, with body motion to match. "Yeah... oh yeah... aw shatz!"

The genuine laugh his antics received made Arin instantly change his mind about sharing any of his knowledge with them. They'd just have to find out for themselves. "That's not how it works."

"Like you would know," Frost coughed out.

"I do."

Frost gave that declaration a disbelieving huff, but Drake was suddenly very interested. "You got a girl back home?"

Arin instantly regretted not walking away during Frost's juvenile display. "Yes."

"Then what are you doing here, man?" Drake asked, bamboozled.

It was not a question he had anticipated. "I'm here for all the same reasons you are."

"Nah ah. We were all signed up by Moms and Pops. You're just about the only cookie cutter walked in here on his own two feet. Why would you do that when you got something good back home?"

"Maybe she ain't so good," Vasquez said with a brotherly slap to Drake's shoulder.

Frost let out a few barks like an old dog.

"Take that back." Arin cut their laughter short.

Drake got to his feet, suddenly on edge.

Vasquez was glancing back and forth between them.

Cold slurry oozed out between Arin's fingers. At some point, he had crushed the cup.

Frost just gave him a defiant look and let out one long, loud, "Owooooo!"

Arin didn't feel himself launching forward until Frost's chair smacked the ground. He was pretty big. He must have come at him with a lot of speed to take him down, chair and all. Desperate to keep him there, Arin threw a panicked punch across the bridge of his nose.

Drake was rushing into his periphery, reaching out, probably just trying to pull Arin away, but with three of them against one of him, he couldn't take that chance. Arin jabbed his elbow into Drake's rib cage. As soon as he doubled over, Arin shoved him for good measure. Drake splatted onto his back.

Arin threw another barrage of fists at Frost. He couldn't let him get the upper hand. He'd be flattened if he did. Frost's nose released a gush of blood. His eyes swirled around, unfocused. *Good enough for now.*

That's when Vasquez threw herself on Arin's back. She was tiny but made up for it with relentlessness. She tried to lock him into a chokehold. Arin found enough strength in his legs to stand with her attached to his back like a leech. He lurched around. Every muscle in his back screamed in pain, but she lost her grip and went flying into a chair. It looked like it hurt.

They were all on the ground now, but that wouldn't last.

Arin put up his fists and prepared to be beaten to a pulp.

"Arin, Drake, Vasquez, Frost, line up now!" Commander Hudson's voice shook the room.

Everyone scrambled, instantly snapping from their various states of sprawl, up into a neat line in the center of the room.

Commander Hudson walked the line, scrutinizing each tight-lipped face.

Frost sniffed at the blood freely flowing from his nose.

"Vasquez, Drake, escort Mister Frost to patch and repair. Mister Arin, follow me."

This was it, the end of his career before it even started. He would be kicked out of the academy, banned from any training program in any city, destined to mediocrity. Arin's fear of inevitable failure built and built as he followed the Commander through the halls. By the time they entered his office, his skin was crawling with regret. Arin waited at attention as Commander Hudson closed the door behind him. He steeled himself to be yelled at, but the first thing the Commander did was offer him a handkerchief. He responded to Arin's look of confusion with a glance down.

Arin's hand was covered in splatters of blood and crusted nutrient slurry. He accepted the handkerchief with a nod and wiped away the evidence that was going to secure his fate, not that he could deny it anyway. He was no good at lying.

Commander Hudson busied himself by shifting papers across his desk. Outside, the newest recruits were learning their formation marches. The gentle rapping of their feet against stone beat a steady rhythm through the window. It might have been calming if Arin wasn't petrified. Commander Hudson seemed to find the papers he was looking for. He read them in silence.

Arin's fear finally sparked to the surface. "Commander, I—"

He silenced him with the raising of his sizable palm.

Arin snapped his jaw shut and told himself to lock it in place.

Commander Hudson finished his document and finally looked up at him. "Anger loses wars. Have you heard that before, Mister Arin?"

"Yes, sir."

"And who said it?"

"Commander James Grey, sir." Arin had no idea why he was being quizzed, but he was happy to play along. At least he wasn't being yelled at.

"James Grey. One of the greatest strategic minds of this entire century. The very father of Unified Law. And do you know why he said it, Mister Arin?"

"To make the case for mandatory injection in the armed forces, sir."

"That's the most common interpretation, but why did he really say it?" Commander Hudson squinted at him.

Was this a test of his ability to interpret history? To think on his feet? *Just answer him*, Arin internally shouted at himself. "Because anger also starts wars."

"Exactly." Commander Hudson looked him up and down. Had he passed the test? "I see your professors were right about you." He fanned out the pile of papers he had been examining. "History, chemistry, medicine, law. Every professor gave you top marks and commendations. And the physical trainer said you were...." He plucked up the report in question to read from the page. "The fastest animal he'd ever seen running on two legs. They're all recommending you for officer training."

A strange sensation washed through Arin's system. Was it relief, pride, shock? He locked his knees to keep them from buckling.

"Of course," Commander Hudson continued, "the ability to command requires more than intelligence and speed. It requires just the right attitude. That is where my recommendation comes in."

Arin was instantly electrified by fear again. Commander Hudson turned to look out the window. He watched the marching recruits in silence. Arin tried to focus on the gentle beat of their footsteps and prepare for inevitable failure... again.

"What you've learned thus far is only the tip of the iceberg. And the physical training you've experienced up until this point only makes you slightly stronger than my Nana." Commander Hudson turned back around.

Arin straightened up as tall as he could.

"Your intelligence burdens you with daily wrath from your cohorts. Your disdain for stooping to the lowest common denominator certainly doesn't win you any friends, and you're only faster than the rest of them because you know you're never going to be as strong." Commander Hudson's observations confirmed Arin's belief that someone had always been watching. He stepped around his desk, approaching him with a slow stride. Is this when he would start yelling? "But none of that has stopped your determination since the day you arrived here. And none of that stopped you from taking down a fellow recruit who was twice your size simply because he was being an ass." Commander Hudson came face to face with him. Arin had never realized they were the same height. Commander Hudson's presence always seemed mountainous in comparison to his. "You've earned my recommendation."

That same sensation washed right down to Arin's bones, but he had no time to savor it. Commander Hudson was already returning to his file to make his recommendation official.

"You can receive your injection tonight. Tomorrow morning, we will transport you to the Elite Forces Camp."

"Tonight, sir?"

"Yes, Mister Arin. Once I've made my recommendation, you are part of the program. There's nothing else you have to do."

"But, sir, I haven't decided about injection yet." Hadn't he? The speed with which he had gone from abject failure to officer-in-training was certainly alarming, but there was something else that made him suddenly crave time to think, something that had cracked open the window of doubt. The mention of Lia, however obtuse, had not only motivated his rage, it had also awoken his longing.

"You're one of the last ones I would assume to have second thoughts, Mister Arin. You were ready the day you walked in."

"I am, and I couldn't be more honored to have your recommendation, sir. But I would like to receive the same time allotted to everyone else."

Commander Hudson gave him another surmising glance. If only Arin could tell what he was thinking. "Very well. Come back next week and tell me what you've decided."

"Thank you, sir."

"Dismissed." Arin gave him the necessary salute, but before he could turn to leave, Commander Hudson had one last thought to share. "Mister Arin. Think about how much you've accomplished in just a few months, and this is only the beginning. Imagine what you might be capable of in the next few. Keep that in mind while you're mulling it over. You may just have the chance to prove your true strength someday."

Arin felt himself straighten up again. He gave Commander Hudson an affirming nod and marched out, keeping perfect time with the soldiers outside.

LIA ENTERED THE tent to find Roland in the midst of yet another command discussion that had started in her absence.

"We can create choke points to the east and west. It won't take more than fifty soldiers at every passing. If we keep within shouting distance, we form a solid wall," Roland explained as he gestured to the mental map that only he could see.

"What about the main road?" Michaels asked. "We need more than fifty to block that."

"We can't put anyone out in the open yet."

Lia made her presence known by shoving into the circle. "We don't have permission to do any of this yet, let alone block their road."

"We're not on anyone's land," Roland was quick to point out.

"If a fight comes over that ridge, we could get pushed there."

"Any sign of one yet?" Michaels asked.

"I can't see anything past the trees," Lia had to admit. "The only thing I can tell you is that the town isn't on fire."

"We won't let that happen," Roland said firmly. "At the first sign of trouble, we can head back up the ridge or down into the valley."

"They don't want us up on that mountain, and they might not want us in the valley either."

"We don't know that the people of Clearwater are going to feel the same way." Roland's denial was unfounded. Perhaps it was actually hope. Regardless, it offered Lia an opening.

"Why wouldn't they? They trade with each other, share the same road, see the same travelers pass. Even with the foothills separating them, they're practically sister towns. We should send someone in. Find out what we're dealing with before we bring a fight to their territory."

Roland turned to Harris. "Do we have time?"

"Two days at the most."

Lia hid her anticipation in clenched fists as Roland considered.

"Harris, Michaels, go in as travelers, bring back as much information as you can."

"And me." Had she spoken up too quickly, too eagerly? Luckily, Lia was good at summoning reason to serve her desire. "Any story that will explain their passing would be more believable if I was with them. A woman's presence tends to soften a lie."

Roland took another moment to consider. It looked as if he was consulting his mental map again rather than assessing Lia's logic. "All right. Gauge their temperature, but don't start any arguments. You have until sunrise. Whatever you don't know by then will have to remain unknown."

One day to find out if Arin has been there, Lia thought. *Use it wisely.*

Stripping her arms and armor for the simplicity of travel clothes made her feel light and free of the burdens that came with command. She wanted to race down into the valley and ask everyone she encountered about a mysterious traveler with miraculous healing abilities. When she emerged from her tent and saw Michaels and Harris awaiting her, the weight of secrecy was suddenly sitting on her shoulders again. *Patience*, Lia told herself as she approached them.

"So, what's our story?" Harris asked with a shrug.

"You didn't come up with one?"

"You were the one preaching the benefits of a feminine presence."

"And here I thought you were the expert at spinning stories." Lia had let too much suspicion surface in her voice and her words. She glanced away from Harris's insulted look under the guise of giving their odd threesome a once over. "We are... husband and wife. From Hammond Valley, born and raised. We ran before the occupation and are seeking a place to settle, where we could comfortably keep ourselves and your"— she gestured to Michaels, her eyes turned down so she wouldn't have to see his reaction—"doddering father."

"Doddering!"

Of course he didn't like that, but at least she had a reason. "People tend to let loose information around those whom they think won't notice. Since we don't have a child in our ranks, you'll have to take that role, Michaels."

He grumbled but didn't argue.

Harris smirked. Something about it annoyed Lia beyond reason.

"And you"—she pointed an accusatory finger at Harris—"will have to get much dirtier." She kicked a cloud of dirt up around his legs and didn't wait for any complaints to surface before explaining. "You've been on the road for months, remember? It can't look like you just put these clothes on today."

He acquiesced with a sigh. This time, Michaels was the one smirking. Lia didn't mind that, but Harris certainly did.

"Watch it, Pops."

Michaels smirk turned into a scowl of stone.

Traveling with these two was going to be challenging enough, even without her secret search for Arin simmering in the back of her mind. *Patience*, Lia told herself again.

HE KEPT THEM framed in the scope as they walked out of the woods and down the road. Simple clothes, hidden weapons—if any. They were planning to do a little spying in disguise. *Lia's area of expertise*, Arin thought as he watched her disappear around the curve with the others.

Desmond had already made up his mind. He twisted his scar with a scowl again. "We should tell everyone who they really are before they get into town."

"Maybe." Arin drifted into memories of all the alter egos he'd seen Lia don in the past. He wondered what kind of accent and mannerisms this particular persona would bring with them. He shook his head, snapping his mind back to the present. "But there's no point in picking a fight with three soldiers when the entire army is just down the road."

"I don't want their poison near us, no matter how few of them carry it."

Arin chose not to remind Desmond that he also carried the same poison. "Those three aren't just the Commander's grunts. They're important to him. Very important." A plan quickly formulated in Arin's mind. A golden opportunity was walking into town as they spoke. "Get your most trusted together, just a small group. Bring them to the mill. I have an idea."

Desmond was still scowling. "My men will want to drive them out before they even set foot on our road."

Arin responded with a smile. "Not when they realize what we can take from their Commander without firing a single bullet." Desmond had no way of knowing the kind of power Lia held, but Arin did. He had seen it with his own eyes.

He had experienced it in his own heart.

IT WAS BRIGHT enough to make the buttons on his uniform glint in the sunlight. The sight made Arin feel justified for the time he had dedicated to polishing them. He puffed up as he thought about how impressed Lia was bound to be when she saw him in uniform. She would pretend that she wasn't, but he would be able to see through her act. He was so wrapped up in imaginings of what would happen when they saw each other again that he didn't notice until he turned up the main road how oddly quiet Waterford was, particularly for such a lovely day. He stopped and did a slow turn to assess his surroundings. The cobblestone streets, the brightly painted houses, the neatly trimmed gardens all seemed completely devoid of life. It was as if the good people of Waterford had all evaporated.

A dull whine in the distance overtook Arin's musings about the town's subdued air. A flash of sunlight revealed a vehicle approaching at rocket-like speed. The bullet-shaped vehicle zoomed past Arin, tossing up leaf litter along with his neatly combed hair. It whined to a halt, then whirred backward and whined to a full stop beside Arin. He quickly stopped fixing his hair and came to attention when he saw the two Unity soldiers staring at him through the window.

"Fresh meat," the one in the passenger seat said under his breath, though Arin heard it loud and clear.

"You with us, junior?" the driver asked.

"I'm a recruit, sir."

"Sir? Well, la-di-dah," said the passenger. The driver was clearly not his superior.

"Shut up," the driver ordered his passenger before turning back to Arin. "What are you doing off base?"

"Don't you remember basic training?" the passenger spoke up again. "It's his weekend."

"How can we be sure? These little fishies swim away all the time."

"One way to find out," the passenger said. He pulled out his gun and pointed it at Arin.

He instinctively dropped to the ground, ducking out of the path of the would-be bullet. When the sound of a gunshot didn't follow, he knew he'd been tricked. He expected to hear laughter, that's how his classmates would have responded, but all he heard from inside the vehicle was a self-satisfied huff.

"Guess you're right," the driver agreed. "He's too skinny to be juiced up anyway."

Arin stood but didn't dare distract himself with the task of dusting off his knees. They were both still staring at him.

The driver geared the vehicle up but held the break long enough to offer Arin a suggestion. "Have a double golden for me, kid."

The vehicle took off with an ear-piercing scream.

The passenger leaned out the window to shout his own parting remarks. "And get laid!"

They rounded the next corner, and the whine of the vehicle, along with its self-generated wind, disappeared as quickly as it had arrived.

Arin took the time to dust off his uniform and smooth his hair back into place before continuing on his way. He had to look perfect when he arrived.

He made the final turn—thankfully in the opposite direction of the vehicle—and the stately mansion appeared at the end of the road. The brambles that had a tendency to push their way through the fence were particularly overgrown. Mayor McMillan never did enjoy paying a gardener for what he considered to be aesthetic gain only, but he did peel open his pockets whenever nature had begun to take too much of his land. It looked as if his definition of too much had loosened a bit.

Arin stared up at the high windows as he approached. Would Lia sense his presence and look out? Would she run down the stairs and burst out onto the street to greet him with open arms? These visions kept him looking up, hoping to see her face. He even considered climbing straight up to her window, as he had done on many nights before he left for the academy, but the high windows remained black, and her face never appeared.

He turned his eyes to what little of the yard he could see between breaks in the brambles. The broad tree stump stood alone in the center of the overgrown lawn. Tiny shoots, the beginnings of new trees, grew up around its gnarled gray roots. The brambles thinned out as the house itself slid into view, and then dead ended in harshly chopped branches where the entry gate stood. He double-checked that his hair was still in place before unlatching the gate.

The iron hinges shrieked, but the sound seemed dull after the whine of the Unity vehicle. Arin closed the gate behind him and made sure it was latched, just as he'd been instructed to do since he was barely tall enough to reach. He marched with confidence down the path, up the steps, onto the porch, and gave three brisk swings to the knocker.

The loud clacks subsided. Nothing sounded out from inside. No footsteps. No voices.

Arin considered announcing himself through the door. Perhaps the Mayor had become more cautious since the town became unified. He opened his mouth to shout out, but didn't seem to have enough air to make even a small noise. He shook off his nerves and reached for the knocker again. His fingertips had just grazed the iron when the door swung open.

Mayor McMillan's broad-shouldered shape filled the doorway. The distinct lines around his mouth that came from many years of both laughing and shouting were firmly turned down.

"Hello, Mayor," Arin said with a squeak. "I came to—"

"Get off my porch."

"Sir, I just wanted to—"

"I don't care what you want. Get off my property." He stomped out of the doorway, forcing Arin back to teetering on the edge of the top step.

"I came to see Lia," Arin forced out.

Mayor McMillan stepped right up into his face.

Arin hadn't realized until then that he'd grown just as tall as the man he had once seen as an angry, red-faced giant. Of course, the mayor could still toss him down the steps if he wanted to, but Arin would not be deterred. He stared right back as the mayor frowned at him.

"You're too late," he said through bared teeth and then turned back toward the house.

"What do you mean? Where is she?"

He was already swinging the door shut.

Arin slapped his arm against it.

Mayor McMillan didn't try to shove it shut on any of his appendages, but he didn't bother to turn around. "I don't know, and even if I did, I wouldn't tell a sorry excuse for a human like you." He practically spat the words out.

Arin was genuinely flabbergasted. "How can you not know?"

The mayor whirled around. "She left!" He charged out the door and shoved Arin stumbling down the steps. "After your weak little ass went off to become one of those tin cans, she picked up and left this house, this town, this territory. She left every little thing that your worthless life ever touched!"

His angry gesticulation forced Arin backward down the path until his spine made contact with the iron gate. Once he had nowhere else to go, Mayor McMillan seemed to grow exponentially.

"She left her own father because of the pathetic little scab that you are." He turned and stomped back toward the door.

Arin barely had the capacity to absorb what he had just heard, but he knew that the closing of the door would represent the end of any chance he had at seeing Lia. His mouth squeezed out the first thought his desperate mind conjured. "Maybe she left because you unified the town!"

The mayor turned back with a look in his eyes that would ignite kindling. "How dare you stand there in that black and silver shroud and say that to me."

Being reminded that he was in uniform instilled Arin with enough confidence to stand up straight again. "This uniform gives me the means to find her. I can bring her home."

"That uniform is nothing but a security blanket for your fearful little soul." He turned away, crossed the threshold and reached for the doorknob.

The creaking hinges awoke Arin's desperation again, but this time it came out as a plea. "Mayor please. I want to find her. Let me help."

He didn't charge out. He didn't even turn around. He only turned his head enough to be heard. "It's no longer Mayor. And you, as always, are incapable of helping anyone but yourself."

The hinges creaked. The door boomed. Arin's last chance at seeing Lia before facing the unknown effects of injection was stolen away from him.

Arin didn't pick a direction. He just walked. With each stomp, with each vibration up his leg, with every breath he forced out of his nostrils, another thought would surface.

How dare he insult me when he's the coward who surrendered an entire town. How dare he judge my capability when he has no idea what I've achieved in the last few months. How dare he tell me what I can't do when I'll soon have more authority than he ever did.

The bitter brew in his brain was starting to churn up the acid in his stomach. He told himself he would feel better if he just calmed down, but as soon as he allowed enough of a pause for a deep inhale, another thought jumped up from the depths.

How could she leave me?

Suddenly, the thumping of his heart outweighed the churning of his stomach. The toxic combination made him so lightheaded that he had to stop and brace against his knees. He stared at the ground, breathing through the blurriness. When his own shiny boots came back into focus, it occurred to him what a terrible look this was for a uniformed soldier, especially if his friends in the vehicle were to speed past. He straightened up and swallowed back the last of his rising bile.

Arin found himself standing next to the very same train station at which he had arrived. It represented a new and wonderfully tidy addition to the town of Waterford, a sleek and speedy transport system the likes of which this sleepy little area had never seen. And why was it here? Because the Unity built it. Unification had brought with it efficiency and progress, just as it had promised. He compared the neat planters along the station wall to the overgrown mess taking over Mayor McMillan's seat of pride.

The momentary satisfaction he gained from their contrast was quickly overtaken by the return of his incessantly thunderous heartbeat when he remembered how much time he and Lia had spent together in that yard. Why did thoughts of her quicken his pulse like that, when the excitement of seeing her had been twisted out of his grip? It didn't take him long to reason out an answer.

I'm afraid I'll never see her again.

The Unity had promised and delivered progress to Waterford. It had promised Arin the opportunity to prove his true strength. All he had to do now was seize it. Doing so would also offer him deliverance from that acid churning anger, from that pulse pounding fear, even from the instinct to flee a bullet. He would never have to live through another day like this ever again.

He hadn't visited his parents yet. He hadn't even announced his arrival. Seeing Lia had been his only goal, and it could no longer be achieved. So, with nothing more holding him to the cobblestone streets of Waterford, Arin entered the station, patiently awaited the next train, and returned to the academy to receive his injection.

SEVEN

A HAIRPIN TURN led them down the last slope and into the valley. The center of town was a broad patch of bald land, bordered by the trees on one side and a river on the other, with an odd mix of buildings scattered throughout.

Harris was already supporting Michaels with one arm as he faked a wobbling gait around the last turn. It was quite convincing. Lia wondered if Michaels might even outshine her act. As they came within view of the first few windows that could have peering eyes behind them, Harris offered his other arm to Lia. Her instinct was to remain free from attachment, but as the author of their fiction she felt obliged to respond to his attempt to enrich it. She hooked her arm around his, and their threesome walked at the slow and wobbly pace Michaels had set, down into the town center.

The streets were surprisingly scant for what should have been a well-populated natural bastion. The few people who were out and about followed with distrusting eyes as they passed, as if they were predatory beasts that might strike at anything. Lia made a few attempts at greeting with a smile but quickly gave up when no one gave so much as a nod in return.

"Well, they may not have scattered in the woods, but this reception feels a bit too familiar for my liking," Harris muttered.

"This isn't the same thing. They don't know who we are. At least, they shouldn't." Lia's mind bubbled away with ideas about what—or who—might have given them away.

"Maybe they just don't take too kindly to travelers around here," Michaels said.

"Then we have a lot of charming to do." Lia's determination set in.

"Well, I'll just leave that to you two youngsters," Michaels croaked out in an old man's voice. "All I need is a sturdy seat and a warm fire for my old bones." It was half act, half complaint.

"It's going to be a long while before you let me forget this, isn't it?" Lia sighed out.

Michaels responded with a wobbling nod. He really was very good.

"That looks like a promising destination." Harris pointed his chin toward a two-story building dominating the center of the town. A dangling sign advertised it as the "MILLHILL INN."

Oddly large for a town that doesn't seem to like visitors, Lia thought.

"Let's go find you that fire, Pops," Harris suggested with a smile.

Michaels responded with a grumpy grumble.

The inn was double height inside, with a rectangular bar in the center surrounded by many tables and chairs, doubtlessly the town's social center. The rooms on the second floor were connected by a long balcony with bold numbers painted on each door. Yes, they must be used to travelers. So, what was wrong with them? There was a stone fireplace near the entry, the perfect place to watch all comings and goings, and to converse with whomever might venture to talk to them. Getting anyone to acknowledge them with more than just a stare was the first challenge.

Harris put on the act of a caring son who was helping his delicate father into a comfortable seat. Lia took advantage of their detachment to do a little investigation. There was a celestial clock hung over the center of the bar, quite old by the look of its brass dials and elaborately painted depictions of moon phases, the perfect conversation starter.

"Why, I haven't seen one of those since I was shorter than wheatgrass," Lia said to the bartender with a smile.

"No?" His face remained expressionless.

"Still keep to the moon phases, eh?"

"'S'right."

Lia had seen bolder expressions on cows. She put on her most effervescent smile. "It's been a dog's age since we did that in Hammond Valley."

She was only guessing, but the bartender confirmed with a, "True."

She waited for more, some acknowledgment of her supposed origins, some question about her desired destination, but all she got was the same bovine stare. "We'll be needing some rooms, after a few warming brews that is, assuming you have the space to spare."

"All available."

"All?" The surprise in her voice was genuine, even if her accent was not.

"'S'right."

Lia made sure Harris and Michaels were still occupied with their act. She leaned casually on the bar and asked in a voice much quieter than the one she had greeted him with "So, tell me then, do you get many travelers?"

"Some." He followed up that statement with the exciting addition of a blink.

Lia considered pressing him to the point where he might admit something out of sheer annoyance, but the little voice in her head reminded her to be patient, so she ordered three ales and let him go about his business.

The inn filled up as the day wore on. The time to make new friends had arrived. As Lia waited at the bar for another round, a young couple approached the table beside her. The young man pulled the seat out for his companion, another perfect conversation starter.

"Why, that's a true gentleman you've got there, miss. Hold on to him." She gave them her brightest smile.

The young woman returned it by briefly turning up the corners of her mouth, then looked away. It was progress, but hardly an opening for conversation.

Harris appeared to help her collect the drinks and made his own attempt at opening the door. "Ah, what I wouldn't have given to have a good ale like this on the road."

The young man responded by sitting down with his back on them. No luck.

As they headed back to their seats by the fire, they found Michaels in the midst of his own attempt to invite an entire group over. "Don't be shy, plenty of seats and heats for all of us."

How long can he keep up that croaking voice? Lia wondered. It didn't matter. The entire group turned away. It seemed as if none of them would get more than one sentence out for the rest of their stay.

"Charming town," Michaels said under his breath. "I think I'd like a summer home here."

"Makes being relegated to the woods feel like a warm embrace. Think we even need to stay the night?" Harris asked.

"Yes." Lia's firm interjection took them both by surprise. "Something happened here. Something made them feel this way. We have to find out what that was." She hadn't told anyone that she knew why they had been pushed out of Cleanair. The illusion that she was still searching for answers only justified the desperation she was showing now. No one needed to know what she was really searching for.

"Yes, but who here will actually tell us anything?" Michaels asked.

"My money is on the man with the scar," Harris said as his eyes traveled across some new visitors.

A handful of men, alike in stature and dress, each with an equally hard edge, strolled into the inn as a group. The man in the lead had a distinct scar that ran from above his eyebrow down the full length of his face.

Harris and the man with the scar caught each other's eye as he passed, but Harris made no attempt at a friendly opening line. They all knew that man would require a different approach.

ENOUGH TIME PASSED for a small band to set themselves up in the corner and for the locals to claim a dance floor by pushing aside tables. Still, no one had spoken to them. They had resigned themselves to quiet observation.

Harris kept his glances subdued, but as he looked over at Lia, he caught her, once again, staring intensely at each face. He leaned toward her. "By all means, keep staring at them. I'm sure no one will find that suspicious."

"We're supposed to be looking for the story here."

"Looking. Not examining."

She took his words to heart only through the length of her next sip, then went right back to scrutinizing.

Harris stood up and presented her with an open hand.

"What are you doing?" She sounded annoyed.

"Asking you to dance, dear."

"If you're trying to be funny."

He gave her a gentlemanly bow so he could whisper, "You want to know what motivates these people, let's get closer so we can find out," then rose and offered his hand again.

Lia accepted with a sigh.

Michaels shared his encouragement in well-voiced character. "You two go on. Young people should enjoy a good dance now and then."

Space naturally cleared out as they approached the dance floor. "It's like we smell," Harris said softly, though with obvious annoyance. They made an attempt to spin toward the middle. All the other dancing pairs continued to give them a wide berth.

"We're hardly getting close enough to shout at them, let alone hear a whisper." Lia sounded aggravated enough to start beating answers out of people.

"I've got a better vantage on that lot though." He flicked his eyes toward the bar, where the man with the scar and his passel of friends were throwing back their ales.

"Now who's examining?" she chided.

Harris turned his eyes back to Lia, only to find her scrutinizing gaze turned on him. He attempted to suppress the odd feeling of accusation that came right along with it. "Just keep up the act. Talk to me."

"About what?" she sizzled with impatience.

"You can start by telling me how you got that cut on your arm."

Lia had been attempting to hide the bandage under her sleeve all day, but dancing had exposed both the bandage and the red slash that had bled through to its surface. She vigorously shook her sleeve back into place. "I rode too close to the trees coming down the pass. Got nicked by a branch."

"Why didn't you come to me for treatment?"

"It's just a scratch, Harris. I don't need you to lick all my wounds."

The coldness in her voice embedded that odd feeling of accusation right into his spine.

The musicians slowed their tempo. The dancing couples followed their lead, coming closer together. Lia attempted to break away. Harris tightened his hold on her hand.

"We're not done here." He meant with their conversation, but a flick of the eyes toward Scarman and his friends offered the excuse he needed to keep her there. "Looks like he just bought his friends another round. Means he's a rich man, and probably popular for it."

She acquiesced to being held on the dance floor but shuffled about in complete silence.

"Aren't you going to say anything, darling?" It was more demand than invitation.

Her eyes glanced upward, searching, digging a thought out of the depths of her mind. "I do have a question for you," she finally said.

"Go ahead."

"If you hadn't given Roland that injection, would he have died?"

Harris came to a standstill. "This is hardly the place to—"

"No one can hear us." She took the lead, forcing him back into a rhythmic sway, then leaned into his shoulder to whisper, "Would you have died without it? Would Roland have?"

He leaned in closer, putting them cheek to cheek. "I don't know. But the Doctor obviously didn't want to take that chance, and neither did I."

"What would it take to kill one of us?"

He considered her motivations. Was she simply seeking knowledge, just as she had when she first learned of the formula, or was she searching for something more? He wouldn't find out unless he answered her. "Short of a bullet through the heart or the brain, I don't know. Maybe nothing."

Her breath gently heated his ear as they danced on in silence. It seemed as if her knowledge seeking was over for time being, until she asked, "Has anyone ever survived that?"

He pulled back to look her in the eye. She stared back with a blank expression on her face, betraying no need, no want, no reason at all for her questions. The word "no" hung on the tip of Harris's tongue, but refused to come out.

The musicians jumped into an upbeat tempo. The dance floor filled with lively movement.

Lia took advantage of his stunned silence to break away. "As always, dancing makes me simply parched. Will you get me another, darling?" She gestured to the bar, directing his attention back toward Scarman and friends. They were in the midst of a whispered conversation.

"Of course, dear," he said with a smile. The rest of their conversation would have to wait.

Harris didn't hesitate to put himself right next to Scarman and his companions. Whatever they were planning didn't involve starting a fight in public, or that would have happened already. "Three more if it please you," he said to the bartender.

The side-eye Scarman and his friends kept on Harris was not subtle. Fortunately, Harris's was well practiced. He kept an ear tuned in their direction, but no one said a word.

The bartender returned promptly with his steins and slapped two large keys down on the bar beside them. "Three steins. Two adjoining chambers."

"Are you suggesting I call it night, friend?" Harris gave him his best attempt at an innocent smile.

"Seven and eight. Whenever you're ready, traveler." The bartender showed not a drop of care one way or the other, but his goal had been achieved. Now, Scarman and his friends knew exactly where they would be staying.

"Thanks for the hospitality." He gave the bartender a nod and scooped up the keys. *No matter*, Harris thought. *I'll be ready for them.*

DESMOND'S SILHOUETTE REMAINED framed in the doorway as he packed and lit his pipe. His gestures were bold, bordering on contrived, but just enough to make his reason for stepping out of the inn obvious to any eyes watching from the inside. He took a long drag before walking away from the door, something he would normally never do, but Arin supposed it looked natural enough to anyone who didn't know him.

Arin stood just outside the pool of light spilling out of the inn. Desmond stepped into the darkness beside him. They began a slow walk around its perimeter, cloistered in the shadows.

"Two rooms in the front with a clear view of the street." A waft of smoke came out with his words.

"Perfect."

"Can't be more than one gun on each of them. Might be more hidden on the old man, but he's got the fierce shakes."

"Does he?" *I guess there's more than one great actor in their ranks,* Arin thought. *Nice touch.* "Then he's the one you drop the information around. Make sure he hears. Then, spread out enough to keep eyes on each. Be subtle, but do whatever you can to get them separated."

"What makes you so sure they will?"

"Tempting bait like you? Who could resist?" Arin's brief break from strategy for a friendly jibe encouraged a smokey smirk out of Desmond.

"'T'ain't fair, using this against me." He ran his finger down his scar.

"It makes you distinctive."

"Jealous?" Desmond let out another waft with his next smirk before his face fell back into its usual look of stone. "I'd feel better if we had weapons."

"You won't need any." Arin was certain of that. None of them were there to hurt anyone, just to coerce.

"You might not but—"

"It won't even come to that. Put some faith in my powers of persuasion. After all, I won you over, didn't I?"

Desmond scoffed. "Jury's still debatin' on that."

They had come back around to the front of the inn, forcing them to take a wide arc away from the light. Arin came to a stop where he had a clear view through the door.

Lia's face was a distant dot, flicking in and out of view as people walked past her. It reminded him of when he saw her in the tavern in Witches Leap. He should have approached her then. He should have told her everything, whether or not there were eyes on them. He should have asked her to come with him, whether or not Roland would intervene. Things might be different now, if he hadn't been such a coward then.

"She meant something to you, didn't she?" Arin's eyes must have lingered too long. Desmond looked more concerned now than he did when they first walked into the town.

"That was in the past."

"You're sure you can do this?"

Arin switched on his inner strategist, tamping down thoughts of anything other than the plan in place. "I have always done whatever I needed to. Whatever had to be done, to advance, to succeed. To survive. And this time, I'm doing it for more than just myself."

Desmond sucked the last dregs of smoke out of his ashes as he considered whether or not to believe his assurances.

Arin turned his gaze back to Lia, challenging his own. When his strategist did not step aside, he flicked his eyes back to Desmond and gave him a nod, signaling his readiness to commence the plan.

Whether or not Desmond was reassured, he nodded back, tapped out his ashes, and returned to the inn.

Arin turned away from the inn and walked off into the night.

He was ready.

THE WAITING ROOM was a bare cube. Its white walls practically glowed with sterility. Arin mused over the necessity for such cleanliness in a clinic where the only procedure performed would render the recipient immune to everything. He supposed most would find it reassuring. It obviously wasn't working for the recruit sitting next to him. She was switching between leg jiggling and finger tapping. Arin might be doing the same thing if he hadn't gotten all his nerves out right along with his breakfast that morning.

The jittering recruit turned her nerves in Arin's direction. "Do you suppose it hurts?"

"No more than any other injection." Arin was pleased to hear his own voice sound so calm, and especially pleased that speaking hadn't brought up another wave of half-digested protein porridge.

"See, that's the thing. I've never liked any of them. But at least this is the last one I'll ever need, right?" She let out an uncomfortable chortle, then stilled, but only for a second. She stood and turned her nerves to pacing.

Arin chose not to watch, fearing it might summon up more nausea.

"Why you in early?" the pacing recruit asked.

"I'm going into the officer training program, and I want to leave as soon as possible."

"Officer!" She let out an impressed huff.

"What about you?" Arin summoned up enough stability to look up at her, since it was the polite thing to do.

"Me? I'm just trying to get it over with."

The sound of a vacuum seal breaking made them both jump. It was the door being pushed open by an injection tech, so completely clad in white that his eyes looked like they were hovering in the middle of the hall.

"Timothy James Arin?" he called out in search of the respective recruit.

Arin winced at the sound of his own name. At least this was the last time he would ever have to hear it said like that. Soon, it would be Officer Arin, then Sub-Commander, then Commander Arin. He liked the sound of that. Those thoughts squashed the last of his nausea and gave him the strength to stand up and head for the door.

"Good luck," the jittering recruit called out to him.

He acknowledged her with a nod over his shoulder. She had turned her nerves to picking at her fingernails. *Well, she won't be doing that much longer*, Arin thought as the injection tech sealed the door behind him.

The injection room was somehow even whiter than the hallway. The tech pointed him toward a slab-like seat at the center. "Have a seat and roll up your left sleeve," he instructed, then his disembodied eyes turned away to prepare the procedure.

Arin's thoughts flowed like water. *Is it colder in here, or am I just imagining that? It doesn't matter, minute temperature changes won't even bother me in a few minutes. Or ever again. Are all the injection rooms like this, or just the ones for recruits? How does someone become an injection tech anyway? Do they have medical training? Do they even need any? Are they all injected, too?* These thoughts carried Arin across the room, seated him on the slab, and had him rolling up his left sleeve before he knew it. He really had become quite good at following orders.

The injection tech hung an I.V. bag on one of the many polished steel hooks dangling over Arin's head. He looked up at the bag full of bright green goo and thought about how much it looked like his grandfather's favorite flavor of nutrient jelly.

"Don't be alarmed by the color," the injection tech said in a mono-tone voice. "It's just the—"

"Transference medium. I know."

The tech nodded, seemingly unimpressed by Arin's well-researched knowl-edge. He turned his attention to Arin's arm, sourcing a vein, cleaning his skin.

Suddenly, Arin felt the pressing need to delay, to question, to research and learn more, to discern and weigh-up every option before committing.

"What if—" Arin began, but the needle had punctured his skin, and the bright green goo was flowing down toward his arm. It was about to become a part of him forever.

"Sorry, what was that?" the tech asked him.

Arin watched the green goo fill the vial taped to his arm. It was entering his body now. The time to discern and weigh options had passed. He summoned a question to cover up his moment of doubt. "What if it doesn't take the first time?"

"Don't worry," the monotone voice answered. "It always works."

Time under the I.V. blurred into a cloud as white and glowing as the room itself. Was he nervous? No. Was he nauseated? No. Was he cold? No. Was he stiff? No. Was he tired? No. Did he even feel the minutes passing as he lay against this slab? No.

The needle came out without the token drop of blood he was used to seeing and without any need for a bandage. Arin looked at the would-be bleeding spot on his arm but saw only unbroken skin. Was that sight exciting? No. Was it satisfying? No. Did it make him feel anything? He really didn't know.

Arin was up and headed to the door before he knew it. The once disem-bodied eyes of the tech had the clear outline of a head around them now, and a body clad in scrubs below that. Had his vision improved? Had there been something wrong with it to begin with? He would never know now.

As the door swung open, the nervous recruit's flushed face jumped into his path. "How did it go? Did it hurt?"

Arin gave this some consideration, but soon realized that he could tell her—quite honestly—"I didn't feel a thing."

BY THE TIME Harris got back from his perimeter check, Lia had established his bed area by throwing a pillow and one pathetically thin blanket onto the floor. She, meanwhile, was laying on top of what looked like a particularly hearty blanket on a rather soft bed, staring up at the ceiling in silent contemplation.

All of the back stretching that Harris had done to sell his perimeter check as a light walk to work out the kinks had actually been necessary. Riding a motorcycle and sleeping on the ground for weeks on end hadn't agreed with his body, regardless of how resilient it had become to other much harsher torments. He was actually looking forward to that bed, no matter how little sleep he might be able to acquire that night.

"Don't a husband and wife normally share their bed?"

"Your dear wife was so travel weary that you thought it best to lay your drunken carcass out on the floor, so as not to disturb her," Lia responded without looking away from her meditative spot on the ceiling.

"How considerate of me." Harris's knees made a hollow clunk as he sat down on his floor-bed. *Perfect.* He balled the pillow and blanket together into a mound and lay back against it.

Voices filtered up through the floor, the tone of which he should have been paying attention to, just in case trouble was brewing below them, but his mind kept wandering. He picked his own spot on the ceiling and contemplated all Lia had said to him that day, the look of accusation in her eyes, the deadpan stare that had accompanied her questions. It had all disturbed him. He took more pride than he cared to admit in having won her trust, which now seemed lost, and he cared far more than he'd ever admit about her opinion of him. He felt too compelled not to ask, "What did I do?"

She took a moment to break away from contemplation. "What do you mean?"

"I won't pretend you haven't had decent reasons to be mad at me in the past, but why now? Why today?"

She sat up and threw her legs over the edge of the bed. "If it matters that much to you—"

He jolted upright. "This isn't about the bed, Lia."

"Then what?"

"You've been speaking to me all day like I'm one of your inept guards. And in the one moment of civil conversation we do manage to have, you chose to ask...." He flicked his eyes toward the door of the adjoining chamber. Michaels was on watch, probably too focused on the conversations filtering in through his open door to hear them, but the walls were thin.

Lia clearly didn't care. "Go on," she said in that same cold tone.

"Questions you shouldn't have been asking," he finished in a more subdued voice. "Not here and not now. We're on a mission, and the last time I checked, we were both Sub-Commanders on the same side. Am I wrong?"

"You tell me."

"That's exactly what I'm talking about." His volume rocketed up. He stood.

She followed, looking as if she was ready to deliver the first punch if he got too close.

"You've been talking to me like I'm a Uni P.O.W., acting like nothing I say or do can be trusted. And you've been that way ever since...." He didn't trail out for fear of being overheard but because the missing piece had clicked into place. "Ever since we left Cleanair." He closed the space between them and looked at her with interrogating eyes. "What really happened in that bar? What did he tell you?"

Lia's face remained stoic, betraying nothing, but the minute step she took back, the slight and nearly imperceptible way in which she shrank away from him, told him he was right. If Harris chose to press, she would tell him, but if he pressed too hard, she might never trust him again. He wavered in indecision, until the cracking open of the adjoining door burst their bubble of tension.

Michaels poked his head into the room. "Sub-Commander?"

Harris responded by holding a halting hand in front of Lia and heading toward the adjoining chamber alone. Michaels had, after all, only asked for one Sub-Commander.

"Aren't we on the same side?" she called out to him, her tone more facetious than cold.

He glanced back at her. "You tell me." He closed the door between them.

Michaels ushered Harris into the far corner of the room, as if it were more private than the others that were mere steps away. "There's some kind of a meet planned at high moon in the mill. The man with the scar is going to be there."

"You're sure about that?"

"I heard it clear as day," Michaels said in a throaty whisper. His old man voice had worn out his actual voice.

"All right. I'll head over and keep an eye on them. There's bound to be answers there."

"I'll go with you."

"No. We need to keep our cover until we know what we're up against. I'll come back if I need you."

"I'd rather have your back, sir."

The thought of support from someone else reminded him of how little he was receiving from Lia. "Then do me a favor. Keep McMillan here. Make up whatever excuse you need, just make sure she doesn't leave without my authorization."

Doubt leapt into Michaels's eyes, probably because keeping Lia in line was a job only a fool would ever volunteer for. "She's my superior, sir."

"And I am hers. So, you're both going to have to follow my orders tonight."

It looked as if he wanted to ask why, but chose instead to confirm with a nod. "Yes, sir."

Lia whirled around to face Harris as he reentered their chamber.

She was still prepared for battle, but Harris suddenly felt no need to explain or excuse anything to her. "Get some sleep. I'll take first watch."

She unclenched her jaw long enough to ask, "What did he hear?"

"Nothing important. Get some rest while you can."

"You said yourself if there's a fight to be had, it will come to us."

"Those men are far from swimming to the bottom of their last pitcher. I'll watch them." He made his intent to remain inert clear by lying back on his floor-bed, and staring up at the ceiling.

Lia let out her tension with a long sigh as she returned to the bed and did the same.

Eventually, she turned on her side with her back toward him. He watched the gentle rise and fall of her lungs, waiting for the tell-tale signs of sleep, so he could make his move.

ARIN KEPT HIS eyes fixed on the small dial on the celestial clock, waiting for the shape of the full moon to emerge into the little window at the top. The kitchen was dark, the house quiet. He tapped out his impatience with the pads of his fingers, so as not to disturb the silence. A slight shuffling drifted into one ear from over his shoulder, the sound of tiny feet attempting to tiptoe around unnoticed.

"I seem to remember your mother putting you in bed a few hours ago," Arin said in a soft voice without turning around.

A small breath drew in. The shuffling stopped.

"Don't worry. Your secret is safe with me." Arin pulled out the chair beside his and pat the seat.

Ewan plodded over and slid into the chair.

"What's the matter?" Arin asked without shifting his eyes from the clock.

"Can't sleep when Papa's not home."

"Your mother is here to look after you."

"But who's gonna look after her? And my little sister?"

Arin turned his eyes away from the clock. Ewan looked so small with his bare feet dangling above the floor. "Sister? How do you know she's going to have a girl?"

"Cause 's what I want."

Arin smiled. The logic of children was always uniquely unpredictable. "It doesn't actually work like that, but I'm sure you'll be just as happy with a little brother."

"Maybe." He began to draw imaginary circles on the table top with his short fingers. "Do you have any kids?"

"No."

"Do you think that if you did they'd be like you?" Ewan looked up at him with big, curious eyes that looked exactly like Jania's.

"Children are always a bit like their parents."

"I mean…." He looked back down at his circling finger. "Would they heal like you?"

Arin found himself struck silent. Doctor Lau's words came floating up from his memory. "They are our brothers, tied by blood with us for as long as the blood continues to flow." It had been the intent of his newly perfect formula to simply pass on to the next generation, but would that include the unique combination that was now swimming through Arin's blood?

He had to admit, "I don't know." But it was certainly possible.

Arin looked back up at the clock. The arced edge of the full moon had appeared in the corner of the window. "You'd better get back to bed. Your father will be home soon enough. I promise to watch over you until he gets back."

Ewan obligingly slid out of his seat.

As Arin listened to his tiny footsteps walk away, his protective instinct kicked in. "Ewan?"

He looked back over his shoulder.

"No matter what noises you hear from the mill tonight, stay in bed. You, your mother—and your little sister—will be safest here."

Ewan's eyes widened. Arin hadn't meant to frighten him, only to assure his safety, but perhaps that needed to be done with fear. Ewan nodded and shuffled back to his room.

Arin turned his eyes back to the clock and resumed his silent finger drumming, but his patient concentration was now fogged over with thoughts of the mystery that was the generation to come. Even though the little boy that waved goodbye to Lia from the fortress balcony as she charged off to war by Roland's side was barely beginning life out in the world, she must know what the formula had done for him. Or perhaps he was just like Ewan, nothing but a small, curious child, with eyes just like his mother's. Arin found himself wondering what his own child's eyes would look like someday, if that day would ever come.

A jolt of realization straightened Arin's spine. He was letting his strategist get shoved aside by the intangible thoughts of a child. *What do questions about the future matter if I don't do anything to shape it for myself?* He pressed his palms into the table, breathed the rest of his intangible thoughts out through clenched teeth, and fixed his eyes back on the clock.

He would do whatever it took to advance, to succeed, to survive. Just as he always had.

THERE WERE THREE other recruits already sitting in the transport when Arin entered. He wondered if they were also going for officer training. In other words, his competition. He considered asking one of them, then realized rather quickly he didn't actually care. Would he have cared if this were yesterday morning, before his injection? Did it even matter now?

He took a seat at the back and stared out the window toward the entry gate. What would Drake, Vasquez, and that mouth-breather Frost say if they knew Arin was headed into officer training? Had they even bothered to come back to the academy? Commander Hudson said that an average of only seventy-three percent of the recruits returned for injection, only those who were brave enough. Arin looked up at the Unity flag flapping in the breeze and sat up tall and straight.

Only those who are brave enough.

The gate slid open just enough to allow Commander Hudson through.

Arin could see a sliver of the seventy-three percent that had returned, lined up in formation in the forecourt. There would probably be hours of waiting in line for their injections. Arin commended himself for taking decisive action and getting it over with.

Commander Hudson took his seat at the front, the engine whirred up, and the transport took off, leaving the long lines of recruits behind. *Goodbye, Timothy*, Arin thought as the academy shrank into the distance. *Hello, Commander Arin.*

The last turret of the academy passed out of view as they entered the rolling hills that formed the natural border around Io City. If they hadn't gotten that far, the BOOM would have been much louder. Even with the hills as a buffer, the shock wave still vibrated the windows.

"What was that?" one of the recruits asked as they all plastered their faces to the window.

The answer appeared over the next crest. A funnel of fire shot up into the air.

"It's a fire bomb." Arin had never seen one before but remembered learning about their signature shape.

"Where is it? Where did it go off?" someone else asked.

Arin didn't know that answer, but Commander Hudson did. "The academy."

All formalities were done away with as they arrived at the training center. Whomever might have been there to greet them was otherwise occupied. Commander Hudson led the short line of recruits on a speedy march down the tube-like hall toward the core of the main building.

They emerged into a bright and open gathering hall. Sounds of chaos filled the room, echoing off the high ceilings, but not a peep was coming out of any of the soldiers inside. A sea of black and silver uniforms stood in silence, watching and listening to the scenes from the academy as they played out on large vizos mounted throughout the hall.

Arin looked up to see the hallowed halls he had just left in various states of disintegration. Some of the walls were still standing, flames licking around their edges. Other buildings had been completely destroyed. Some of the screens showed nothing but black smoke choking out its surroundings.

Commander Hudson approached the nearest soldier with an officer's insignia. "Who's responsible for this?"

"The Initiative. They claimed it as soon as the shock wave cleared."

"What have we lost?"

"Two of the three dormitories. The medical center. And the armory went up as soon as the flames reached it." He spoke without looking away from the vizos and without calling him sir. It was behavior Commander Hudson would never normally stand for, but he, too, could not take his eyes off the screens.

"How many accounted for?"

The officer finally looked away from the screen to address him. "They haven't sent us those numbers yet, sir."

Arin and the other recruits joined their superiors in watching the chaos unfold on the screens around them. Arin fixated on an image of a pile of rubble engulfed in flames. He was trying to figure out what it once was, when a human form crawled out of the pile. Whoever it was, they were burning from head to toe. The human shape stumbled away from the rubble, then collapsed on the ground, writhing and twitching.

Arin turned his eyes to the ground. As he stared at the polished floor he thought, *Why?* He didn't feel shocked or horrified. There was no sense that he might faint or vomit. The immediate sensation that had made him look away, the instinct that what he saw was simply not right, evaporated away. He looked to one side and then the other. All of the soldiers were staring up at the vizos, completely expressionless. He looked back up at the burning pile of rubble. Whomever had been on fire had managed to roll out of the flames. They were now lying still but blackened and smoking. *Would whoever that was recover or remain still forever?*

Arin sought out Commander Hudson. "Commander?"

His eyes snapped away from the screen to meet Arin's. "Yes?"

"How many would have been injected when it happened?"

"A third at the most."

Arin nodded. Did that answer achieve anything for him? He wasn't sure, but something had compelled him to ask, nonetheless.

"Mister Arin." Commander Hudson put a hand on his shoulder. "Expectations of greatness carry with them a heavy weight, but you're allowed to disregard that at this moment. You can stop to mourn the passing of your friends."

Arin looked back up at the screens and began to pull apart the meaning of those words. *Friends? Mourn?* He wondered briefly what had happened to the lowbrow threesome that had regularly tortured him, if they had even returned to the academy. He thought of the nervous recruit who would be among the injected third. *Would she be grateful for that? Could she be?*

The thoughts blurred together like watercolors until Arin shaped a realization out of the murky brown. He turned back to Commander Hudson. "No, sir. I can't"

EIGHT

VIBRATION TRAVELED RIGHT up through Lia's pillow. She jolted up and listened. Hands pounded rhythmically on the bar. Voices rose in inebriated song. Those men were still downstairs, but she turned to discover Harris was no longer in the room. She shouldn't have even lay down, let alone closed her eyes. The previous sleepless nights had made her far too vulnerable, and Harris had taken advantage of that. But why?

Lia jumped out of bed and cracked open the chamber door to peer out.

Scarman and his friends were still gathered in a clump at the bar, filling the otherwise empty inn with loud, off-key singing. He spun around to raise his nearly empty stein at the peak of the song and looked right up at Lia. She might have believed it was a passing glance if he hadn't winked.

Shatz! She ducked back inside and closed the door. If Harris wasn't watching them, then where had he gone?

Lia burst into the adjoining chamber.

Michaels was very clearly on watch at the window. He spun around in surprise, then attempted a casual—albeit transparent—excuse for his alertness. "I couldn't sleep a wink. You hear that racket they're making?"

"Who did he tell you to keep eyes on?"

"What do you mean?"

"Where is Harris?"

Michaels stammered, made a few attempts at starting a sentence, then seemed to give up the fight altogether. "He's following a lead."

"What lead?"

"It's probably nothing. That's why he wants us to stay." Michaels attempted nonchalance, but it was not a natural part of his demeanor.

"Where is he?"

"I can't tell you."

Lia approached with speed, backing Michaels right up against the window. "I am a superior officer Michaels, and I expect you to answer me."

"It's because of my superior that I can't."

Lia let out a frustrated grunt. There was no point in fighting against Michaels's annoyingly resolute loyalty.

A lone voice drifted up to the window. Scarman was standing just below them, swaying and singing unevenly as he lit his pipe. He took a long drag.

Lia's eyes followed the puff of smoke as it rose up past the window. "Is that who you're watching?"

Michaels said nothing.

Lia watched Scarman slowly meander away from the inn. She silently lifted the window sash.

"Sub-Commander, please!" Michaels grasped her arm but quickly retracted his hand as soon as he saw the look in her eyes. "We can't risk blowing what little cover we have if we're seen."

"Who said anything about being seen?" Lia did a quick survey of the clearing in front of the inn—empty. She sat on the window ledge, swung her legs out, and turned around to lower herself down.

Michaels attempted to hold her back with a firm point instead of a grab this time. "I am under direct orders to keep you here," he said as loudly as he dared.

"Don't worry. I won't hold that against you." Lia lowered herself until his petrified face disappeared from view, then dropped to the ground. She did another quick survey of her surroundings—still empty—then slinked away to follow Scarman to his mystery destination.

THE MILL REMAINED dark, silent, and by all appearances empty. Harris glanced up at the rising moon in the sky above. It had yet to completely clear the trees. Still too early. The crooked house that was joined to the mill also looked empty, but something told him to sneak in closer just to be certain.

The gushing waterfall and the sloshing wheel were more than loud enough to conceal his approach. He crawled along the precarious ledge that led past the first window, trying not to look down into the churning water below. He had never been a fan of the water. It was more powerful than he would ever be. He both respected and feared that.

Harris crawled along under the first window, then leaned his back against the house and peered through the lower corner. The light of the rising moon revealed someone sleeping inside, a woman, if the long dark hair spread out over the pillows was any indication. She certainly didn't look like anyone who was preparing for an ambush. Harris didn't know whether or not that put him at ease.

He turned away from the large window and began to crawl along to the next. His hand made unexpected contact with a patch of wet moss. The soft bank beneath gave way. Harris threw his back against the house in a desperate attempt to keep from falling.

A tiny landslide cascaded from where his hand had been, down into the river below. Whatever sound it might have made when it hit the water was absorbed by the gurgling and sloshing.

Harris let out a sigh of relief and continued his precarious crawl along the edge of the house. He was about to check the next window when the reflection of faint light appeared on the surface of the river. He peered down the length of the house.

The soft yellow light of a lamp was traveling in and out of the windows that led up toward the mill. Someone was heading inside to prepare for the meeting.

IF THE SOFT ground hadn't allowed Lia to follow Scarman's sinuous path, the gentle singing in the distance would have told her exactly where he was. She followed at a fair distance, taking long, slow, silent strides so she could listen. The song was the same, but the voice sounded far less inebriated than the man had appeared. She thought of how quickly he had spotted her face hovering in the doorway above the bar, something he would never have achieved through a veil of ale. It had to be a ploy.

Sure enough, the trail of footprints straightened out as it reached an upward slope. It would have been difficult to maintain sideways steps in the slipping dirt. In fact, the footsteps became broad and intentional.

We must be close to his destination, Lia thought.

She was about to pick up her own pace to assure he wouldn't slip out of sight but was stopped in her tracks by the creeping feeling of eyes on her back. It only took one glance over her shoulder to spot the shape of a human silhouette peering around one of the tree trunks.

Scarman had at least five friends in tow. It was safe to assume they were all on her tail, unless they had left one behind to watch Michaels. Regardless, Lia was confident she could shake them, but it would mean abandoning Scarman's trail, for now.

ARIN TOOK ANOTHER lap around the gently grinding mill. Waiting for Desmond had been easy enough, but now that he was there, watching him walk in circles, Arin's patience was wearing down.

"You're certain he heard every word?" he asked Desmond as he paced past him.

"We all but shouted it. There's no reason he wouldn't have."

"And you gave her the chance to follow?"

"We won't know if she did until the others get back, but she had eyes on me like a hawk. Can't imagine she'd give up the hunt easy. Even if she lost sight of me, she'd still know where I was headed."

"Unless he didn't tell her what he heard," Arin said as he paced past Desmond again. "But why wouldn't he?" he asked himself.

The barrel of a gun pointed into his face.

"Because he reports to me," Harris responded as he stepped out from behind one of the pillars.

Arin obligingly put his hands up and backed around the mill.

Desmond jumped to his feet as soon as Harris and his gun cleared into view.

"Don't worry," Arin assured him. "This one knows that shooting me won't do him any good. Or do you still think I find that threatening?"

"You're hardly invincible."

"Even you have no idea what I'm capable of."

Harris's eyes flickered with doubt, or was it a desire to know more? Either would keep him from pulling the trigger. "What did you do to these people? To this entire town?" he demanded with the flick of his gun.

Desmond twitched as if he was about to dive at Harris. Arin froze him in place with a shake of the head. He slowly lowered his hands. This was not the encounter he had planned to have that night, but one he had prepared for nonetheless.

"I only told them the truth. I am not responsible for how they reacted to it."

"What about Lia? What happened to protecting her?"

"She made her choice." Arin had raised his voice louder than intended. Harris's elbow stiffened.

Desmond straightened up, looking ready to pounce again, but his feet remained fixed.

"Is that what this is? Petty revenge. You would risk the lives of every person in this town just to spite Roland?"

Arin suppressed the desire to punch Harris right in the nose. How dare he call his actions petty. He loosened the fingers that had clenched into a fist. "I don't ask anyone to risk anything. I only give them the choice to remain what they are or to become one of you. Yes, some have chosen to fight against you, but what they decide is up to them."

"How many towns? Territories? How much land have you crawled across in the last few years?"

Arin chose not to respond. *Let him wonder until it drives him mad.*

Harris pressed the barrel of his gun into Arin's forehead, trying to force an answer.

"It won't do you any good," Arin said with calm confidence. He was preparing to push Harris to his limit mentally, physically if need be, when the door leading in from the house opened.

Desmond raced around the mill. He would have succeeded in slamming the door shut, or at least putting himself in Harris's way, if he hadn't produced a second gun, freezing him in place.

The doorknob slipped from Jania's grip as soon as she saw Harris and his weapons. She froze like a fear-struck deer.

HARRIS HAD PREPARED for a fight, but not to have his guns pointed at an unarmed man and a pregnant woman. Arin stood in between them. If he had intended to take Harris out, now would be the perfect time, but he didn't move a muscle.

"He won't hurt anyone," Arin said to the room. "This one doesn't share his Commander's blood lust." He felt compelled to reassure them, which meant he cared about them. Arin may not have been threatened by a bullet, but having these two at the end of the barrel would certainly keep him talking.

"Into the corner, both of you." Harris directed them with his guns. "Get down."

They huddled down together, the pregnant woman nestled into Scarman's arms. With that rogue element out of the way, Harris could turn his attention to unraveling Arin's plans, but he didn't even have to begin an interrogation. Arin was too proud to keep quiet.

"You're wondering right now, how you can tell your commander about my sudden, unexplained appearance and treacherous plot against him without incriminating yourself."

"I hardly need his help to take out one vengeful little pest."

"You're wrong about that. Even if you pulled out his sword and sliced off my head right now, you'd still have to explain to Roland, and to every living experiment in your army, why they're suddenly enemies of their own people."

"We don't have to go where we're not wanted. And then the people you poisoned against us won't have our protection when the Unity arrives. Are you prepared to live with that?"

"Who says they can't protect themselves?"

Harris let out a huff of disbelief. "Are you telling me you're raising an army?"

"Why not? You did."

The enormity of his ego was astounding. Harris wondered how much of it he had brought into being himself. He had told Arin what made him unique. He had given him the chance to escape. He was the reason Arin was still alive in the first place. Harris's guns were pointed at the ground, but his fingertips lightly caressed the triggers as he considered what it would take to eliminate the problem altogether.

"So, you've thrown a few stumbling blocks into our road, made a few friends along the way, played a little spy game, but this is hardly an ambush." Harris gestured to the other two with his guns.

The woman let out a light whimper that made him immediately regret it.

He turned his attention away from them and began to circle Arin. "Why construct this elaborate set-up if you're not going to use it against me?" Then, Harris remembered there was only one person Arin had been asking his scar-faced friend about. "What do you want with Lia?"

Arin's jaw tensed up, but he said nothing.

"Do you intend to turn her against us?"

He still said nothing.

"Is it something more than that?" Harris asked as he approached, keeping his eyes fixed on Arin's stoic face. "How deep is your need for revenge?"

There was a tiny twitch in the corner of his mouth. Harris had either touched a nerve or dug out a grain of truth.

That was all he needed to know. Harris stepped back and pointed both of his guns square into Arin's face. "I don't care how hard it is. I am going to kill you."

Unfortunately, he had forgotten to keep an eye on his hostages.

SIDEWINDING THROUGH THE trees, on and off the road, in and out of the moonlight had to be annoying her followers at the very least. Lia had certainly had her fill of it.

A deep bellow sounded out from the sky. Rain was approaching. If she didn't get back to the road soon, Scarman's trail would wash away.

Lia had just started to circle back to where she left the last footprint behind when another sound cracked through the air. It was gunshots, two, back-to-back, and they were close. She took off in the direction of the sound at full speed. Whoever was still following would just have to chase her now.

THE HOT STING of two bullets entering his chest was shocking enough to cause a moment of breathlessness, but as his body started to force them out, the pain dulled enough for Arin to sit up.

Desmond was grappled onto Harris's back. The timing of his leap had at least saved Arin two bullets to the face. Harris dropped to his knees under Desmond's weight. He was about to gain the upper hand when Harris threw a blind punch over his shoulder with his fist wrapped around his gun. The sound of steel cracking into bone was undeniable.

Jania shrieked. Desmond's nose gushed blood. His body went slack and slid to the floor.

Arin jumped up and bolted to the back of the room.

Harris marched over to where he had gone down. There was a tingle of satisfaction in watching him discover nothing but two bloody bullets where he expected Arin to be laying.

"Like I said, you have no idea what I'm capable of," Arin called over the grinding mill wheel.

Harris had a look in his eyes that told Arin he was determined to find out. He raised his guns and raced toward him.

Let him keep shooting, Arin thought.

Desmond had other ideas. He leapt at Harris and shoved him into the mill wheel.

The one shot he got out zipped into Arin's shoulder. It was less of a shock that time.

Harris grunted as his side smacked hard into the stone. One of his guns tumbled away, but Desmond's plans went instantly awry when he lost his own footing. The grinding millstones took hold of his collar. He flailed in panic as the millstones tightened their hold.

Jania screamed and raced to his side.

Arin lurched forward to help but found Harris in his path.

They locked into a struggle. Harris pushed him back toward the window, shuffling and scrambling closer to the edge.

Once the river came into view, Arin greeted it with a smile. "Go ahead!" Arin challenged, but his smile dropped as soon as he saw what was over Harris's shoulder.

Ewan was standing in the doorway, watching his father flail and his mother struggle, with wide, frightened eyes.

"Ewan don't!" Arin shouted, but Ewan was already racing toward them.

Desmond scrambled backward, trying to move with the mill stones as they held him captive. Jania crawled along with him, crying out her frustration in bursts with every attempt to pull him free. Ewan raced alongside them in panicked tears.

Still, Harris did not relent. He twisted his gun hand in Arin's grip, doing all he could to aim up into his face.

Arin had no choice but to hold on. He might survive another shot to the head, but it would cause far more than a moment of breathlessness.

Desmond's fight against the mill wheel brought him scrambling toward them. Ewan came racing around with his parents, eyes too blurred with tears to see where he was going.

There was a tiny thud as Harris's knee made contact with Ewan's back. The next thing they heard was Ewan's scream as he went careening out the window and splashed into the river.

A split second of unspoken conversation took place between Arin and Harris. Neither of them was about to let a child drown, but Harris didn't care one way or the other what happened to Desmond. Arin had no choice but to let him go and dive to Desmond's side.

ANOTHER GUNSHOT. A light up ahead. Lia raced toward both, following a narrow footpath that ran along the river and banked up toward a mill house by a waterfall. There was another boom from above as the sky broke open. Heavy droplets pounded down. The next sound froze her in place.

A high-pitched scream. A splash. There was just enough light spilling out of the mill to highlight the small head of a child as it surfaced and then got sucked back into the racing river. Another splash followed. Another head surfaced, arms attempted to swim with the current. It was Harris. Both of their splashing, struggling bodies sped right past Lia.

She spun around and ran after them, leaving the mystery in the mill house behind.

THE ICY WATER was instantly numbing. Harris's second gun was lost to the rapids. It didn't matter. That little boy wouldn't last long. He had to get to him.

Swimming didn't make him go any faster. All it provided was arms to brace against the rocks as they raced up to meet him. The last gargantuan boulder forced him under. The river sucked him around its side. He spluttered back up to the surface.

The little boy was just ahead, his arms flapping to try to keep him afloat. Harris dared to take a nosedive under the surface. He made a blind grab, felt the boy's floating clothes. He balled the fabric into his fist and yanked the boy back into his arms.

They surfaced together. The rocks were gone, but the river was only getting deeper. Harris made a desperate grab at the riverbank with one arm, holding tight to the boy with the other. The slippery mud gave way. The ceaseless rain forced it sliding into the river. He lost his grip.

They managed to stay above the surface, but a dark curve toward unknown conditions was rapidly approaching. Harris swam back toward the bank with kicking legs and one rapidly tiring arm. He made another attempt, clutching a fistful of reeds. His hand slipped. With another flail, he managed to catch a tree root.

Harris held on with all the strength in one hand and pushed the boy up onto the bank with the other. His little feet slipped up through the mud, then scrambled away to safety.

Harris's fingers began to give way. He threw his other arm at the bank, hoping to catch anything he could find. What he found was another hand. Lia was kneeling on the bank, reaching toward the water. Harris released his other hand and swung it around to meet hers.

With a groan of effort, she hauled him up onto the bank. Harris scrambled up until his feet were no longer slipping down the bank, then collapsed onto his back. He tried to suck in a breath but found it accompanied by a mouthful of rain. He rolled over onto all fours and coughed out as much water as he could.

"Ewan, get away from them! Now!" a gruff voice shouted. The same little feet raced past.

Harris turned his eyes up to find several pairs of well-worn boots surrounding him. Scarman's friends had arrived.

One of the men scooped the little boy up and raced off with him. The other four were busy brandishing their weapons. Harris took a visual inventory as he stood. One crossbow, one club, and two very mean looking axes.

Lia was already standing with her hands in the air. Her face was branch-whipped and bleeding, her clothes just as soaked and muddy as Harris's. He was already starting to shiver beyond control. Armed or not, neither of them were fit for a fight.

"You saved the boy's life," said the man with the club. "And for that we will grant you yours. But give us one good reason why we should let you return to your godforsaken army."

"I can give you about twelve." Michaels emerged from the trees at their backs with his two favorite six-shooters, his "pair of ladies," armed and aimed.

In the split second of distraction he provided, Lia pulled out her own gun and aimed it at the man with the crossbow.

The foursome remained undaunted. The men with axes tightened their grip. The man with the crossbow sharpened his aim on Lia.

"Stop!" Harris shivered in a breath, filling his lungs up enough to be heard over the roar of rain. "We didn't come here to take your land, or your town, or your people. If you don't want us here, we'll leave. We don't want a fight."

"Then you best go before you find yourselves one." The man with the club stepped aside. The others followed his lead, lowering their weapons.

Lia and Michaels did the same.

The man with the club pointed it at the road leading away from the town.

They obliged and took it.

ARIN WRAPPED THE cold pack around Desmond's bruised up neck. He might end up with another scar, not to mention a crooked nose, but at least he was safe. Ewan was, too, with Jania already warming him up in the bath. There would be nightmares and tears, but those would pass in time.

But what of the man who went after him, the man Arin had stared vengeful promises at before they had broken apart to help the others? The kitchen door opened, and with it the possibility of answers, but all that entered were the four men he was expecting, unaccompanied.

"You let them leave." That was all Arin said in greeting.

"There's thousands of them over the ridge. If we tried to take those three—"

"We only needed one! One woman who could've stopped that entire army in its tracks."

"She was too well protected by the others. We can't set our axes and arrows against their guns. We're not like you."

It was true. He should have done it himself. Foregoing the bait, foregoing the trap, Arin should have just walked into that inn and told her the truth. It didn't matter how many guns were against him. He could stand up to them. Arin collapsed in frustration, landing in the chair he had been so patiently waiting in hours earlier.

Desmond wrapped a fist on the table to get his attention. "We will get another chance," he said in a raspy voice that was struggling out of his trachea. "We will find another way."

Arin considered his words, knowing what it felt like to have the desire to prove yourself so embedded into your being. He couldn't dismiss the motivation—and the inventiveness—that it provided. "Perhaps we will."

BEING IN LESS-then-stellar condition as they walked the road in the rain spared Harris from having to explain what had happened. By the time the rain stopped and the sun was promising to arrive, he had conjured up a decently believable account of the events.

Lia hadn't said much. It was hard to tell if she believed any of it.

"They were awfully touchy about one man's mill," Michaels said. Maybe he didn't believe it either.

"It wasn't just his mill. It was their livelihood."

"But we don't aim to take anything, property or otherwise, from any of them."

"My attempts to explain that obviously didn't go so well." Harris breathed a bit more heat into his hands. He didn't need to do it as much now, but it had become a way to compensate for the gaps in his storytelling.

"Still can't figure how they found us out," Michaels commented to the air.

Harris stole a glance over at Lia. Had she figured out how? Her unblinking stare at the road ahead indicated nothing.

"So, we just walk away from another town?" Michaels asked what might have been the air again, but Harris felt the need to answer.

"What else would you have done?"

"I wouldn't have taken off on a lead alone to begin with." It was the first thing Lia had said for what felt like hours. Her tone was accusatory, but she was still looking only at the road.

"Cheers to that," Michaels added.

Harris had nothing to say in response, so he just warmed his fingertips with another puff of air.

After a few more steps and a few more minutes of rising light, Lia spoke up again. "You did the right thing, going after the kid." She was actually looking at him this time. She may not have believed his story, but that grain of praise was genuine.

"Of course," he said in one short, quiet breath.

Her eyes lingered on his a moment longer, searching. She still knew something she wasn't willing to admit to, but so did he. The secrets they were each carrying were going to remain unspoken… for the time being.

They didn't get far into the trees before the frantic movement in and out of the trunks revealed the camp—or rather where the camp had been. Everybody in sight was busy breaking tents down and packing up supplies.

Harris, Lia and Michaels quickly parted their way through the chaos toward the command tent. They found Roland inside in the midst of his own controlled hurry. He only gave their bedraggled appearances a momentary glance before launching into an explanation.

"We've received intel form the borderlands. Martrim has redirected his entire troop. They're marching around this mountain range instead of over it."

"That doesn't make any sense. They're skipping around parces of valuable land to trace a path over nothing." Harris was stumped.

"He doesn't want the land. He's playing cat and mouse. Instead of chasing us, now we have to chase him."

Harris kicked out his frustration on a supply box. At least anger had finally warmed up his core.

Roland acknowledged Lia's injuries with a light caress to her cheek. She mouthed out, "I'm fine."

Of course she was. She wasn't the one in the river.

Roland switched back into command mode and began to lay out their rather dire situation. "We must assume he will remain one move and several steps ahead of us. Just out of reach. He will follow an unpredictable path and put eyes on ours. From this point forward, we might as well be chasing a ghost."

You have no idea how right you are, Harris thought, but that truth was going to remain unspoken for the time being.

NINE

SUNLIGHT GLITTERED ON the surface of the water. Gentle babbling filled the air. It was hard to believe this was the same river that seemed determined to kill him the other night, until Harris stuck his hand under the surface to dunk his canteen. The icy chill rushed back into his bones. *Yeah, that feels about right.* Sunlight winked off of something farther along the shore. He capped his canteen, shook off the water, and wandered downriver to investigate.

The something turned out to be a rifle—Lia's rifle—propped up against a rock and abandoned, right along with her pistols, her armor, and all of her clothes, as if she'd turned to smoke. Harris picked up her rifle and shook his head.

"Problem, sir?" Lia's voice called out from the river. She was floating on her back in the middle of a silty pool, stark naked.

Harris turned his eyes to the sky. "You left your weapons unattended."

"They're hardly unattended. You're holding one right now."

"You have no idea who might have stumbled on these. We're in the middle of no man's land here."

"And have been for several days. A few more without taking advantage of this river, and Martrim will be able to smell our approach."

Harris shook his head again for emphasis and returned her rifle to the ground without looking down.

She splashed closer to him, becoming a flesh-colored blur in the corner of his eye.

"You've got to be freezing."

"It's life affirming." Her words were accompanied by short shudders of breath. "Care to join me?"

"I've had enough affirmation lately, thanks." Another splash made him certain she was about to emerge. Harris turned away, determined not to be caught standing next to her, then a cold slap of river muck hit him right in the neck. He whipped around.

She ducked her muck throwing hand back under the water. He should have known presenting Lia with any boundary, even an invisible one, would make her determined to destroy it.

Walking away would have been the intelligent thing to do. He must not have been feeling very intelligent. Harris crouched by the bank, scooped up a handful of mud, and pitched it right back at her.

Lia ducked under the water just in time. She swam to the depths of the silty pool, obscuring her flesh briefly under a clouded layer, then surfaced with another fistful of river bottom.

An easy lean avoided her slow pitch. Harris bent to scoop up his next weapon.

"Sub-Commander." The sound of Roland's voice, especially addressing him by rank, instantly straightened him up. Harris shook the slime off his hand as he turned to face him.

Lia was splashing away, probably to an innocently distant bit of the bank.

Roland's face didn't show anger, or even annoyance, but consternation. "We have a problem."

He was right. There was a solid cap of snow on the peak. "Shatz," Harris muttered as he lowered his scope.

"I thought we had a month before the snow came in." Roland sounded like he'd been betrayed, as if what Harris said had any control over the weather.

"Well, winter came early this year."

"Can we still cross them?"

"With extra time, maybe."

"Which we don't have."

"I know that."

"Are there alternatives?" Roland was practically breathing down his neck but turned his head as Lia approached.

She was fully reassembled but still ringing the river water out of her hair. It provided enough of a distraction from Roland's ceaseless questions for Harris's decision making skills—hopefully intelligent ones—to return.

"Get the others, and I'll tell you." He headed to his tent without looking back. It wasn't often that he gave an order to Roland, but he liked to take advantage of the opportunity when it presented itself.

Harris laid out his patched together maps on the flattest rock he could find. Roland, Lia, Emmett, and Michaels circled around.

"Eight days. That's how long it will take to go around those mountains." He pointed out the trail as he spoke.

"Those Unis will be right on top of us when we come around," Michaels said.

"If it's going to take that long anyway, then why not go over?" Emmett asked.

"Going over would take longer in the snow, if we didn't get lost, which we will. Not a single person here has ever crossed those mountains with snow covering the trail markers." Harris may have been laying down a bit of extra pessimism, but it was not without reason.

"Should we risk it anyway?" Lia asked.

"No. We might all come back down too weak to face the fight waiting for us at the bottom." Roland took a pause. Harris waited for the inevitable next question. "Is there an alternative?"

"There is one. Only one." Harris slid his finger around to the other side of the mountain. "If we head the other direction. It will take us two, maybe three days to pass. But we'll have to go through Olympus." He could feel Roland's eyes turn his direction. He kept his fixed on the map.

"Uh, Olympus? As in the massacre of?" Leave it to Emmett to ask the obvious.

"The very same," Roland confirmed.

"So, it's a town full of Scavs. We can take them." Leave it to Michaels to underestimate the situation.

"It's a city," Roland corrected. "Almost the entire population of which was gassed and turned. They doubtlessly outnumber us."

"We can still take them," Michaels said.

"That doesn't mean we should. We've never touched a Scav city before. Why start with this one?" Lia seemed oddly sympathetic about the twisted creatures that had tried to eat her the last time she encountered them.

"We may not have a choice. But we can't afford any unnecessary injuries when we're this close, even from a seemingly minor scuffle." Roland was downplaying the risks a bit too much for Harris.

"Which it won't be." Harris finally turned his eyes up from the map, meeting with Roland's consternation again, though for an entirely different reason now. "You and I know that better than anyone."

There was a pregnant pause before Emmett asked, "How?"

Harris chose to let Roland answer. "Because we were there when it happened."

Harris walked away, leaving them to the discussion that would follow. He didn't want to hear any apology or sympathy. He needed time to think, time to plan, time to chastise himself for every stupid decision in his life that had brought him around to this moment. He walked until he found a tree that seemed welcoming enough, leaned his back against it, and slid down to the ground. The breeze was too gentle, the birdsong too beautiful. Harris briefly considered a life affirming dunk in the river, but chose instead to muddy the air with the sound of his own voice.

"Welcome home, you idealistic, little arsehole."

THE FATE OF OLYMPUS

WE CAN WIN this thing!" Harris's voice echoed around the underground chamber. All the other residents of Utopia were still out and about, plying their trade. Without them there was nothing to soak up the sound that bounced around the copper arches.

Switch finished breathing out the last drag from his hookah, then sneered, exposing the gold tooth that his others had yellowed out to match. "Win what? There's no war, and there ain't nobody taking this city. It's ours. Always has been. Always will be."

"Don't you get it? These aren't the bucket heads who couldn't arrest us if they tried. Unity soldiers don't get soft. We can't outrun them, and once they take over, we sure as hell won't be able to hide."

"I don't hide. I live right here just the way I choose. It don't matter who runs this city by law, we still run it for real." Switch sucked another drag out of the long coil. His ego knew no bounds.

Harris began pacing. He didn't care how much of a racket his echoing footfalls made. He needed to do something to make his point as hard to ignore as possible. "They don't enforce their laws with thirty days of rest in a clean prison bed. They send you to work. If we don't fall in line, we won't be living down here. We'll be working down here."

Switch sat upright, abandoning the elbow he'd been casually leaning on as he smoked. Perhaps he was finally starting to take Harris seriously. "So, you suggest we fight a bunch of uniforms we can't outrun, can't kill, can't even hurt, and who are going to rule over every pissed on footpath in this city?"

"Yes." What more could he say?

Switch burst into laughter. It made a bigger racket than Harris's pacing.

Wince and Lash waltzed into the chamber while he was still in the throes of it. They were wearing the exact same color again. It didn't seem to matter how often Harris told them that it made them stand out like identical sore thumbs. The already comically lanky brother and sister kept choosing to do it anyway. Must be a twin thing.

"What's so funny?" Wince asked with a goofy smile on his face, ready to join in.

"Oh, you know Harris, here. Always spinning the yarn."

"Care to share?" Lash asked.

"It's a private joke, just between the two of us. Ain't that right, H?" Switch gave him a wink with a world of pressure behind it.

"Yeah."

Wince and Lash didn't pry. They had already moved on to the task of emptying their pockets into the share basin. Watches, jewelry, and coins clinked into the bottom.

"Good haul tonight. People are feeling drunk and generous. Mostly just drunk." Lash sounded like she'd had a good night.

"Maybe you ought to go back up and join them?" Switch suggested.

"You mean this ain't a good showing for a night's work?" Wince sounded like he'd had a less profitable evening.

Switch actually bothered to stand up. "I mean go have a little fun, and take Harris with you. He needs to loosen up, relax."

"You don't have to tell me twice." Lash took Harris and her brother by the sleeve and hauled them off.

Harris glanced back as he was being carted away.

Switch shooed him off with an upward sweep of his arms "Go. You'll see, ain't nothing gonna change about this city. It's ours tonight. Still will be tomorrow."

The Acro was decently full, but Harris still managed to usher his friends to a quiet table in one of the tavern's danker corners. He didn't care how much Switch had said with that wink, he had a lot more ranting to let loose. "I'm telling you, this city is rolling over like a beat dog. Pretty soon it'll be whatever the Unity says goes. They'll tell people they're going to clean up the streets, and you know what happens to us then? Work camps, hard labor, no freedom."

"No way. They can't do that, man. We outnumber 'em. This is our city, all the way." Wince's confidence was born out of ignorance rather than ego.

"There's no shortage of Unis out there, and it's not like they're a dying breed."

Lash leaned in like she was sharing a secret. "I heard they already got control of every town between here and Redville. They claim there ain't nothing but the most law abiding citizens there now."

"You mean robots. I'm not signing up for that." Harris punctuated his statement by throwing back his drink and slapping down the glass.

The door opened, and along with the breeze that blew in some cryptic litter, came a stranger in a long duster. He was tall and striking. There was an intensity in his eyes that looked like it belonged to a man twice his age. His collar was raised even though this season's frost had yet to begin. It wasn't a shield against the cold, but against recognition. Whoever this man was, he was trying not to stand out.

Harris's eyes followed him to the bar. "Either of you seen this chap before?"

"Nope," they both said in twinny tandem.

"Merchant maybe?" Wince suggested.

"Selling what to who in this crap part of town?"

"He looks local," said Lash.

"He's trying to, but that coat's never seen a winter in this city. If it had, there'd be shatz stains all over the tails." Harris only gave them a token glance as he spoke. He was too busy watching the stranger.

"So, maybe he's got a new coat. Makes him a man of means," Lash said hungrily.

"Yeah, Harris. What do you say you let our new friend buy us a couple drinks?" Wince added, practically starving.

They had missed the point, but at least they had given him a decent excuse to get closer. Harris gave them a salute and headed for the bar.

The stranger had walked in, sat down, ordered his drink with confidence, and was now hunched over the glass. To anyone else, it would have looked like he was gently pickling away in his own little world, but Harris noticed the ear tipped up just above his collar. He was listening, spying.

Harris casually leaned onto the bar beside him. "'Nother round, mate."

The stranger didn't move a muscle.

The bartender barely regarded Harris with a glance. "Show me some money, sooty."

Sooty. The word stood his hairs on end. Did he look like he had so much as a smudge of soot on him, let alone any of the other mysterious stains you could collect off these streets? Harris dug into his pockets and dropped a fistful of bills on the bar. "Clean enough? Or do you want me to go out back and give them a rinse?"

The bartender counted out the bills he needed with a grumble, then shoved the rest back at him. The bills were at the perfect spread to explain the wide elbow motions Harris made snatching them back up. He gently elbowed the stranger.

He eyed Harris over his collar.

"'Scuse," Harris said with a passing glance at his face. He was even younger than he thought, no more than a couple of years older than him. Harris leaned on the bar, elbows crossed, hands draped over the front edge. It was his go-to position. He slacked his fingers and casually lowered one hand down into the stranger's pocket.

Harris's view of the Acro spun around so fast he had no idea what had happened until his back smacked the bar. He stifled the urge to say, "Ow!" and channeled his effort into scrambling his hands up onto the bar so he could hold up his own weight. The stranger had already stretched his collar with the lift and spin. He didn't want the slack to become permanent.

The stranger stared down his nose at him with a look that Harris found absolutely fascinating. It said, "I could snap your neck if I choose, but you're not what I'm after." People had tried to kill Harris before—once or twice—but no one had ever looked at him like that.

The sound of many chairs scraping the floor finally broke the stranger's gaze. He flicked his eyes one way, then the other. Harris didn't have to look. He knew who was there and what they had on them. The stranger looked back at him with a burning stare. He wasn't afraid, but he was definitely annoyed.

Harris turned his chin up and smiled.

The stranger dropped him.

Harris immediately straightened his clothes and smoothed his collar down.

The stranger backed toward the door, hands in the air, careful not to turn around too fast as he left. No, he wasn't afraid. This just wasn't what he was after.

Harris didn't wait long before he followed him out into the streets. "Hold up there, hero," he called out as the stranger walked off between the rising steam clouds. "You can't do something like that and not tell me who you are."

The stranger didn't stop walking, but he wasn't too shy to start talking. "You expect me to stand here and chat, while your buddies sneak up and surround me for another shot at a fair fight?" His voice had the same intensity as his eyes.

"Nah, we wouldn't do that. Wouldn't be any fun now that we spoiled the surprise." Harris took a couple of jogging strides to catch up to him. "How many did you count when you took that glance around the place?"

"I have no idea what you mean."

"You were calculating, I saw it. You determined the odds weren't in your favor and left."

"A fact that could have been observed by anyone who can count higher than one." The stranger turned out to have a sense of humor.

"Come on. How many? I'll tell you if you're right."

He finally stopped walking. He really wanted to know. "Eleven. Five on my right, four on my left, and two behind me. And between you all, there were four knives, two chains, and two brass hands. Nothing on you though, or you'd weigh more than a sack of corn."

Truly impressive. Harris couldn't suppress his excitement. "Spot on. Which proves it. You're a Resistance fighter, aren't you?"

He started walking again.

Harris trotted alongside him. "No other reason for someone like you to be in a shatzhole like this. You aim to take out the occupation, don't you?"

"I have no aim."

"No need to hide your intentions from me. If you want to fight the Unis, I want in."

"We have no need for petty thieves."

"Hah! You are Resistance," Harris declared with a point. "And I'm no thief. I just wanted to see who you were. Only took a second to see you had no I.D. on you. Just this." Harris revealed the one thing he had pilfered from the stranger's pocket, a burlap bag full of what felt like seeds.

The stranger's face turned to stone. He snatched the bag back in one quick grab, wrenching Harris's wrist with his speed.

Harris raised his hands up in supplication. "Tell me your name, and I promise never to take it again."

The stranger gave his proposition decent consideration before answering. "It's Roland."

"Harris."

They regarded each other with a mirrored raising of chins, then the stranger named Roland turned and walked away.

Harris gave a light rub to his sprained wrist. He felt the urge to make it clear this would not be their last meeting. "There's nothing that goes on in this town that I don't know about, Roland. You can't hide whatever you're up to from me, no matter where you go. My people will find you."

Roland turned around but kept walking backward at a steady pace, flicking in and out of the yellow funnels of light spilling from the lampposts. "Your people? Am I supposed to believe you're some sort of gang leader?"

"Am I supposed to believe you're a farmer?"

Roland responded with a smile. "So, find me."

ROLAND KNEW IT was a story he would end up telling someday, even though he didn't think it was a place he would ever have to return to. "They had already decided that Olympus's citizens were only worth unifying if they cooperated. They secretly shipped in enough gas to take out the whole city and were authorized to use it in the event of any resistance. We just gave them the excuse."

The mood was somber even though he hadn't shared any of the gruesome details, nor the internal monologue that had come rushing back with the memories. *We were the only two left standing, the only two to make it out of those walls, and we were responsible for all of it.*

"I don't get it," Michaels said, breaking through Roland's punitive thought pattern. "Why not take the city then, if that's what they wanted all along?"

"By then, half of it was destroyed, burning to the ground. It was no longer worth it to them. All that death amounted to nothing." *And it was all our fault.*

"Have any of you ever fought the Scavs before?" Emmett asked, offering a change of subject.

"Ran from. Once." Lia sounded as if she had drudged up her own internal monologue with that memory. "But it wasn't easy. And it was nowhere near the numbers we might face in Olympus."

"How do we know how many that could even be?" Emmett asked.

"There's only one way to find out." Harris had returned from whatever inward journey he'd been taking in the interim. Perhaps he simply didn't want to hear the story told out loud. He already knew how it ended. "There are plenty of people in this army who had to travel through Scav territory to get to Cambria. We may not have much experience with the Scavs, but they do. So, we talk to them, gather intel, paint a picture of what we're dealing with. We also need to figure out how many are left. If we're outnumbered, we should know by how much. Lia and I will go to the edge of the city and do some reconnaissance."

"You need Lianna for that?" Roland wasn't sure why he asked. He knew what he'd seen that morning was entirely her doing, and innocent enough in her own unique view of the world. He supposed it was a knee jerk reaction.

"I need sharp eyes, and hers are the best. Plus, it wouldn't hurt to have a shooter with me just in case we get too close." Harris's logic was sound enough. Roland only wondered what else was going on in his head.

"Fine. Lianna, prep supplies and pack enough to spend the night if need be. I don't want anyone traveling this territory in the dark."

"Yes, sir." She took off to prepare.

"Emmett, Michaels, gather anyone who has ever set foot in Scav territory, anyone with even a grain of information about them."

"Yes, sir." They left side by side.

Harris hung back, knowing their conversation was not yet finished.

"Tell me you've thought this through," Roland said.

"It's my job, isn't it?"

"So, we gather our intel, and then what?" What he really wanted to know was if Harris had already made his own plans.

Harris responded with a shrug. "That's what the intel is for." He took off without waiting to be dismissed.

BY THE TIME they got back, Utopia was not only full but already lost in a haze of smoke and dense with an air of sedation.

Harris didn't care how much noise he made as he raced in from the adjoining tunnel. "They're here! The Resistors are right here in Olympus and ready to fight!"

His shout only brought about squirming and whining from most of them, but Switch sat up with a jolt. "How much did you drink?"

"Not nearly enough," Lash said as she followed him into the chamber. "I met one. He was in the Acro. Big guy with one hell of a grip. Young, too. Nowhere near the age most of these codgers are pushing from what I hear."

"You met who?" Switch said with another gold-toothed sneer.

"A Resistance fighter. I knew it, too, even before he confirmed it. He was alone, maybe a scout or something, but I'm sure there's more where he came from."

The others were starting to tune into the conversation.

Logan launched one of his scuzzy pillows at Harris. "Can it, would you? Some of us are trying to relax." Tuning in, but not caring.

"How can you relax? This city is about to light up!" Harris's excitement was turning into a natural high.

"What are you going on about?" Dee asked. At least her voice had a bit of clarity to it.

Harris was about to explain to the only person who seemed to care, when Grant chimed in.

"Harris is just excited cause he met some new dude." He laughed at his own joke.

Harris launched the scuzzy pillow at his face. "I'm telling you, he was Resistance. And if we track them down, we can join them. We can fight the poker faces and get them out of our city. For good."

"Wait a minute." Logan finally sat up. "Are you telling me there's a war about to start in this city? 'Cause I'm not sticking around for that."

"All right. All right." Switch's voice echoed around the chamber. Everyone else went silent. He pushed himself up to standing and put his arms out like he was instructing everyone else to remain seated. "Let's not jump to conclusions. So, there was a new bloke in the tavern. Big deal." Wince and Lash were standing on either side of Harris. Switch directed his first question at Wince. "You see him, too?"

"He wasn't imaginary."

Switch walked down the line like he was inspecting his troops. He threw the next question at Lash. "And he was unusual?"

"Most def for this part of town."

He circled back to Wince "And did he look like a fighter?"

"Sure acted like one."

Switch brought his inspection around to Harris, taking his time as he turned to face him for the next question. "Was he bigger than me?"

Harris didn't have to wait for the cocky smile that followed to know he was being toyed with.

Switch turned out to address the rest of the chamber. "Enough about these so-called fighters. Ain't no war ever come to Olympus, and no war ever will. Them Unis are just gonna slide on out of our city one day and leave us to the dogs like they always have. And I don't care how many weirdos come through our streets these days, ain't none of you joining any crackpots in their scheme to fight."

"I'm not wrong about this," Harris said.

Wince and Lash both took a giant step away from him, as if convinced his comeback was going to earn a violent retribution.

All Switch did was shake his head. "End of discussion." He returned to his lounging and his hookah. The other Utopians followed his lead.

Harris was the only one left standing. Instead of joining them on their horizontal plane, he chose to turn around and walk away.

"Where you goin', H?" Switch called out after him.

"To relax," he shouted back over his shoulder.

Harris relished what little time he ever had to himself, even when he knew it would only be minutes. He sat on the stone perch built into the tunnel wall and stared up at the new moon through the steam grate above. He went in for another swig of the top shelf golden he'd managed to sneak out of the tavern, only to find the bottle snatched out of his hand.

Switch held the bottle up the way you would hold something dangerous out of a child's reach, as if Harris couldn't take it right back. "What was all that about, huh? What are you trying to do to me?" Switch asked with a slosh of the bottle.

"I dropped it. Left you and your doped up masses to go about your businesses. What more do you want?"

"I want you to get these visions of yourself as some war hero out of your head. You ain't a revolutionary. You're a sooty, just like the rest of us, and you always will be. Don't you know that?"

Harris didn't know what aggravated him more—being told what he wasn't, or being told what he was. "Well, excuse me for thinking we're better than all the other shatz on the street. I won't make that mistake again." He hopped off his perch and started to walk away.

"Don't you trash us like that. And don't you dare walk away from me." Switch's voice echoed down the tunnel.

Harris kept walking until a SMASH froze his feet in place. He turned back around. Switch breathed out his frustration and tossed what was left of the bottle to the ground. *What a waste of good golden.*

"Try to understand. I'm only doing this to protect you, to protect everybody." Switch approached him, slow and steady, like he was closing in on an alley cat. "I don't want you to fight because I don't want you to die. And you know, without one hell of a miracle, that's what's gonna happen." Switch put his hands on Harris's shoulders and gave them a needlessly tight squeeze. "You're my family, H. And I always take care of my family. Ain't that right?"

Knowing words might betray him, Harris chose to nod.

"So, you gonna listen when I tell you to get that Resistance crap out of your head?"

He nodded again.

"And you ain't gonna go looking for that bloke from the tavern, are you?"

Just try and stop me. "No."

Switch gave him a self-satisfied smile and two firm pats on the cheek. "That's my boy."

Harris followed him down the tunnel, past the splattered remains of the liquor he would have liked to continue drinking, and back into Utopia. He had plenty of time to plan his next move.

TREE COVER THINNED out at the top of the ridge. Harris ducked down low as he scrambled up the last few steps. Lia did the same. It probably wasn't necessary, but better to be safe than eaten.

There in the valley below them sat the huge looming gate of Olympus. The bold stone letters above the archway had collected a healthy crop of moss, even a miniature tree in the dip of the *M*, but they were still broadcasting the city's name, loud and clear, out toward the empty road. Harris had actually never seen the gate like this. The first time in his life he was ever outside of it, his view had been obscured by smoke.

Lia pulled out her scope to examine the details. "The gate is open just a crack but wide enough for a person."

"Guess we forgot to lock up when we left."

She should have at least smiled. It was a good one, but all Lia did was flick him a glance before returning to her scan. "Nature has taken the road. No one has been in or out this way for a long time."

"Olympites were never too big on travel. Real homebodies by nature." He didn't bother to check whether or not that had elicited a smile.

"We need to get closer to the city center, somewhere they won't have much cover."

"I know just the place."

Finding it from the outside proved to be a bit of a challenge. The walls were taller than he remembered, the straight runs of uninterrupted stone much longer. Wasn't your childhood home supposed to feel smaller when you went back to it? Harris ran his hands along the wall, as if vibrations might come through the stone to tell him exactly what was on the other side. Eventually, they found a spot they both agreed was worth the climb.

The stones were weather worn, but hearty vines provided ropes wherever decent footing was lost to decay. Harris had only ever climbed the walls from the inside, just for fun. He had only ever been arrested for it twice. He was just starting to wonder how much longer the old walls had in them, when a crack sounded out from below.

Lia snatched at the closest bundle of vines as the stone under her foot fell away. They both stilled as the chunk of stone cracked down the wall and thudded onto the forest floor. Nothing but silence followed. *Guess no one cares what happens outside the wall,* Harris thought. *They never did.*

The top had just enough depth for them to sit without being spotted by eyes on the inside, assuming none of the Scavs had taken to living in the penthouses.

Harris was pleased to discover his instinctual map had been right. "Dead ahead. Central Square."

Lia lay on her stomach and leaned on her elbows, giving a steady base to the scope, which was now attached to her rifle. Better safe than eaten. "I see movement."

"It always was the place to be." Harris could see them, too, tiny, hunched shapes scurrying along the streets like roaches.

"I count at least eighty, and that's just in that open patch. If that's any indication, then there could be—"

"Thousands upon thousands." Harris suspected what they discovered might be bad, just not that bad.

Lia looked away from her scope as she processed.

Harris continued to watch the little roaches below. A group of them were clumped together in what was almost a lumpy circle. "Those in the huddle there, what are they doing?"

Lia refocused her scope. "Maybe it's food of some kind, why else would they…?" Her mouth hovered open, eyes squinted as she double-checked. "It's a fire. They're gathered around, sharing the warmth."

Harris thought she might be attempting a joke. "That's not possible." He lowered himself down beside her and forced his way behind the scope. There it was, the orange glow of flames, with the huddled bodies peacefully circled around it.

"That must be how they've survived winters out here." Lia was dismissing this discovery a bit too quickly for his liking.

"Wonderful. Now if they realize fire is also a great weapon, we're even more axed."

"Something isn't right about this. They're not behaving like the animals that tried to tear me off my bike."

"Maybe big city Scavs are more sophisticated."

That comment elicited more of a scowl than a smile. She squeezed him aside.

Harris observed what he could with his own eyes, while Lia took another survey with the scope. She began to gently rotate her aim as she followed one of the little moving shapes across the square. Harris sharpened his gaze in the same direction.

One of them was carrying something big enough to slow it down to a walk rather than a scurry. It couldn't have been something edible, or the others would swarm. Generating a fire was one thing, but Scavs didn't farm, Scavs didn't build, Scavs didn't possess anything but the rags on their bodies, so what would one of them be toting across the square?

Lia took in a shocked breath, and then breathed out the answer. "They have children." She slid herself over to let him take a look.

The heavy bundle being carried across the square had little legs dangling below it, and little arms were wrapped around the bearer's shoulders. The bundle-carrying Scav, who did have a vaguely woman-shaped body beneath her layers, reached the middle of the square and lowered it to the ground. The child scampered off on its own, racing off to explore the world, the way any child would.

They weren't just looking at the former citizens of Olympus. They were looking at an entirely new generation of them.

TEN

CENTRAL SQUARE WAS the most logical place to look for the stranger named Roland. If reconnaissance was his goal, then his travels would inevitably cross him through the square. Even if he was trying to remain unseen, he wouldn't slip past Harris. If any of the Utopians spotted him and wondered why he wasn't hustling in the tavern as usual, he would simply tell them he was looking for a more high-class mark that night.

It was decently chilly, but Harris had a pocket-sized bottle of double golden to provide the insulation his body lacked. The early tavern-going crowd thinned out as the ladies and gentlemen of the night took to the streets. Once their show pony strutting and cockatoo cackling had found profitable company, the only stragglers left on the street were the early drunks. The late drunks wouldn't emerge until sunrise.

Harris was just about to give up his hunt and return to the warmth of the underground, when a formidable stranger crossed into the square. He was even bigger than Roland, and significantly older, but had the same intensity in his eyes. There was a hint of ruddiness in the tufts of white hair that stuck out from under his hat. He, too, was trying not to be noticed, but had no chance at succeeding. Two formidable strangers in two days was no coincidence. Harris decided to follow.

The ginger giant turned down an alley charmingly known to the locals as Red Stain. You only walked down there in broad daylight, or if you were capable of killing a man with your little finger.

The night was pitch black, and Harris was likely to get snapped in half before he could so much as lift a finger. He told himself that tonight might be an exception and dared to follow him into the alley. He had only followed the ginger-haired stranger past the first steam cloud when the residents of Red Stain showed up to maintain their reputation.

The first two dropped down from the fire escapes. The other two emerged from the shadows of deep-set doors. The ginger-haired stranger was instantly surrounded.

Harris ducked behind the nearest dumpster. Being invisible was his only defense. The meaty sounds of heavy body blows soon followed. Harris pawed around in the mysterious piles behind the dumpster for a potential weapon. A wooden plank splintered in half. A stone block proved too heavy to move.

The oofs and ughs of gut pounding continued on the other side of the dumpster.

Harris finally turned to the only thing in his pocket, the bottle of double golden. He gave it a goodbye kiss, smashed the glass against the street, took a tightfisted hold of the broken bottle neck, and popped out of hiding.

One of the Red Stainers was lying on the street, completely unconscious. Another was racing away to hide in the darkness. The third was standing by in open-mounted silence as he watched the fourth being repeatedly punched in the face by the ginger giant. After receiving the final bone-crunching blow, the fourth man collapsed in a heap next to his friend. The only one left standing seemed to suddenly wake up when he realized he was next. He whipped out a knife and slashed at the air in front of him.

The ginger giant shook his head. He pulled out a gun and pointed it at the knife-wielding Red Stainer, who immediately pissed himself.

"Bang," said the ginger-haired stranger.

The Red Stainer let out a tiny scream and fell down. Realizing that it was only his reputation that had been shot, he scrambled up and ran away.

The ginger giant slid his gun back into its hidden holster and continued on his way.

Harris was standing out in the open, jagged bottle neck in hand, open mouth drying out in the night air, but no one had seen him. He let out a little laugh of manic relief, tossed the bottle neck into the dumpster, and followed the ginger giant to his destination.

He wasn't surprised to see the ginger giant ducking into the Nike Hostel. Its total lack of windows made it the perfect place for anyone who didn't want to be seen doing whatever their activity of choice happened to be. It was the perfect place for a clandestine group of Resistors to stay.

Luckily, Harris knew how to get up to the skylights, and it was through the very first one that he spotted Roland. He was hunched over a large set of engineering plans. The ginger giant stomped into the room, slammed the door behind him, and sat down on one of the rickety beds with such gusto that Harris was surprised it didn't collapse. He leaned gently against the angled pane of glass and pressed his ear down to listen.

"Can't believe the Unity even wants to take this city. What are they going to do with all these speed bumps? Injections won't reprogram them. They'll still be nothing but a bunch of pinkies and thieves." *A bit judgmental*, but Harris supposed it was an understandable reaction to the night that ginger giant had been having.

"Robot pinkies and thieves are a lot easier to control. Besides, it's not the people they want. Within these rotting buildings and stinking streets is everything the Unis need to build a shiny new city, with citizens as squeaky clean as the buildings they'll lock them in." Harris thought Roland was being too judgmental as well, but the skylight creaked, as if agreeing with him.

"I'm starting to think we ought to let them do it. Maybe the world is better off with one less shatz city and a hell of a lot less shatz people."

Harris wrestled with the instinct to jump in through the skylight and tell the judgmental ginger exactly where he could shove his opinions of Olympus, versus his survival instinct. It was always better not to piss off a giant man with a gun.

The skylight made up his mind for him. The metal frame groaned, the glass panel he was leaning on gave way, and Harris fell head first into the room. Shards were still tinkling to the floor as he looked up into the barrel of not one, but two guns.

Harris focused on Roland's face behind one of the barrels. "Found you."

"And how did you do that?" Roland asked without the tiniest shift in his aim.

"Gramps here just made the city a little less dangerous for my fellow citizens. I wanted to thank him."

"Friend of yours?" the ginger giant asked.

"Hardly."

"Give me a little credit, farmer."

The guns backed away, though their aim stayed at the ready. Roland gestured for Harris to stand.

Harris felt a sting of pain and warm drips of blood running down one arm, but he wasn't about to look away from either of those guns. He kept his hands up and let the blood pool in his sleeve. "If you two are trying to blend in, then you ought to let yourselves take a punch every once in a while. Black eyes are like a nice hat around here, very fashionable."

"So, you found us. Where are your people, big shot?"

Harris was incensed. "Where are yours?"

The door swung open. A hard-edged man with a scarred-up face dragged Wince and Lash into the room by their hair. "Got a couple of grade school spies on our hands." He took a quick survey of the destruction in the room. "What in the hell happened?"

"A guest dropped in." At least Roland still had a sense of humor. "These two belong to you?"

"That depends." Harris dared to look away from the guns toward the ensnared twins. "Did Switch ask you to follow me?"

"No, man, no!" Wince said from his taut sideways position. "We saw you ducking into Red Stain, thought you might get jumped. We just wanted to keep an eye on you."

"Like these two would do you any good. I picked 'em up as easy as newborn kittens." The scar-faced man pulled their hair for emphasis, to which they both responded with kittenish whines.

"That's shatz, Wince. You'd never turn that corner with only your sister for backup."

"We weren't alone," Lash said between whimpers.

The door on the other side of the chamber swung open. A tall, lanky man tossed Logan into the room, then planted his boot firmly in the middle of his back. "I found this sneaky little sooty out... by... the...." He trailed out as he saw the odd collection of people in the room.

Harris didn't wait for anyone to explain. "Now I know you're lying. There's no way Logan would do a damn thing Switch didn't tell him to do."

"Hey, I didn't do nothing wrong," Logan said into the floorboards. "I was just following everyone else."

"And who is everyone else?" Roland asked Harris as he cocked back the safety on his gun.

Harris was about to stammer about his ignorance of this entire operation, when another person marched in through the door behind the lanky man. She was curvy and stout, and she had Dee's head wedged firmly under her arm.

"Dee?" Harris was truly dumbfounded.

"Hey, Harris." She gave him a blind wave, her voice muffled by the arm around her face.

"Please tell me this is the last of your circus act." Roland sounded more than impatient.

"'Fraid not," said the stout woman holding Dee. "One of them knocked himself out cold when he slipped off the fire escape." She gestured to the door with her chin.

Logan had just gotten himself up onto all fours. The lanky man gave him another swift kick in the arse, assuring he stayed sprawled out on his stomach as he went to check the door.

The lanky man dragged in yet another Utopian. It was Grant, slack jawed and totally unconscious.

Harris looked around at the odd scene in the room as he considered what he could say to the rather large and increasingly impatient men with guns pointed at him, and their—very likely—gun toting companions.

Wince and Lash were both going red-faced in their book-ended sideways positions. Logan had no chance at getting up with the giant foot planted on his arse. Dee was about to pass out from oxygen deprivation, and Grant was nothing but a pile on the floor.

Harris swallowed and said the first thing that popped into his mind. "Well, I guess your people have met my people."

ROLAND'S FIRST INTERVIEWEE was a tiny woman named Palmer. She seemed to shrink to an even smaller size as she entered the tent. He opted to invite her to sit, assuring they were eye to eye as they spoke. "You crossed Balarathon to get to Cambria, is that right?"

She sucked a breath in through her nostrils before answering. "Yes, sir."

"What can you tell me about the Scavs you encountered there?"

"I can't say I remember much."

He could see that she did. "Anything you remember would help."

"It's all such a blur." Her eyes were glassy. She was probably more worried about appearing fearful in front of him than about reliving those memories.

He put a reassuring hand on her shoulder. "Try, please."

She siphoned up another breath. "They're crazed, like rabid animals. And stronger than any other creature I've seen living. Some say fearless. They'll face bullets again and again, no hesitation. They don't stop till they're dead."

"But what have you seen with your own eyes?"

"Enough to know to stay away from them. Ain't no tellin' when they'll attack or why. They see another living thing in their way, and they just...." The glassiness returned to her eyes, but this time it was the memories that brought it on.

"They just what?"

"Tear it to shreds."

The other interviews were more of the same.

"They come out of nowhere. Surround like locusts."

"Fierce. Terrible."

"Soulless."

"You won't hear anything until they're right on top of you. You won't see anything but a flash of movement."

"They chase you down and never stop. Your only chance is to get outside the city walls. They never go beyond them. But inside those walls it's...."

"Hell. I wouldn't go back for all the grain in the world. Not there, not anywhere near them."

Emmett and Michaels had heard similar stories. No one had taken their encounters with the Scavs lightly. Many of them had lost friends along the way. As evening approached, Roland, Emmett, and Michaels cloistered themselves in the command tent to try to make sense of what they had heard.

"The only thing that wasn't clear is whether or not they eat the ones they take. None of the survivors stuck around long enough to find out," Michaels said.

Roland was fairly certain they did. Perhaps Michaels was just in denial.

"I'm liking our chances in the snow better," Emmett said, though he knew that option was off the table. Perhaps he was just exercising wishful thinking.

"It just doesn't add up. Beings driven by strength without reason, violence without cause, yet they survive to this day. How? And they never leave the cities in which they were turned. Why?" Roland paced out his confusion.

"Most of them were more afraid of the Scavs than the Unis. How are we supposed to convince them to head into a nest the size of Olympus?" Emmett asked.

Nest. Something about that word shook all the loose pieces into place. Everything Roland knew about the Scavs, everything they had heard that day, suddenly made perfect sense. "That's it, Emmett. You've got it."

"Got? What? How?" Emmett was genuinely perplexed.

"There's a first time for everything, son," Michaels said with a smile.

"Olympus is a nest. All of those Scav cities are. If we enter it in the right way, we may not have to fight them at all."

All Roland had to do now was formulate a plan, and hold out hope that it would play out better than the last one he had attempted within those walls.

THEIR ODD HANDFUL of unexpected visitors was easy to round up. Roland doubted anyone even needed the weapons they were wielding to keep them captive in the corner of the room. Mere words would have done the job. The one that had just awoken from his self-inflicted stupor was still trying to figure out where he was.

Harris was clearly the most intrepid—and probably the most troublesome—among them. Though the calm with which he had handled the fairly serious slash on his arm was worth respecting. All he asked for was a needle, thread, and whatever liquor they had lying around. A splash of the bottle had been used to clean the wound. About a quarter of it had gone down his gullet. His pain tolerance seemed only outweighed by his liver tolerance.

When Roland approached, he was in the midst of pulling the needle through his skin. He breathed the pain out through clenched teeth, then sucked the breath back in as he pulled the thread along behind it. Not only had he managed to keep from passing out, but he had neatly sealed the cleft through his skin with even ties down its length. He tied off the thread with a dexterous maneuver of one hand, then snipped the end with a tug of his teeth.

Roland sat in the chair opposite his. "Looks as if you've done this before."

He leaned back and sighed away the last of his pain. "Not myself, but I spent some time in a hospital once."

"That's hardly surprising."

He smiled and took another healthy swig of medicine. "It was clean, comfortable, three squares a day. Can't say I didn't fake a pain or two so I could stay longer. Nurses took to me. Let me follow them around like a lost dog. I learned a thing or two."

"It obviously didn't sway you from your path."

"Hey, sometimes the path chooses us. Ain't that right, hero?"

"What about the rest of these sooties?"

He slapped the bottle down. "We're not sooties! We're not beggars, we're not thugs, and we're not the stinkin' speed bumps you see on the street. We're better than that. Understood?"

Harris certainly had a chip on his shoulder, but he also carried a sense of pride that Roland understood very well. "Is that what you came here to prove? You think dropping in through the ceiling while your buddies get rounded up like sheep impresses me?"

"You think you're so impressive? Where's your army? Where's your stockpile of weapons, your master plan? Where's a single thing that gives you the advantage over the poker faces?" He scooped the bottle back up.

Roland yanked it out of his hand. "You're far from having any advantages yourself. You can't even trail each other without getting caught." He threw a glance over his shoulder at the five inconveniences cowering in the corner.

Harris gave him a smile oozing with intent. "You're wrong about that. We can tell you how many Unis are in the city right now and how many more show up each day. Where they go, what they do, what taverns they eat at, which whores they pink. And if you're real nice, we can even bring you back some I.D.s, security keys, top secret documents. Anything not tied to their skin. And I—" He slapped his hand down on the pile of city plans Roland had just managed to acquire. "I can tell you that all the information you've got is wrong."

Roland gave him his most interrogating stare. "Is it?"

"Those plans are nearly ten years old. Created for some big city beautification project. Shatz idea anyway. It went belly up when the last mayor took off with all the dosh. Most of those tunnels are half built, some of them never even started." He flicked the plans with a touch of disdain. "You're already outnumbered a hundred to one easy. Do you really think you and your army of four is going to take out the occupation alone?"

"Do you really think you six are going to make up the difference?"

"Those are just pocket jockeys who followed me out here, and far from the brightest of the bunch, as you can tell. But we all still know more than you'll ever know about this city, even if you camped here till you were as old as ginger gramps over there. And there are enough of us to outnumber the Unis for the next year."

Roland looked Harris up and down, assessing his sincerity. Something about his illogical combination of self-abasement and unflappable confidence won Roland over. "Prove it then. Show me an army of master spies, and maybe we'll find a job for you."

If only it had been that simple.

HARRIS TOSSED TINY sticks into the sparking flames, barely keeping the fire alive. The approaching footsteps could have only been Lia's, and the way in which she tore through the brush could only mean she had encountered no threats.

"No movement. No sound. Not so much as a spider crawling around out there," she said as she plunked herself down by the fire.

"Good." Harris celebrated her declaration of safety by throwing a fat branch onto the meager flame so it would breathe up into a decent fire. He watched the flames caress up around the bottom of the branch attempting to kiss together at the top. The blissful warmth had just started to defrost his fingers when he felt Lia looking at him over the fire. He invited her to speak her mind with an open hand.

"What was it like when you were growing up?" she asked.

"Like any other city."

"How descriptive."

He could tell by the tone of her voice that she would not easily accept his dismissal of conversation, so he shared the most harmless memory that came to mind. "It stank."

"Be serious."

"I mean it. Between the rusted steam system, occasional burst sewer pipe, and less than stellar hygiene of the locals, stench usually hung around the streets like fog." *Does it smell the same now?* he wondered.

"Charming."

"I didn't, of course. Kept myself as clean as the mayor's spats." When was the last time he had even thought about the mayor's spats?

"So I'm sure." Lia turned her eyes to the fire, satisfied by the single superficial detail he was willing to share.

Remembering that distinct Olympian smell triggered something in Harris's brain. As it wafted into his imagination, it carried with it the sights, sounds, and feeling of being on those streets again. It was an odd sensation. He didn't realize he had laughed out loud until he saw Lia's raised eyebrows on the other side of the fire.

"I was just thinking how poorly named the city was. Home of the gods. What a load of shatz." That was all he had to say to excuse the laugh, but something compelled him to keep talking. "Then again, the gods were also cheaters, liars, and murderers. They spent as much time pinking around as our mayor did. Olympites, however, lacked the flair and creativity of the gods. Our squabbles usually resulted in fist fights and occasional hair pulling between pinkies. Of course, I always found that pretty entertaining." To that, she responded with the smile he had been trying to coax out earlier, along with a subtle eye roll. It would have been the perfect way to conclude the conversation, but he couldn't stop talking. "It's ironic, actually."

"What is?"

"That lung injury, that's what saved my life that day. If I'd been able to take full panicked breaths the way I can now, I also would have breathed in the gas." He laughed again. He really couldn't help it. "Can you imagine it? A genius like me in a shroud of rags, sitting in the gutter, gnawing on my own toenails."

"Would have been a tragic waste."

They shared a smile. He looked down at the fire, felt as his smile faded, and hoped she hadn't noticed.

"It wasn't your fault." She had noticed.

"You weren't there," he said without looking up.

"You told me what happened."

"But you weren't there." He finally looked up.

She was trying to conceal her concern, but Harris could see it flickering behind the reflection of the flames in her eyes.

"Get some rest. I'll take first watch." He didn't wait for her acknowledgment. He got to his feet and turned to look out into the woods, leaving his memories to sit by the fire.

THE TUNNEL HAD never looked so dark. The patterned pool of yellow light, a beacon signaling the way up and out of that darkness, seemed so far away. Harris's own rasping breath flooded out the echoes of his footfalls. Sweat poured down his neck, soaking his already wet collar. A loud clang made him stop in his tracks. He stifled his rasping and listened.

A mechanical HISS in the distance was followed by the appearance of red gas. It crept across the pool of light, billowing toward him.

Harris turned and ran.

A right, a left, and a scramble through the broken sleuth gate left the cloud of gas behind, but it was getting harder and harder to breathe. Harris leaned against the tunnel wall, trying to suck in oxygen.

The rattle of gunfire echoed over from another tunnel. Screams and yells signaled the approach of the crowd. The black blob of their combined silhouettes rushed toward him. Harris flattened himself against the wall to prevent the racing horde from trampling him.

A familiar face emerged from the blob. It was Dee, her eyes wide with panic. "Harris run! They're coming!" She reached out to him.

He reached back, tried to yell a warning about the gas, but there was no air to force out the sound. "Not that way," came out as a wheeze, drowned out by the echoes of running feet. Their fingertips touched. His attempt at a clasp found nothing but air, and then they were gone.

He tried to run but could only manage a few steps before black spots filled his vision. His hands and knees smacked onto the tunnel floor. At least he could still move. Harris crawled, heaving in breaths between each lift of his knees.

With a long reach forward, his hand found another pool of patterned light. Escape was overhead. Harris hoisted himself up, rung after rung, threw his body against the steam grate at the top, and pulled himself up onto the street.

Along with the rush of fresh air came the indiscernible cries from every direction.

The orange light of raging fires filled the square. People raced past.

Arms clasped around Harris and lifted him to his feet.

He flung his fists around, trying to fight off his capture.

The same arms spun him around. It was Roland. "We have to get out of the city! Now!"

"They're... still down there...." Harris wheezed. "Thousands... in the gas...."

"We can't help them."

Harris gave Roland a hard shove, breaking his hold. He wanted to scream at him for his cowardice, but he didn't have the strength for rage. He finally saw the chaos surrounding them.

A wall of Unity soldiers marched into the square, blanketing gunfire across any living thing that dared to cross their paths.

One of the burning buildings exploded, rocketing flaming debris into the air.

Harris spun around, desperate to find the fighters among them, but everywhere he looked there was nothing but fear and destruction.

He knew they were beyond hope, but he still heard himself say "We have... to save them...."

Roland grabbed his shoulders. "They're gone! Do you hear me Harris? They're lost! All of them."

He finally saw the panic and pain in Roland's eyes. He was alone in the world now. So was Harris. They both ran from Olympus, leaving the city to burn.

HARRIS STARED UP at the treetops as the light of approaching dawn began to pick out the leaves. With nothing but sky and untamed nature in his view, he could almost be anywhere. He let himself wander away until the light rustling of Lia's packing overtook the silence. He sat up and rubbed the sting of sleep out of his eyes.

"Just in time," Lia said as she cinched up her pack. "It's almost light enough now."

Harris stood, ignoring the stiffness in his body.

In the distance, the tallest tower of Olympus was poking up between the trees. He focused on the few ornate details he could pick out at that distance, a scroll here, a deep arch there.

He felt Lia's eyes settle on him and knew he had to say something. "It was beautiful once."

She joined him in meditating on the tiny tower among the treetops

"It was pretty run-down by the time I was born, but you could still tell. There was a grandeur in the old buildings. Solid foundations, big arches, towers, statues everywhere. It had once been a great city."

They watched until the sunlight broke over the horizon and touched the tip of the tower.

"Do you think we'll be going in?" Lia asked

"Can you see it happening any other way?"

She didn't have to answer. She gave a light brush to his arm, indicating it was time to head back. They walked off together, leaving the lonely tower to bask in the rising sun.

ELEVEN

WHAT HARRIS AND Lianna had seen only affirmed Roland's belief. The challenge that faced him now was convincing the others. "Think about it. Everyone we spoke to compared the Scavs to animals. Packs, swarms, rabid, claws."

"Not to mention crazed, deadly, impossibly strong, completely unpredictable," Michaels added with his usual flair for the negative.

"But they are predictable. They swarm against intruders, often after being triggered by a loud noise like the firing of a gun. If you run, they'll chase, but they never give chase beyond the city walls. And they're far from crazed if they're building fires and raising children."

"So, what are they then? A pack of wolves?" asked Lianna.

"No less human than they ever were. The gas didn't turn them, it touched them. It awoke something deep, instinctual. It's the animal nature in all of us, just enhanced, strengthened." It seemed to be sinking in. Or perhaps, like Roland, they realized how much of their own animal nature it had taken to get them where they were. "They act only when threatened. They're just protecting their territories, their nests."

Roland mused on what he would do if his nest—if his child—seemed threatened. He may not claw apart the threat with his bare hands, but his response would be no less animal.

"So, you're saying that if we just let them stand their ground…." Lianna was already convinced.

"We pose no threat. They won't fight. And we won't have to." Roland took a pause to read the room. Were they ready for the rest? "We approach slowly, with no visible weapons. And we go in on foot."

"We just leave the bikes?" Emmett was the only one to ask the question out loud, but they were all equally incredulous.

"No engines. No speed. Nothing loud, nothing sudden, nothing that could be perceived as a threat in any way. Not even running."

Harris finally joined the conversation. "We have thousands of people at our back. How can we keep those numbers from being seen as a threat?"

"One group goes in first. We gain their trust. We ask their permission. When we have it, the others follow."

"How are we supposed to ask for anything?" Lianna asked.

"There will be a way. We just have to find out what it is. And the only way to do that is from the inside."

Harris looked off to the side, as if he were considering the plan, but Roland could tell he simply didn't like it. Was it because of the risk involved, or because he wasn't the one who had come up with it? He finally looked up at Roland. "What's our fallback?"

"To fight. As always."

To that plan, Harris nodded his acceptance.

Of course, Roland didn't want that to become their only option. It was one thing to kill a threat of equal strength. It was another thing entirely to harm a child. He found himself wondering how many of them were the same age as Malcolm.

Roland brought his thoughts back to the mission at hand. "Inform your squads. No visible weapons. Not even a handle. Lianna, your snipers are our perimeter. Weapons hidden but at the ready. I want eyes completely surrounding us at all times."

With nods and affirmations, they headed out of the tent.

Harris didn't have to be told to wait behind.

"Harris, you're our map. I want the straightest shot right into the heart of Olympus and out the other side."

"Sounds familiar."

Roland waited for words of protest, of doubt, of whatever it was that was on Harris's mind, but he said nothing more.

"We've learned a great deal since then." Roland had wanted to make that point more eloquently, but that was all he had been able to say.

"Cautious approach or not, I know we'll survive. We always do."

"What is it you're doubtful about, then?"

Harris looked down at the outline he had drawn on the map indicating the border walls of Olympus. "You know that everyone you left behind died that day. I don't."

HARRIS

HE WAS STILL holding the knife when he raced out the door. Harris hadn't thought about how that made him look until the kids on the stoop ran away screaming. Even though the blood was still warm on his hands, their reaction seemed a bit extreme. That's when he realized he had been followed. The man Harris had deemed a pig-faced waste of flesh stumbled out behind him, clutching his gut wound.

"You're going to pay for this you little shatz stain!" The strength of his voice didn't seem at all impacted by the knife wound. Of course, it wasn't very deep. Harris's meatless, adolescent arms didn't have a lot of strength, and the knife he had managed to grab on time would barely dent a protein block. That didn't stop him from slashing at the air as he backed away from his pig-faced pursuer.

"Go ahead and hit me!" Harris challenged. "They'll put your arse right back in that box."

"You're the one who's going back where you came from. You can be someone else's problem."

"That's right because you're not my father!" The vibrations from shouting left a satisfying tingle in the back of Harris's throat.

"No." Pig-face grunted. "Your father paid his whore and left."

Harris let out a roar and dove, knife first, at pig-face only to meet with his cement block of a fist. He splatted onto the street. The next drips of warm blood he felt were flooding from his own nose.

"Go on then! Get out of here!" Pig-face shouted.

Harris didn't hesitate. He scrambled up and ran off beyond the steam cloud at the end of the street. He cut through the market, squeezing between bodies. He crossed Central Square, oblivious to whatever traffic was about to run him over. He didn't stop until the arched entry of a quiet lane-way invited him to depart from the bustling of the city.

Harris ducked into the cloistered canyon between the buildings, and stopped to catch his breath. The knife was still in his hand. There was no point in trying to dispose of it now that half the city had seen it in his bloody fist, so he pocketed it. It was, after all, his only possession now, apart from the clothes on his back.

A gentle whooshing from the end of the lane-way called to him. A bit of exploring beneath the rubbish revealed one of the ornate steam grates that peppered the city streets. As stale and metallic as the air humming up through it smelled, its warmth was enticing. It took considerable effort to pry up the iron grate, but Harris was rewarded with another waft of heat once it came loose. He stared down into the blackness beneath. It looked quiet down there... and safe. He threw his legs over the side of the hole and lowered himself into the tunnel.

Harris remained in the spot of light from above. The black of the tunnels beyond was still a bit too intimidating to explore. He was curled in a tight ball, holding in every whiff of warmth, nearing the edge of sleep, when sudden, raucous laughter jolted him upright. It bounced down the tunnel, echoed over his head, and degraded back into silence. More noises followed, indiscernible mumbles, several people walking in unison.

"Hello?" Harris called out.

The sounds stopped.

He got to his feet and fished the knife from his pocket. Harris squinted into the darkness in one direction, but it was too dense, his eyes too reliant on the light from above that was now flickering off the blade. He turned the other direction.

A face popped into his pool of light. "Boo!" said the face.

Harris fell over and landed hard on his back. The knife slid away into the darkness.

The disembodied face turned out to belong to a stout bodied teenager, whose fits of laughter rocked his entire body as he stepped into the light.

"Man, that never gets old." He breathed out the last of his laughter and wiped away the happy tear it had brought to his eyes. "Don't piss yourself, kid. I'm just messin'." He extended a hand out to help Harris up, but he was still too stunned to move. "I don't bite," he said with a little sneer that exposed a single gold tooth.

Harris allowed himself to be lifted.

"Name's Switch."

"Ha... Harris."

"H, huh? That's new. We don't have any other H's down here."

"Down here?"

"That's right. What brings you to Sootyville, H?" He opened his arms, indicating the tunnel itself.

Harris didn't have an answer. All he did was glance around and stammer.

Switch's thick fingers took a hold of his chin. He turned Harris's face to one side, examining it in the light.

Harris remembered the steam train punch that had probably swelled up his face by now.

Switch released his hold. "Lemme guess. You need some food, some company, and a little bit of the hard stuff to warm up the engines. Is that it?"

Harris wasn't sure if that was an invitation, but it sounded exactly like what he needed, so he nodded.

Switched draped a heavy arm over his shoulder. "Let me show you a little place I call Utopia," he said and led him away from his secure pool of light into the darkness of the tunnel.

THEY STAYED UPRIGHT as they approached the ridge this time. It was clear by now that any danger to them remained within the city walls.

Harris examined the gate of Olympus. It was just ajar enough to allow a single file line through.

"No one has been in for a very long time," Roland observed. "Neither in nor out."

"Do you suppose that works for us or against us?" Harris asked.

"There's only one way to know."

"I'm starting to realize how uncomfortable I get when you improvise."

Roland reached over his shoulder and lifted his concealed sword just enough to show Harris it was there.

"That's a little better."

"And yours?"

"Two sidearms, a knife, easy enough to reach if I have to."

"Let's hope it doesn't come to that." That was Roland's way of saying don't let it happen. "Have you got us, Lianna?"

"You're covered from here to about seven blocks into the city. Then, we lose visibility. From that point forward, we'll have to join you on the ground," she said through their radios.

"Time to head in," Roland said.

Harris was happy to let him take the lead. First one in, first one eaten. He signaled to the soldiers waiting below the ridge, then followed on Roland's heels even though he knew he might end up being dessert.

Olympus didn't smell the same. It wouldn't without the mechanics of the underground pushing the steam around to blend all the smells, good and bad, into one dense cloud. There were also no markets, no restaurants, no breweries, no drunks, no stinking speed bumps, and no brothels drowned in incense anymore. The city smelled the way it looked—empty.

The large, stone facades, blackened by ash and age, loomed over them. Harris swore Olympus had actually gotten bigger over the years. They peered into every crack and crevice they passed, knowing that the dark spots might contain a vicious enemy, ready to pounce, but each opening remained as dead as the stone surrounding it.

They reached the end of the first corridor without hearing so much as a whisper. The intersection opened up corridors on either side of them. Harris and Roland took a back-to-back scan of their surroundings. The long stretches of cobblestone reaching out in all four directions remained empty.

"Clear," Roland declared.

"Same here," Harris confirmed.

"No sign of movement around any of you yet," Lia said through their radios. *"You're clear for another block."*

Roland signaled to the long snake of soldiers following behind them, then nodded his readiness to move forward.

In the middle of the next block, one of the ornate facades had collapsed onto the street. The empty innards of what was once a grand block of flats was exposed to the elements, molding away with age. The facade itself created a wall of rubble, blocking their path.

"What do you think?" Harris asked.

"The dust hasn't been disturbed. They're not living in this part of the city."

Roland and Harris approached the rubble. Each tested a foothold, then climbed up to the top. The straight line of street on the other side sloped gently downhill and ended with a distant view of the fountain that sat in the middle of Central Square.

"Straight shot to the square." Harris pointed down their path. "And that's definitely where they live."

"Then we'd better arrive before dark." They signaled to their train of followers, climbed down, and continued on their way.

Roland continued to glance up at the buildings, examining each colonnade, each twisted gargoyle face. *Is he sight-seeing?* Harris was a bit more concerned with potential ground level threats.

Roland eventually shared his observations. "I had forgotten how closed in the city is, how claustrophobic. You can barely see the sky. Did that ever bother you?"

Harris had to make a conscious effort to switch from a strategic mindset to a conversational one. "It's all I knew back then. I guess it was comforting."

"Is that why you lived in the underground? Comfort?"

He scoffed, surprising himself with his own volume. "I wouldn't call it comfortable. I'm not sure I would even call it living."

"What was it then?"

Roland should never have asked. Harris's strategic mindset was completely dampened now, buried under the rubble of memory. He didn't want the conversation to continue, but he answered, nonetheless. "Purgatory."

THE SMASH OF the bottle hitting the metal wall was somewhat relieving, but the degrading echoes of tinkling glass that followed only gave him the chills.

"Whore!" Harris yelled in an attempt to gain a bit more relief. It didn't last long. He started pacing out his anger.

Switch was just sitting back and sucking his pipe as always.

"She's nothing but a pinky. Only difference is pinkies get paid. No wait, she did get paid because I was stupid enough to give her half my dosh every time I saw her."

"I tried to warn you," Switch said as he let out his exhaust.

"She wasn't even decent enough to take that taint outside before she started climbing all over him." Harris could feel himself losing his voice but wasn't ready to stop yelling yet. "The Acro is a tiny place. It's not like I wasn't going to notice. They were practically on the bar for shatz sake!"

"She was trying to tick you off, H."

"Whore!" His voice cracked. That was the last shout he had in him.

"You want another bottle to throw?"

"It doesn't help." Harris plopped onto the other end of the chaise Switch had chosen as his lounge for the evening.

Switch huffed out a few lazy smoke rings. "You want my advice?"

"No." Harris didn't want anything but the contents of the bottle he had thrown at the wall.

Switch sat up. "What, you think I'm not going to help you out? You think after all these years I spent watching out for your arse that I'm gonna give you bad advice?" He was waving his pipe around as he spoke.

Harris wasn't going to live it down if he didn't let him get his point out. He really wished he hadn't thrown that bottle. "I didn't mean that. Go ahead."

He was relieved to see Switch resume his lounging. "Forget about her. Forget about all women. They ain't nothing but a pain in your arse and a drain on your dosh, so ax 'em!"

Harris waited for more, but all that came out were a few more smoke rings. "That's it?"

"Yeah, that's it. What more do you want, H? You want me to tell you that the next one will be different, that she's not gonna screw you over, too? I ain't gonna do that 'cause it'd be a lie."

"So, I just avoid women for the rest of my life." He had to laugh. "How in the hell am I supposed to do that?"

Switch took a moment to tap out his ashes. Harris thought he might have to wait while he reloaded his pipe before getting an answer, but Switch stood up and cleared his throat like he was preparing to address a crowd.

"Allow me to use this opportunity to teach you a little something about life, H. Women only serve two purposes in this world. One is to make babies. Some crazy button in their brain makes it so they can't get enough of those screaming shatz factories, but the only men you see in this world hauling around those little meat sacks are the ones who can't get away. 'Cause let's face it, if men wanted babies then there wouldn't be an entire group of us sooties who never knew a man named Papa. But you know what? We're better for it. 'Cause Papa was an arsehole anyway." He stood up tall and pointed a finger into the air. "The second purpose women have is pleasure." He sat on the arm of chaise next to Harris.

Harris leaned back. Not only was his proximity unexpected, but Switch's pipe breath was not something he felt like absorbing.

It only made Switch lean in closer. "Now, that's where things get complicated. 'Cause we men, we need a little release now and then. And when presented with an opportunity to get that release, we tend to lose our heads. You learned the hard way that you won't notice how light your pockets are getting until it's too late. You go too long without a little release, and it'll just keep happening, over and over again. But we… we have an advantage."

Switch was waiting for a prompt. Harris had no choice but to give it to him or face another potential argument. "Which is?"

"We don't need women for pleasure." A momentary pause followed. Harris could see Switch looking at him out of the corner of his eye, but he didn't want to turn around. He jumped when he felt Switch's hand give him a solid pat on the shoulder.

"Just think about that." Switch stood up, returned to his seat at the other end of the chaise, and reloaded his pipe.

Harris didn't turn to look at him until a curl of smoke indicated that he had gone back to lounging, but as their eyes met, he shared his final thought. "When women serve no purpose, they can easily be avoided."

"IT'S NORTHWEST OF *your position,"* Lia informed them through the radio. *"Looks like a small campfire, less than ten parces out. You could be coming up on them any moment now."*

"Visibility?" Harris asked, hoping she might say it was still perfect. He felt better knowing there were snipers on their side.

"Spotty at best. We can't keep you completely covered anymore."

"Your team better join us on the ground then. We'll hold," Roland ordered.

At least they were waiting in an open intersection. Nothing could sneak up on them faster than they could draw their weapons. On the other hand, the soldiers behind them could be attacked from any number of hiding spots along the street. Harris tried not to let himself imagine what that might look—and sound—like.

He stood back-to-back with Roland, waiting for the signal from the snipers. "Why do you suppose they're all concentrated in the center, when they could have the whole city?"

"Same reason we all gather in cities, towns, and tribes. They need each other for survival. Their suspicion of outsiders is no different from ours either. We accept them only when we come to understand them and to believe they won't harm us." Roland really had put a lot of thought into his theory about the instinctual nature of the Scavs. Even if he was right about everything, there was still a veritable canyon of understanding between them, and they had no idea how to bridge it. "I have visual over here," Roland declared.

Harris was relieved to see the triple flash of light from his side. "Here, too." He didn't intend to move until he could count the snipers on his flank, but Roland turned him around with an unexpected tug on the arm.

The street ahead of them was filling up with Scavs.

Hunched figures crept out of the shadows, dragging the long, ragged tails of their well-worn clothes behind them. Sunken eyes, set deep into pale faces, examined them. Gnarled hands supported bony frames as the Scavs crawled out of the buildings and into the street.

"Hold positions. Steady," Roland said half into the radio and half to himself.

The group of Scavs fleshed out as more of them scrabbled out into the open, but they didn't push into the intersection. It was as if there was an invisible wall between them and the Scavs, but the numbers emerging behind that wall grew and grew.

"Many more, and we'll be outnumbered," Harris whispered.

"We hold our ground. Just look straight into their eyes." Roland sounded surprisingly calm.

Harris clenched his fist up where his guns should have been. "Which set of eyes?"

Just as he asked, several of the shadowy faces turned to watch the snipers arrive. They walked over slowly enough to keep the Scavs from launching into an attack, but now all eyes were on them.

Roland ushered Lia into the intersection with a gentle flick of his fingers. "Come forward slowly."

Each pair of sunken eyes followed as the snipers crept into their flanking positions. Lia took up the position in front, just as they had planned, though Roland flinched as if he wanted to yank her back.

The Scavs finally stopped emerging onto the street. That was either all of the ones in this neighborhood, or the ones that would start off the feasting.

Each group stilled and waited in silence.

A ripple of movement began at the back of the Scav horde, slight but unnerving. It sent a line of motion through the crowd headed straight toward them.

Roland tensed, but there was nothing to fight, nothing to target. They couldn't even tell what had caused the movement until a child raced out into the open.

The skinny arm of the child's mother reached out to snatch it back, but the child was too fast. The mother let out a slight whimper of panic as the child crossed the invisible wall and entered the open street between them. The child stopped in the middle of the intersection and stared up at them with glowing red eyes.

Their children have red eyes! That sight alone made Harris want to race out of the city.

The next movement came from their side as Lia stepped forward.

Roland reached out for her, words of warning on the tip of his tongue, but she was beyond the reach he dared to extend while the Scavs were watching.

Lia put herself at the same distance from the army as the child was from its mother. Lia and the child examined each other at arm's length. She must have smiled because the little pale face of the child did the same. It looked almost like any other child when it smiled, apart from its eerie red eyes.

Lia slowly dropped to her knees, putting them eye to eye. She remained still and calm as the child approached her. Tiny, ice-white hands reached out of their shroud of rags and poked at her body armor. The hands traveled up and plucked at a lock of her hair. Lia dared to reach forward and gently lift one of the thick black ropes that were the child's hair.

A little giggle emerged. The child wrapped its pale little fingers around Lia's wrist and pulled her up to her feet.

Lia walked toward the Scavs, being dragged along by her little leader. Roland took a step forward.

There was a snarl from somewhere in the Scav crowd.

"Steady," Harris reminded him.

The child stopped when it arrived in front of its mother. Its little head turned back and forth, glancing between them.

The mother remained frozen.

Lia lifted her wrist, and with it the child's hand, then gently cupped it into her own.

The mother whimpered but didn't dare move.

Lia gently passed the child's tiny hand over to its mother.

The mother clasped it back in her own trembling mitt, then Lia stepped away. She walked backward, slow and steady, then raised her hand and gave the child a little wave.

The child smiled again, just as sweet and happy and eerie-eyed as before, and waved back. Murmurs and movements from the Scavs behind them soon followed.

"That was genius," Harris heard himself mutter.

"That was a mother's instinct," Roland replied.

Lia's steady backward walk ended at a standstill between them. "What now?" she asked in a whisper.

The Scavs answered.

The child tugged on its mother's hand and pulled her beyond the wall. Her hesitant steps began a trickle of movement from the horde of Scavs as they crept toward them.

"We're being approached. Hold steady," Roland said softly into the radio.

The Scavs closed in and surrounded them with examining hands and eyes. Lia maintained a smile even though there was fright beneath it. One of Scavs stretched up to his full height as he approached, putting himself eye to eye with Roland. Harris didn't realize he had raised his hands up as if he didn't want them immersed.

"Put your hands down. It's not a police search," Lia said in a harsh whisper.

Feels about the same, Harris thought. He slowly lowered his hands down to his side but kept his fists closed tight.

The first few Scavs continued past them down the street, but the flow of hands and eyes didn't stop as the rest of the horde followed their lead.

"Keep your focus. They're still assessing us," Roland said.

"How will we know when they're done?" Lia asked.

"I think all of us have to pass the test." He turned to look back at the long line of soldiers waiting behind them. "Do not engage. Let them surround," he instructed through the radio.

"Maintain eye contact," Lia added.

Harris had no instructions to give. The only logical plan was to do absolutely nothing. They remained still—though not necessarily calm—as the crowd of creeping hands finished their examinations and thinned out as they approached the rest of the soldiers. He hoped none of them were feeling too jumpy.

IT WAS AFTERNOON by the time they were allowed to continue their slow forward march, but the sun had emerged to bless them with the occasional shaft of light and warmth between the long shadows.

The lengthy examination had spread them out like a long line of ants, and their entire army had Scav escorts along every few steps. They were watching their every move with curiosity and caution. The streets were full of movement, but everyone maintained a measured silence.

Harris took another glance over his shoulder.

"Stop looking back. You'll only raise suspicion," Roland said in a rather impatient way.

"We're so spread out they could be taking us one by one."

"Every soldier has another looking after them. Have faith in your army."

Harris wondered where Roland's faith in him had disappeared to. He usually accepted his words of caution. How had these creatures won such trust so quickly? He tried to fix his eyes—and his mind—on their destination.

Lia took a brief glance down the canyon of streets with her scope. She had subtly pulled it from her under her jacket little by little, so its brass finish would not be perceived as that of a weapon. "I can see them in the square. It's very well populated."

"Let's hope our escorts properly introduce us," said Roland.

They were entering another slit of sunlight as Lia clipped her scope onto her belt.

A wink of light flashed off the brass and captured the attention of a young looking Scav. He approached her with a finger pointed toward the scope.

Harris snapped his arms into ready to draw position, but Roland didn't even twitch.

Lia stopped walking.

The young Scav poked the scope, running the point of a twisted finger along its surface.

Lia looked down at the scope and then up into his face. She gave him a shrug of the shoulders, hoping it would translate to, "I don't know what you want."

Something about that universal gesture of confusion must have clicked. He pointed to a narrow street that veered away from their path and gestured for her to follow. She looked to Roland.

"No. Don't," Harris said on instinct, but Roland nodded.

"How are we supposed to understand them if we refuse what they share with us?" he said to Harris without taking his eyes off Lia.

The young Scav continued to insist with gesturing arms.

"Go ahead. We'll follow," Roland said. He sent the signal to keep going down the line, gestured for Harris to follow him, and just like that he had been volunteered to turn down a narrow street that was bathed in shadow and mystery.

Once they rounded the corner, they could see the tall, sagging shape of a dilapidated house of worship at the dead end of the street. The Scav scampered toward it.

"Did you know this was here?" Roland asked Harris.

"You think I ever went to services?"

The young Scav climbed up the stairs, stopped in the pointed doorway, and turned to usher Lia along. She followed him into the black void behind the smashed doorway, with Roland and Harris just a few steps behind.

The proudly painted walls were still standing, but the once colorful stained glass windows were smashed to bits, and a collapsed roof had allowed a pool of rainwater to collect in the center.

"Do you think they worship here?" Lia asked.

"That would be news to me. The people of Olympus find faith, and all they had to do was become rabid leapers."

"Civil words, Harris." Roland had definitely lost his patience. "They may not speak to us, but that doesn't mean they don't understand us."

The young Scav pointed toward the main altar at the end of the hall. They skirted around the pool of water and followed him toward it.

Whether Roland appreciated it or not, Harris still had a job to do. "This is as good a spot as any for an ambush," he pointed out.

"They had their chance to do that."

"To the entire army in a bloody mess, yes. But this would be the perfect way to pick off its leaders without anyone else noticing."

Roland was too busy examining his surroundings to even give Harris an impatient glance. He just shook his head. "There is something else here. Something important."

"I think you're right," Lia agreed as she arrived at the altar.

The elevated platform, its resident sculptures, and every surface surrounding them, was covered in bits of glass and metal. Piles of machine parts formed metal cairns, and odd assortments of small shiny objects, keys, toys, and jewelry filled the urns and bowls that would have once contained holy liquids.

As they stepped up onto the altar, the young Scav reached for Lia's scope and tried to pull it from her belt.

Harris was a hair away from drawing his concealed gun. He was already certain these objects had been taken from people who had entered the city only to become a hearty meal.

Roland stepped in without any weapon. He gently put one hand over the scope and said, "Please. She needs that."

Harris scoffed in disbelief, louder than he had intended, but the young Scav seemed to understand. He released the scope and took a step back.

They explored the shimmering contents of the altar as the young Scav stood off to one side.

Lia's multiple reflections danced in the bits of glass covering one of the statues. "This place serves some purpose. Everything was put here in a specific way for a reason."

"You want to fill us in?" Harris said to the Scav. Talking had worked for Roland, so he figured he would give it a shot.

The young Scav just scowled at him.

Roland and Lia were still lost in their tour of this mystery, but Harris's unease was beginning to eat into his skin. Why did this place suddenly matter more than the thousands of lives they had turned into a literal chain of food for the beasts who were now watching them? They had come to Olympus to survive a war, not to contemplate why these ugly, red-eyed things would have taken up the habit of decorating with rubbish. They were creatures of nonsense before they were turned. That simply hadn't changed.

"I'm going back to watch the line," Harris announced, then left without waiting for any agreement or approval.

HARRIS ESCAPED TO his favorite stone perch. He sat with his knees clutched to his chest and stared up through the grate. He was hoping to see the moon, but it had yet to make an appearance. It would have been difficult to see through tears anyway.

He drank down about a quarter of the bottle in one go. The acidic burn in his throat provided a bit of relief, but only for as long as the sensation lasted.

Switch's stout silhouette appeared at the end of the tunnel.

Harris leapt off his perch and marched off the opposite direction. He didn't want to see his face. He didn't want to hear his voice. He didn't want to do anything but sit in the steamy quiet of the tunnels and drink until his body violently rejected its contents.

"Hey," was all Switch began with. It was soft enough that Harris could pretend he hadn't heard it, but the shouting soon followed. "Hey! Don't you walk away from me. You turn around and look at me when I'm talking to you!"

He turned around, but only so he could make it known that he had no fear.

Switch approached, slow and steady.

Harris watched him with a hard-edged stare.

"You don't have to run, H. Not from me." He reached out and put a hand on Harris's cheek.

He didn't know whether to slap it away or turn around and run, so he stayed perfectly still.

Switch's fat thumb brushed one of his tears aside. "You know it's supposed to hurt the first time."

"Ax off!" Harris's voice echoed around the tunnel. He shoved Switch with all his might, knocking him into the slimy little river of condensation. He marched off again. He wanted to run but was afraid it would make him look like a coward.

"How dare you treat me that way after everything I've done for you!" Switch shouted from the tunnel floor.

Harris kept walking.

Switch sloshed up to his feet and marched after him. "At least I care! At least I'm not going to pink you raw and leave you lying in a gutter like some cheap whore! You think I liked that, huh? You think it felt good? You think I ever want you to feel the way I did? Ax!"

He must have kicked the tunnel wall. The sound rattled right into Harris's skull and made him freeze up. When the echoes dispersed into nothingness, a soft sniffing sounded out from over his shoulder. He dared to turn around.

Switch was crumpled against the tunnel wall, snorting back tears. Somehow all of Harris's motivation to run smacked right into a wall. Before he knew how it had happened, he was kneeling by Switch's side.

"Where you gonna go anyway, huh?" Switch asked without looking up. "What would you do without us? Without me?"

"I don't know." It was true, but that didn't mean he couldn't figure it out if he tried.

Switch turned his swollen eyes up to face him. "You're my family, H. You know that, don't you?"

"Yeah."

Switch reached up and caressed his cheek. His hands were clammy with tunnel moisture.

Harris resisted the urge to pull back.

Switch clapped a hand on his other cheek and pulled him forward into a hard kiss. He smelled like mildew and cheap tobacco.

Harris's adrenaline was just about to force out another hard shove, but Switch released him and stood up.

"Come on," he said without a hint of tears. "Everyone will be back soon. Don't want to miss the start of the party." Switch walked off, leaving Harris kneeling on the tunnel floor.

He looked at the bottle that was still clutched in his hand, swallowed down another quarter of what was left, then stood up to follow Switch back to Utopia.

CENTRAL SQUARE WAS just as active as it had always been, but instead of merchants, shoppers, dealers, pinkies, and hustlers, the square was full of tight-knit groups of soldiers, each being watched by a ring of pale-faced Scavs.

Harris stepped up onto the wall surrounding the long dried out fountain in the middle. He walked along the wall, taking a full survey of the odd scene he found himself in the middle of.

Somewhere in that wide field of stone was the steam grate he had escaped this city through. It seemed so definitive then. Everything he had known was burning to the ground, but somehow those blackened skeletons of his past had drawn him right back to the very place he'd tried to abandon them.

Roland approached and ushered him down into close conversation. "Each group has located and established watch through sunrise. They've also picked strategic positions to fortify from should things go sour with the locals."

Harris nodded. There was no reason to question that plan.

"Have you located one for us?"

Harris pointed up at the wide turret that stood at the center of the fountain.

Roland looked up with an air of doubt. "It's not very high."

"High enough to keep eyes on the entire square and will fit twenty standing." Harris waited for Roland to counter his plan, but he just nodded. Harris stepped back up onto the fountain wall to continue his slow circle.

Roland followed along from the ground. "One night is all this will take. We'll be well past these walls by sunset tomorrow."

If we survive the night, Harris thought, though he wouldn't say it out loud. Everything he had experienced that day confirmed that Roland's confidence was in no mood to be questioned, so all he said was, "We won't be certain of that until tomorrow."

TWELVE

THE RED-LIGHT DISTRICT was particularly busy that night. Something about the frost of winter made people want to cozy up with whomever their pockets could acquire. Harris had to take a sideways scuttle to avoid a collision with one of the patrons being booted down the stairs. He landed face-first on the cobblestone. *Guess his pockets were a bit light.*

Some of the objects of desire flaunting themselves in the windows were particularly enticing, but Harris had already set his mind on a destination. Aphrodisia's palace may have been one of the older—and far less recently repainted—establishments, but there was a certain charm to its well-worn decor.

Harris was about to do his routine double-check of the surrounding streets to assure he hadn't been followed, when the door at the top of the stairs opened.

Nymph, the very well-endowed madame of the house, sauntered out to greet him. "Why, if it isn't our favorite paperboy. You bring us good news?" While it was true that his wealth of information often earned him a discount, he could tell she was after a different type of paper delivery that evening.

He gave a pat to his coat pocket. "As always."

"Then come on in." She stepped aside and slipped her silken robe off one shoulder, exposing a rather ill fitting—in just the right way—red slip. He was instantly too distracted to remember to double-check the surrounding streets.

Nymph and the skinny redhead named Ariel joined Harris on

the client lounge as he downed his complimentary golden and surveyed his options.

"So, what suits your fancy tonight?" asked Nymph.

He could smell an up-sell coming his way.

Ariel ran her sharp fingernails through his hair. "Don't be afraid to try something new, sweetie."

She had attempted to win his patronage before, but Harris preferred a more full-bodied experience. Rather than offend her with an immediate no, he let his eyes wander over every selection in the room. The most exposed of them all was a young man, about his age, standing by the fireplace. Harris didn't realize how long he had watched the dancing shadows created by his well-formed stomach muscles until Nymph leaned in to whisper in his ear.

"Is that what you're in the mood for tonight?"

"Shatz! He's a knob polisher." Ariel spat the words out. It felt worse than being called a sooty.

"I am not," he said as firmly as he dared. In a brothel, raising your voice to any level that could be perceived as even remotely threatening would result in your face hitting cobblestone. They didn't need anyone's business bad enough to tolerate that shatz.

"It's too bad," Ariel sighed out. "I'd heard good things about you." She walked off without making another attempt at him.

He wanted to yell out in his defense but didn't dare try.

Nymph turned his face toward hers with a red-tipped finger. "Hey, in my place you can have whatever you want. Me, him, and for the right price… both of us."

It was an up-sell worth considering. Then, he remembered, "I only brought one pay day."

"Just one then. Go ahead and take your pick."

Harris focused on his drink rather than his options, hoping to find a decision at the bottom of the glass. What he discovered there was less of a conscious decision and more of an impulse to walk over to the fireplace and introduce himself to the young man standing there.

His legs felt like jelly as they ascended the stairs. Once they were inside the room, he found himself stuck to the floor. Was that fear? The four-poster bed, hideous lace curtains, and gaudy glass lamps were all the same, but something felt different about that room tonight, as if it were watching him.

The young man, whose name of choice was Hermes, was obviously used to taking charge in these situations. Harris felt his jacket slide off his shoulders. Hermes tossed it aside, gave him a seductive smile, and began unbuttoning his shirt. He peeled away that layer and dropped to his knees in one fluid motion.

Harris broke out in goosebumps as the air touched his bare skin. It was both terrifying and exhilarating. He unstuck his feet to step out of his boots, then suddenly found himself able to move again. Fingers clawed off his belt. Hands yanked off his pants as he backed toward the bed.

Hermes lowered him back with a gentle push on the chest. The surface of the sateen bed covers was cold but warmed up quickly. Hermes straddled him and began to kiss his way down his chest.

Harris lay back and closed his eyes. That's when he heard the noises in the hallway.

Voices, several of them, all shouting, closed in quick. Harris had barely opened his eyes when the door smashed in.

Switch shook off all the painted hands attempting to hold him back and charged into the room like an angry bull. He hauled Hermes off the bed and flung him into the corner. There was another smash, probably the table breaking under his weight, but Harris was too focused on Switch's seething face to see anything else.

He leapt up, ready to make a dash for the door, but Switch pulled out a knife. The screams and shouts all blended together as Switch backed Harris into the corner.

"You dirty little sooty!" Angry spittle flew out of Switch's mouth.

"Don't!" Harris backed into the narrow corridor between the bed and the window. There was nowhere to run.

"You traitor!" Switch took a forceful jab at him.

Harris snatched his arm, twisted it to one side, but the cold shock of pain soon followed. He looked down to see the knife buried in his side.

Switch yanked it out with a jerk, and a lightning bolt shot up Harris's body.

Harris fell to his hands and knees and screamed out in a voice he had never heard before. "Stop! Please!"

"It's too late for you to beg, you ungrateful little bastard!" The next jolt of pain came from Switch's boot as he kicked it into Harris's stomach.

Suddenly, he was on his back, with Switch and his knife poised to pounce on him. He held up his arms, his only shield, as the knife came down from above.

"I trusted you! I gave you everything! You're a liar! A cheat!" Every shout came with a jab, and every jab made another slash into the meat of his arms. All he could do was hold up his narrow shield, but Switch's final manic jab pushed right past it.

There was a strange wet popping sound followed by a sudden tightness in his body, as if every muscle tensed at once. Harris could see the handle of the knife sticking out of his chest.

Switch's face snapped into panic. He pulled the knife out. "No. No," Switch whispered as he stared at the bloody knife.

The air in the room was suddenly too thick to breathe. Harris's pain morphed into the sensation of ice water filling his veins. He wanted to shiver but couldn't move. He wanted to cry out for help but couldn't take in enough air to force out a sound.

Switch hovered, looking more petrified than he ever seemed capable of. He opened his mouth, but no sound came out, or perhaps Harris just couldn't hear anymore.

Something outside made him snap his head toward the window. It must have been sirens, but all Harris could hear was a muted drone.

Switch bolted up and climbed out the window. The last thing Harris saw was a bloody smear on the ugly lace curtains.

SMALL FIRES WERE dotted evenly over the square and into the streets beyond. Each fire had a neat ring of soldiers around it and a clump of

Scavs nearby. None of them had bothered to make their own fires. The body heat of this many people was probably already more warmth than they were used to. There were murmurs of conversation in the air, but none of them were too loud or too animated. It wasn't worth the risk.

Harris kept his eyes on the fire, and only the fire. He was tired of looking at the city, and he was definitely tired of looking at Scav faces. There was a little whirl of motion in the corner of his eye.

Lia was turning her scope over in her hands, examining it in detail, as if it were new to her. She was still trying to piece together the mystery they'd been presented with that afternoon.

Good luck, Harris thought.

"That man over there," Roland said softly. "Do you see the symbol on his coat?" He flicked a subtle look over the fire.

The Scav on the other side was large, strong, and ancient looking, with long gray hair framing an ashen face covered in purple scars.

"It's a Resistance symbol," Lia correctly observed, though she'd probably rarely seen one. They had never chosen to don the symbol themselves. It was the kind of self-important behavior they associated with the Unis, not to mention the fact that it was also like painting a target on your back.

"Those scars are from before he was turned. Probably from the first war, back when they were fighting in the open," Roland said with an air of reverence. "I just never knew any of them were in Olympus."

"He was probably hiding." Harris shouldn't have said that out loud, but he had. He finally turned his eyes up from the fire. "That's what brought most people here, criminals and vets alike. I bet he threw his uniform on the second the fighting started again. He's probably been like that ever since."

"It's too bad we can't convince them to fight with us now." It was an odd notion, particularly coming from Lia. At what point had she decided that these twisted things were her allies?

"Even if you could sit down and have a chat with them, you'd never convince a soul to come with us. It's fighting that turned them into this. Hell, some of them weren't even fighting, just standing in the wrong place at the wrong time." Looking away from the fire had filled Harris with a pressing need to move. Several sets of glowing eyes followed him as he stood up.

"Where are you going?" There was a wary edge in Roland's voice. It only made Harris want to walk away faster.

"To the tavern. Care to join? I'll buy this time."

"Harris—"

"I'll be fine." He walked off, ignoring all eyes that followed, including Roland's.

Harris let memory guide him to the ring road that encompassed the square and had off-shoots leading toward every other part of the city. Scavs darted in and out of the crevices around him like rodents but otherwise just quietly observed him from the shadows. He didn't look at them. He didn't break his pace. As long as they didn't have a problem with his late night stroll, he wouldn't have a problem with their incessant scampering.

Cobblestone turned to brick, brick turned to slate, and slate turned back into cobblestone. The monotony of cold, lifeless streetscapes was suddenly broken up by a bronze medallion in the middle of the footpath.

Harris came to a stop at the medallion. It had gone green with age, but the symbol at its center was still easy enough to see, even in the dark of night. It was a caduceus. He was outside the hospital. Harris turned his eyes up and faced the burnt-out shell of the sturdy, brick building.

Even after all this time, he remembered which window had been his.

THE KNOCK ON the window jolted Harris out of his drugged-up slumber. Wince was pushing his goofy face up against the dingy glass. He waved Lash over, and she did the same. Together, they slowly pushed up the sash and crawled inside like a matched pair of invading spiders.

Harris did his best to blink away the opiate haze, but it was still hard to tell them apart.

"Finally found you, man," said a masculine voice. It must have been Wince.

"You could have gone in through the front door." Harris didn't realize how dry his mouth was until he spoke.

"You think those white coats are going to let us past the waiting room? I thought we might try a sob story, but no way they were going to believe you're our older brother," said Lash.

"Besides, why bother when they don't lock the windows?" Wince's smile dropped as he reached Harris's bedside. "Whoa." He was staring at the blood that had soaked through Harris's bandages.

"We didn't know. I mean, we heard, but we didn't really know for sure," Lash stammered.

"Know what?" Harris asked.

"How bad it was. You hear fight, and you think one thing, but between you and Switch? We figured he just gave you a few bruises is all. We assumed those pinkies were lying. Just trying to make up a good story."

"What did you do to him, man?" Wince sounded genuinely confused.

Even in his inebriated state, the question made Harris's blood boil. "Me? I'm the one with a punctured lung, and you want to know what I did to him?"

"I'm sorry. I didn't mean it like that, man. It's just... look at you."

"They caught him, you know, a few hours later." Lash didn't lean in the way she usually did when sharing gossip. She was probably afraid she might break him. "They got him locked in one of those underground boxes. Might even be for good if... if you press charges. At least, that's what I heard."

There was a pause as they waited for Harris to share his thoughts.

"So... are you gonna?" Wince eventually asked.

Harris gave this as much consideration as his compromised brain would allow. He would have to report it in full, every embarrassing detail, every scandalous nuance of what had occurred. It would all come out into the open eventually. The law did not have the power to keep anything sacred, not in Olympus. He would have to tell them why Switch had done it. Even if he didn't, no one would accept it as a random act of violence. Everything had a reason, and this reason would be dug up by force if necessary. Then, everyone would know.

There was a slim chance they would think Switch was just plain crazy. A slim chance they would keep him in a comfortable institution for the rest of his life. Perhaps that was better for everyone. The odds were much greater that he would end up back on the street. What would happen then? Thinking about it made Harris dizzy.

"Why bother?" he said before closing his eyes.

GINGER WAS, BY far, his favorite nurse. They had all been kinder and more tolerant than anyone he'd ever met before, but Ginger was also easy on the eyes and good at throwing his jokes right back at him. It was as healing as it was entertaining. Harris was in the midst of scraping up the last of the glucose pudding when she entered. She took the tray away before he managed to shovel in the last bite.

"Honestly, I've never seen anyone like the food here, let alone put on a few bales eating it." She gabbed as she went about her routine. She was good at talking her way through everything. "Of course, most of them don't need it the way you did. I guess I should be happy there's more padding on those bones now, even if it did come from twice processed greens."

"Tastes better than the fake ale nuts in the tavern."

"That I don't doubt." She tugged at the shade, and it retracted with a snap.

Harris grumbled. Daylight felt like a smack in the face.

"You quit that whining. You need light as much as you do nutrition. Now, lift up your shirt and let me take a look."

"You did that yesterday."

"Don't get shy on me now, young man. You know it's a waste of your breath. It's nothing I didn't see when they brought you in here, naked as—"

"The day I was hatched. I know. You've told me that story. You all have. A lot."

"And it never stops being funny."

Her smile and wink won him over. He lifted his shirt. She rubbed a bit of heat into her hands before pulling back the bandages. She was very thoughtful indeed. He hated being examined, but at least she was the one doing it.

She smoothed the bandages back down and straightened his shirt with a tug. "Well, short of you developing any more sharp pains in your spleen, or any other organs you happen to learn the proper names of the day before something seems to go wrong with them, you'll be ready to leave tomorrow."

"I wasn't lying when I said my kidney hurt. Right here."

"Yes, I know where the kidneys are, dear. At least you're a good student." She gave him a warm smile.

He felt it coming, the speech she had been holding back until his last night in the hospital. He held out on smart-mouthed replies to give her the space she needed to begin.

"My offer still stands. My sister has got a big place, more than enough room for another bed. All you'd ever have to do is a bit of housework once in a blue moon."

"I've never done housework in my life, and I don't intend to start now."

"You could get a job then. You'd earn good money, smart as you are. You'd have your own place before you knew it."

"No. Thank you. The clothes are more than generous. Hey, I'm lucky enough to not be walking out of here the way I came in, right?"

He thought she would laugh, but her face just crinkled with worry. She perched on the bed beside him, something busy nurses would never do unless they were about to tell someone they were dying. He was pretty sure that wasn't the case.

"Listen, I know the kind of life you've been leading. I know it because it's the kind that usually ends in here. You're young. You've got the chance to lead a proper life now, but you won't be able to do it without a little help, and without the support of a family."

He wasn't sure he liked the word family anymore. It was family that had put him in that hospital. It wasn't the kind of family she was talking about. A sweet spirit like her probably couldn't even comprehend the kind of families he'd had throughout his life, but he wouldn't try to explain. He just knew he would be better off without any kind of family at all.

She needed some kind of reassurance, but the best he could offer was "I'll be fine."

They let him wait until the afternoon shift came in before hustling him to checkout. Ginger was there to say goodbye, along with most of the other nurses that had tolerated him shadowing them during their shifts. He was certain they were the most generous souls in all of Olympus. They were still watching him through the front window when he turned back. He gave them a proud salute and walked off with confidence.

He knew that's what they needed to see.

HARRIS DIDN'T WANT to think about what might have happened to Ginger. Whether or not she was long gone, or still out there in the city, she deserved better. They all did. He turned away before the picture of their faces watching him through the window could solidify in his mind.

Should I walk the same path? Can I even remember it? Will I recognize what it has become? Harris's feet were moving again before he had answered any of those questions, but the answers turned out to be *yes*, *yes*, and *yes*.

He left the hospital behind and took a right turn into the shopping district. The once busy streets were empty. Even the Scavs seemed to have abandoned them. The shop fronts were all smashed in, though the glass was nowhere to be seen. It had probably been relocated into a Scav house of refuse worship. Everything beyond what had once been windows was nothing but a tangled mess of dusty detritus.

The bar at the end of the row, where he had tried—and failed—to hustle his way into his first post recovery drink, had been burnt to the ground. *Good*, Harris thought, and walked on.

The next landmark he found was the junior school he had watched the kids happily race out of that afternoon. It was still standing, an un-touched monument to education, sealed in by rusted gates. He didn't remember how close the next landmark was until he circled around the back of the school.

The entrance to the lane-way looked like a gaping black maw, waiting to swallow him whole. He slowed as he neared, half because he didn't want to accidentally sneak up on a Scav, and half because he imagined being sucked into it like a vortex. The lane-way was as lifeless as a tomb. The sleeping speed bumps he had once skirted around were long gone, but the steam grate was still there.

That was the one he had pried up that day. That was the entrance he had used to go right back to the family he'd sworn he was going to leave behind forever. He hadn't lasted more than a few hours on his own. He did leave them behind eventually, but it was under very different circumstances.

Harris turned away and marched off at a much faster pace. He kept his eyes on the ground and watched the paving stones flick past. He wasn't sure if he was headed back to camp or away from it. Did it matter? There was only so far you could go in a walled city. He walked on and on, certain he had gone even beyond the unofficial boundary of Scav territory, until he heard a snarl from around the next corner.

He stopped and listened.

Low guttural growls and cat-like hisses emanated from the street ahead. Curiosity kept him from turning away.

In the middle of the street ahead, several Scavs were tugging away at the leathery remains of some long-dead animal. They fought for their share by flashing teeth and swiping fingernails at each other. Where that failed to impress, a good old fashioned shove seemed to do the trick.

Harris found himself creeping toward them, drawn to the morbidity of the scene.

A large Scav in the middle of the huddle let out what could only be described as a combination of a roar and a scream. It sent a shiver down Harris's spine and stuck his feet to the flagstones. The other Scavs scampered away and resigned themselves to waiting in the shadows. The victor hunched over his prize and tore into the shriveled shape with his claws.

Harris began walking again, certain he could quietly tiptoe past him while he was feasting, but the large Scav raised his head and sniffed the air.

Harris froze.

The Scav rose and slowly turned to face him. His face was scarred, his frayed hair crisscrossed over his eyes, but in the center of his rotting sneer was a single gold tooth.

Harris couldn't stop staring. He had to know for sure.

The Scav stared back at him, and something behind his yellow eyes sparked with the light of recognition.

Harris hadn't just found Switch. Switch had found Harris.

Abandoning his prize, Switch crept slowly toward him. He was hunched, his bones twisted by a combination of chemicals and hard living. His numerous scars looked like they had come from many fights over many years. Some of them still had the mean red hue of infection. He was a pitiful creature.

He straightened up as much as his spine would allow and reached out a hand with ragged flesh still dangling from its nails. It looked as if he was trying to embrace the air between them.

A strange sensation traveled down Harris's legs. What felt at first like a desire run was actually every drop of sympathy draining out of his body and washing into the gutter. The void it left behind swiftly filled with rage.

Without a second thought, Harris dropped a hand to his ankle holster, yanked out his gun, secured his aim, and pulled the trigger.

Switch was nothing but a lump of rags on the street.

A curl of smoke escaped the barrel of the gun.

The echoes of the bang rattled away into the side streets. A split second of silence followed.

Then, the city itself boiled with movement. Dark figures raced out of the shadows. Growls and shrieks filled the air.

Harris was swiftly enclosed in hurricane of rags. His back hit the cold stone. Teeth snapped. Claws snatched. Angry eyes glowed in the darkness. Spurts of blood shot up into the air. It all became one blur of movement until everything turned black.

GROWLS WERE STILL vibrating the air when Harris's vision came back. There was a dark circle of figures surrounding him, but they were all facing away, creating a wall of protection.

One of the figures popped into his eyeline. "He's conscious!" It was Emmett's voice.

Harris forced his eyes to focus. Between the legs surrounding him was a sea of snarling Scav faces below, just out of snatching height. He was back in Central Square, lying on top of the turret in the middle of the fountain.

"How?" he began to ask.

Emmett put a hand to his chest. "Don't try to speak." He was frantically winding a bandage around Harris's head. There was moisture cascading down his face. Was that blood? Harris raised a hand up to touch it, only to discover a perfect crescent-shaped bite mark where two fingers had once been.

Emmett turned a bit greenish as he haphazardly wound the last of the bandages around Harris's three-fingered hand.

"Talk to me, Emmett!" Roland's voice called out. He was standing behind Harris, one of the many people in the circle. They were keeping the undulating horde of Scavs at bay by constantly flicking their aim into one face, then another, and another.

"He's okay!" Emmett shouted back, though it didn't sound like he believed it. "You're going to be okay, sir. Just don't move." Emmett stood and joined the defensive circle.

Harris examined his body. Every bit of flesh not covered by armor was bleeding through loosely tied bandages. He looked around at the legs surrounding him.

One of them had a trickle of blood dripping down the back, pooling at the heel. He followed the blood up to its source. There was a deep claw wound on the back of Lia's neck. She must have followed him. She must have brought him back.

"No... why?" he whispered.

Something fuzzed in his ear. His radio was still there, cracked and shoved hard into the canal. *"There are too many to take!"* a voice shouted through the static.

"We need to retreat," said another.

"There is no retreat!"

"We hold!" Roland shouted.

Somewhere beyond the Scavs filling the square were other cloisters of soldiers, trapped in buildings and on rooftops, desperate to make sure they didn't end life as a meal. Why was Roland telling them to hold?

"We can take the close ones, but the others will move too fast for precise kills. We would have to blanket the square from every angle," Emmett said as he slid his aim around, making sure nothing crept into his periphery.

"We don't fire unless given no choice," Roland responded.

"Why not?" Harris called from the ground. He pushed up to seated. "We've killed… every other force that stands in our way. Why stop now? Why them?"

Roland didn't respond. He just flicked his chin at Emmett. He dropped back to Harris's side and tried to gently encourage him to lie back.

Harris shook him off and struggled up to his feet. Everything went gray, but he managed to stay upright. "We can do it, Roland. We can end this… right now."

"There wouldn't be anything to end if you hadn't shot one of them in the face!" Lia shouted over her shoulder.

Roland shot a seething look back at Harris.

The sun was beginning to rise, bathing the square in purple light. It made the Scavs look even more alien than they did before.

Harris stumbled toward Roland on jelly legs. "What are you waiting for? We're stronger. We get to win this one."

"They're still human beings. We can't just slaughter them," Lia said.

Harris leaned into Roland's ear. "If we won't kill them because they're human, then why do we kill anybody at all?"

His lip twitched. His finger traced the trigger of his gun. Roland agreed with him. "We wait for more light."

"No. We can't," Lia whispered.

"Pick your starting targets," Roland ordered. "This is going to take considerable speed."

"There has to be another way." Lia was still arguing.

"Why does it even matter?" Harris said through his teeth.

"It could have been you!" she shouted back at him. "It could have been you down there with your children!"

"Then go ahead and throw me back where I belong." Harris pointed down into the square.

A silence of disbelief followed.

It looked as if Roland was going to change his mind, then he turned to Lia. "We have no other choice. Be ready to move on my mark."

The circle around Harris tightened up, guns held high. His own guns were gone, trampled under Scav feet, but he found his knife still tucked under his chest plate. If he was going to die, right there in the city of his birth, he was going to cut open a few throats on his way out.

The rising sun found a gap between the buildings.

A slash of golden light fell over the turret.

Roland drew in a breath to give the order.

Lia shouted, "Wait!"

She removed the stabilizing hand from the barrel of her rifle, fished into her pocket, and pulled out her signal mirror. With shaking hands, she guided the mirror into the slit of sunlight across the barrel of her gun.

The mirror sent a spot of gold blazing into the square. Every face hit by the light became still and silent.

Lia sent the light gliding back and forth across the sea of Scavs.

Growling ceased. Twisted faces relaxed.

"Signal mirrors," Roland said. "Everyone, find the light."

The soldiers in Harris's protective circle did exactly as ordered. One by one, their own golden spots of light joined Lia's.

The surge of anger below dropped into a placid calm.

"All units do the same. Use your mirrors. Flash the sunlight into the crowd," Roland ordered into the radio.

Towers, balconies, windows, and rooftops all around the square soon lit up with golden flashes. The spots of light danced around. The sunken eyes followed everywhere they went.

Lia stashed her gun, looped the mirror around her neck, and bent, ready to lower herself into the crowd.

Roland snatched her shoulder. "I'll take this one. Just stay ready for anything."

She nodded and stepped back into position.

Roland's climb down the sculptural facade of the turret and into the crowd went unimpeded. No teeth sunk into his flesh. No claws snatched at his limbs. They didn't even touch his weapons, which were now all visible. The Scavs simply stared at him with curious faces.

As he stepped into the crowd, a hunched old lady approached with a gnarled finger pointed at his chest. She poked at the signal mirror around his neck with a long, yellow fingernail.

Roland pulled it over his head and held it in front of her.

The mirror spun, flashing a dance of light over her ashen face.

"Is this what you need?" Roland asked.

She answered with an open palm. Roland lowered the mirror into her hand. She clasped her pointed yellow fingers around it, and he let go of the chain. The hunched old woman shrunk back into the crowd and showed off her prize.

None of the others tried to take it from her. They simply looked at the little piece of golden glass in awe.

Roland's order broadcast softly through the static in Harris's ear. *"We leave an offering. That's how we regain their trust. Relay the order. Tell every other group to do the same."*

"Yes, sir," Emmett said and began his best description of that rather cryptic order.

Harris didn't realize he had slid over to the edge of the turret until Lia pulled him back.

"You should probably stay out of sight for now."

"This won't last. Animals can't be bought off."

"He looks a lot healthier than you do."

Harris took a look at his three-fingered hand and then down at Roland strolling, untouched, among the Scavs. He couldn't disagree.

Emmett cleaned up the worst of the blood, or so he said. There were no mirrors left for Harris to double-check. Nonetheless, Lia and Emmett kept firm flanking positions on him as they walked out of the city from the center of the line rather than the front. They also hadn't bothered to restore any of his weapons. He was too much of a liability.

The line of soldiers was significantly tighter now, and their Scav escorts, few and far between, but all conversation was still kept to a minimum.

"What do you suppose they've done with them all?" Emmett asked in a hushed voice.

"That place we saw couldn't have been the only one like that. There must be spots all over the city where they gather together any objects that reflect light," Lia said.

"But why?"

"The buildings are packed in tight, made entirely of stone. You would never see much sunlight at all unless you collected it somehow. I guess that's what places like that are for. Most every living creature needs sunlight. Scavs included." It sounded as if Lia's thinking by fireside had yielded some answers. Either that or she just got lucky.

They passed a handful of Scavs who were sitting together in a clump on top of a pile of rubble. They looked like vultures waiting for something nearby to drop dead. Their eyes followed Harris.

Emmett and Lia both took up slightly tighter flanking positions. He couldn't be sure, but it felt like they started walking a bit faster, too.

Harris waited until they were well past the walls of Olympus before performing his own medical check. He picked a spot away from prying eyes and judgmental whispers, though he could still see the tail end of the line in the valley below snaking its way out of the city. No one appeared to be running. They might all make it out after all.

Between bites, gashes, scratches, abrasions, and contusions, he counted twenty-four injuries altogether, not including the missing fingers. That was the last bandage he dared to unwrap. The flesh and bone must have come off in one clean snap. The crescent left behind had an impression of practically every tooth involved. He was almost too fascinated to be disgusted, until he thought of his fingers digesting away in the acid pit of some Scav's stomach.

Harris had brought more than just the basic medical supplies with him. He had brought the box of injection needles. *Surely a small dose will do more good than harm.* He double-checked his surroundings for watchful eyes. Finding none, he snapped open the box and pulled out one of the needles full of the precious silver liquid.

With the needle clasped firmly in his dominant hand—which was thankfully intact—he aimed the point into the middle of the wound and pressed lightly on the plunger.

His hand felt like it had burst into flames. He dropped the needle and tried to shake the pain away with violent jerks. Harris was on the verge of crying out, of making anyone within earshot aware of what he had done, when the pain dropped down into a dull electric storm, followed by the sensation of pins and needles. He clasped his own shaking wrist and turned his hand over to look at the wound.

The flesh had sealed shut, leaving nothing but a blob of purple where the skin had been torn open.

"Can't grow fingers, huh?" Harris said to the needle in a shaky voice. "Good to know."

He sealed the needle back in the box and quickly masked his miraculously healed hand under a bandage. He had just finished concealing the evidence and was ready to begin picking up the many discarded bits of bloody bandage when Roland approached.

"Did you check on Lianna?"

"She's okay. Emmett did well dressing her wounds." Harris didn't mention that she had also flat out refused his help. If she hadn't shared that with Roland, then he didn't need to know.

"If you'd been much farther away—"

"You know I would have done the same for her."

Roland nodded and turned his gaze down into the valley. The line of soldiers had finished trickling out of the city walls. They had made it out unscathed—most of them anyway. There was a long silence as they watched the line wind around the base of the hill.

Roland became the first to break it. "I don't need to know. Just add it to the list of things you've kept from me over the years."

"That's not…." What could he say? Harris hadn't intended to tell him what happened. He hadn't intended to live long enough to tell anyone.

"It doesn't matter. I forgive you. I always forgive you."

"Always?"

"The first time we met, you tried to steal from me, but I forgave you."

Harris felt himself smile. As odd as it was, it had become one of his fonder memories.

"You keep more secrets under your hat than anyone I know, but I forgive that because you're the only man I trust with my own."

He felt his smile fade.

Roland took in a breath before going on. "You tried to take my wife from me, and still I forgave you."

A surge of guilt rose up with a bit of stomach acid. Harris swallowed them both back.

"But"—Roland turned to look at him—"if you ever lose faith in our mission again, that is something I will not forgive."

Roland didn't give him the chance to respond. He just turned and headed back toward the line, leaving Harris to clean up his own bloody mess.

THIRTEEN

THE TUNNEL WALLS glistened in what little light filtered down through the air shafts. The occasional slosh of his boot indicated water had been gathering, possibly over many years. Roland hoped it hadn't compromised the integrity of the tunnels. They were already too deep in the mountain to turn back. The spots from their flashlights soon disappeared into a void ahead. They had reached the junction.

Roland, Harris, and Lianna each took in the full circle as they entered. Four tunnels verged off into the unknown.

Harris consulted the map. The bold lines certainly looked like they had been drawn by a steady hand. Hopefully the memories it had been drawn from were just as sharp.

"Western surface point. Northern surface point. Peak of the mountain. Deeper in." Harris shined his light down each corresponding tunnel. "We take each surface point, and we have a fair chance at surrounding Martrim's troops."

Roland didn't like the sound of "fair chance." They had been chasing Martrim for what felt like years, though it had only been months. All he wanted now was an opportunity to shoot at him, or better yet, sever a limb. Fair chance or not, this was the only chance they had. "All right. Snipers to the high ground at the peak. Your unit to the west. Mine will take the north."

They lit their flares, compared to make sure each color was distinct enough to be recognized by the soldiers following, and marked the corresponding tunnels.

"Radios on at all times," Roland ordered. Separating was risky. Keeping in contact would be essential. He took another survey of the junction before giving the order, "Move out," and they each walked into their corresponding tunnels.

Walking the northern tunnel demanded patience. Curve after curve presented itself as he went along, and behind each could be another obstacle, another setback. Roland had had his fill of setbacks. His line of soldiers followed close behind but must have been spreading out farther and farther as each curve narrowed the tunnel down to allow only one at a time to squeeze through.

Roland rounded another curve, only to see yet another one ahead of him. His patience was wearing thin. "I'm getting a fair amount of turns here. Are you sure this is headed north?"

HARRIS KNEW IT was only a matter of time before Roland would bring that up. "Did I not mention? Our former miner drew that tunnel as nothing but a long squiggle. He said he'd never gotten an accurate count of the number of turns."

"Then how can you be sure his map is accurate at all?" Roland's voice sounded more annoyed than wary.

"Miners don't forget their mental maps when getting lost means ending up dead. The tunnels are right, we just have to get to the other end of them."

"A little warning would have been appreciated." He was definitely annoyed.

Of course, Roland had no idea what Harris had been dealing with. His tunnel had shrunk and shrunk until he had no choice but to crawl along the length of it.

"I certainly didn't get any warning about the coffin-like conditions of my tunnel." Harris took another check of the tunnel ahead with his flashlight. More of the same. At least it didn't appear to get any smaller. "What kind of conditions are you getting, Lia?"

"Oh, I have no doubt I'm heading up." Her voice was winded.

"At least one of us is getting what we expected." Harris said with a sigh.

"AND THEN SOME." Lia's tunnel had presented an upward climb right out of the junction. It had only gotten more and more vertical as she went. The section ahead was about to require a scramble up a rock face. "It always has to be the high ground, doesn't it."

"You wanted sniper sub-command. It comes with the territory," Harris responded.

Lia took the first step up onto the rock face. This wasn't going to be easy. "You're just punishing me for being a better shot than you," she said between breaths.

"Believe me, I wish I was climbing right now."

Roland's voice cracked into the conversation. *"Save your energy. Keep the chatter to a minimum."*

Then, a fourth person entered the conversation. *"Don't be a spoil sport, Roland."* It was the cold, slithering sound of Martrim's voice.

Lia came to a dead stop mid-climb.

"Your Sub-Commander's friendly dialogue is the only thing keeping me entertained while I wait for you up here on the surface."

There was a pause before anyone responded.

"MARTRIM, I PRESUME?" Roland said with confidence. "I can't be certain from the sound of your voice alone, since I didn't give you the chance to use it when we last met."

"You presume correctly, only I prefer to be addressed as Commander Martrim *now."*

Roland came to a standstill at the point of the next hairpin turn. There was no reason to keep moving until they settled this. "Then I guess some thanks is in order."

"Was it you who pinned the stars on my uniform?" There was an air of smugness in Martrim's voice, particularly odd for a tin can.

Roland decided to throw it right back at him. "I might as well have. It was only after my army proved its strength that you gained command. Up until that point, your superiors probably saw you as a paranoid, delusional waste of nanites."

"A formidable army and an ego to match. We're more alike than you think, Roland."

That suggestion only made him want to sever more of Martrim's limbs. "Am I really meant to believe that you have soldiers at every surface point out of this mine? You'd be thinned out over parces. Even a Unity Commander doesn't have that many troops at his disposal."

"Oh, not every surface point. I agree, that would be a waste of resources. No, I've chosen to cover the western, the northern, and the peak, the very three you're aiming for as we speak. The good news is, you're all at about the halfway mark, so I won't have much longer to wait. Except for you, Roland. Those curves give you about twice the distance to cover."

HE HAD TO be posturing. He was only listening. He was just guessing.

"I'm calling your bluff," Roland's voice said. He had obviously thought the same. *"You're either at our backs or on the surface, blind to our position."*

A bead of sweat dripped off the end of Harris's nose. Crawling along had been hard enough work. Now the tunnel seemed to be heating up like an oven.

"Even you can't see through a mountain, Martrim," Roland added.

Or can he? Harris pressed the radio hard into his ear. A low hum vibrated against his eardrum.

"Then how do I know our little discourse just brought you all to a standstill?" Martrim responded. Yes, he could see them.

"Back now!" Harris commanded to the soldiers behind him. He wasn't about to get stuck in this maze only to emerge, freshly spit roasted, right into Martrim's grasp. There was no way Roland would let that happen either.

"Sub-commanders to the last checkpoint," Roland ordered. *"Radios off."*

HEARING MARTRIM'S VOICE hit Lia like a punch to the eye. Hearing Roland order them back winded her like a kick in the stomach.

She descended and dropped off the rock wall, her soldiers following. Then, she let the gravity of the mountain help her race back down to the junction. The flares were still glowing, though their colors had all muddied to gray.

Lia was the first to arrive. Her unit was the smallest and easiest to navigate through.

Harris arrived soon after, sweat dripping down his brow.

"How did he do it?" she asked.

"It's the radios," Harris said between pants. "He's not just listening, he's using them to calibrate our positions."

Roland wasted no time as he marched into the junction. "How can he do that through all this rock? The signal would bounce everywhere."

Harris had no response other than a shrug. It was tech they didn't have, but that didn't mean it didn't exist.

"So, we go on without them," Lia suggested. "He won't know when any of us are going to hit the surface."

"Neither will we. If we don't coordinate our attack, if any one of our units engages without the others, we'll be outnumbered." That was Roland's way of saying they would get picked off one by one. "Is there any other way to get to the surface?"

Harris was already consulting the map. "Only one." He pointed to the tunnel that led farther into the heart of the mountain. "There is an exit halfway down. It's a goods lift, a skyway system leading down to the valley floor."

"I'm not running for the valley when I know he's up on that mountain," Roland firmly declared

"We can get off at the first drop point. Circle back through the woods. He won't see us coming through those trees."

Roland looked around at the growing numbers of soldiers backing up into the junction as he considered. "All right. Harris's unit in the lead. Radios off. We travel as one."

It all seemed too simple.

Lia grasped Roland's arm. "He's up there baiting us to make our next move. He'll figure out where we're headed soon enough, or just flood the tunnel with Unis… unless we offer up an alternative."

"What alternative?"

The plan seemed to come to her in a flash. "Send soldiers carrying half the radios in every direction, including the way we came in. Then, leave the rest of the radios here in the junction. It will look like we've sent scouts to find another way out."

"He'll know it's a ruse," Harris said.

"But he'll have no choice but to keep watch on our signals, just in case one of them is the real thing. It may keep him distracted long enough to get everyone out before he finds our exit. Especially if I stay and talk to him."

"Why would you do that?" Roland was seething.

"He didn't have to talk to us. He didn't have to admit he knew where we were. He's toying with us. So, let's make sure he has something to play with. Knowing he has your wife on the line will definitely hold his interest."

Roland took another look at the clump of soldiers gathering around the junction. He was trying to think of a better way to use Martrim's mind games to their advantage. There wasn't one. He turned back to Lia. "How will you find us?"

"Mark the tunnel. I'll know when to follow."

Roland's orders went filtering down each tunnel. They had to hope there was nothing lost in translation as it traveled by word of mouth down the line into the darkness.

Harris stomped out the other flares and lit a bright green one at the entrance to the tunnel heading deep into the mountain. "Ready," he declared.

They each switched their radios back on. Roland pulled his out of his ear and tossed it to the ground.

Harris was about to do the same, then reconsidered. He said in a loud and clear voice, "You're a twisted excuse for a human, and I look forward to watching Roland skin you like a rabbit," then pulled the radio out of his ear and tossed it aside. "He's all yours," he said to Lia as he headed into the tunnel.

Roland took Lia's hand before following. She gave him a reassuring smile, trying to convince him—and herself—that there was only so much harm Martrim could inflict over a radio. She let his hand slide out of hers, then turned her attention to the conversation she had tasked herself with.

"Was that the colorful Sub-Commander I just heard?" Martrim's voice slithered into her ear as she donned her radio.

"He just wanted to make sure our next conversation got off to a good start." Lia stepped to the side of the junction to let the flood of soldiers filter past her and into the tunnel marked with the green flare.

"Ah, Lia, isn't it? What a pleasure it is to hear your sweet, feminine tones after such a gruff greeting from your cohort. Don't I get a rebuttal?"

"Debate isn't really his style."

One by one each officer was dropping their radios to the ground as they passed.

"Then what about your illustrious leader? Can't I have a word with him?" Martrim asked with a heavily put-on politeness.

"Seems they're both bored of you. But I'm still here."

"And I have no doubt you'll keep me very entertained, Miss McMillan."

Lia froze up.

"Am I to take it from your sudden lack of witty retorts that you didn't expect me to know your full name? It is Miss Lianna McMillan of the Waterford township if I'm not mistaken."

The line of soldiers was thinning out. Lia focused on the growing constellation of little orange lights from the radios around her feet, centering, calming. "Am I supposed to be impressed by your ability to read a birth certificate? Family records are no challenge for a Unity bloodhound to track down. Any one of your drones could have dug that up."

"What impresses, Miss McMillan, is your lengthy record of anti-Unity crimes. There are certainly a lot of uniformed bodies in your wake, including those of one hundred and eighty-three hopeful young recruits, killed in

the most infamous operation conducted by those who called themselves the Initiative, a name which lacks creativity if you ask me. Fails to strike fear."

Creative or not, the Initiative was a name she never wanted to hear again. She hoped none of the officers that had yet to relinquish their radios were actually listening. She was tired of explaining that particular part of her past. At least it was a topic that would keep Martrim occupied.

"If you truly are such a good investigator, then you would have figured out by now that my fingerprints weren't on any of those bombs."

"Don't worry, Miss McMillan. Your pathetically mortal soul was saved from damnation by one"—he paused as if he were consulting notes—*"Toban Willis. Do you recall that name?"*

All too well, Lia thought. She let herself sink to the ground. "I do."

"He pledged to your ignorance of their plans just before he was sentenced to death. Seems an awfully moral thing for a baby killer to do."

She didn't disagree. She had spent so much of her life certain that she had been blamed for the entire operation as punishment for daring to leave. That seemed much more likely than a tearful confession, not out of Toban. She paused long enough for the last of the feet to march past her, and the last of the radios to be left behind.

She was alone now, with nothing but the orange glow of radios and Martrim's cold voice for company.

"Was he a good man, Miss McMillan?"

Lia gave this fair consideration, taking into account the information that Martrim had just shared with her, but it hadn't changed her feelings about Toban. "No."

EARNING A BOUNTY

HE PRESSED HER hard into the mattress with an oxygen depleting kiss. Lia dug her nails into the meat of his thick forearm. He was either going to like that or get pissed off at her. Toban responded by slap-grabbing her thighs and twisting her legs around him like twine.

Guess he liked it. She could feel them approaching the line between passion and mania. She pulled back a bit, relaxing her legs back down. Mania was not a pleasant place to visit.

A door slammed downstairs. Toban stopped all at once, one ear perked up to listen. Male voices murmured up through the floorboards.

"They're back!" he said excitedly to the air around Lia. He pushed off the mattress, scooped up his clothes, and was leaping into them as he left the room.

Lia lay back to catch her breath. The morning light filtering through the window was lovely. The old sheet it had to pass through was not. Suddenly, she wanted nothing more than to leave that room.

Toban's wide shoulders were hunched over something on the counter when she entered the kitchen. Wilson's hard-edged face was looking down from the other side. Lia could see a peek of what looked like engineering plans for a massive building.

"Morning, Lia." It was James's soft voice, an unusual match to his giant body. He was always nice to her.

"Hi, James." She was always nice back. Being the two youngest people in the house had given them an unspoken desire to look out for each other. As always, the rest of the activity went on without acknowledging either of them.

"Vents. Pipes. Storage," Toban muttered as he scanned the plans. "It's perfect." He launched himself over the counter to grab Wilson's face in enthusiastic thanks.

Wilson shoved him back. "Yeah, it's great. We still need a way to get in," he said in his usual monotone way.

"Don't worry, boys. You can leave that part to us." Lia's presence finally got acknowledged with an arm around her waist.

"Us?" she asked.

Toban dismissed the others before he even began to explain.

It was appallingly simple. So simple that Lia marveled at how it had not been immediately dismissed. These so-called revolutionaries were supposed to be the most undermining force against the Unis since the war of Resistance, the infected thorn in their sides, and this was the best their master planner could come up with?

"You wanted to be included. You've practically been begging for it, and now I'm giving you the most important job of all. What's your problem?" Toban threw his arms out wide, as if she were aggravating him beyond his capacity to cope. Really, she had said very little.

"I don't beg. And I don't believe this is the best plan."

"Academy guards keep their keys on their uniforms. Easiest way to get keys off them is get them out of uniform," he explained as if the concept were somehow beyond her comprehension. "It's a no fail plan. Even if he keeps his keys up his ass, he'd unclench for you, babe." He reached a hand out to her hip.

She slapped it back. "Easiest way to get the keys would be to stick a gun in his face and ask for them."

"Then he runs off, raises the alarm, and boom. We're finished. But if we sneak them away, he might not even notice till he goes to work the next morning. But by then...."

"Yes, what exactly would have happened by then?" she asked, one eyebrow raised.

"It's better if you don't know."

"I won't say anything."

"But you can't say anything if you don't know anything!" Toban's volume encouraged the slamming of a door from somewhere else in the house. He chose to calm himself by putting his hands on her hips and giving them a squeeze.

"At least give me a gun for protection."

Toban shook his head vigorously "No, absolutely not. You get caught with a gun, we're all axed."

"That won't happen."

"Oh, yeah? Where you gonna hide it?" He pulled her body up against his.

"I don't understand why you would want me to do this. Why it doesn't bother you."

"You think it doesn't bother me? That's crazy. I can't stand to think about any other man touching you, let alone Uni scum. It kills me babe." He demonstrated his pain with another hip squeeze. "But no sacrifice is too great." He wrapped his arms around the small of her back and locked his hands together. His eyes were sparkling with a wild energy. "Tell me yes."

Lia considered the notion of sacrifices. She had already made a few. Doing so had only made her stronger. What was one more? Perhaps the simplest plan was the best plan. "Fine."

Toban pulled her in for another suction enforced kiss, then threw a victorious fist into the air and ran off to tell the others.

Lia stood alone in the kitchen, preparing herself to make yet another sacrifice.

THIS TUNNEL WAS significantly more welcoming than the sinuous northern tunnel had been, wide and flat, with a steady downward slope. They were able to walk along at a good clip, and would be on their way to ambushing Martrim soon enough, assuming Harris was right about there being an exit. Roland tried not to focus on what might happen if there wasn't.

Harris stopped to light another flare. The flash of green highlighted the concern on his brow. Perhaps he wasn't sure if they would find the exit either. Then again, there might be something else concerning him. It had certainly been weighing on Roland's mind.

"You're sure you're leaving enough?"

"She'll see them. All she has to do is leave before the first one dies out," Harris responded as he carefully laid the flare off to one side, well out of the path of the marching feet that would follow behind them.

They lead on. The sound of footfalls and the low murmurs of conversation bounced around the tunnel behind them.

It wasn't long before Harris said what was on his mind. "No bikes. No signal mirrors. No radios. And pretty soon, no flares." He took a pause, letting it sink in. "Should we just hand over our weapons and body armor and go home?"

Their growing list of disadvantages had not escaped Roland's attention, but it was not as dire as Harris thought. They had fought with less. They had won with less. All they had to do now was believe they could do it again. All Roland had to do was remind him of that. "Tell me it's not worth the chance to put a gun to the back of his head."

Harris responded with a smile.

"**YOU WOULD SPEAK** *so ill of your ex-lover?*" Martrim's voice asked of her.

Lia's stomach did a flip. She wasn't sure if it was referring to Toban as her lover or the sound of those words coming out of Martrim's mouth that nauseated her more. "Most people do, but I doubt that's something you have any experience with." Finding a way to add insult to her response had prevented the nausea from rising.

"The joys, pleasures, and pains of youth are a universal experience, darling."

She wasn't sure what was worse, when he called her Miss McMillan, or darling. She stifled her disgust in another insult. "Please don't share any of your personal experiences, unless you're attempting to kill me with laughter."

"No, Miss McMillan. I'd rather keep talking about you." Miss McMillan was worse. It felt as if she were a child again, being spoken to by some saccharine schoolmarm. *"Tell me then,"* Martrim continued. *"If it wasn't the affections of your bed fellow that kept you on the Initiative's side, then what did?"*

She gave this another moment's consideration. She wouldn't say naivety. There was no weakness worth admitting to that snake. She wouldn't say teenage hormones combined with pent-up aggression. That would just make him reminisce again. And she definitely wouldn't say that she actually liked surmounting every horrific challenge that Toban presented to her. That would only excite his not-so-inner sadist.

She simply said, "The thrill of the hunt."

THE ONLY PLACE to check how she looked was in the darkened window behind the sheet. The dress might have covered enough flesh, but the material was thin enough to caress and highlight every curve, both defining and diminutive. Even in her translucent reflection, Lia could pick out the details that were bound to catch the attention of any person with a penchant for the female form. She thought of Toban having to take her place if they discovered their target of choice had other inclinations. She was still laughing about it when he entered the room.

"You're going to kill it, babe," he said in the darkened reflection.

She dropped the sheet and turned around. "It's not very subtle."

"What about you is?" He stepped in closer to inspect her with wandering eyes and hands. "Now you remember everything? 'Cause this ain't gonna do us any good if you go for the wrong mark."

"Name, rank, age, weight, hair color, eye color, drink of choice, though what good it does him, I have no idea. Yeah. I got it."

"All right. No need to get touchy. I just want to make sure this goes as smooth as all your little silky bits." He ran his fingers down her sides, wrapped his arms around her, and pulled her into a slow dance, swaying to the music humming in his own head. He stepped away suddenly, straight back to business. "James is waiting outside."

Lia nodded and turned away.

He pulled her back for one final word of encouragement, which he whispered straight into her ear. "He won't even know what hit him."

James drove her into the city on his old, well-traveled motorcycle. It seemed a less than fitting choice, given how little protection the dress offered from the elements, not to mention the road. Luckily, James was their most responsible wheel-man. It didn't take them long to get on the highway.

The Initiative kept quarters in the bad part of the city, but not too far from the respectable center. The road became smooth and pristine as they took the final turn toward the block of towers that surrounded Io City Center. Lights filled the city. The towers shimmered, catching every color from below like facets in a giant gem.

"It's almost pretty at night," James said over the roar of the engine. "Looks like stars."

"Sure, but do you ever look up?"

He was already looking up before Lia could reconsider suggesting that her driver take his eyes off the road, but they remained stable and smooth, so she dared to join him.

The sky above was glowing a sickly yellow in the flood of lights from below.

"I don't see anything," he said as he returned his eyes to the road.

"Exactly. They put all the stars down here so you would forget they used to be up there."

James remained in silent contemplation throughout the rest of their drive.

The stuttering of the engine bounced around the narrow lane-ways as they drove into what was clearly the hub of Io City nightlife. Lia found it rather ironic how many people were out and about, dressed up and jaunting from one booming club to another. How many of them were even capable of enjoying themselves?

James pulled over and clicked off the engine at the far end of one of the quieter lane-ways.

Lia could see the sign for her destination garishly flashing in the distance.

"This is as far as I can take you. If any of them see a heap like this pull up to one of those classy joints, they'll get suspicious," James said.

"You're telling me this is the classy part of town?" Lia pulled the wind knots out of her hair and smoothed down the might-as-well-be-invisible dress. "Where will you be if I need backup?"

"Here." He sheepishly pointed to the ground he was standing on.

"Oh. Okay." Lia was truly on her own. There was only one thing to do—turn her chin up and march off to the club with confidence. She could feel James's eyes on her back as she walked away. He was worried.

Lights spun. Music vibrated the floor. The center of the club was a frenzy of movement. Lia examined the people in the crowd. No matter how frenetic their bodies, their faces remained expressionless. They might as well have been dead.

If the Unity Guards hadn't stood out in their light absorbing uniforms, their total lack of movement would have given them away. They were standing together in a clump by the bar.

What for? Lia thought. All the liquor in the city wouldn't even give them a light buzz.

She decided to spot her target before walking past with her best attention-seeking stride. He looked a bit younger than he was. Perhaps the nanites had preserving benefits. Still, he was old enough not to take for granted the advances of an attractive eighteen-year-old.

She was in the midst of her strut when a flash of light off a piece of metal caught her attention. The keys were hanging from his belt.

By then, several sets of eyes were following her across the room. She chose to pretend she hadn't noticed and casually approached the bar. She picked a spot just out of conversation range and hoped they might go back into their quiet clump of non-movement.

Half a drink later, no one was watching her. Now all she had to do was decide if she could pull off a snatch and grab, or if a slow brush and a bit of flirtation would do the trick. The mere thought of how itchy the fabric of his uniform probably was reminded her of how little she liked this plan to begin with. Snatch and grab it was.

She ran one hand along the bar as she marched toward them, feigned a light, accidental bump, and had the keys palmed before she knew it. Her target looked at her.

Is he annoyed that he was bumped into? Pleased to see who did it? Is he feeling anything at all? She didn't stick around long enough to find out. With an apology and a wink, she turned and walked off. She could feel eyes on her back as she walked away. Perhaps he was a little pleased after all.

TOBAN HELD THE victory keys up like a torch. Everyone in the room cheered. "This, my fellows of the Initiative, signals the dawning of a new day. Those robots will finally know the true price of their unworthy pride."

Another cheer went up. It was as if Toban had manifested the keys out of thin air.

"Don't you want to know how I got them?" Lia asked, seeking her piece of the glory.

"Oh, we know," Wilson said with a wry smile.

"Only you would think it would be that quick," she said back, happy to see his smug smile drop away.

"Later, babe. Right now, we have a lot of planning to do." Toban gave her a quick squeeze as he swept past. "I need my crew in the basement."

Everyone flooded out of the room.

Lia's brief moment of victory was over before it had even arrived. She sat down and slipped off her shoes before she noticed James was still sitting in the corner. "Don't you belong downstairs?"

"I've been put in the 'better if I don't know' category. I'm just the driver." At least she wasn't the only one.

"Your way was definitely better than Toban's," James said with a chuckle.

"I just got lucky."

"Good thing, too. I mean, sure he might not have noticed his keys were gone till he needed 'em, but he sure would have known who took 'em when he did notice."

The brutal truth James had just spoken hit Lia like a smack in the face. He was right. She was bait. Sacrificial bait. Her mouth fell open. Her fingers began to tremble.

James looked at her with wide eyes. "Wait. I didn't mean it to sound like that. Toban wouldn't let anything bad happen to you." James didn't even sound convinced of that as he said it.

Lia let out a manic giggle. The heat of tears stung her eyes. All those months, and she hadn't seen the ugly face of reality looking her right in the eye.

"Okay, he made a mistake," James continued to stammer. "I'm sure he didn't realize—"

"He never realizes." Saying it out loud brought up another manic giggle. She couldn't hold them back. Lia had to stand up and walk out her nerves.

"Maybe he was too focused on the big picture." James didn't sound convinced of anything he said on Toban's behalf.

"And neither of us has any idea what that big picture is, do we? Are you so sure it's something worth glossing over the details for?"

"You're not a detail."

"No. I'm a pawn." Her mania melted into tears. She let them stream out, slow, steady, and silent.

James squirmed. "Okay. He was wrong. No excuses. It's not like it hasn't happened before. It's not the first time he's treated you like you're...."

What was he going to say? Disposable? Convenient? Worthless? Whatever it was, she didn't need to hear it. Lia stopped her tears and her trembles with one long, slow breath, then turned to face James. "Then help me teach him a lesson."

LIA EYED THE flare. It was beginning to dim, but Martrim was far from finished prying up the boards she had nailed over the door to her past. She would keep him talking as long as it took. He wouldn't have the chance to hack anyone up as long as she was keeping him amused.

"You can't possibly think it was all so terrible, Miss McMillan. After all, it was those loyal members of the Initiative that gave you your first taste of anarchy."

"Not to mention the gift of a price on my head."

"You are, indeed, worth a tidy bundle." He sounded vaguely impressed. She fought the urge to ask how much her bounty was. *"Do you not find that flattering?"*

"I prefer to earn my stars rather than be branded with them."

"Funny you should work so hard to distance yourself from the murder of a few paltry recruits, when I have no doubt you've lost count of the number of officers you've assassinated by now. Not to mention a bounty hunter or two who died under rather mysterious circumstances in your wake."

"First, they were hopeful recruits, and now they're paltry? I didn't think poker faces could be so fickle."

"I am also capable of impatience, Miss McMillan."

Don't tempt me, she thought. "Ask me a direct question, and you'll get a direct answer. I have nothing to hide."

There was a pause, as if he were consulting his script. Maybe he didn't know what to say when she wasn't giving him the run around. Maybe honesty would try his patience even more than attitude. *Good.*

"Well, you've made your feelings for the rather predatory Mister Willis quite clear. What about the rest of them? Were they all bad people, Miss McMillan?"

"No. Some of them were just very easy to manipulate."

"Not you, though."

"We have met." What she heard through the radio sounded almost like a chuckle.

"You are trying indeed." He took a breath, as if nearly laughing had been a great effort for him. *"They must have been awfully upset when their little gang lost your unique skill set."*

"That's one way to put it."

TOBAN'S GREAT PLAN must have gone into action the next morning. He was gone before sunrise, along with all of his favorite cronies, James, and the big truck they kept parked under the dead tree in the back.

Lia had enough time to get in a bit of quick draw practice and pack her bag. She had just thrown the last ball of clothing in when she heard the truck pull up.

Outside, Toban and his cronies flooded out of the back gate. James stumbled out of the cabin. His face looked like ash. His knees wobbled. He fell onto all fours. Toban and Wilson scooped him up, swearing as they went, and forced him to stumble into the house.

Lia still had the chance to slip out the back before anyone thought to look for her, but she had to know what had happened. She rushed into the living room just as Toban and Wilson were tossing James onto a chair. He was sweating and panting in panic.

"What happened?" Lia asked.

"He's a pussy. That's what happened." That was all the information Wilson had to offer.

Toban had already made his way across the room and was tuning in the vizo.

Lia knelt down to look into James's face. He was just about to say something when the vizo focused and the sound blared on. He fixed his horrified eyes on the screen. Lia's gaze followed.

A distant image showed a massive blaze consuming a huge compound of fortified buildings. *"The flames then reached the armory, setting off a series of explosions. Burning shrapnel flew across the campus, alighting other structures,"* said the voice coming from the vizo. *"Eight hundred and seventy two recruits are currently training at the Academy, though we have yet to confirm how many were on campus this morning."*

"You firebombed the Academy!" Lia had marched over to Toban's side without even noticing. He was kneeling in front of the screen, fists clenched in excitement as he soaked it all in.

He responded without shifting his eyes from the vizo. "Come on, babe. You knew you were yanking keys off an Academy Guard."

"I thought you were going to steal their weapons, sabotage their pipes, not kill the students!" She was being shushed. Someone was trying to shove her out of the way. She didn't care.

"Plenty of 'em were juiced. They won't all die. Some of them will just have a really bad day." He smiled. A few people in the room chuckled. They were drinking in the pain they had caused like it was top shelf golden.

Lia sunk to her knees and stared at the screen. Somewhere among those buildings, somewhere in that midst of that chaos, somewhere lost in the flames, was Arin. Her tears would have broken loose if not for the distraction of James vomiting all over the floor behind them.

"Weak, man." Again, that was all Wilson had to say.

Lia leapt up the stairs two at a time. There was no need to sneak. There was no time to wait. She was leaving now. She raced back down, but Toban was in her path before she could reach the door.

"Whoa. Where are you off to?"

"I'm gone. I want no part of this."

"No, no, no. It's too late now. You wanted in. Remember? You got us the keys. You're full Initiative, babe. You're not going anywhere." He was sliding forward so gradually, she didn't notice she had been backing away from the door.

Lia planted her feet. "I will never be one of you twisted freaks." She took a step around him.

He snatched her wrist and yanked her back.

"Let go!"

"I'm afraid I can do that." He sounded colder and angrier than he ever had before. He had just killed. He had just enjoyed it. She wasn't about to be next.

Lia's quick draw went exactly as she had practiced. She had her gun pointed at Toban's forehead before he drew in his next breath.

"I think you can." Her voice was as steady as her hand.

"Which one of you bucket heads gave her a gun?" Wilson yelled.

She hoped James was still too busy being sick to give himself away.

"It doesn't matter," Toban said. "She doesn't know how to use it." He was still clamped on to her wrist. *Good thing he picked the wrong hand.*

Lia flicked her aim up at the ceiling. Three bangs in sequence were followed by the shattering of three lights in a row.

She turned her aim back to his forehead. "I'm a pretty quick learner."

Toban released her wrist with a little smile of satisfaction on his face. "All right, I underestimated you. That only makes you more valuable to our cause."

"Your cause has turned you into the same sick, soulless robots you've been fighting. Worse, because you actually enjoy what you do." She backed toward the door.

Toban stood perfectly still with that same smile on his face. "This is the wrong move, babe. You step out that door, and you're on your own. But stay with us, and we can protect you."

She laughed the same manic laugh, only it came this time without the nerves and without the tears. "If I stay, I end up being a human shield. You all will," she announced to the whole room.

James was looking up at her with fear-filled eyes, but he didn't move a muscle.

She turned her eyes back to Toban. He was still smiling. If she had to guess, she'd say he was turned on. He really was twisted. She felt out the doorknob without shifting her eyes or her aim. The fresh air that came rushing into that stale house felt like the embrace of freedom.

Lia smiled right back at Toban and offered him one final thought. "Goodbye… babe."

FOURTEEN

LIA HAD TO stand. The chill of the rock was starting to travel up her spine. She wanted to walk in some warmth but couldn't risk moving. If Martrim could tell there was only one signal in the junction, pacing in circles, he would know exactly where she was.

"This discussion reminds me of the one we had all those years ago. Do you remember?" Martrim asked.

"You mean when you told me you were a gentleman? Yes, I think of it whenever I need a good laugh."

"Cheeky, Miss McMillan." He almost sounded as if he were enjoying himself. *"No, I mean when I told you there were other paths you could have chosen for yourself."*

"Is this going to end with another attempt at recruitment?" She was starting to get the shivers. Lia marched in place and rubbed the heat back into her arms. She wasn't about to let him hear even a hint of it in her voice.

"Certainly not. You're far too passionate for my army."

"That goes without saying."

"You're far too emotional for any army, darling. Your actions are driven by love, hate, and who knows what other nonsense goes on in that head of yours."

"It's called human nature."

"It's called weakness, and it loses wars."

"Of course, you never get distracted by anything, do you?"

"Even the pleasure of your company has yet to pull me away from watching your little display. How do you decide who goes and who stays? Do you draw straws?"

Lia took a glance at the flare. Nearly out. She transferred a bit of chill into laughter. "That's it. You've figured out our greatest strategic secret."

"You sound as if you're enjoying yourself, Miss McMillan. Or, should I be addressing you as Missus…?"

He was waiting for her to fill in the blank. Suddenly, she was no longer cold. "It's quite clear whose records you haven't found. You're still after that one big catch, aren't you, Martrim? But all you've fished up so far are guppies."

"Chum does eventually attract the shark."

"That shark will bite your head off before you ever see him coming."

"Oh, I doubt that." He took another moment to consult his unseen record of Lia's life. *"Rumor has it you two have been blessed with a little resistor."*

Lia froze up again. The thought of any mention of her son on Martrim's lips made her want to reach through the radio and strangle him. She waited too long to respond.

"What? No clever confirmation or well phrased denial, Miss McMillan? Have I, as you emotional types say, struck a nerve?"

"I just don't believe in dragging children into war, even if only through conversation," Lia responded without giving away the sudden shuddering of her teeth.

"So, it is true." He sounded as deeply satisfied as a tin can could ever get. *"I suppose it's best I send one of you home alive then, lest I continue the ill reputation set by my predecessors."*

He had struck something deeper than a nerve. The thought of home, the notion of not making it back to the child she had left there, shook loose a part of Lia's foundation. She summoned enough stability for a response. "And how are you going to decide which? Draw straws?"

"I'm sure fate will deliver a decision soon enough." There was another pause, another consultation of some piece of information. *"I wonder if Roland is going to wish he had those few soldiers you sent off with the radios at his back when we ambush him on the skyway."*

Lia was running before she knew it. She flew past the flare just as it went out.

Martrim's voice slithered into her ear. *"Like I said, far too emotional. I can see you, Miss McMillan."*

She stopped long enough to switch off and pocket her radio. She pulled out her flashlight. There was nothing ahead but an empty tunnel, and the dim light of a single dying flare in the distance.

The flare snuffed out.

Lia raced into the darkness.

A SPILL OF light ahead revealed another tunnel branching softly to the right. Roland blinked as his eyes adjusted to the return of daylight.

The short offshoot ended at a sheer drop, straight down the cliff face. Just a leap beyond the drop, an aged wooden platform hung from thick ropes. The complex system of ropes and pulleys overhead was supported by wooden towers jutting out of a gorge between two ridges. Identical platforms dangled at even intervals along the ropes, an unknown number of them, leading down to the valley floor in the invisible distance.

"How reliable is this?" Roland asked, though he knew it was too late to consider any other option.

"It was built to transport raw minerals by the baleful. Each platform should hold as many of us as it can fit. Assuming the ropes aren't rotted." Harris looked up as he said it.

Roland's eyes followed. The ropes looked sound enough. That was the most they could assess from where they were standing. "And how fast will we travel?"

"Depends on whether or not the brakes still work."

That, they wouldn't know until they were moving. "Send word down the line. Groups of at least thirty. And tell everyone to be prepared to jump."

They prepared themselves by backing into the cave a bit before racing to the platform, if only to help alleviate the unease of having to cross that would-be-fatal gap. The platform sped into view and, one by one, they each took the leap. Boots clunked onto the wooden slab. Ropes squeaked. The platform shuddered. They spread out quickly to even out their weight. The slight swaying and worrisome creaking subsided.

"Weapons up. Stay alert," Roland reminded them.

Harris pulled the brake.

The platform jiggled and began a slow, shaky descent toward the valley. They focused eyes and aim on the ridges at either side of the skyway. The next platform swayed past them and up to the exit. The next group of soldiers jumped on. No screams indicating any of them had fallen. No sounds at all, aside from the creaking of ropes and clunking of old mechanics.

"Something about this doesn't sit right," Roland had to admit.

"You mean the eerie silence coming from a mountain that we know ought to be crawling with Unis," Harris said.

"It's too silent altogether. There's not even any… birdsong." It was a trap! "Get down, now!" Roland shouted just as a line of Unity soldiers popped up on both ridges. Bullets rained down on them, cracking into the wood, pinging off their armor. "Return fire!"

They clumped into a defensive huddle and blanketed the ridges with gunfire. The cracks and booms of battle filled the gorge.

LIA SHOUTED AS she ran, though the sound of her voice was swallowed by the emptiness ahead of her. Another dim flare appeared. She doubled her pace, managing to pass before it snuffed out of existence.

She was about to shout again when another sound bounced down the tunnel toward her. She slid to a stop and listened. For a moment she was certain it was the sound of the tunnel collapsing in on itself.

No, the distant cracks were not rocks hitting rocks. It was gunfire slicing through the air.

Lia ran faster than she ever had before.

ONE OF THEM dropped, just a shoulder wound. The others closed in to protect her as they fired back. The gunfire only increased as more and more of their soldiers flew out of the tunnel and onto the platforms. Rocks along the ridge shattered. Bodies in dark uniforms dropped out of sight.

Roland spotted a single man who stood higher than all the others. It was Martrim. He held up his rifle with one hand and waved with the other one.

Roland took aim at Martrim.

Martrim took aim at Roland.

The hot sting of a bullet zipped past Roland's ear.

Martrim's arm jerked back, probably a shot to the bicep.

Not good enough. Roland took aim again.

Martrim ducked out of sight.

"Cut the main brake!" Harris yelled over the barrage. "Speed us up!" He pointed to the brake above Roland's head.

Roland glanced back up the line of platforms. Their soldiers were still leaping out of the tunnel. "What about the rest of them?"

"They'll make it. I have a plan."

Roland pulled out his sword and sliced off the brake.

ANOTHER FLARE APPEARED, and another. Lia's thighs burned. Her lungs felt as if they were about to explode. Another light appeared, not a dim spot but a soft glow. *Daylight!* Lia's own momentum sent her stumbling into the wall as she rounded the curve.

Fuzzy silhouettes ahead of her raced toward the bright glow.

"Wait!" Lia shouted, but they had leapt into the light before her shout could be heard.

Her eyes adjusted as she raced to follow and found focus just as the edge of the tunnel sped into view. Lia came to a sliding stop where the tunnel dropped off. Loose shale slid out from under her and careened into the valley. She looked up.

Unity soldiers lined both sides of the gorge. Platforms carrying the Resistors were speeding down toward the unknown.

Lia prepared herself to jump, but the Unis got there first. They sprung like deer over the ridge and onto the empty platforms. She was still standing in the open when a platform covered in black uniforms whooshed past.

A barrage of gunfire sent Lia ducking back into the tunnel. She watched from the shadows as the platform turned and began to descend. Another followed, and another, each covered in Unity soldiers, chasing their soldiers down into the valley.

She could take out one or two as they passed, but what difference would it make? One gun alone was nothing against those numbers. She crept as close as she dared to the sharp edge of sunlight on the tunnel wall.

Another platform passed, and another. It seemed as if the Unis would never stop coming. Then, an empty platform flew past, and another. Lia dared to creep toward the edge.

The ridges were vacant. The Unis were racing into the valley, the sounds of gunfire descending right along with them.

Now was her chance. Lia backed into position, counted out the seconds, and raced for the next platform. She landed on her knees, stabilized her position, and prepared her rifle. Even if it was only one or two tin cans she could shoot off the last platform, that was one or two less. She readied her aim.

ZIP! A bullet nicked one of the ropes holding her platform. She scanned the ridge. Nothing. The platform ahead. None of them were even looking in her direction.

Three more ZIPS and three more bullets shot through the same rope. It unraveled like a tornado. Lia had just enough time to grasp the edge of the platform before the rope snapped.

One corner of the platform dropped away. Lia held on with one hand and made a desperate grab for her rifle with the other. It slid into the trees below.

She reached up to grab the edge with the other hand, but bullets cracked into the wood all around her. Whoever was shooting wasn't trying to hit her but trying to make her fall.

She whipped a pistol out of her holster and peppered the ridge with bullets. Nothing.

Her other hand was burning. Her fingers felt like they were being yanked right out of their sockets. She reached up and tried to claw her way to stability.

Another bullet, another crack, and the aged board she was gripping splintered in half.

Lia screamed as the platform shrank away, and the forest floor raced up to meet her.

CEASELESS GUNFIRE HAD died down to only opportune shots. The Unis were at their back now. The shooting would begin again, only after their chase came to an end.

"That's our exit!" Harris pointed to the drop-off point below. Where one of the support towers sat in the middle of the gorge, a narrow wooden bridge extended from either side, linking the shaky platforms to the stable land.

"That's a small target!" Roland shouted, but what else were they going to do?

"We made it on, didn't we?"

Just as they prepared to take the leap, a distant sound floated down the valley and into Roland's ears, a shrill scream, fading into nothing.

It was Lianna. She was falling.

Roland would have missed the drop-off altogether if Harris hadn't shouted, "Now!"

The bridge came within reach. They made the leap just as the platform raced away from them. Now every other soldier speeding down on every other platform had to do the same.

They formed a gauntlet, arms to reach out and snatch their fellow soldiers, guns to shoot their enemies. One by one, they each leapt. Platform by platform, the Unis were closing in. The last platform of Resistors neared. The one behind it carried the first hoard of black-clad soldiers.

"Ready! Aim!" Roland shouted to the soldiers forming the wall of guns. The last platform arrived, their soldiers began leaping, and Roland gave the order. *"FIRE!"*

Bullets riddled the support tower at the center of the valley. Gears and ropes tore. Wood shattered.

Just as the last Resistance soldier made the leap, grasped to safety by the others, the top of the tower tilted to one side and tore away. The approaching Unis only got in a few stray shots before their platform dropped out from under them.

The weight of the crashing tower and the dropping platforms yanked the ropes down to the earth, sending a shockwave of destruction in both directions. The dark uniforms fell away like rocks in a landslide.

LIA'S HEAD FELT flattened at the back. Her entire spine pulsed in pain. She wheezed life back into her deflated lungs and waited for her vision to return.

A rumbling, a vibration, not from inside her own body but coming up through the ground, told her something big was headed her way. Her vision came back just in time to see a fat rope closing in from above.

She couldn't run. She could only roll.

THWACK! The rope hit the ground beside her. Its length whipped through the trees, showering branches down over her curled up body. The thunderous vibrations moved on.

Lia rolled onto her back and heaved in as much air as she could. Leaves were still gently drifting down around her when her vision grayed away.

ROLAND STOOD AT the end of the bridge and stared at the destruction below. Even in the dim light of the evening, it was quite a sight to behold. Crushed trees, shattered platforms, coils of rope strewn up and down the gorge, and somewhere down there was Lianna.

He felt Harris arrive at his back.

"How many did we lose?" Roland asked.

"Less than you'd think."

"A few is still too many."

Harris joined him in surveying the chaos they had created. "Think the fall got any of them?"

"Not enough."

"It will still take Martrim a while to pick up all the pieces."

"It may take me just as long to find Lianna."

"She said she'd find us."

Roland finally pried his eyes away from the destruction in the gorge to face Harris. "It was her. I know it was. And from what I heard, she was falling well before we took out the tower. Whether that was by chance or by design, she's down there with that monster now."

"She'll be gone before they even finish dusting off their uniforms. No one is going to lay a hand on her, not if she has anything to do with it." His confidence was genuine.

Roland should have felt the same way, but something about how it had all happened felt insidious. This wasn't an accident. "We can make camp halfway down. Our injured can rest while I search."

"You mean, while we search." Harris put a hand on his shoulder, drawing him away from the destruction below.

FOR A SPLIT second, Lia thought she had been buried alive. She sprung up to discover that it was just a light layer of foliage covering her face, darkened by the evening gloom that was settling into the valley floor.

She did a quick check. Her body, though throbbing, was intact, but all of her weapons had been lost in the fall. She was just preparing herself to stand when a nearby branch snapped. It was the kind of sound that only the movement of a large animal, like a human, could produce.

Lia glanced around to see not just one, but three hooded figures approaching through the trees. Every joint in her legs cracked as she leapt to her feet. She tossed aside branches in a frantic search for a fallen gun. Nothing but more branches.

The figures came closer, their faces lost in shadow, but their intent all too clear. Lia watched as their circle closed in on her, waiting for a weakness to reveal itself. A slight limp slowed one of them down. *Good enough.*

Lia barreled through the gap created by the limping figure, but their cohort's speed made up the difference. Arms snatched her waist and pulled her down. With frantic flailing, she freed up one leg and sent it flying into the chest of her captor, but as one grip loosened, two more sets of hands took hold. Her arms were pinned to the ground, her flying legs grasped in a bear grip. Lia was still squirming against them when a fourth figure emerged.

His hand appeared first and pushed a noxious smelling cloth against her nose and mouth. Then, his head hovered, upside down, obscured by the dark of the evening, but for a split second Lia could see his eyes. They were deeply familiar and incredibly haunting. Something about them made her want to scream.

FIFTEEN

LIA'S EYES OPENED onto pitch black. She tried to move, only to discover the arms twisted behind her back were also tied firmly to some unseen object. The ground was cold and dusty, the air around her stale and still. She calmed her breathing and struggled up into a seated position.

The blackness became a dim glow filtering through fabric. A blindfold. She put her face to her knee and pushed it up onto her forehead. The glow turned out to be a steady flame, licking away inside a single lamp that dangled overhead. She was in a round room, dug deep into rock and lined with wooden benches. She must have been somewhere within the mountain she had just emerged from.

Small niches carved into the wall bore a few long-abandoned personal effects of the miners who would have once rested on those benches. A narrow, arched doorway into a tunnel served as the only entrance and exit to the room. The tunnel beyond was dark, quiet, and as far as she could tell, empty.

Lia assessed her bonds. Thick ropes looped her wrists together and traced back to an iron ring mounted into the rock. She fingered the loops around her wrist. No give. She geared up her strength and took one hard tug at the ring. Steadfast. The only thing that might weaken either of them would be time and determination. How long she would be there alone, she couldn't know, but her determination was sound, so she began to pull on the ropes.

She tugged against the ring until her shoulders burned, then kept pulling until they went numb. She strained the rope by shuffling forward on her knees until blisters formed, then kept pulling until she had worn away her last layer of protective fabric. She twisted the ropes until her wrists were raw, then kept twisting until they were bleeding. Time lasted longer than determination.

Lia rested her back against the stone wall, her head on her knee, and considered her present fate. Martrim was the kind of man to inflict this type of torture, but not the kind who would let it unfold in his absence. She had been brought here by another hand, but whose? She was here for a reason, but what?

Footsteps sounded out in the tunnel. A single person was making a steady approach toward her. Lia turned her eyes up, firmed her jaw, and prepared to face her kidnapper. As he entered the room she found herself confronted by those same eyes, deeply familiar and incredibly haunting.

The man she was facing was Arin.

CONFRONTING THE GHOSTS

SHE HELD HER breath as he approached. They came toe to toe. He knelt to face her.

"Hello, Lia."

She drew in a sharp breath at the sound of his voice. This was no delusion created by her stint of painful isolation. This was real. Arin was alive. Arin was here. Arin was the one who had taken her.

He gently removed her blindfold and used it to brush the dust from her cheek. It was such a simple, such an intimate gesture, as if they had seen each other yesterday, as if he hadn't kept her tied up in a cave for hours, as if she had never watched him die. "Are you hurt?"

She felt her mouth open, but no sound came out.

"Were you injured when you fell?"

"No," she whispered.

Arin stood up and backed away.

Lia took in his head to toe appearance, his inscrutable face. "How… how are you here?"

"It seems your mad doctor's formula is stronger than even he realized. Works miracles."

"I saw the blood. I felt it happen. I watched you die."

"Yes. You watched your husband pull the trigger, and then what? That's exactly what I was wondering when I woke up in an underground cell. That is, after I could put two thoughts together without going half blind from the pain. Fortunately, your commander's right-hand man was too proud of himself not to share the answers."

Lia's head was spinning. She wanted to close her eyes but was afraid Arin might evaporate the second she lost sight of him. "Harris. You're saying he saved you?"

"If you could call it that. I was more of a specimen, one he'd still have locked up under a bell jar if he had his way."

Lia knew she'd been lied to. She had already drawn out Roland's ignorance of that lie, but to have it confirmed that Harris had been the one who kept the truth hidden, through years of friendship, of trust, of a connection far deeper than either of them was willing to admit to, was more than she could believe. That didn't sound like something Harris could do, not to her.

Lia's body was reeling. She dropped her head to her knee and spoke to the air, hoping it would continue to answer back in Arin's voice. "How did he do it? Why?"

"The how is apparently my unique attribute. A healing ability derived from a combination of the Unity nanites and the ones that are also in your blood. They make a very strong team. And the why? He was looking to duplicate the results, with or without my cooperation."

That sounded very much like Harris. Her shock channeled into the pain of betrayal, her pain into anger, and her anger into renewed determination. She raised her head up to face Arin. "Why didn't you come to me? Why didn't you tell me you were still alive?"

"What was I supposed to do? Walk into your fortress, shake Roland's hand, congratulate him on winning the last round?"

"You come to me, Arin. You find me. The one you've known your whole life! The one who could have died right by your side that day."

The sudden strength in her voice sent him back a step. "Yet you didn't. You didn't have to escape prison. You didn't have to rebuild your mind from the shattered pieces that were left behind."

"You have no idea what I felt that day. You have no idea what I've been through since."

He knelt, bringing them eye to eye again. "Tell me then. Tell me how terribly you've suffered, living in your palace, following your brave leader, catering to his every whim."

"I fought against him. Against every lie!" Lia jerked forward as she spat the words out.

Arin backed off and stared down the bridge of his nose at her. "Fighting? Is that what you were doing when you rode into Cleanair by his side? Or when you walked into Clearwater with your fellow soldiers in disguise? Were you fighting when you rushed to Roland's aid on the skyway?"

For a moment, she thought she might be insane. How could he know so much unless she had conjured him out of her own imagination? "How do you know all that?"

"An entire army isn't exactly easy to hide, even inside a mountain." He fished into his front pocket, and pulled out one of their earpiece radios. "Harris was kind enough to keep his radio on your command frequency."

Dizziness rushed back into Lia's body. He had been spying on them like an enemy. While she was suffering under the weight of his demise, he had been watching. While she continued to risk her life in battle, he had been watching. While she had been desperately seeking to unravel the mystery of his survival, he had simply been watching. The whole room felt as if it was spinning.

"I don't understand. Why are you sneaking around, watching us from the shadows?"

He stepped forward and leaned over her. "Because the day you had your child and your freedom within your grasp, but chose to let him ride away with all of it, was the day you stopped fighting, and the day that I started."

Arin turned his back and marched off into the tunnel.

"ARIN! DON'T LEAVE me here!" Her pleas followed him into the tunnel, shrill cries echoing all the way down and around the curve.

With every yell, he felt as if his own lungs were emptying. He had to stop and lean against the wall to catch his breath. His fingers were trembling. He clenched them into fists.

"Please... please don't leave." Her cries degraded into sobs.

He let himself sink to the ground and sat, just out of sight, listening to every soft whimper, every shuddering breath. He knew she was in pain, though she would never admit it. He knew she was frightened, though she would never show it. How could he do this to her?

"The one you've known your whole life!" Those words stung. She was so much more than just a means to an end. She could be still, but he couldn't let himself think about that. Not yet.

Her crying died down into silence, probably out of exhaustion. Arin let his own set in. He wanted to stay sharp, focused on the task at hand, but seeing her, so close, so damaged by his own actions, had been harder than he prepared for.

He sat alone in the tunnel and reminded himself of his own words of reassurance. "I have always done what I needed to. To advance, to succeed, to survive. I'm doing it for more than just myself."

LIA SAT UP straight when she heard the footsteps returning. After her shouts went unanswered, she used her time alone to rebuild her determination. If all Arin wanted was a prisoner, then he wouldn't have gone to such lengths to take her. He was planning something. She would find out what it was.

Her eyes followed as he walked into the room. He placed a jug of water on the ground, doubtlessly his bargaining tool.

She flicked her gaze away from the light of the flame dancing on its quenching surface and refused to look back. Answers would have to satiate her for the time being.

"Thirsty?" he asked as he sat on the bench opposite her.

"Why are you going from town to town, poisoning people against us?"

"I don't poison anyone. I tell them the truth. What they decide to do with it is entirely up to them."

"They're choosing to give up. To bypass their chance to fight against the Unity."

"Some have left. Some have stayed. Some are preparing to fight. Some haven't even believed a word I said. But none of them have given up."

"This is the last chance they have at keeping their land."

"So, it's turn or be turned? Become one of you or one of them? Those are the only options?" His questions were eerily similar to Martrim's. Perhaps it was a Unity interrogation tactic still hard wired into his brain.

"Do you think they can survive this war without our help?"

He stood up and pointed an accusatory finger at her. "You used to believe that they could." He took a step toward her. "You used to believe that all your strength came simply from your determination, drive, passion."

He took another step, passing beside the jug.

Lia kept her eyes fixed on his face so she wouldn't be at all tempted by its presence.

"You used to believe that every ounce of your humanity was all that you needed to survive." He crouched down to face her. "Even when you thought I was stronger than you, you still held a gun to my head and told me you knew exactly where to put a hole that wouldn't heal. Do you remember?"

"Yes."

"Were you afraid of me then?"

"No."

"Now I really am stronger than you. Are you afraid?"

"No."

He straightened up and held his arms out. "Then why hide behind your glorious army?"

"I don't hide. I lead. I lead, I fight, and I win."

"For your cause, or for his?"

"We're on the same side! Everything I wanted for the world then is still what I want now, is still what I'm fighting for." Her voice cracked out through her parched throat. She didn't have to look at the jug for him to know it was still in play.

He slid it away with his foot. All that did was ignite a fire that she didn't want quenched.

"What about you Arin? Whose side are you on this week?"

To that, he said nothing and did nothing.

It only fueled her fire. "Which force is it more convenient, more prestigious, to be a part of now? Which enemy the easiest to destroy?"

"I'm not attempting to destroy anything. I'm simply building something of my own."

"What? Your own army?"

He didn't have to answer. The smug look on his face told her everything.

"That's why you're undermining us? Why you're picking apart everything Roland has built?"

"Is it Roland's army now? A second ago, it was yours."

Her instinct to yell was stifled by her inability to, but she realized her words would be more meaningful if she simply said them. "You're tearing away at a force stronger than any one of us. And for what? So you can conquer your enemies? So you can tie them up in caves?" An angry tear escaped the corner of her eye.

His inscrutable face finally broke. He looked at the ground. "You're not my enemy."

"What am I then?"

He sat down on the bench and took a moment before answering. "A means of communication."

"To Roland?"

He nodded.

"So, you're sending him a message. What is it that me being here says? That you're strong? That you're a force to be reckoned with?"

"Can you say otherwise from where you're sitting?"

"So, you and a few goons managed to tie me up. Does that mean I should be afraid of you? That he should?"

"It's been years, Lia. You've got to be asking yourself how many towns, how many territories I've traveled across in that time, and how many people I now have at my back."

What she found herself wondering about more than any of that was where the goodhearted boy she once loved more than anything else in the world was hiding under that stoic facade. "What would that matter to Roland? To any of us?"

"If I can get to you, don't you think I can get to anyone in your ranks? Did you ever stop to think what would happen if any of your soldiers found out what they really are?"

The thought had haunted her regularly. Knowing a truth so powerful made her want to shout it out to the world, then sent chills down her spine whenever she thought about the chaos that would yield. But that wasn't why she was there. Arin was talking her in circles, employing whatever strategy he had set out to undertake when he walked into the room with that jug.

Lia was too exhausted to continue prying apart his intentions but still had a spark of anger left, so she used it. "This is just posturing and empty threats. These ropes, this cave, none of it proves you're powerful. None of it proves you're strong. Roland will find me, and you will regret ever bringing me here."

"I have yet to hear a knock on the door."

"He will come, and he will finish what he started."

Arin stood and shouted, "Then let him come!" and smashed the jug with his foot. "I'll be ready." He walked away.

Lia didn't call after him this time. She couldn't. All she had the strength to do was watch the water dribble away between the smashed bits of clay and wonder where the Arin she once knew had gone.

THE LAMP CONTAINED nothing but a low flame flickering over a pile of embers by the time Arin returned. Its light failed to reach the edges of the room, leaving them obscured in splotches of shadow.

Lia lay in one of those splotches, twisted up and perfectly still. He would have thought she was asleep if the flame hadn't thrown a shine into her eyes as they followed him into the room.

He placed the bottle of water on the ground in front of her. This time, she didn't take her eyes off the water. She stared through the glass, into the liquid waiting inside, as Arin backed away. He was still trying to figure out where to begin when she spoke.

"This isn't you, Arin. You never tortured anyone, even when you were a Uni Commander. You said so yourself. Do you remember?"

Of course he did. He remembered every word they had said to each other from the very moment he discovered her under that helmet. "It's not my intent to torture you."

She looked up at him without shifting her body. The tiny highlights in her eyes made her look like a nocturnal creature staring down her prey. "Who shot me off the platform?"

"The fall was shallow where I took the shots."

"Who drugged me?"

"It's a natural sedative, completely harmless."

"How long have I been here?"

He hesitated.

She insisted. "How long?"

"Twenty-eight hours."

"Perhaps we have different definitions of the word."

She looked off into one of the shadows. He waited for more words of accusation to be thrown his way, but she didn't seem to have any left. She didn't even seem to have the will the move.

Arin broke with his plans and approached her. She still didn't move, nor did she make a sound as he looped his arms under hers and lifted her into a seated position. He reached for the bottle of water and held it to her lips.

Lia leaned her head back and took in a few quenching sips before stopping to breathe.

He sat on the ground in front of her. They stared at each other through shadow.

"Is this all I am to you now? A pawn to start a war game?" The water had refreshed her voice, and by the sound of it, a bit of her will.

"You're far more valuable than that."

"The queen then. It doesn't matter. I'm still just a piece on the board."

He put the bottle down and looked up into the little flame as he thought of what to say. Suddenly, all his plans seemed fruitless, moving forward with the next tactic pointless.

Lia, however exhausted, was no longer holding back. "If this isn't torture, then perhaps it's revenge. I just don't know what for."

"You were the one who brought me to the doctor to turn into yet another one of his inventions."

"I thought I was saving you. As far as I knew, it was the only chance you had. You can't blame me for what I didn't know, for the secrets that were kept from me."

"Yet when I told you the truth, you put a gun to my head."

"I wasn't the first to draw, and I'm not the one who pulled the trigger."

"No. Not on me, and not on Roland either."

"You have no idea how close I came."

"And no idea how hard you've fought, so you've said. But I have yet to see any evidence of this great struggle. His army grows bigger, his power stronger, and the source of all that miraculous strength remains a secret."

"What was I supposed to do? You were dead, Arin. I was the only one who knew, the only person who hadn't agreed to hide the formula's existence. How many people do you think would have believed me? How far do you think I could have gotten without Roland finding me? I was completely alone." The dim flame highlighted a tear as it ran down her cheek.

Arin fought his instinct to wipe it away. "So, you just gave up?"

"I never give up."

The renewed strength in her voice helped him to summon up some of his own. "You watched him murder me. Yet you stayed by his side. You fought on his orders. You had his child!"

Even in shadow, he could see the look on her face change. Her fiery stare melted into a sudden fear that arose in tandem with fresh tears. "I don't know that I did."

Arin felt like he'd just received an electric shock. His spine tingled. His legs weakened. "How can you not know?"

"Why would I want to? My child's father was either dead or a murderer. But every time I look into my son's eyes, it's not Roland's I see looking back at me."

Lia leaned her head back, closed her eyes, and let the tears flow, as if she were suddenly relieved of a monumental burden.

Arin had to look away as he puzzled it together. This was no tactic, no ploy to manipulate him. Those were words she had waited years to say. The child-to-be she had so affectionately caressed on the balcony, the little bundle in her arms in Witches Leap, the tiny boy she had waved goodbye to months ago, was no longer a disdainful symbol of her loyalty to Roland.

Arin wanted to erase so many of the ugly thoughts that had crossed his mind in those last few years. He couldn't bring himself to look at her yet but felt the need to know. "What's his name?"

"Malcolm," she said softly.

He looked up as he realized, "After your grandfather."

Lia nodded.

They stared at each other in silence.

Arin didn't need the confirmation of any science to know. He could feel it down to his very core. They had a child, and his name was Malcolm.

LIA LET OUT a small gasp when Arin flicked up the knife. It was her instinctual reaction to the sight of any blade, no matter how small. Under those circumstances, it was less than controllable.

Arin looked hurt, as if he expected her trust, but how could she trust him now? He kept his eyes on her face, bringing them nose to nose as he reached around behind her back and began sawing away the ropes.

What if she hadn't said anything about Malcolm? Was her value suddenly defined through him? Did Arin care about her at all anymore? She felt the last twine of fiber snap.

Arin leaned back as she desperately unwound the coils, peeling them away with what felt like a layer of skin. He stashed the knife back in his pocket and held the bottle of water in front of her.

Her fingers were trembling as she reached for it. The water rushed down her throat, washing away the pain of those last few hours. She was running out of breath but didn't stop drinking until she'd tipped out the last drop. She pulled the bottle away from her lips and panted in oxygen.

Arin's look was no longer inscrutable. His face had softened. His eyes were wrinkled with regret. Was what she saw in them real, or was it another tactic, another part of his plan? With the refreshment of the water had come another dose of determination. If it was a tactic, she wouldn't give him the chance to use it.

He was about to say something when she smashed the bottle over his head.

There was an instant gush of blood from his forehead. He fell back.

Lia tried to stand, but her legs had gone numb from being twisted up underneath her. She slapped down onto her stomach.

Arin's arms grasped her legs and climbed up her body.

"Please don't fight me!" he shouted.

Her pleas had gone unanswered. So would his.

She whirled around and punched him in the nose. He only flinched but didn't lose his grip. She sent a barrage of fists and elbows at him, but he kept coming. She twisted and flailed but soon found herself pinned to the ground.

"You were right!" he shouted as he hovered over her. "I can't torture you. I can't hurt you. I never wanted to. I'm sorry, Lia. You have to believe that, please!"

If her strength hadn't already given out, then her struggle would have naturally subsided when she saw his face. There was nothing but a little dribble of blood where she swore the bottle had torn a gash in his forehead. There was no sign of damage to the nose she was certain she had felt crack under her fist. All she saw was a panicked look on his undamaged face.

"You're not just a piece on the board, Lia. Not to me." His grip loosened.

She scrambled out from under him.

"I just wanted you to understand." He leaned back and held up his hands.

He was giving her a choice. She could run for the tunnel, or she could ask, "Understand what?"

"Things are more complicated now. I'm… different."

"How?"

He glanced around and picked up a shard of the broken bottle. He held his palm up and sliced into it with the shard, tearing open his skin. Before Lia could react, he wrapped his bloody palm around her wrist.

She tried to yank it back.

He held on tight. "Just wait," was all he said. A moment later, he released her wrist.

The angry red rope burns were gone, the tears through her skin completely healed.

Arin showed her his palm. The slice he had taken through his own skin had disappeared. "This ability grows stronger every day. That cut, a hundred others like it, have caused me no pain. Given a few more months, years, who knows what I might be capable of?"

Lia was already dizzy and disoriented from fighting. Seeing what she had just seen, hearing what she had just heard, made her feel like she was delusional all over again. Denial was her only defense. "You're just reverting, turning right back into the tin can you used to be."

"That's not true."

"You're one of those heartless robots already. How else could you have kept me locked up in this hole?"

"I am not." He reached out to her.

She backed away, but there was only so far she could go.

He grasped her shoulders. "Lia, look at me. Look into my eyes and tell me that I don't feel anything right now."

She couldn't. There was pain in them, and fear, and regret, and longing, and every feeling she had come to know so well over those last few years. It was as real as the hands that were clasped around her shoulders. But was this the Arin she once knew? "Then how could you leave me?"

"I didn't have a choice."

"You did when you saw me in the tavern. We looked right at each other, and then you were gone. Why did you make me believe I was chasing nothing but a ghost?"

His posture went slack. His hands dropped. "Because I was a coward."

"But you're… different now."

"Very." He pulled the knife from his pocket, flipped up the blade, and sliced open the tip of his finger. He touched it gently to her other wrist.

Lia watched as the dot of blood absorbed into her and healed every bit of raw flesh, leaving nothing but healthy skin behind. The whole thing took seconds. She felt nothing but a warm tingle.

His hand hovered over hers with an air of uncertainty. He was staring at the gold ring Roland had given her.

Lia pulled her hand back, breaking his gaze. She rubbed the skin of her wrists. No pain. She gave herself a light pinch until it stung. This was no delusion.

"Lia." Even in the dim light, she could see the sudden worry in Arin's eyes. "If Malcolm really is—he might be like me. He might heal the way that I do."

She already knew he was going to be different, and he had been. Malcolm was a child that didn't cry, didn't fuss. He seemed to always understand where he was and what was expected of him. Those traits alone made her wary of what else she might discover about him over the years. This added a level of fear she didn't think she could feel, not about her own child.

"Has he ever been hurt?" Arin asked.

Lia vigorously shook her head. "He's never even fallen from his crib. I don't know—I've never wanted to know what he might be capable of." Now she not only wondered but feared what kind of child he would have grown into by the time she returned to him.

Arin was watching her through the shadows with those same hauntingly familiar eyes.

If I'm right, she wondered, *will he grow up to look like him? Does it matter?* None of it changed how she felt about her son, or how hard she was willing to fight to get back to him. The only question that remained was whether or not Arin was one of the forces she would have to fight.

SHE REMAINED SITTING in quiet thought as he went to get the supplies. She could walk out of that room anytime, but Arin knew she wouldn't. There was still too much unspoken between them. Lia was always one to take the risk rather than not know its reward.

He put the plate in front of her. The food was meager, but at least it was real. He also brought another bottle of water. She knew it wasn't a worthwhile weapon. He refueled the lamp, sat across from her, and let her ask questions as they came to her. They came slowly at first, but as she became revived by the food, so did the ease with which she was able to speak to him.

"Do you just show them this miraculous healing power of yours?" she asked.

"No. I don't want anyone to think it's a trick or that I'm some Uni spy." He also didn't want to feel like a traveling sideshow. "I've only shown a few people. Those who weren't going to believe me without any evidence."

"Manny?"

"The bartender in Cleanair?"

She nodded.

He nodded back. "I could tell he was too sound, too logical to believe in anything sight unseen."

"And rather influential in his town. You can't say that didn't have anything to do with it."

"No, I can't."

"So, there is some strategy in your great quest to reveal the truth."

"I never said there wasn't."

Their exchange, though stilted and rife with suspicion, felt almost like the competitive back and forth they would have once exchanged for fun and excitement. Arin had to remind himself that they were far from what they had once been to each other, then felt a pang of guilt at the fact that the rift between them was now entirely his doing.

She tore her last bit of meat into little pieces as thought brought her to her next question. "Don't we want the same things for the world?"

He nodded.

"Doesn't that mean we're fighting on the same side, against the same enemy?"

"It does."

"Then why haven't you appeared on the battlefield?"

Arin took a moment to think of how to explain his logic. "Let me put it to you this way. Do you have any idea how many places I've been? How many towns I've traveled through, how many people I've spoken to?"

"No."

"Did you see the faces of any of the men in the woods? Would you recognize any of them if you saw them again?"

She took another bite before she admitted, "No."

"Do you have any idea how many of them are sitting at the other end of that tunnel?"

She turned her eyes toward the tunnel, as if the answer might reveal itself.

"You see, appearing on the battlefield just gives your enemies a chance to shoot at you."

"So, you're an army of ghosts." Lia looked down at the plate as she mused over the thought. "Then why take me? Having me here hardly makes you invisible."

Arin turned his eyes away too quickly. He waited too long to answer.

"I should have known." She tossed down her last morsel and got to her feet. "This is nothing but a standoff. It has nothing to do with your master plans, your sanctimonious fight for the truth. You're so desperate to show off your new superpowers that you're baiting Roland into a fight." She paced.

Arin remained still, calm. "That's not true."

"But it's what you do, Arin. You sold your own humanity just for the chance to be stronger. And when you had no choice but to give that up, you leapt into an army you knew nothing about just to prove that you were still strong."

It was getting harder to stay calm. He stood and tried to think of how he could explain why she was really there, what he could say to make her believe him.

Lia continued pacing and seething. "This power, it's your dream come true. The ultimate revenge against anyone who has ever taken advantage of you, anyone who dares to treat you like you're weak."

"That's not who I am. Not anymore."

"How am I supposed to believe that?"

"Because before, I never would have admitted that I needed you!" Perhaps he knew how to explain it after all. "I need you, Lia."

She was taken aback.

"I need your knowledge of this world. I need your strength, just as much as my own. I need your leadership, right by my side."

"So, you're looking for, what, a partner? A fellow Commander for your crusade?"

"No. Just you." He approached her.

She didn't shy away.

"I need your uncanny charm. I need your infectious energy, your unparalleled stubbornness."

She started as he put his hands on her arms, but she didn't pull away from him.

"I need you."

They looked at each other in silence. Arin held in his desperation as he waited for her response. Whether he was about to see trust reappear in her eyes or watch her walk out of the tunnel, at least he would know.

She didn't have a chance to do either before the explosion rocked the cave.

THE BOOM RATTLED up through Lia's legs and shook dust from the walls. The explosion was close. The entrance must have been at the other end of the tunnel the entire time.

"That was your knock on the door," she said to Arin.

He turned his attention to the tunnel as many sets of footsteps raced toward them. The shapes of the three bodies that appeared looked familiar. They were her kidnappers, and one of them was the man from Clearwater with the scar on his face.

They acknowledged each other with a brief, even if contentious look, before he spoke to Arin. "They're at the blockade."

"How much time do we have?"

"Maybe ten minutes with what they're throwing at it. Do we lead them in, or do we head for the river?"

"That means fight or flee, doesn't it?" Lia asked. She could see Arin's mind was calculating, weighing.

"Arin!" the man with the scar insisted.

"Go back and watch the blockade. We'll meet you at the entrance." There was an air of doubt. He didn't want to wait.

"Go!" Arin insisted.

The men funneled back into the tunnel.

"I don't know what you put in their way, but Michaels can make bombs out of shoe leather if he has to. This will not stop until they get through." What she really wanted to tell him was not to be standing in Roland's path when he did.

"You can't go back."

Another boom rattled the tunnel. Debris showered from above.

"I can't go with you. This will follow us wherever we are."

"Not if I stop it now."

Another boom sent the lamp crashing to the floor. Orange embers exploded up around them.

"That's not one man out there. That's an entire army!"

"What do I have to say? What do I have to do to convince you I'm telling the truth?"

The next boom nearly shook them off their feet. That cave wasn't going to be safe much longer.

Arin squeezed her arms, pleading with his hands for an answer.

"You have to run. If you meant what you said, if you really want to help people, if you really want to use your strength to better this world, then you have to run. You have to leave this fight behind so you can go on fighting."

A split second of doubt flashed across his eyes before the light of determination leapt into them. Lia was certain she had gotten through. He would leave. He would survive. He would go on fighting, and this would all be over… for now.

With the next boom came shouts of panic from the other end of the tunnel.

Arin clasped Lia's hand and pulled her into the tunnel with him. The three men stood at the other end, silhouetted by a growing shaft of daylight. The large entry chamber was capped off by a formidable pile of rocks, but the pile was crumbling, sunlight and shouts pouring in from the other side. The three men were brandishing meager weapons, but they were not ready for this fight.

Scarman asked again, "Which direction?"

"We head for the river," Arin answered with confidence. He would leave, he would survive, and he would go on fighting.

"It's the river out!" Scarman shouted into a radio, and the three men launched into a speedy retreat.

Lia prepared to watch Arin do the same, but instead of saying his goodbyes, he tightened his grip on her hand. She found herself being pulled away as one final explosion made the rock wall collapse. Roland would not be far behind them.

Their retreat took them down another darkened tunnel, past one junction and another. Mysterious figures appeared from the darkness and joined in their retreat. Lamps and flashlights danced ahead and behind them. Lia, bewildered by the growing number of people, could barely feel her own body racing along with them.

"Prep the boats," Scarman ordered into his radio. "We're almost there."

The tunnel opened up into a huge chamber which capped an underground lake. Even more figures of mystery awaited them in a small fleet of boats, each lit by a single lantern. A steep downward slope led toward the water.

Lia was scrambling down with Arin and the mysterious crowd that traveled with him before she could take it all in. People filed into the boats and began rowing away into the darkness. More tunnels led away from the lake into underground rivers, and who knew where beyond those.

Lia found herself standing at the water's edge.

Arin clasped her other hand and held them both close to his chest. "Once we leave this cave, we will disappear, all of us. Roland will not be able to find us, and neither will you. Unless you come with me."

A part of her felt like leaping into the boat, but something else deep within stuck her feet to the ground and made her utter, "I can't."

"Don't you believe me?" he asked with a squeeze of her hands.

She did. Despite all he had put her through, she believed everything he had said to her, but that didn't matter. "I have to go back. For Malcolm."

The other boats were already disappearing, their lamplight being swallowed by the darkness.

"This is our last chance!" Scarman shouted to him from the boat.

Arin didn't seem to be able to move.

"Go. Please," Lia whispered.

When Arin did finally move, he pulled her into a kiss. It was soft and gentle and perfectly formed.

"I'll find you." Arin released her hands, jumped into the boat, and turned back. "I'll find both of you." And with that promise, he left.

Lia watched the boat glide away. She watched Arin turn back for one final look before it disappeared into dark mystery.

There was nothing left in the giant cavern but Lia and the single lamp by her side. She sank to the ground and watched the ripples of water dissipate into stillness. She was staring at her own reflection on the glassy surface of the lake when the shouts started behind her.

"Here! Down here!" Roland's voice called out. Feet scrambled down the slope. "Fan out. Pick up the trail," he ordered as he neared.

She was still looking at her reflection when Roland's boot hit the water's edge, making her face distort into a wavy blur.

He dropped to his knees beside her. "Lianna."

She wanted to turn her head, but it seemed too difficult.

"Lianna, please say something."

She broke her gaze on the water and managed to find her voice. "I'm all right."

Roland wrapped his arms around her, holding her in an air tight embrace as the chamber filled with the shouts of their searching soldiers.

WHEN HARRIS ARRIVED, Roland was standing outside of his own tent like a sentry. The sight put him on edge. What had he discovered? He didn't move as Harris approached, only acknowledging him with a glance to one side.

Harris felt compelled to speak first. He gestured to the medical kit he had brought. "You didn't tell me what she needed."

Roland responded with a subtle signal to keep his voice down and flicked a glance at the nearest group of soldiers. Their fire-lit silhouettes were eyeing the tent and exchanging whispers, most likely scandalous conjecture about what might have happened to Lia while she was gone. It was already an idiotic thing to do without Roland watching. Those brains weren't doing themselves any favors.

Harris turned his face toward the tent and spoke in a low voice. "I thought she wasn't injured."

"She's not as far as I can see."

"What do you know?"

"Nothing."

That seemed incredibly unlikely. "What has she said?"

"Nothing."

That seemed ludicrous. "Nothing at all?"

Roland turned to face him, abandoning sentry duty. "Not one word since we left the caves. She hasn't eaten. She's barely moved. If that psychopath had her, kept her in those caves for two days, there's no telling what he could have put her through." There was panic behind his eyes.

"She's back, Roland. Safe."

"Those ropes had blood on them."

"There's not a scratch on her."

"It's not visible wounds I'm worried about." Roland turned his gaze back out toward the camp, though his eyes didn't seem to be focused on anything in particular.

"What do you need me to do?"

"Talk to her. Try to get something out of her. Anything at all."

"If she hasn't said anything to you, what makes you think she'll talk to me?"

"She trusts you." It was hard for him to say.

Harris couldn't tell him that he didn't think that was true anymore. Roland needed him too badly. He gave him a nod and entered the tent.

Lia lay in the far corner, curled up under the blankets. The lamp by her side threw a sharp shadow of the immobile heap that she was against the canvas. She didn't appear to have heard him come in.

"Lia?"

She didn't move.

"Lia I'm here to…." What was he there for? He remembered the medical kit in his hand. "Give you a medical exam. Commander's orders."

She turned over and pushed herself up into a seated position. He had to assume that was acceptance.

Harris knelt by her side and opened the kit. What good was that going to do? He gently held one of her wrists, pretending to check her pulse. "Did any of them hurt you, in a fight or while you were in the cave?"

"No." Her voice was clear enough.

He pushed up her sleeves, examining farther up her arms. There had to be rope burns somewhere, but there was no sign. Not even a scrape. "How many of them were there?"

"Is this an exam or an interrogation?" She was looking right at him, but her eyes were telling him nothing.

"Are you dehydrated? In any kind of pain?"

"No." There was still nothing apparent on her face.

He turned his eyes back to his exam and peeled away the layer of blankets, exposing her bare legs. There were sores on her knees. It didn't explain the ropes, but at least it gave him a reason to be there. He gently cleaned her sores before asking his next question. "Were your tortured?"

"No." There was enough hesitance in her voice to plant the seed of doubt, but he didn't bother looking up to see what had surfaced in her eyes. He focused on dressing the wounds, as he tried to think of another question, but Lia asked hers first. "What do you really want to know?"

He finally looked up at her. "Who took you?"

"Let's just call him an old friend."

The look in her eyes finally told him everything. He knew exactly who she meant. Instinct made him want to jump up and retreat, but she pounced on him before he could move.

"How could you do it? How could you lie to me about that?" She spoke through clenched teeth, holding back the shouts that would have brought Roland into the tent. She threw a barrage of fists at him, knocking him onto his back. "I trusted you! You made me trust you!"

The hits that were slapping against his shielding arms would be heard any minute. He grasped her flying fists, pulling her off balance. Lia fell onto his chest, fought for release, but he held on tight.

"What would I have said?" Harris asked in as loud a whisper as he dared. "What could I have told you that would have kept you from going after him? What would have kept Roland from going after you?"

"Don't you dare act like this was for the greater good. You did it for you, and you alone." The words sizzled out of her.

"Don't pretend you weren't grateful to see him alive."

Lia's muscles went slack enough for him to trust releasing her arms.

She got to her feet and pointed a shaking finger at him. The light of the lamp threw its exaggerated shadow overhead, assuring its accusation didn't go unnoticed. "You have no idea what I felt. No idea what I experienced."

Harris stood to face her. "More than you're willing to tell Roland, that much is certain."

"You have no idea what you even created." She stepped up close. He prepared to be hit again, but all she threw at him were words. "It doesn't matter how I feel, if it ever even did to you. You took a man's life. You twisted it into something you didn't understand. Now, the result of your self-centered quest is out in the world. He's stronger than you know. He has more allies than any of us know. He had the power to take me. Me, Harris, right out from under Roland's nose, and still disappear into thin air. And all of that happened because of your lies."

There was suddenly very little air in that tent. He wanted to pace like a caged animal but couldn't move his legs. His entire body was awash with defeat. "You're right."

She stepped back, allowing him to find some air. "What are we supposed to do now?"

His mind raced, but there was only one clear solution. "Tell the truth." What else was left?

Lia's face dropped into a look of panic. She flicked her eyes toward Roland's sentry post outside the tent. "He's dangerous."

Harris was certain she couldn't have meant that. "Not to me."

"That's what I thought." The look on her face didn't change. "When he found me in Witches Leap, I told him he didn't deserve to be Malcolm's father. He choked me."

Harris wanted to believe she couldn't possibly be remembering that right, that the stress and fear of the moment had to have tainted the truth. All he found himself able to say was, "He wouldn't."

She turned her eyes down. "It wasn't him, not entirely. Something within." She looked back up, her panic replaced with a cold acceptance. "It's the thing that makes him capable of looking a man in the eye while he runs him through with a sword. The thing that made him murder Arin in cold blood, right in front of me. And you're about to tell him you're the one who brought him back to life."

Harris couldn't explain those words away as a tainted memory. He knew what was within Roland. He just thought he'd never have to confront it himself. Lia obviously had. Perhaps it was simply his turn. "I was bound to pay the price someday."

Harris removed his weapons, dropped them into the med kit, sealed them inside, and backed away. Lia was staring at him like it was the last time they were ever going to see each other. He couldn't stand it.

He turned away and left the tent to tell Roland what he had discovered.

SIXTEEN

HIS BACK WHAMMED against the cliff face, followed by the back of his skull. Strange and almost musical plonking sounds rained down around him. It was probably loose shale falling from the rock face. Either that or Harris's eardrums had disconnected from the impact.

Roland closed in on him. Harris held up his hands. He wasn't going to fight. He wasn't going to run. He was going to face whatever came his way. His skull hit the cliff again as Roland took hold of his neck.

"How could I have ever trusted such a selfish, manipulative liar!" Roland's voice vibrated his eardrums.

"Roland, please...." Harris had to force air past Roland's chokehold to keep talking. "I want to... explain." After a third and very rattling slam against the cliff, Roland released his neck. Harris felt his knees wobble but stayed upright. He sucked in oxygen.

"What kind of lies are you going to conjure up?"

"I brought you here to tell the truth about everything."

Roland backed off. Harris had just convinced himself that he wouldn't have to take any more punishment, when Roland slid out his sword. "Give me one good reason not to gut you right now."

"We are still allies!" Panic surfaced in his voice.

The light of approaching dawn highlighted the edges Roland's figure as he circled with his sword. "You kept a deadly secret hidden under my city. You are no ally of mine."

Harris didn't want to back away but couldn't help it. This wasn't the first time Roland had thought about making someone disappear.

Harris never thought it would be him. "Think of the questions then. How are you going to explain my disappearance?"

"Accidents happen."

Perhaps he was going to run after all.

Harris attempted to duck away. Roland grabbed his arm.

Harris loosened it with a hard elbow to the stomach and made a dash for safety. Roland's sword side-slapped against his leg with a painful crack and took him to the ground.

Harris had just enough time to turn over before Roland and his sword had him pinned to the ground.

Cold steel pushed against his neck.

"I'm still your friend. Your oldest, most loyal!" Harris shouted.

"What is that worth now?" Roland pressed down.

Harris felt the sting of the blade breaking skin. "Everything to me! I did it for us!"

Whether it was the panic in his plea or the words he chose, Roland stopped pressing.

Blood trickled down the side of Harris's neck.

Roland stared down at him, nostrils flaring, eyes burning, but that thing within him was being held at bay.

Harris fixed his eyes on Roland's, hoping to keep it there.

Whether it was his words or his eyes, something made Roland relent.

Harris scrambled up. He felt his neck, still intact, but screaming in pain.

Roland pointed his freshly bloodied sword at him. "You nursed an unbreakable enemy, with nothing but vengeance on his mind, back to full health. You set him free in the world, gave him years to undermine our cause. And now he has the means to kidnap my wife! How could you have possibly done that for us?"

"He was still human but completely bulletproof, in a way that has never been matched. If I'd had the chance to figure out how it happened, how to replicate it—"

"You would have injected yourself long before anyone else had the slightest notion of what you were doing."

"I would have used it for us, Roland. All of us." Warm blood was soaking into his collar. Harris hoped he wasn't about to drain out of consciousness before Roland had decided his fate.

Roland shook his head. "You're just starting to believe your own lies."

"It's the truth!" Shouting only forced the blood to flow faster. Harris held a hand against his neck and tried to calm his breathing. "I let it get out of my control. I compromised everything we worked for. This is the worst mistake I could have made. And now, we've all paid for it. I will not deny that."

Roland hadn't moved. He was listening.

This was his chance—maybe his only chance—to regain his trust. "If I could have done it. If I had him in my grasp, right now, I would make it worth the risk. For all of us."

Roland squeezed the handle of his sword but did not otherwise move. "How unfortunate you won't have the chance to prove that."

"You can't go after him. It's exactly what he wants."

"More stories, Harris?"

Harris dared to take a step closer. "He put himself in the path of this army more than once. His aim was to be seen and recognized. And not just by anyone, but by Lia. You already killed him once for her. He knows you'd do it a thousand times over if you had to."

"Once more ought to suffice." His hand pulsed on the sword again.

"He also knows that while you're busy trailing him, your army goes nowhere. Think of the two days we already lost. How many more are you willing to sacrifice?"

Roland flicked the point of his sword up under Harris's chin. "Those two days are on your head."

Harris resisted the urge to step back. He fixed his eyes on Roland's again, hoping that if all else failed, he would at least know his last words had been honest ones.

"You're right. But don't let vengeance kill our mission. Don't give him the satisfaction." Harris could tell he was reaching the reason that had been pushed out of Roland's body the moment he told him who had taken Lia. "If you won't trust me as your friend, then trust me as your Sub-commander. Do not let him in."

"I will accept that as your final advisement."

Harris fought the urge to step back again when he heard the word "final."

Roland became the first to back away, slow and steady. "You're demoted to third officer of operations."

Something about the loss of rank made Harris instantly forget his fear. "I'm your head of operations."

"You no longer command anyone but yourself. That ought to suit you." Roland whirled his sword toward the ground and turned away.

Harris's confession had saved him but had also turned him into nothing but another body on the battlefield. That didn't suit him at all. "Please, don't do this."

Roland stopped walking but only turned enough to throw a glance down the length of his sword. "Consider the alternative."

He continued on his way, trying to force an end to their discourse.

"Then who will be your second?" Harris called after him. "Who will be your second, Roland? One of the men who still have no idea what makes this army so miraculously unstoppable? Or the wife who didn't want to tell you who she'd been with for the last two days?"

Roland turned back. The intensity in his eyes had melted into what Harris could only describe as bitter disappointment. "Anyone but you."

THE SHAPE OF THE FUTURE

LIA HAD WAITED with her guns at the ready for so long that the handles had gone hot and slick as her hands clammed up under the stress of the unknown. She didn't want to need them, but there was no telling what she was going to face when the tent flaps parted again. The silence of the night had drawn on, the light of dawn was starting to creep up, and neither of them had returned.

When the tent flaps finally opened, it was for Roland and his sword. He gave her and her guns a weary look. "Haven't we done this dance before?"

She eyed the sliver of blood on the edge of his blade. "Where's Harris?"

"Soldier Wilson is intact and confined to quarters, as are you, until further notice." He took in a deep breath, like he was preparing for a fight should one come his way. "Put the guns down, Lianna."

She lowered both guns to the ground and placed them in front of her feet. "I want a chance to explain," she said as she rose.

"I've heard quite enough explanations for one day." He approached with an air of interrogation. "For days now, for hours still, even after we found you, I believed… far worse things than I ever want to believe. And you would have let me go on believing them."

"I didn't mean for that to happen. I just didn't know what to say." She made sure to hold his gaze as she said, "I'm sorry." Whether or not it had any impact, she couldn't tell.

"I can't blame you for not wanting to tell me. You know better than anyone what I would have done." He slid one of her guns away with the tip of his sword and put his foot on the other.

She ignored the guns and held her gaze on his. "And now that you do know, what are you going to do?"

"Should I have the opportunity, I will eliminate the problem." That look was much less cryptic. "But until that day arrives, you can thank Harris for convincing me to focus on less… trivial matters."

Lia stifled what would have been a sigh of relief.

"But if I ever get the slightest sense, from anything at all, even something as substance-less as a whisper in the wind, that you have a notion of joining him, my priorities will shift."

She stifled what would have been a chill down her spine.

"Did he show you these miraculous abilities of his?"

Lia's mind flashed back to the moment Arin healed her wrist with just a drop of his blood. "He told me about them."

"Did he tell you why he took you?"

She could still hear his voice saying that he needed her. "He was trying to draw you out."

"Then why run when I arrive?"

She heard her own voice telling him to run from this fight so he could go on fighting. "He was outgunned, outnumbered. It was the only option."

"Did he give you any notion of his intentions?"

He said he would find her. She didn't know how, but she had no doubt he would. "No."

"Did he touch you?"

She felt Roland's eyes burning into her with the arrival of that question. She hoped he couldn't tell that she could still feel Arin's kiss. "Only when he released me."

Roland gave her an examining gaze. He took a step back and slid his sword back into its sheath, even though Harris's blood was still fresh on the blade.

"I could have gone with him." She didn't know why, but she felt Roland had to know that.

He tilted his head as if letting that grain of information settle. "And by what twist of fate did you choose not to?"

"We have a mission to finish. Land to gain, people to free from Unity control. To get to the coast and back, that's what I'm here to do."

"Tell me then, what will happen once we've completed that mission."

"I will return home to my family."

His eyes traced over her face, reading, analyzing. Whether satisfied by what he saw there or not, he turned around and left the tent.

HARRIS EXAMINED HIS neck in the mirror. The thin slice looked almost black in the dim light of the tent. There would be no concealing it. He pulled off his shirt and took a disdainful look at the blood soaked into the collar. He tossed it aside and began to gently clean his wound.

The mirror revealed the tent flaps parting behind him. Lia entered with his medical kit in her hands.

"Aren't you confined to quarters?" he asked without turning to look at her.

"Roland is gathering a reconnaissance group. I have a few minutes."

"This is hardly the time to exercise your rebellion."

"You're hardly the one to be sharing words of caution."

He turned around, took the kit back, and opened it up. His guns were still there. That was something at least. He decided to take advantage of having her ear. "I'll say it a thousand times if I have to, Lia. There are no more secrets left to uncover."

"Someday I might believe that." That was the best reaction he could expect.

He grabbed a swab from the kit, turned toward the mirror, and wiped away as much blood as he could in one painful swoop.

She was still standing behind him. "Are you all right?"

At least she still cared about his well-being, even if she would never trust him again. "I've survived worse."

"I guess I should thank you for convincing him not to go after Arin."

"If you have the slightest idea I did that for you, get it out of your head. It's only what's best for this army. Roland knows that too, or he wouldn't have listened to me."

"He's not our enemy."

Harris whipped around. "How can you believe that now?"

"We're both fighting the Unity."

"Then why take you? Why lead us on a two day chase?" His voice was raising, but what did that matter now? "What do you think he'd do if Roland caught him? Engage him in friendly debate?"

"He'd only do what he had to, to survive."

"He used you, Lia! He manipulated you, twisted you until your emotions were on his side."

"Not everyone functions the way you do, Harris."

Her naivety was beyond his comprehension. More than that, it was dangerous. "How long did he keep you in that cave? Was it long enough for you to have whipped yourself up into a panic? Long enough that you had already devised an escape plan and were just waiting for the chance to use it, despite any risk? Long enough to be exhausted, starved, too weak to fight?"

She entered a tight-lipped silence.

He stepped in close to her and said in a low voice, "You're forgetting, that I have that man's brain on file. He was a Unity strategist, well trained in enemy negotiations. And recruitment tactics."

He leaned back, letting it sink in. He knew there was something behind her pause when he asked about torture. Arin was twisting her toward something. It didn't matter what. He wasn't going to let it work.

Her lips finally loosened with a question. "Then why did he let me go?"

Harris let out a little huff that was close to laughter. "It's you, Lia. You have an astounding ability to steer men away from their grand plans and better intentions."

She looked wounded. It was hard to take.

He turned away. "Go back to your tent."

Harris waited for the brief appearance and disappearance of sunlight to tell him she had left. He turned back to the mirror. The wound on his neck was still oozing. He looked to the medical kit for the solution. The little box containing injections of the formula seemed to stare back at him. "Temptress." He kicked the lid shut.

Another flash of light indicated yet another visitor. Harris looked up to see Emmett standing just inside the entrance. Apparently, being confined to quarters was not going to provide him any peace.

Emmett's mouth dropped open as his eyes focused on Harris's neck. "Are… are you all right, sir?"

"Never better. You're here for…?"

"I'm sorry to bother you, sir. I just needed your advice."

"It's no longer sir. You outrank me now. It's just Soldier Wilson."

"I still um…."

Harris gestured for Emmett to take a seat, lest he stammer himself lightheaded. He wrapped a single loop of bandage around his neck before joining him. He didn't want to have his nearly severed arteries stared at. He invited Emmett to speak with open arms.

"The Commander is having me lead the tracking team looking for traces of Martrim's troop, and um… I'm not sure what I'm looking for."

"You used to hunt."

"Yes, but animals follow predictable patterns. They don't backtrack or circle around. They don't set traps for the hunters."

"The fact that you know that's what you're likely to see means you're already halfway to finding him. Look for what you're not expecting, then another step beyond that. That's where Martrim will be."

Emmett nodded, looking only slightly reassured. He stood to leave, but hesitated.

"Emmett?"

"Yes-s?" Stifling the instinct to call him sir resulted in an oddly elongated *s*.

"You're one of our top trackers. You've been doing it since you were a kid. What did you really come to say to me?"

Emmett went red. "The Commander sent me with orders."

Harris gave him another open armed invitation.

"He said you are to follow the ravine. There's signs of a small village a few parces away. He wants you to seek them out about whatever food and supplies they can offer." He swallowed like he was having trouble stomaching the words.

Harris responded with a short and simple, "Yes, sir."

LIA PACED THE length of the tent. She wanted to run, to race away from her fog of confusion, her brewing storm of anger. More memories were floating into her mind now.

Arin had come down the tunnel only after she had exhausted every attempt she could make at escape, but the tunnel was too short to have stifled the sounds of her struggle. He had heard them all.

Arin's words echoed in her mind. "Tell me then. Tell me how terribly you've suffered, living in your palace, following your brave leader, catering to his every whim."

Pace. Pace. Pace.

"Now I really am stronger than you. Are you afraid?"

Pace. Pace. Pace.

"Then let him come!" She could still hear the sound of the water jug smashing under his foot. The jarring memory filled Lia with a sudden mad energy.

She began to tear apart the tent.

She tossed the bedding aside. Too soft to feel. She kicked over the flimsy planning table. It's weak clatter only made her angrier. She kicked the supply crates, not relenting until the sides cracked open and they spilled out their innards. Still not good enough. She barreled toward the largest one and shoved it on its side. The top fell open, and a mixed supply of swords slid out.

The loud clangs of cascading metal finally brought her to a standstill.

Lia closed her eyes and soaked in the little spike of adrenaline. As its rush filtered from her chest out into her limbs, she remembered the wash of relief she experienced when she admitted to what she had never known—the truth she had been too afraid to face—about Malcolm.

That reveal had changed everything about Arin. It stripped away all the posturing and threats of hours before. Was that too a ploy, another recruitment tactic? She once told Roland that he didn't deserve to be his father, yet he had spent every moment of Malcolm's life proving otherwise. Arin had spent every moment of his life hiding in the shadows. The catharsis of her admission began to twist in her memory into a moment rife with doubt. The adrenaline was starting to make her dizzy.

As Lia parted her lids, the first thing she saw was a tiny glimmer of light. A gentle breeze was pushing through the tent flaps, allowing a stream of morning light to fall upon the swords. A single point was glinting off one of the swords.

Lia bent over the deadly pile of metal, took hold of the handle, and slid out the blade that was signaling to her. She let her eyes trace up and down the swath of steel. She held it in front of her, staring down its length the way she would look through her scope. It was heavy, just heavy enough to be challenging to swing.

She stepped into the center of the tent, ignoring whatever discarded bits were crunching under her feet, readied her grip, and took one broad swing. The whoosh of air, the feeling of her muscles locking to try and stop it in midair, was more satisfying than the destruction of anything at her fingertips. As Lia took another swing, she felt the dizzying doubt begin to leave her body, so she kept swinging.

HARRIS HAD TO side-wind his way down the steep incline leading into the ravine. The branches underfoot crunched with every step. It had been a long time since this valley had seen any rain. The sound helped to calm him, to keep him from thinking about the questionable future that Arin's reemergence had created. After every five crunches, he took a turn, bringing him steadily closer to the floor of the ravine. The trees thinned out, wooden roofs appeared below, and his next turn brought about a clunk instead of a crunch. He stooped, pushed aside the brambles, and pulled up the wooden sign he had stepped on. What was left of its aged post crumbled in his hand. The faded paint on its flaky surface read "SANCTUARY."

If only, Harris thought. He tossed the sign aside and continued crunching his way downward. He ran the last few steps, half with intent and half forced by gravity, but slowed to a stop as the first few buildings in the village came into view. The wooden structures were rotting away and just as faded as the long-buried sign. The stone pathways running between them were rife with a healthy population of weeds. The tiny village was long abandoned. Harris kept one hand on his gun—just in case—as he entered the little forest of buildings. Not a soul, not a sound, not a single sign of life appeared.

"Is anyone here?" he asked the air.

It responded with silence.

Just as Harris was about to return to camp, a skinny curl of smoke appeared between the buildings. It was snaking up from some unseen chimney in the trees. He decided to investigate.

The next slope was even steeper, forcing Harris to lean into it as he headed toward the smoke. The air was quiet, except for birdsong, and another sound that rose gently above it as Harris got closer to the smoke. It was humming. A woman's voice absentmindedly hummed, no tune in particular, from somewhere among the trees.

Abandoning the direction of the smoke, Harris followed the voice.

She wasn't hard to spot. Her fiery red locks, though tied back, were the brightest spot of color in the desiccated landscape, zipping up and down as she deftly collected firewood. Something about her made Harris decide not to approach without a plan. She didn't seem dangerous. Quite the opposite, more easy to scare, like one of the vulnerable forest creatures. He didn't want to send her scampering into hiding.

He followed at a distance, watching her swift and efficient movements. She knew exactly where to step so the slope wouldn't overtake her balance. She picked fallen branches with care, knowing which would best feed the fire that was doubtlessly responsible for the curl of smoke that had called him there. She had no idea she was being followed. What reason would she have to suspect it? It had probably never happened before.

He spotted a simple stone home through a break in the trees, most likely her destination. The plan came together. He would announce himself, offer a hand in taking her firewood back, and talk with her as long as she would let him. Something made him feel like he wouldn't easily grow tired of it. He didn't exactly have any pressing reason to go back to camp anyway.

He was about to call out when he spotted the movement around her house. Unity soldiers had also found it.

Harris did a quick assessment. They hadn't seen him. They hadn't seen her. They would any second. The redheaded songbird would not stay hidden. His next plan came together only after he had already started running. He swept toward her as silently as he could, grabbed her around the waist, and threw them both behind the nearest tree.

Her would-be-scream was stifled under his hand, but the firewood flew from her grip, and the birds above scattered into the sky. The Unis would have heard that. They had to stay invisible. She struggled against him but was not too challenging to hold on to.

"Shh. Don't struggle. They'll hear you," he whispered. It didn't get through to her. He took a chance, and leaned their locked-together bodies around the tree, just enough to see the house. "Look."

The Unis were continuing to arrive, though they didn't appear to have heard the firewood scatter, and seemed only interested in the house.

Her struggle subsided so swiftly it felt like she had melted in his arms. "Is that your house?" Harris asked without loosening his grip.

She nodded.

"Is there anyone inside?"

She shook her head, freeing up a flaming lock of hair.

"Do you have any weapons in there? Anything hidden in the woods?"

She shook again, sending the lock ticking into his chin.

"You understand this means that when I let you go, you can't go running back to your house or take off into the woods, right? That the best thing to do is stay quiet and hidden."

She nodded.

As soon as he let go, she shrunk as far away as she could without leaving the security of their hide. She stared at him with the most beguiling eyes he had ever seen. It took him a moment to remember that they were still in danger.

"Did you know they were here?" he asked.

"I heard the shots at the top of the valley a few days back. I thought that they'd pass. That I'd be safe." Her voice was gentle, just like her humming. Her welling eyes were darting back and forth between Harris and the Unis below. "That's my home."

"Don't worry. The only thing they'll part you from is the contents of your pantry. But I count at least thirty, with more coming still. I'm afraid two guns isn't going to take care of it."

"You're a soldier," she said rather breathlessly as her eyes traveled over his body armor.

And only that now, Harris thought. "So they tell me."

She froze up and didn't seem to be able to say anything else. Fear was petrifying her in place.

He needed to distract her from it. "I'm Harris." He extended a hand.

She looked a bit alarmed at first, but then reached hers back. "I'm May."

"My favorite time of year." He smiled.

Her posture relaxed ever so slightly.

"Let's get you somewhere safe, May. But first." He reached toward the hem of her dress.

She lurched back.

"Relax." Though whispered, the word came out like an order. It had the effect of making her freeze up again. It hadn't been his aim, but at least she wasn't about to run. He felt around to where the edge had already been loosened from being stepped on one too many times and tore off a strip of fabric.

She stared at him wide-eyed as he held it in front of her.

"Tie that around your hair. There aren't too many red-headed forest creatures around here." He said it with a smile, bringing about another modicum of relaxation.

She tied the fabric tight around her hair.

He found himself a little disappointed to see it all disappear. He had to remind himself again about the danger just below them. "Now follow me, and do exactly what I do. Every single move I make, you make the same. Got it?"

She nodded.

He ducked down low into the underbrush and began to crawl back the way he came, with the red-headed songbird named May following along behind him.

ROLAND ATTEMPTED TO fix his focus into the valley. Noting an oddity in the bark of any tree, the placement of any rock, would be the only way to find a slippery worm like Martrim. No matter where his eyes traveled, Roland's mind wandered elsewhere.

Martrim had once been his only true enemy, the only one that stood out in the faceless mass of others who were nothing more than obstacles to him. Now he had another, one that had been shaped and shielded by his most trusted. Did that make them enemies as well?

All the doubts he had confronted through all the setbacks they had surmounted over those last few months seemed conquerable because he wasn't alone in his burden of leadership. At that moment, he felt entirely and irrevocably alone. Was the future he had set out to secure for the world, for its next generation, for Malcolm, now completely his to shape?

The thought sent a shudder into his jaw. He clamped it tight and turned back to Emmett.

Being a better tracker than he ever gave himself credit for made Emmett the right person for this tricky task, but his lack of confidence made him slow to commit to his discoveries. He was still scrutinizing the same broken branch, lifting it, letting it drop back into its natural position over and over again.

"Direction?" Roland asked. They didn't have time to coax out his confidence.

"I can't tell." Roland didn't have to ask Emmett to say more. One glance kept him talking. "I can tell you that they were here. No animal is this clumsy, but this mess is nothing but... well, mess."

"Meaning, he's derailing us."

"I think so. I mean, yes, he is. But he's covered his tracks in the process. Very, very well."

That had once been only their area of expertise. Martrim was the first Unity Commander Roland had ever known to use the same clandestine tactics that they did. It would have been flattering if it wasn't so dangerous.

He turned his attention back to the valley, just in time to see a narrow funnel of fire shoot up into the sky.

"A firebomb," Emmett muttered.

"We know whose signature that is." The other soldiers were calling out to each other, regrouping and arming up to retaliate, but fire alone was nothing to relate against. Still, someone was down there. Someone would be waiting for them to arrive. There was only one way to find out if it was Martrim.

Roland gathered the recon group in close for orders. "We head down from the west, low and tight. Stay armed, and stay alert."

At least he had a potential fight to focus on now. Getting through this one, and the next, and the next, would at least keep him moving toward the future, whether or not he was alone in his fight.

They snaked a quick path down toward the rising puff of smoke. The fire seemed to have run out of fuel quickly, either because it had hit rock or been doused. If the latter were the case, they still had time to get there before the hand responsible had a chance to hide.

Roland doubled his speed until the edge of the burnt patch came into view. The fire had in fact hit the rocky sides at a bottleneck leading out of the valley and into the open land beyond. The trees were gone. What few bushes remained were still being consumed by tiny—but hungry—flames. There was no one in sight.

Roland signaled for everyone to drop into hiding and crept in closer with Emmett. He scanned the land with his scope. Roland held out hope that he would spot something, but Emmett didn't second guess himself this time.

"Nothing, not even a footprint."

"He didn't burn that patch to walk across it. He burnt it so he'd have a clear view of us when we do."

"So, we circle around."

Roland shook his head. "We can't if we trail him out of the valley. It's too steep on either side. That's a bottleneck we have no choice but to go through. He's flushing us out like rabbits."

"Of course, rabbits would have run from the fire. We headed straight—" Emmett gripped onto his arm. "It's a diversion. He must have put a timer on it. He's not drawing us out, he's drawing us away!" Not only had Emmett not second guessed himself, he had ripped Martrim's plan right out of its burrow.

Now Roland knew. "He's headed into the ravine."

HARRIS DIDN'T HESITATE to stand when they reached the edge of the village. Had the Unis found it, they would already be making themselves comfortable in what was left of the town, but it was just as quiet and empty as he left it. May was still down on her elbows when he turned around, and looked too petrified to move.

"It's okay, you can stand up now."

"Are you sure?"

"The only trail I see was the one I made getting down here." He offered her a hand.

Every branch she'd snagged along the way came up with her as she stood. Her face was scratched from the stray ends that couldn't be avoided.

"I'm sorry about the necessary mode of transit." He reached out to help brush the leaves from her clothing.

She shied away. "I'm fine."

"I can get those scratches cleaned up when we get back to camp." As he pointed up to her face, her eyes zeroed in on his three fingered hand, then quickly discovered the bandage around his neck. Her shock was palpable. He tucked the hand into his belt but couldn't do anything to erase the wound on his neck, so he backed away. "We'd better get moving."

Her footsteps were treading lightly over the stone pathways beside him. His suddenly sounded—and felt—very heavy. "How long have you been a soldier?" she quietly asked.

"I guess since the day my home filled up with Unis, like yours." He answered without turning to look at her, lest he reveal another disfiguring scar he'd forgotten he had. "How long have you lived there?"

"All my life."

"So, you must know what happened here." He gestured toward the vacant buildings surrounding them.

"Everyone took off when the mines dried up some years back."

"Why didn't you?"

"Papa refused to leave. 'Twas his grandfather that built our home. He said it was too much history to walk away from."

"And where is he now?"

"At peace."

"Sorry."

Her footsteps slowed, forcing him to finally look her way. There were tears welling in those beguiling eyes again.

"We'll do whatever we can to get them out of your house."

"It's just... those gunshots, that was more than close enough for me. I've never taken to warfare. I stayed here to be away from it all, and now... I'm standing here with an armed soldier. The fight has entered through my front door. What am I meant to do?"

Harris's hand had come to rest on one of his sidearms. It was a habit he suddenly felt very self-conscious about. He slid his guns around behind his back. "You don't have to do anything. We want them out of there as much as you do. We'll do everything in our power to make it happen. We will have to fight, yes. But only once, and it will be over. I promise."

"How many of you are there?"

"More than enough." That was something he felt no need to hide.

It didn't take long for him to realize he was better off following her up the next slope. He pointed toward their camp and let her figure out which steps were solid enough to not have their feet scrambling for purchase. He also didn't mind being in a position to watch her. She was a pleasing sight to behold.

When they reached the top, he felt obligated to step back into the lead. It was a good thing he did, too, because voices were floating over from the next clearing. He pointed May to the closest hiding place. The cover was thin, but it would do in a pinch. Then, he armed himself and pushed into the clearing.

As he raised his gun to the first shape he saw on the other side, he found himself staring down the barrel of Roland's gun. They both pulled their guns back in unison. Emmett and the reconnaissance group were standing behind him.

"Martrim's troop is in the ravine," Roland announced instead of offering any kind of greeting.

"I noticed."

"You saw traces?"

"More than traces. They found themselves a cozy headquarters." Harris called back to May "You can come out. It's safe." He was pleased to see that she did. Not only had she not run, she had believed his assurance of her safety. They were getting somewhere. "This is May. She has a few unwanted house guests. May, this is Roland, our Commander."

Her eyes grew wide again. Roland had a tendency to have that effect on people, but there seemed to be something more behind her doe-like stare.

"Come with us, May. We'll take care of you." Roland took off without another word.

May remained frozen as the other soldiers flooded past her to follow him. She didn't snap back until Harris spoke again.

"We're almost there."

"Is that *the* Commander? The one who leads all of you?"

"Always has been."

"I didn't realize you were that kind of soldier, that you were with the Resistance army."

He thought about asking if she had heard of any other, but realized it might be too soon to open up that door with May, especially if she were to say that she had. And it was far too soon to open that still oozing wound with Roland. "You said you stayed away from all the fighting."

"Traders come past. They tell me of the news beyond Sanctuary, about the wars, about your army. They've spoken of him, of his skill, his fearlessness. They speak of him as legend."

Harris already knew that to be true, but he didn't enjoy being reminded of it. Then, an entirely different question popped into his mind. "Do they ever speak of anyone else? Any other commanders at his side?"

He prepared himself to hear about the legend of the great unknown assassin that Lia had managed to spread with her travels, but all May said was, "No."

Of course not, Harris thought. None of that mattered now anyway. He offered her the lead again. There were other soldiers for her to follow now. At least he could continue to enjoy the view.

WHOOSH! THE SOUND of the blade slicing through the air was getting louder and more satisfying with every stroke. With the ache in her muscles surpassed hours ago, Lia felt like her body was growing stronger with every swing. So, too, was her spirit.

She would not be a piece on the board. She would not be manipulated by words. She would be as unyielding as the steel in her hand and no longer bend, even for love. She was cleansing away Arin's effect on her with every drop of sweat.

Lia jabbed the point into her invisible opponent, telling herself she felt its impact. Missed the heart. No matter. She jabbed it again and again until there was no room for doubt. Her unseen enemy would never rise again.

But what about the tin can coming from behind? With a twist of her spine and lurch of steel, she spun around to face her next fight. She raised the blade high overhead and brought it crushing down on his skull. With a snap of her elbows, she yanked it free, leaving a gruesome mess behind.

Did another opponent dare to take her on? Lia let the weight of the steel spin her around to find her next imaginary foe, only to discover she was no longer alone in the tent.

Roland was looking at her with what appeared to be a sparkle of pride in his eye. No one else would have noticed, but there was also the hint of a smile on his face.

Emmett was standing next to him in a typical slack-jawed pose, Harris just behind him, and someone else was lurking in his shadow.

Lia took a wide sidestep so she could see the face of their cowering visitor. A comely redhead with giant eyes stared back at her.

Lia had forgotten she still had hold of the sword until she felt the weight of the steel pull back as she raised her arm and pointed with it. "Who's she?" The wide-eyed woman took a frightened hop back. Apparently, she scared easy.

SEVENTEEN

AFTER THE INITIAL shock of being greeted by a sword-wielding madwoman passed, May settled into her task. Her hand was shaking as she drew out the plan of her little house. Being watched by several sets of eyes would have made anyone uncomfortable, but it was Roland hovering over her shoulder that seemed to have the strongest effect on her.

Harris knelt down beside her, hoping that if anyone's presence would bring her some comfort, it would be his.

"And there's another window here. That's the kitchen," she said as she marked the room with a little flame where the hearth was.

"Coal stove?" Roland asked.

"'Twas before the mines dried up. I use wood chips now."

"Still, no one is fitting in through that chimney," Lia said.

May shrunk away from her. Perhaps she was having the strongest effect on her.

"Anything above that?" Roland asked.

"Only attic space. Just storage, no windows."

"But the perfect place to hide for an ambush," Harris said.

Roland either didn't think it was relevant or was simply ignoring him. He took a circle around the group before asking his next question. "Is there coal storage inside the house?"

"Aye, under the kitchen. But it's small. Not even room to stand."

"How do you get the coal in?"

"Wheelbarrow down an access shoot. It's probably grown over after all these years."

"Where?" Roland leaned over her.

She gulped back her nerves and turned back to the drawing. She drew a shaky line that arced up toward the slope behind her house where Harris had found her.

"That's the winner," Harris said.

"You mean to get in there? But it couldn't fit more than one person at a crawl."

"We'll figure out a way. Thank you for your help," Roland said as he straightened up. He looked to Harris, but not for confirmation or advice. "Soldier Wilson, will you please see that May is taken care of. Treat those scratches and find her a comfortable place to rest."

Harris opened his mouth to argue. How could he leave now when their tactical conversation hadn't even begun. Then, he remembered that was no longer his job. His mouth had been hanging open for what felt like an inordinately long time before her finally uttered, "Yes, sir."

Though everyone else averted their eyes, Roland watched as Harris escorted May from the tent, assuring his orders were being followed.

May tilted her eyes up as Harris cleaned the cuts on her face, as if she were too shy to look at him so closely. She had probably been told it was rude to stare. He smiled at the thought of her as a young girl being taught how to live in the world. He'd had no such training. What would they have thought of each other back then?

"You're very kind to look after me like this," she said without altering her upward stare. "Are you the doctor?"

"Among other things." Or was that all he was now?

"I'm not sure I like that man."

"Who? Roland?"

She gently nodded.

Harris was genuinely surprised. Intimidation aside, Roland's presence usually reassured people, if not downright impressed them. This was a first.

"I'm not sure I like any of them very much. Being so cloaked, so secretive. I'm glad you're not like that."

Fortunately, she wasn't looking his way. If she had been, she would have seen the heat of shame he felt rise to the surface. He pushed it

down with a clearing of his throat. "All done. You'll be healed up soon."
He leaned back, giving her the room to move her gaze.

It only turned down to the ground. "I fear otherwise."

"You couldn't be safer than you are right here."

She finally looked at him, bewitching him into stillness with those
eyes of hers. "That I do believe. As hard as it is to be in the presence of
so much weaponry, I know it's for the best. It's just… my home. No
matter how this ends, I'll have so many pieces to pick up. If any at all."

"Regardless of what happens, I promise I will be there to help you
pick up the pieces." He had said it without a second thought.

"You really mean that?"

He must have because his tendency to be already planning his escape
route was nowhere to be found. "You have my word."

Her eyes went glassy again, but this time it was with the threat of
grateful tears.

Rather than watch them emerge, he chose to leave her in peace.
"You can rest here. I won't be far if you need anything."

"Thank you again." Her voice wavered.

He fought the urge to wrap her up in his arms and left the tent.

Harris paced the short distance between his tent and the one Roland
was discussing tactics inside of. He wouldn't let himself leave May's line of
sight, but he also desperately wanted to know what they were planning.

As Emmett emerged, Harris didn't hesitate to step into his path.
"What's the plan, sir?"

"We move after the moon drops out of sight, so we have maximum
darkness for cover."

"And then?"

"That's all I can say." Emmett's muscles tensed like he was preparing
to take a punch.

"What do you mean?"

"The Commander said it would be better not to share too many details."

Roland probably didn't mean for that suggestion to slip out either.

Harris didn't want to push Emmett to say anything that would get him
into trouble, but he had to know more. "I still need to know my position, sir."

"Third flank." Emmett swallowed loudly.

"I'm third flank?" The mere suggestion of it made it impossible for Harris to remember his "Yes sirs."

"You're to hold the perimeter. That's all you need to know." Emmett turned away and marched off as quickly as he could.

AFTER THE OTHERS left, Lianna began to reassemble the tent without a word about it, as if its contents had been destroyed in the course of a normal day. She averted Roland's gaze as she picked up the bits and pieces, most of which had been stepped on, if not skewered by a blade. She did not attempt to restore the swords to their case, nor did she even pick up the one she had been wielding, which lay abandoned in the corner.

Roland chose to pick up the sword himself. He gave it a light swing, testing its weight. Seeing Lianna's will and determination return to her reassured him. Seeing it return in the form of a sword-wielding warrior excited him.

"Was it boredom that drove you to take up steel, or something else?" he asked with another swing of the sword.

She answered without looking up from her task. "I figured it was about time that I learned. I was just taking advantage of the day."

"You never expressed an interest in close combat before, especially not with a blade."

"Still doesn't hurt to know, just in case I end up on the ground again."

Meaning she would never let anyone get their hands on her again. Roland let a smile sneak out. "This one isn't right for you. It's too heavy."

"I can handle it."

"Of that I have no doubt." He waited for the seed of pride he planted with that statement to germinate. No one else would have noticed, but there was the hint of a smile on her face. "However, sword fighting is not a matter of strength."

He could feel her watching as he approached the pile of fallen swords. He searched through the blades until the right one called to him. It was long and slim, with a gentle curve.

"The sword should act as an extension of your body. You move and fight as one." Her eyes focused on the blade as he turned to face her. "Lean, fast, much deadlier than it looks. No one will see this one coming."

She wrapped her palm around the handle, a perfect fit. He stepped back, allowing the space for her to take a few swings. Lianna and the sword already appeared to be dancing together, perfect partners. He took another step back, pulled out his own sword, and took up ready position.

The doubt that would normally make Lianna refuse such a suggestion only surfaced in her words. "Don't you have a battle to prepare for?" But her body remained firm, ready to fight.

"And too many hours left before I get to it. I prefer not to be idle while I wait."

Another near invisible smile appeared on her face as she mirrored his stance. "I'm not sure what to do."

"Just follow my lead."

For the next few hours, she did exactly that.

HARRIS SETTLED INTO position at the top of the steep grade leading down to the little house. The lamplight spilling out of the windows made it look like a distant beacon in the black of night. The Unity guards, standing at compass points around the house, were so small they looked like nocturnal rodents waiting for insects to pounce upon.

He felt so far away.

What would he have planned? Harris wondered, assuming that whatever Roland came up with wouldn't be too far off his own ideas. Snipers take out the guards. First flank moves in on signal. *But what is the signal?*

He watched the subtle movement through the brush taper off as the last of them settled into place. The Unis were surrounded. It was only a matter of making the first move. But what was it going to be? There was an extended wait in silence before Harris received the answer.

A muffled shout called out from inside the house. A window flung open. Blackened smoke funneled out of the window. The first soldier to lean out and shout took a shot to the head and tumbled out onto the ground.

Just as the guards turned their attention out toward the woods, the snipers took over. A perfect circle of shots neatly took out the surrounding guards. Lia would be pretty proud of her unit for that performance. The soldiers left inside soon poured out the front door along with a billow of smoke.

The firing began.

Gunshots echoed around the ravine as the first flank emerged from hiding and closed in to surround the house. Harris armed his gun, ready to move, but the fighting remained far below him. A few of the Unis ducked back into the house, sealing themselves in with the smoke. True, sucking up smoke wouldn't do nearly as much damage as being shot in the head. So, how would they get those tin cans out of cover?

Harris saw the first flank running back into the trees. He didn't have time to wonder why.

A huge BOOM vibrated up the ravine. Fireballs shot out through the windows and up through the little chimney. The Unis poured back out of the house, all of them engulfed in flames. None of them got very far before another explosion blasted apart the walls of the house and sent fiery rubble rocketing into the trees.

May's home was gone.

The first flank surrounded again as the fire-beaten Unis attempted to flee. The ground below rippled with sound and movement as the Resistors tore them down one by one. Harris watched in shock as the house continued to crumble and burn, as their soldiers closed closer and closer in, lit by the beacon of burning rubble.

He felt so far away.

Harris abandoned his position and raced down the slope. His gravity-forced run brought him barreling toward one of the flaming soldiers. He shot him in the head, ending their fight before it started. Now down where he belonged, Harris determined to kill every one of those tin cans that had made themselves welcome in May's home. It was not long before he lost count of the number of bodies that dropped before him.

Roland had been doing the same with his sword. As they came around to the same side of the flaming foundation, Roland took out the last Uni between them with a slash across the neck. The body fell, allowing them a clear view of each other. The field of death and destruction at their feet was bathed in orange by the flaming wreckage that had once been a peaceful home.

"You didn't have to destroy it!" Harris yelled over the roar of the fire.

"Would you have thought of another way?" Roland yelled back.

Would he have? Did it matter? He wasn't given the chance.

Roland backed away, returning to regroup for whatever part of the plan happened next.

Harris remained right where he was standing and watched May's home burn to the ground.

SOMETHING HAD CHANGED within Roland by the time they got back to the tent. Lia watched as he dropped his weapons and stripped off his armor without saying a word. He stood with his back facing her, his head turned down, breathing in and out, in a slow, calming rhythm.

There had been no Martrim, no officers of any rank, just a unit of decoys amounting to a pile of bodies. Everything he was after was still out of his reach. Defeat was creeping in on him. It was a frightening sight.

As she watched his shoulders rise and fall with each breath, she remembered how that day had begun, and how much of that defeat she was responsible for. She couldn't change what happened on the battlefield, but she could restore at least one thing he felt robbed of.

Lia touched his arm as she approached. Roland didn't move. She circled around to face him. His eyes were closed, his brow knit together. She ran a single finger down the contour of his profile, relaxing his face. His eyes remained shut.

She guided his arms around her, first one, then the other. His hands made no attempt to hold on, but his arms gently rested on her hips. She wrapped her own around his waist, letting her fingers find the dip in the small of his back, and rested her head on his chest. He smelled like the fire they'd sent raging through that house, that fire that had amounted to nothing. She closed her eyes and breathed in deep, finding his smell beneath the acrid stench of smoke.

Lia listened to Roland's heart. It beat with the same strong and steady thumping she'd heard over all their years together. The familiarity of it, the consistency of it, helped to remove some of her fright. His arms began to wrap around her. His fingertips pressed into her flesh.

She looked up. His eyes were finally open, looking down at hers, questioning. She answered his question with a kiss. It was returned with a grateful release of longing, of tension, of fear. They made love until the sun rose.

Lia would no longer bend for love, but that didn't mean she wouldn't let it bend for her.

EVEN IN THE rising light, Harris could find nothing that remained of the life May had once lived in that home. He had picked through the rubble since the second it was palpable, hoping that some treasure, some meaningful object, even some banal everyday thing could be taken back to her. Now, with the gray light of dawn seeping into the ravine, it was undeniable.

Everything had been destroyed.

He had openly ignored what would have been one of his obligations as a soldier in the third flank, to strip weapons and pile up bodies, but when Emmett approached, it wasn't to discipline him. He had trouble beginning the conversation, so Harris began for him. "What's the report, sir?"

"No Martrim. No officers at all. It would seem this unit was just—"

"A distraction." Harris tossed away the last charred chunk he had attempted to identify.

"They were his soldiers. He left them here to keep us busy, but…."

"Don't trick yourself into believing that he didn't know he was sacrificing them."

"He really is sick, isn't he?" Emmett looked disgusted. Harris found it both comforting and bewildering that even after all these years of fighting, Emmett hadn't desensitized to violence, at least not the type he considered to be committed without reasonable purpose.

"He was just focused on the bigger picture." Harris looked down at the charred remains surrounding them. "And apparently, so were we." Emmett wanted to say something, to argue on behalf of Roland's plan, but Harris didn't want to hear it. "Permission to return to camp, sir."

Emmett stifled his argument. "Granted."

There was no point in trying to wipe the ash from his body. He would have to tell May what had happened to her home. At least his appearance would do some of the talking for him. He did, however, check to make sure there was no blood on him.

She was standing just outside his tent, a blanket wrapped around her against the chill of morning. Her giant doe-eyes flooded over as soon as she saw him.

"I'm sorry." That was all he could think to say.

He prepared to be screamed at, accused of lying to her, but all she did was collapse against him and sob. He was taken aback at first, afraid that she might crack like a crystalline glass if he touched her, but she needed to be touched. She needed to be comforted. He wrapped his arms around her.

She let herself be drawn in close. He let her sob until she had no tears left.

THERE WAS NO time to rest. There was no time to regroup. There was no time to do anything but chase that black-eyed snake to the next fight. And the next. And the next.

Roland had relayed the orders. The camp was nearly packed up, ready to be shouldered to their next destination. He could only guess what that was, but he had no doubt of Martrim's intentions. He wouldn't run forever. He would face them when the time was right and the advantages were all his. That's when Roland would get the chance he had been chasing for months, the chance to watch him die.

Roland was on his way to collect his own belongings when Harris's voice called out to him. "I need to speak to you, Commander."

He should have cut him off. He should have told him it wasn't the time for petty arguments, but he wanted to know what Harris would dare to say to him now. Roland acknowledged him without breaking his pace. "If you came to discuss optional strategies, I'm not interested."

"I came to ask permission, sir."

"Permission for what?"

"To bring May with us."

Those words brought him to a standstill. "We don't tend to pick up strays."

"We don't?" Harris didn't have to flick his eyes toward their tent for Roland to know what he meant.

"If you're telling me she'd shape into a top tier soldier—"

"She won't fight."

"Then why do we need her?"

"We owe her."

Roland turned back to his march across the camp. He was not about to let Harris, of all people, lecture him about moral duty.

"She either comes with us, or I stay and help her rebuild her home."

Roland's momentum slammed to another halt. Now, Harris had gone from enforcing moral duty to making threats. "And by what logic would you abandon your post, just like that?"

"I gave her my word."

Roland stepped in close to him and examined the intent in his face. It was no threat. He meant what he said. "She's your responsibility, wholly and solely."

"Understood, sir."

Being properly addressed only made Roland angrier. He wanted to walk away, but there was more behind Harris's eyes. "Is there anything else, Soldier Wilson?"

"I'm too skilled to be pushed back to third flank. If you don't want me in your tactical discussions, fine. But don't waste me on the field."

Roland's knuckles cracked with the sudden contraction of his fists. "Duly noted, soldier. Now get back to work."

Harris walked off without the proper sign off, but Roland would rather see him leave than engage in further argument. There was no longer time for that.

LIA WAS IN the throes of haphazard packing, yet again, when May's birdlike voice chirped out from behind her. "Excuse me. I'm sorry to—"

"Yes?" Lia found herself both wanting to get this conversation over with as fast as possible, and very curious about what could possibly be compelling May to talk to her in the first place.

"Harris told me you might have some clothes I could use. Something that would be better suited for travel."

"Travel." Lia took a moment to absorb the notion of May following them along like a lost dog. "Emmett's in charge of supplies. He's got plenty of clothes."

"Which Harris did say, but I don't want to look like one of the soldiers if I can help it. He said you might have something else, something for when you're—"

"Playing dress-up?"

"A disguise, he said."

May was retracting into herself, trying to shy away from the conversation, but Lia was far too curious to let her get away that easy.

"I do have some dresses." It didn't take Lia long to find the bag she kept her "disguises" in. She held it out to her at arm's length. "Most of those only fit when I was pregnant anyway."

She expected May to practically run away after that comment, but her giant eyes only squinted in curiosity. "You have a child?"

"Try to hide your shock." Now Lia really did want nothing more than to get this conversation over with.

"I'm sorry. I didn't mean anything by that. It's just... it must be quite hard to be a soldier and a mother."

Lia found herself staring into May's eyes. There was nothing but honesty in them.

"It is." As she said the words, it felt as if a little hand squeezed her heart.

"Do you have a boy or—"

"His name is Malcolm. He's…." A ripple of sadness washed through her entire body. "He's four now." His second birthday was the last one she'd spent with him. It felt like both yesterday and a lifetime ago.

May gave her a look of entirely unabashed empathy. It was very unnerving. "I'll hold onto hopes of a swift reunion for you both."

"Guess I will, too." What else could she do? She entered this war thinking fighting alone was what would get her back to him. Now, she knew a little hope was also necessary.

May gathered the bag of clothes against her chest. "Thank you for these. I'll repay you in time." She returned to where Harris was packing and joined him in his task.

So, Harris has found himself a travel companion. Lia hid her smirk by turning back to her own packing. She donned her gun belt and then slipped on her jacket. As she tugged down to hook it together at the front, she felt a round, hard nodule inside her pocket. She didn't have to look to know it was her earpiece.

Another memory came rushing back. Arin had one of their radios. It was how he had found her. It was how he would do it again, if he chose to.

She continued to hook together her jacket without acknowledging the lump in her pocket, but she let the possibilities it presented play through her mind. Would she want him to find her? Would she want to see him again? Could she drop it now and let the chance slip through her fingers? Even then, would that one little stumbling block stop him?

No, it wouldn't.

Perhaps it was better to have control in her own hands—or rather her pocket. She was letting the thoughts flow through as she slipped her rifle over her shoulder, but only one thought took over as she reached down to pick up her sword.

I will not bend.

She slipped the sheath of the "deadlier than it looks" sword over her other shoulder and felt the weight of it settle against her.

Let him do what he would. She would do what was right.

The next thing she felt settle onto her shoulder was Roland's hand. "Are you ready?" he asked.

She looked up at him and said, "Yes."

She was ready for anything.

WRITER AND FILMMAKER Margaret M. MacDonald is passionate about telling stories which transport people into other worlds and make this one a little more extraordinary. Her visual writing style, shaped by her background as a designer, conveys a tangible sense of place, inviting readers into the story world. Born and raised in the United States and currently living in Australia, Margaret likes to bring a mix of both cultures into her work. She has written a library of screenplays and novels in a mix of genres, has directed several short films, and has been lucky enough to win a few awards along the way. She enjoys embracing a creative challenge and wants, more than anything else, to tell a story audiences will love.